Praise for *The Daug…* *the Lost Col…*

Elinor

Being long intrigued by the Lost Colony … …noke, I was eager to read *Elinor*, Shannon McNear's novelization of this true historical mystery. I wasn't disappointed! The setting, one familiar to me, felt authentically painted. The characters, Elinor and Sees Far in particular, were vivid and sympathetic in their courage to adapt to challenging circumstances and new ideas. To call the research behind this story thorough is an understatement. By the end, I couldn't turn pages fast enough yet didn't want the story to end. Readers of Elinor will be glad there's more to look forward to in this series.

–Lori Benton, Christy Award-winning author of
Mountain Laurel and *Shiloh*

A riveting, romantic, and redemptive story that shines hopeful light on what might have happened to the Lost Colony of Roanoke. *Elinor* is beautifully told, and Shannon McNear is sure to win historical hearts with this stirring, well-researched tale of early America.

–Laura Frantz, Christy Award-winning author of *A Heart Adrift*

Mary

With *Mary: Daughters of the Lost Colony*, author Shannon McNear blurs the demarcation between history and fiction in such a way that the saga is both fully believable and beautifully written. I loved how the story questions deepen as McNear picks up where her novel *Elinor* ends, twining the fates of two women from different cultures and beliefs who hold the same needs and yearnings. *Mary* pulses with drama, romance, and spiritual insight. I highly recommend it to any lover of historical fiction who has ever pondered the mysteries surrounding the Lost Colony of Roanoke.

–Naomi Musch, author of *Season of My Enemy (Heroines of WWII)*,
Song for the Hunter (sequel to *Mist O'er the Voyageur*),
and *Lumberjacks and Ladies (Not for Love)*

Shannon McNear once again transports readers to the 1590s in the wilds of a yet unexplored continent. Her new book, *Mary,* returns to the lost people of Roanoke and explores what might have happened using their known history and expanding into the possibilities. Readers reengage with the characters they grew to love in *Elinor* and follow their lives as they adapt to the strange and wonderful place they learn to call home. Experience their struggles to survive in both body and spirit alongside these brave men and women of two very different cultures. A captivating read for anyone with a love of history, mystery, and imagination.

–Pegg Thomas, award-winning author of *Abigail's Peace*

Rebecca

Set during a time of great cultural clash, one brave woman dares to bring peace. Everyone knows the name of Pocahontas but this retelling is a whole new experience. Lush in history, conflict, and romance, *Rebecca* is an exquisitely written story that will stay with you long after you close the book.

–Michelle Griep, Christy Award-winning author of *The Bride of Blackfriars Lane*

Rebecca brings a heart-rending conclusion to Shannon McNear's Daughters of the Lost Colony trilogy. And what an ending it is, watching Pocahontas, the daughter of the Powhatan king, grow from childhood to adulthood and navigate the turbulent relationships between her Native culture and that of the English. A bittersweet ending, but full of hope too. I can't praise this highly enough.

–Jennifer Uhlarik, award-winning author of *Sand Creek Serenade* and *Love's Fortress*

DAUGHTERS OF THE LOST COLONY
1607

Rebecca

A Riveting Story Based on the Lost Colony of Roanoke

Shannon McNear

BARBOUR
PUBLISHING

Print ISBN 978-1-63609-589-9
Adobe Digital Edition (.epub) 978-1-63609-590-5

Cover Design: Kirk DouPonce, DogEared Design

Published by Barbour Publishing, Inc., 1810 Barbour Drive, Uhrichsville, Ohio 44683, www.barbourbooks.com

Our mission is to inspire the world with the life-changing message of the Bible.

ecpa Member of the Evangelical Christian Publishers Association

Printed in the United States of America.

Dedication

To Mato'aka. . .
May we someday meet in the Golden City

And to Becky. . .
Thank you again for taking a chance on a nobody writer ten years ago. . .and for the opportunity to write these stories in particular. I hope I've done your vision justice!

The Lord is my shepherd, I shall not want.
He maketh me to rest in green pasture, and leadeth me by the still waters.
He restoreth my soul, and leadeth me in the paths of
righteousness for his Name's sake.
Yea, though I should walk through the valley of the shadow of death,
I will fear no evil; for thou art with me: thy rod and thy staff,
they comfort me.
Thou dost prepare a table before me in the sight of mine adversaries:
thou dost anoint mine head with oil, and my cup runneth over.
Doubtless kindness and mercy shall follow me all the days of my life,
and I shall remain a long season in the house of the Lord.
(Psalm 23, the 1599 Geneva Bible)

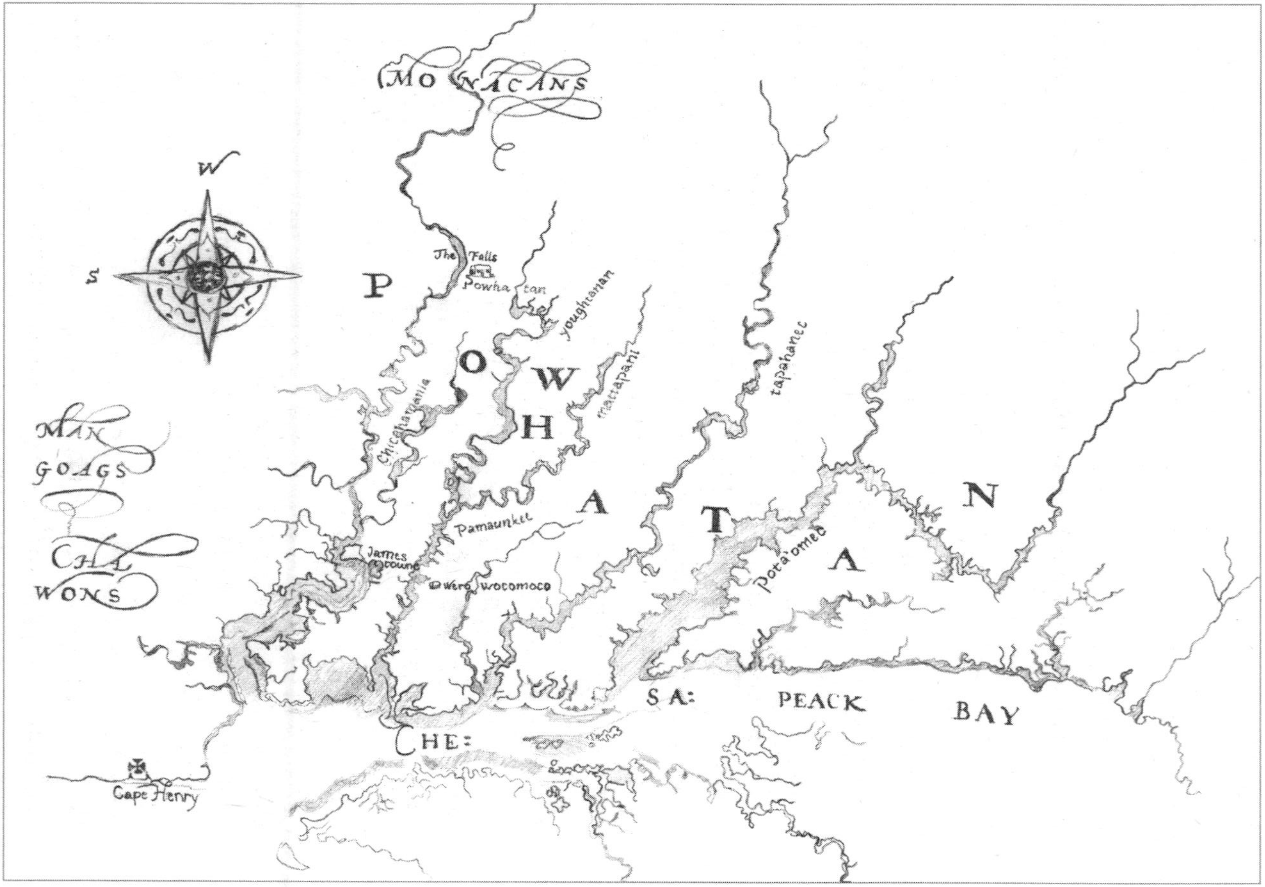

MONACANS
W
S
The Falls
Powhatan
youghtanan
mattapani
tapahanec
Chickahamania
Pamaunkee
James towne
Wero wocomoco
Pota'omeo
POWHATAN
MANGOAGS
CHAWONS
CHE: SA: PEACK BAY
Cape Henry

Dear Reader,

The story of the Lost Colony flows naturally into that of the settlement of Jamestown. Even after the conflict between England and Spain simmered down, England still craved supremacy in the New World and the wealth that new holdings with rich natural resources would bring her. Exploration and settlement also provided a solution for the overcrowding and poverty of London and other cities—and while the Anglo-Spanish War might have been officially over, the unrelenting competition with Spain continued.

And so, although one settlement had been "lost" (or abandoned, depending upon your perspective), the dream of English holdings in the New World never quite died. At the same time, when the Virginia Company of London sent out three ships to once again attempt settlement, that original colony was not forgotten. One of their directives, in fact, was to discover what had become of the Roanoke Colony, and the experiences of those original voyages were kept firmly in mind, especially since another such expedition seeking the whereabouts of the Roanoke Colony had ended in failure.

Times had changed, however, since the days of Queen Elizabeth. Her longtime favorite, Sir Walter Raleigh (spelled Ralegh in my stories, in accordance with his own accounts), had fallen out of favor with her successor, King James, and was thrown into prison on the accusation of treason. Although Catholicism was still viewed with suspicion as well, movements arose in criticism of the Church of England and the Crown, some wishing to purify the Church of its corruption and others wishing to separate entirely (aka Puritans and Separatists). The Geneva Bible, in widespread use among English speakers of the time, was also disliked by Church and Crown for its repudiation of the divine right of kings (or clergy), which would lead to the commissioning of a new translation by King James.

And so onto this stage—set not by the star playwrights of the day, William Shakespeare and Ben Jonson, but by the winds and tides of kings and politics—stepped men who were both adventurers and scholars, some with formal education and some self-taught, all of whom felt they had a crucial role to play in the shaping of a new settlement and the New

World. Some of whom doubtlessly lived their professed faith in God with more integrity than others. I leave it for you, dear reader, to draw your own conclusions about individuals, where that is concerned.

I would beg you, however—as I have cautioned before—not to project Christian morality on those who have never even heard of Jesus, much less accepted Him as Savior. John Smith commented, interestingly enough, that the Indians showed more signs of true Christianity than those reared in the faith, but no human is without flaws, and never is that more evident than in the history of our country.

By the same token, I crave grace for using certain historical terms and attitudes that would never fly in our time. We do have much in our history to answer for. Understand, however, that the use of "savage" as applied to Indigenous peoples was in their time simply a colloquial word, much as we use "Native" today. Sometimes it was a judgment on the perceived lack of progress or sophistication of a particular people group, but sometimes not. Please know that I often do not condone the words and actions of my characters, yet I feel it needful to portray known history as accurately as possible.

Finally, this story can, if necessary, stand on its own as speculative history of Pocahontas and the original Jamestown, but your understanding will be enriched by the reading of the two stories it follows: *Elinor* and *Mary*. Pay special attention to the epilogue of *Mary*, as it sets the stage for this one.

As always, thank you for joining me on this journey!

My most earnest regards,
Shannon

Prologue

Tsenacomoco, Cohattayough (Planting and Weeding Season), 1606 by English reckoning

She stood in the middle of the floor, glancing about in a near panic. It had been—oh, so long!—since he had either sent for her or come to her, night or day. And now—*waugh!* He would come, and soon.

Wahunsenecawh. Greater than all the *weroances* now, called *mamanatowic* by the People.

The Powhatan.

She had belonged to him for fourteen summers and winters. Every time she'd given up the thought of meriting further attention from him, he came, and her traitor heart crumbled under the heat of their passion. He always provided well for her, making sure she had house and food and deerskins.

And status. The other women might grumble—some did—but none could deny the favor he showed her. Even when he himself did not visit.

The first thing was to prepare something to eat. Dried, ground walnuts stewed with dried squash would please him. As was the way of the People, she always kept a little food by, simmering either for him or other visitors as well as themselves. Being nearer the beginning of the growing season, her store had dwindled, but there remained enough nuts and squash for one meal with which to honor him.

Fourteen turnings of the leaves. She'd been with the True People now for sixteen, longer than she had lived among those she'd once called her own people. How distant were those memories of a land across the sea, of a crowded and filthy city, of the people who had sailed across with such high hopes, scrabbling to make a life on these shores while so ignorant of the ways of the land and the People, of the richness to be found.

Once, years ago, Wahunsenecawh had asked her to tell him of her life before. He'd suffered but a short description, growing restless either from disbelief or boredom. He did ask her what her name had been, but snorted his disdain when she told him. "*Ay-mah.* So plain and ugly. It does not even have meaning." He'd flashed her his best smile, leaning in a little. "You need more. Something that speaks of who you are."

"More than 'the Crane'?" she'd returned pertly, and he laughed.

"You are *Woanagusso*," he murmured, and his dark eyes glittered in that way which never failed to send a thrill through her body.

A swan. Graceful and beautiful, fierce and formidable. She'd accept that.

He had then declared that name to the entire town, and she carried herself with even more pride than before. Once a captive and a slave, now a favored wife to a weroance and a new name as well. Some of the women scoffed, saying it was not proper for anything but a milk name, being called after a bird. *Boasts Much* would be far better.

Woanagusso only smiled. She had not chosen it, after all. And who would gainsay Wahunsenecawh?

The stewed walnuts and squash simmered happily now over her fire, prepared while the girls ran in and out. She allowed each a small taste, setting a separate pot to cook with squash and peas, both foodstuffs more readily obtainable and stored than the walnuts. But they would enjoy leftovers, provided Wahunsenecawh did not devour the entire pot—or give it to his men who attended outside.

Voices heralded his approach. Woanagusso ducked outside to greet him, as was proper. He waited, muscled arms folded across his chest, while one of his men slid past her to inspect the interior of her *yehakan*, then came back out with a firm nod.

Beneath the ornaments woven into the knotted length of his hair, more silver glinted than she recalled had been there last time he'd come to her. The right side of his head gleamed smooth, a thin, roached crest separating the two from front to back. Sparse strands, likewise silver, adorned his chin and upper lip, a concession to his advancing years. He'd been not a very young man when he'd claimed her. And yet, the familiar sparkle of his dark eyes drew a shiver from her. As always. She summoned a smile. "*Wingapo*, husband. I have food. Will you eat?"

His mouth curved in response. "When have I ever refused to eat at your hand?"

A laugh bubbled out of her, and when he gestured for her to go first, she led him inside. A word to his attendants, and they remained outside, doubtless arrayed at the door to keep others away.

The town would soon be abuzz with talk of the visit.

He towered for but a moment in the middle of the yehakan floor, then, at her invitation, seated himself on the woven mats she had stacked on the bed frame.

"*Sá keyd wingan*?" she asked, while dishing him a bowl of the stew.

He nodded, his gaze flicking here and there before resting again upon her. "I am well. Are you also well, my wife?"

"I also am well."

"And the girls?"

She shot him a smile. "Do you not see them more often than I? Channa is a woman now and goes where she wills, but even Mato'aka and Little Flower are barely here, busy running about with all the other children in tow."

He laughed softly. "That Mato'aka. Well is she called Pocahuntas. She is never still and ever into mischief."

"That she is." Rising, she held out the bowl. "She is much like her father in that, I suspect—save for the mischief. It will make her a most formidable woman."

Wahunsenecawh accepted the dish but caught one of her hands in his. "She is not unlike her mother as well."

She could not help her lingering smile. "You honor me."

He gave a little dip of his head and released her. "I speak truth." With nimble fingers, he scooped a generous morsel from the dish to his mouth. "Mm. You excel at this, as always."

With a half bow, she withdrew a pace and settled on her own mat, halfway between him and the fire. He was all gleam and glitter while he ate, even in the dimness, with the oils on his skin and the loops of copper and pearls about his neck.

"Have you spoken with Channa?" he asked, once his first, greedy bites were past.

Mattachanna, older than Mato'aka, was his daughter by another woman but stayed often with Woanagusso, since her own mother lived too far for easy travel. As was the custom, Wahunsenecawh had brought the girl here once she was weaned and old enough to be cared for elsewhere.

All too aware that she also could be sent away, yet having no family to be sent to, Woanagusso did not mind the arrangement. "Yes. She told me Tomakin has asked her to be his wife."

One of his dark eyebrows ticked upward. "And what are your thoughts about that?"

"His position is highly respected."

The corner of his mouth lifted. "It is said he will be an elder of the *quiakrosoc* before long."

It was more than respectable—it was highly sought after, and she'd no reason to quibble on the girl's choice of a husband.

Except for one, and it was a reason she was not permitted to speak of. She must take the diplomatic path.

Dipping her head, she flashed a quick smile. "That would be noteworthy indeed."

Wahunsenecawh watched her closely. Too closely. "Is that your only thought?"

She blinked at him. "Should it not be?"

He sat back and gave full attention to his bowl for a few moments. When it was empty, he set it aside and, after licking his fingers, reached for her. When she was cuddled across his lap, head tucked under his chin and against his shoulder, he spoke at last, the rumble of his voice vibrating against her cheek. "I wonder sometimes if you truly believe in our gods or if you still follow the god of your own people."

She tried to sit up, but he held her against him. "Your people are my people," she said. "They are *Tunapewoc*."

There could be no other reply than that.

"Hmm." Again, that wonderful, deep rumble. "You know my kindness too well to say otherwise."

She caught a smile before betraying herself. He would feel the motion of her cheek on his chest. "You are mamanatowic."

At that, he did tug her into a sitting position, his dark eyes grave. "Recall that I have told you never to mention your god to anyone. I will not hesitate to send you away."

"Kuppeh." The assent came without thought. He would indeed make good on that threat—she had seen it with others. And she knew also why he demanded this—because of all the awfulness with the Spanish.

Releasing a great sigh, he pulled her close again, this time to nuzzle her neck and smooth one of his great, strong hands down the length of her bare leg. "Good. Now then, wife, you have fed me with walnut stew. Have you other dainties for me?"

The summer night was nothing short of magical.

She crept through the outskirts of the town, past her father's field, tall now with *pegatawah*, where fireflies rose and blinked in all solemnity. Tempted as she was to stop and watch them—as she did many a night before—something more drew her beyond, deeper under the trees surrounding the town. It did not matter that she was being followed, her father's guards like silent shadows trailing behind. Thus they always did, as was their duty. They would report her actions to *Nohsh*, but they dared not hinder her steps. Not on such a night as this.

Besides, how could they fail to be as charmed by its beauty as she?

She took her time, stepping lightly and with care in the way she had been taught as long as she could recall, making as little sound as possible. No fear touched her of the dark of night. Not only could she see quite well under the glimmer of stars and a slip of a moon, but the men shadowing her would not allow her to come to harm.

At last she came to the place—a circle of trees that grew impossibly tall, where, in addition to fireflies, the air fairly shimmered with power. With *powa*, the essence of dreams and visions, that for which it was said their very people—and Nohsh himself—took their name and title.

This place, with its circle of stones inside that of the trees, was her own refuge, a place to dance and make prayers and soak in the energy of the spirits who watched over her people, the way Nohsh's guards watched over her. A place to retreat and think about the words that swirled through her head. *Manito'inini. Machicómoco. Midéwiwin.* The People of the *manito*, or Great Spirits. The Great Council. The Great Medicine Dance.

And her own names. *Amonute. Mato'aka.* Beloved Woman. White Feather.

Those of whom she was born. Those who had seen her destiny, through dreams and visions, before her birth. The Sacred Hoop of life itself, inside which she was to move and live. The destiny in which she was being taught even now.

And lastly, the symbol of such a destiny, marking her place amongst her people.

Her mind spun. How could she bear it all? They assured her that she would grow and learn the way as she went, that those marked with such a path before them indeed became worthy in the very doing of great deeds.

Because in this moment, in the day to day, she was only *Pocahuntas*. The wild one, the Maker of Mischief.

But something deep inside craved for more.

Drifting to the center of the circle, she raised her arms and closed her eyes. "Give me strength. Make me worthy. Let me not fail."

Part One

Captain John Smith

Chapter One

England, 1606

"And above all, take care not to offend the Naturals."

Naturals. What absurdity, to call them such a thing. A mere kindness, Smith was sure.

Still, he must not be disrespectful of age and experience. The former, in Reverend Hakluyt, shoulders bent, hair nearly snowy for all that his visage was yet unlined. The latter, in Master Harriot, his hair yet dark and back unbowed, though deep creases traced his features.

'Twas all part of the process for the venture—to meet with those who had gone before or who had interest somehow in this and previous expeditions. Wisdom could be found in such things, and part of his impatience with those in positions of authority was their unwillingness to receive anything from those they perceived as beneath them.

Yet in this moment he could not help but chafe. The room seemed overwarm. Reverend Hakluyt had, in his turn, droned on and on, his voice a single, thready tone.

"There may be other worthy endeavors to which to put your hand on this venture, and I do not say the investors are amiss in seeking a return upon their monies. But remember that material wealth means nothing if deceived souls are not brought into the kingdom of God along the way. In fact, such concern should be paramount."

'Twas the same preached at them by ministers offering spiritual preparation in advance of their voyage. And though Smith understood—was all they did not for the glory of God?—the constant reminder grated upon his nerves. He did not need hounded to know his duty, much less to remember it.

He did, however, wish for the meeting to be done so he could speak with Master Harriot privately. He was the one who best would know how to approach these—these *Naturals*.

All knew, however, that in reality they were but savages. Still, if he could learn something of their tongue, 'twould make their way easier. And perhaps they, unlike those who had gone before, not quite twenty years ago now, would not disappear into the wilderness as if they'd never been.

The meeting ended, and as the other men dispersed into small huddles of conversation, Smith made his way toward Master Harriot.

His plain black suit hung on a lean frame, the gauntness of which hollowed his face as well. Sharp-featured, with dark eyes alive despite the gravity of his expression as he listened and nodded in response to what Edward Wingfield was saying to him at the moment. Or babbling might be the proper term. The older man, self-important in his position amongst the venture because he had been both a soldier and member of Parliament, spoke so quickly and emphatically that hardly a breath was taken between sentences. Master Harriot proved the very model of graciousness in suffering such treatment.

Smith stood back and waited his turn. Apparently sensing Smith's eyes upon himself, Master Wingfield abruptly stopped and swung toward him then muttered a hasty conclusion to his speech and moved away.

Master Harriot shook his head, the slightest smile curving his thin mouth as his gaze settled upon Smith. "And you would be the adventurer all are talking about. Captain John Smith! What honor to make your acquaintance. I greatly admire one who could endure captivity by the Turks and Moors and come away unscathed."

He could not help it—Smith's chest puffed a little. "My thanks, Master Harriot. I only hope I can be not only of use to this venture but an advantage as well. Thus why I have sought you out."

Master Harriot's smile widened. "Is it, now? What might I do for you, good sir?"

Smith half bowed. "Your lexicon of the savage's tongue, sir. I am most desirous to have a peek at it."

"Are you? Is there time for such a thing?"

"We have a fortnight until we sail. I am quick enough at languages and plan to give all spare moments to study on the voyage."

"That would require you have your own copy, as I am most loath to release mine."

Another bow. "As you wish. I have a good hand and do not mind the labor."

Master Harriot lifted one brow. "Indeed? When shall suit you to come?"

"As soon as is convenient for you."

The brow went higher. "This evening? You may sup with me if you please."

Nothing would please him more. "I would cause you no expense."

"'Tis none. I assure you, 'twould be a delight."

And thus he found himself later at Master Harriot's apartments, in the story above a bookshop. The rooms were crammed full of books and papers and various scientific instruments—at least, Smith presumed they were scientific. Either that or instruments of sorcery, and he preferred to think them the former, despite rumors noised about concerning the man. But all was clean enough to Smith's eyes, even tidy.

Master Harriot fixed him with a look, so obviously eager that he might as well be rubbing his hands together in glee. Smith had the impression he was, in truth, holding himself back from that very thing.

"Shall we begin? I have laid the book out on the table, here, and provided writing materials if you lack them."

Smith dipped his head in thanks. "I would be happy to reimburse you for those."

A bit of friendly dickering over the matter followed. Smith most certainly would not allow the older man to just give him what he could afford. Then he set to work.

Master Harriot did not simply leave him to it, however. After the first flicker of annoyance at the man's hovering, Smith came to the realization that this tongue was not only different from any other he had been exposed to, but learning it could mean the difference between life and death in the New World.

He would endeavor to be a most attentive student, while he could.

The New World, 1607

Twenty weeks at sea.

Six, still within sight of England's shores because of foul weather. They should never have set out in December.

Fourteen more along the Canary Isles, the West Indies, and to Virginia, of the New World.

Thirteen of those fourteen spent under guard on the *Susan Constant*, largest of the three ships sent on this voyage.

Not that he hadn't made good use of them. Praying and reciting catechism and the Holy Scriptures. Forced humility was good for his soul. He was no stranger to trials that brought a man such as him to his knees, and God had always brought him through. In addition to these, studying the lexicon of the savages' tongue, because he was also nothing if not an optimist.

He oft grew weary of study, particularly in the early days when they were not being tossed about by some storm, and in the moment flung down his book and paced about, one step square. How could they have done this? Imprisoning him for suspected mutiny. Him! Mutiny! Was he not ever the model of duty? He would see that they rued it sooner rather than late. He vowed it with every fiber of his being.

Then he would return to his senses and remind himself that he must—as always!—possess his soul in patience and rest his hope in God alone. Through the turns of day into night and back again, then the tempests, one after another, which tossed their small ship and stole all shred of comfort, and sometimes most of hope.

The last, however, drove them right up to the coast of Virginia and to the opening of what appeared to be a fair bay. Another token of God's providence. But still they kept him imprisoned.

Vindicate me, O God. I wait wholly on You.

Heavy footfalls echoed among the bales and crates of provisions, followed by the exchange of a greeting with his guard, and then from around the corner came Captain Bartholomew Gosnold, master of the larger of their companion ships, *Godspeed*, trailed by the guard. Smith stopped his pacing and stood at attention.

"We are going ashore," Gosnold said. "It has been agreed to release you, but you must give your word to forbear any sort of vengeance."

He held up his hands. "What matter my word if they think me guilty of mutiny?"

Gosnold clucked his tongue and reached to unlock the irons. "Methinks you've been too long in the hold. That is not the Captain John Smith I know."

Rubbing his wrists and ankles, Smith flashed him a look. He must tread very carefully indeed if he did not wish to return here. 'Twas not in his nature to pretend to be what he was not—but he could, and must be, on his best behavior. "My thanks," he said.

The other man gave a half smile. "At least they recognize your worth as a soldier. Do your best to prove them wrong about the remainder of their opinions."

Smith gathered his belongings and stowed them in his haversack then slung it across his body. "Have they yet discovered who is appointed to the first council?"

"No. There is talk of doing so after our landing." Gosnold smiled again, but tightly. "Come."

Smith emerged above deck and drew a deep breath of the sweet spring breeze. Calls of seabirds filled the air, and tall trees lined the shore, their leaves such a brilliant green they dazzled his eyes. There was scarce time to enjoy the view, however, with Wingfield and Captain Newport both regarding him with sour expressions.

"If we restore to you your pieces," Wingfield said, ever haughty, "do you promise to behave as befits a Christian and a soldier of the Crown?"

Newport made no comment, but combed his beard with the hook he wore as a relic of losing his hand in a battle years before—a disquieting gesture. Smith bit back a snarl and resisted the urge to plant his feet with fists on hips. "I promise to act only in defense of this venture."

He could say neither more nor less. Newport turned away, but Wingfield nodded after a moment's consideration. "Very well." He motioned for Smith's arquebus and French pistol to be returned, along with shot and powder.

The handful appointed to go ashore finished readying themselves, the shallop was lowered, and they climbed down into it.

Smith kept close watch as they neared land. Nothing on the water except their own ship. No movement except vegetation and shorebirds at water's edge.

"Matches lit!" Gosnold said, very low, and they all complied, making sure the slow-burning fuses on their guns were alive in preparation for the possible need to fire.

They drove the shallop in as close as they could, then the first man out dragged it nearer still.

A thrill coursed through Smith as his feet touched dry ground. The New World! Soon, God willing, to be the Colony of Virginia.

They pressed in under cover of the trees—and such goodly, fair trees they were, oak and diverse other kinds he did not know. Some were as wide as a man's arms could stretch. All colors of flowering plants lay below, and lush glades here and there. Birdsong filled the air, along with the hum of bees, and butterflies and dragonflies lent an air of enchantment.

"I am almost ravished at the sight of such beauty," murmured George Percy, behind him, as they traced the edge of a gurgling brook that they'd tasted and found fresh and sweet.

Smith agreed but would not say so in the hearing of an adversary. In the meantime, he remained watchful.

They spent most of the day ashore, exploring the land and the water's edge. Near dark they finally reboarded the shallop, so to return to the ship, when Smith spied movement of men scuttling through the bushes on all fours like bears—

"Be 'ware!"

They all went to attention, arms up and ready.

Heads half shaven and bodies covered only in deerskins about their middle and red and black paint, the wild men attacked hard and fast, letting loose a rain of arrows toward the English. Smith and his companions were ready and answered with a sharp fire in return.

The savages fled into the forest, screeching and howling. The sailors pushed the shallop out into the current and rowed as quickly as they could. Gabriel Archer clutched bleeding hands together, and one of the sailors, lacking armor, had two arrows through his body.

Why they had sent anyone along who was not properly fitted, he did not know. But he supposed the sailors had thought it unnecessary.

They regained the ship, and once wounds were tended, Captain Newport commanded that they open the box containing the names of those appointed to the first council.

"They are as follows. Myself—Captain Newport. Edward Maria Wingfield. Bartholomew Gosnold. John Ratcliffe. Captain John Martin. Captain George Kendall. And finally, Captain John Smith."

A murmur went up from the crowd, and Wingfield was, predictably, the first to protest. "Not Smith! How can he be on this list? I refuse to allow him to be brought onto the council."

Smith looked over and caught the smallest shake of the head from Gosnold, so he set his jaw and resolved to be quiet and biddable.

After much argument, they made Master Hunt, minister of the gospel, a council member in his place, and Wingfield was elected president.

It did not matter. He was here for the good of the colony regardless. And Hunt was a good man.

An immediate action was to plant a cross on the place of their first landing, which they named Cape Henry. The worthy Master Hunt broke out the furnishings for their first communion on land and preached a heartfelt sermon.

Happy enough to hear the Word of God under open skies, Smith again kept watch. Brief movements in the trees and bushes around them made it clear—they were being observed.

Smith's heart leaped into his throat. He was the one who had devoted the most study to the savages' tongue. He was the one who should lead in treating with them. But he must yet hold himself in check.

Over the next weeks, however, he had ample opportunity to test his knowledge as they continued their explorations and made contact with the wild people of the land. At nearly every place, they were met by the inhabitants of the various towns, sometimes by the leaders—their weroances—themselves. The savages seemed to favor long orations, of which the English could understand nothing, accompanied by great feasts and dancing. To the surprise of all, their food was good, despite its strangeness, and they were fed with such an abundance and entertained so gladly, many of the men let down their guard. But Smith continued to keep watch, not trusting the smiles and openness of these people who wore not much more than a sort of deerskin apron and all manner of beads and ornaments made of shells, feathers, and whatnot. Captain Newport had brought along many trade goods—beads, needles, hatchets—which much delighted the savages, and they traded for as much of the native grain as they could.

In the midst of it all, they settled upon a location to begin building their own town—although that not without argument as well. It seemed a fair enough spot, an uninhabited island adjacent to the mainland, with enough trees to provide cover from incoming ships, on the north side of what they called the King's River. They would name both the river and the town after King James.

Smith knew the illusion of peace could not hold long. And after one exploration upriver to a great falls, where stood a town of the savages named Powhatan for their own king who had been born there, they returned to find that Jamestowne had been attacked, with only the ship's ordinance effecting a good defense. One of the ship's boys, Richard Mutton, had taken an arrow to the thigh and bled out, and while others were also wounded, they were recovering, if slowly.

Among other work, they began planting corn as soon as they'd settled, and the attack spurred the building of a palisade about the town. A few skirmishes arose, mostly thwarted from close watch, but a handful of savages came, indicating friendship. Two such men took the time to impart which of the Indians were friends to the English and which were enemies. Smith made careful notes.

In a little more than a fortnight, they'd completed the palisade. Smith thought he might breathe a bit better, especially as more weroances sent words of peace and gifts of food.

But then the sickness began. This was one happenstance he could do nothing about.

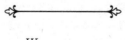

Werowocomoco

"There are visitors to Tsenacomoco, Mamanatowic. Dressed strangely, as the *Span-ish*—yet different. They have the fire sticks with great noise. The only good that can be said about them is that they have come to stay upon an island that is useless for living upon for long, where the water is not good at certain times and the insects are terrible."

Wahunsenecawh sat forward, hands upon his knees. "Visitors, you say." And not the Span-ish. He thought back to those others of whom he had heard tales, ten and twenty years before, to the south of them.

The ones of whom Woanagusso, his *Ay-mah*, had come.

"And you are certain they are not of the Span-ish?"

"Their colors are different. And the sound of their tongue, harsher."

"Hmm."

The three warriors stood before him, unbent despite the scuffs and wounds upon their bodies.

So many things to consider with this. "Why are they here? Do they intend to stay? We must find out. Which means someone must go speak with them."

"We have tried. Some towns have offered them food, but those of us who did not have any to spare—at least not in the moment—were driven away with their loud weapons."

He rubbed his chin. "We will watch," he said at last. "The towns may give pegatawah as they wish—or not—but we will keep watch. Spread the word to keep me informed of all they do."

In the meantime, he would go see his White Swan.

He gathered six of the warriors who served as his retinue and made his way through the town to her yehakan. Usually he gave her warning—time enough to prepare a proper welcome, including food—but this matter niggled at him.

And he wished a fresh look at her and to ask certain questions of her with no one to warn or interfere.

She met him at the doorway with eyes wide, her already too-pale cheeks going even more pale and then pink. It always pleased and amused him when she responded with such obvious changes of skin color, but such had lessened as she grew more accustomed to him—and as her skin grew browner with the sun and with the colored oils their people rubbed into their skin.

No matter how brown she became, however, deep into the summer, the shade of her skin never quite matched that of the other women. It both fascinated and repelled him.

She stared at him a heartbeat or two more then sank to a kneeling position, head bent. Her dark hair, bound at the nape and adorned with a single blue jay feather, gleamed in the sun with glints of red. Not the absolute black of most of the People, with the exception of the occasional spawn of the Span-ish.

"Wahunsenecawh. Mamanatowic. How may I serve your pleasure today?"

Her voice, soft and even now not without that particular inflection which came with her being born of a foreign tongue, swept across him like the brush of a feathered wing. She had always stirred him with the craving to possess her—and did even now, thus why he kept her near even after bearing him not one but two children.

"Stand, Woanagusso. I wish to speak with you awhile."

She rose, her gaze sparkling and limbs shifting in a manner that betrayed her lingering unease and reminding him for a moment of Mato'aka. They both waited while two of his attendants ducked inside to inspect the dwelling.

"This is unexpected."

Her lashes fell and her cheeks reddened again, no doubt at having blurted the obvious, but it only drew a smile from him.

How could she still charm him so?

"What, I may not simply drop in on one of my favorite wives?"

The shade of her cheeks deepened. "Of course you may."

His attendants reemerged. "All is well, Mamanatowic."

He bent to enter the yehakan, and she followed after. The smoky-dark interior wrapped him about, fragrant with the small pot of stew simmering at the central fire and drying bunches of various plants hanging about. He drew a deep breath, savoring the smells, while she arranged a pile of mats and furs on her sleeping bench. "The girls are away?"

"Granny Snow is instructing Mato'aka today, along with Channa. Little Flower tags along as the shadow she always is. I do not expect them until after dark." She made a sound in her throat, half a laugh. "As if anyone could tear Mato'aka away from the evening dancing."

When she stood back, he settled onto the stack. Very comfortable, as always.

She swayed, fingering the fringe of her doeskin apron. "Do you wish food?"

He smiled again. "I would not refuse a morsel made under your hand."

She scooped a serving from the simmering pot into a small bowl and handed it to him then stood back while he ate, watching him as he watched her.

When he'd swallowed the last bit and wiped his fingers, he set the bowl aside. "Tell me again of your people, Ay-mah."

Her eyes widened and her lips flattened, no doubt at his use of her old name. Exotic eyes, they were. Brown but not as dark as those of the other women, and with a slight uptilt at the corners. One brow lifted. "Why do you ask?"

Such impertinence. He set his hands on his knees. "I am curious."

She tipped her head, measuring him. "They are from across *yapám*."

He nodded. That much she had told him.

"Their land is cold and—and grey. They wear much more clothing than the People. Some of that is because of the cold, some because they feel it more—proper."

"Proper?"

"Yes." Her gaze darted away and back then lingered on his chest and shoulders. "They think our bodies should be covered because—because they are evil and cause us to do wrong."

He leaned toward her. "Does my body cause you to do wrong?"

Her expression did not change, and for a moment she did not respond, even as the color crept up her face. But she did not either smile or show shock. "I am your wife, Mamanatowic."

"Call me by my name," he said, with deliberate gruffness.

Her eyes came to his. "Wahunsenecawh."

The stirring swept through him. Surely she felt it as well. But he had more questions to ask.

"When your people came across yapám," he said, "on their great winged *kanoes*, was it by chance, or did they mean to send more later?"

The first glimmer of understanding and suspicion of where he intended to take the conversation dawned in her face. Her small mouth thinned again. She blinked. "I do not know."

He leaned one elbow on a knee. "I think you do know."

She held her silence for a moment. "I was young. Not even a woman yet."

He waited.

At last she huffed and turned a circle. "There was talk of sending more. But the leader who had gone back to bring us help never returned. And I do not know whether they meant to leave us to our fate at that point, or—or what."

"How many years have passed since then?"

"I—I have lost count." Another huff. Did she speak truth or try to evade again? "I think perhaps ten, twice over." Sudden tears sparkled in her eyes. "I have lived in Tsenacomoco for more than half my life."

"You are of the People now." He cleared his throat. "What of their kanoes? What of their weapons? How do they make war?"

She collected herself once more and straightened. "Much they have made war with the Span-ish, in their kanoes upon yapám. They are fierce enough, I suppose, and I have often heard my elders say they are quick to take offense where none is meant. But"—again her eyes flew to his and away—"I have seen the People do the same, when it suits them."

He nodded slowly. It was a fair enough observation. "Are they a great people? Are they many?"

Uncertainty flickered across her face. "They are very many. Our towns were crowded beyond what I can describe to you. We—" She stopped, lips parted, looked at him again. "Many of us longed for an open country, where we could breathe good air and live without sickness and the badness that men will do to each other when they have no real work."

"Real work?" He snorted. "Would you turn men into women?"

Her frown matched his. "No. But there, the men are shut up into the towns and not even allowed to hunt. They must buy or sell things or do work for others. Or go out to fight or sail the ocean."

He sat back and looked at her. It was hard to remember at times that she was the child of a completely different people—one that had come in waves to their neighbors to the south and sought to make their own towns but had been swallowed up by the land and the People. Defeated ultimately by O'ki and the manito.

A chill swept him. Or had they? The Suquoten had taken Ay-mah captive years ago from where her people dwelt with the Kurawoten then carried her to their allies, the Weopomeioc. She was a gift to the Powhatan, a token of victory over the weak aliens. Word had it that the Kurawoten retaliated by taking many Suquoten towns. The Suquoten and Weopomeioc had renewed their efforts to make war. Some said the Kurawoten eventually fled to among the Coree, while others said they also came north to hide among the Chesepioc.

Were the pale-skinned foreigners still among the People to the south? Did their people seek their whereabouts once again?

And if they did, would they demand his own Woanagusso, formerly known as Ay-mah, be returned to them?

She shifted as she sat before him. "Perhaps it is not to be wondered at if they seek other places to dwell."

He blinked. He'd nearly forgotten what they were speaking of.

"Perhaps it is not," he said after a pair of heartbeats.

Her eyes, so strangely set and yet familiar after all these years, held his. What thoughts strayed behind them that she did not speak? She was both exactly like all the other women but not, at the same time.

He leaned toward her. "May I stay with you this night, my wife?"

Surprise sparked in the depths of her gaze, then warmth. "Of course, my husband. I would welcome your presence."

She did not even question it. She dared not. He was, after all, mamanatowic and her husband and, after all these years, the most compelling man she had ever met.

She almost resented falling asleep rather than lying awake to savor his warmth at her back, his arm draped over her, but sleep took her regardless.

Deep into the night, Wahunsenecawh surged upright with a shout, drawing a gasp from her own throat and cries from Mato'aka, Little Flower, and Channa, asleep on adjoining platforms. The inside of the yehakan was dark, the fire burning low, as she struggled to discern what had happened.

While she uncurled from the mantle covering them, he sat on the edge of the platform, breathing hard, cradling his head in both hands. "What is it, my husband?" she murmured.

He did not answer, and Channa ventured, "Nohsh?"

"Go back to sleep," he rumbled, unmoving.

While the girls lay down again with obvious reluctance, she knelt on the bed and smoothed her hands across his shoulders and back. He would tell her if he wished. And if not, no pleading would draw it from him.

He drew in a long breath. "I—dreamed."

She continued kneading his shoulders. He pitched his voice, it seemed, for her ears alone.

"I saw—the deaths of all my people. Only I was left."

Her hands stilled. "Oh, my husband!"

He did not move. "What kind of mamanatowic am I—or even, a man at all—if I cannot keep my people alive?"

An answering fear beat in her own chest, and she had no words for him.

God. Oh, God!

The prayer, or at least the beginnings of one, felt woefully inadequate as well.

At last he unfolded himself and, turning, stretched out on the platform once more, tugging her down beside him. She cuddled in, her back side against his front.

"I must speak to the quiakrosoc," he said. "But it can wait until tomorrow."

Cold settled in the pit of her belly. Even after more than half her life amongst the People, nothing the priests did or said sat well with her. And she could not say exactly why.

The quiakrosoc stared at him. None spoke. Not that he expected immediate responses. Grave matters must be thought through, with plenty of time given for consideration before answers were offered.

Then, one by one, with gathering frowns or pursed mouths, they looked down or away.

"We need to think on this, Wahunsenecawh," said the eldest. "We can give you no insight at this time."

"Of course." He did not bother to keep the irritation from his tone.

Over the coming days, the reports about *Tassantassas* trickled in, and none gave him any cause to rest easy. They had made not only a camp upon that one island but had fortified it with hewn posts. It was clear they had no intentions of leaving anytime soon.

In the meantime, the dream returned twice more. He'd begun to think it nothing more than a product of sleeping beside Woanagusso and breathing the strange air of her yehakan for an entire night, but it came again, once when he was with a younger and newly married wife and once when he slept alone.

That third time, he summoned the quiakrosoc and stood them together before him, sending everyone else outside his personal yehakan. "I am weary of your lack of answers," he told the quiakrosoc. "The dream has come yet again. Three times now I have seen the deaths of our people. Surely you, with an ear open to the manito, can give me at least a hint of what may be happening."

Much averting of eyes and shuffling of feet greeted his demand. But one at last stepped forward, his own gaze haunted. "I have seen, oh Wahunsenecawh. There is a people who will come out of the East and defeat ours."

A murmuring rippled through the group at his pronouncement. His own heart leaped as well, sending the blood jolting through his veins. He scowled, ignoring the feeling. "This is not new. They have been saying thus for two tens of years."

"Even so, Mamanatowic, it will come."

He sat back, hands upon his knees. "What do you propose we do?"

The quiakros met his gaze without wavering. "Go to war. Diminish these people before they rise up against us."

Chapter Two

"You two will be women full grown in the manito. You must keep your eyes and ears open to more than what you can see and hear."

Granny Snow led them through the forest, baskets in hand for gathering berries and medicinal leaves. Mato'aka paused to scratch beneath the edge of her leggings made of *wutapantam* hide worked soft, where the summer's heat drew a trickle of sweat. She understood the necessity of protective clothing against briars and branches during foraging outings, but oh, she missed the freedom of bare limbs.

As always, however, their outings brought more than simple foraging. Granny Snow instructed whenever given opportunity. It wasn't that Mato'aka did not take such instruction seriously, but. . .sometimes she would like to be a simple girl.

Not the daughter of the mamanatowic. And not the next Beloved Woman in training.

Besides, it seemed whenever she actually wanted the attention, the responsibility, the elders were quick to tell her to stay back and remain silent. And then they grew exasperated—or worse, dismissive—of her shenanigans. But she just could not help it. Pranks and jests and little adventures made life so much more interesting.

They waded into a thicket and began the real work of the outing—plucking the juicy, dark purple berries that somehow always came with small but fierce thorns. Mato'aka made it a game to see how many she could pick before getting scratched. Today, the sun grew hot and the berries lay thick in the bottom of her basket when the first prick broke skin and drew blood on her forearm.

An offering to the manito that made the berries so plump, the aunties used to say, laughing. An offering she did not wish to give—but there was nothing for it now.

From the next bush over, Channa's voice rose above the hum of bees. "Nohsh says that when he has returned, Tomakin and I shall be joined at last."

Mato'aka spared her but a glance. "And Tomakin did not stay behind to see your yehakan built?"

Channa tossed her head. "It is all but finished now. Once we have picked berries and set enough to dry, I will see to weaving more mats to cover the walls."

She would expect Mato'aka to help with the weaving of mats. Mato'aka vented a tiny sigh. It wasn't that she minded helping, but weaving was such a tedious task.

"And where has Nohsh gone this time?" she asked, more to distract herself than because she was interested in the answer.

But the glance that Channa and Granny Snow exchanged brought a chill to her skin and set all her senses at alert.

Granny Snow bobbed a nod, and Channa turned to her. "He is gone to war. The quiakrosoc have warned of a grave danger, so he and his warriors went to deal with it."

The chill deepened. All she could do was stare at Channa, and then Granny Snow, who gave a single blink and said, her voice full of calmness and affection, "You must not allow yourself to be troubled by this. Because he goes to war now, our People will avoid war later. From that direction at least."

Mato'aka clutched her basket. She should think of some reply but could not.

"War is part of the life of the People. You know this. Why do you think we tell you, if warriors come and steal you away, resolve only to live and prosper wherever the manito take you?" Having risen to sharpness, her voice gentled again. "But for now, you are safe, little one. If that happens, then O'ki will prepare you. Your own strength will sustain you."

Jamestowne, August 1607

Between the infernal heat and sheer incompetence of those purporting to have their company's best interests at heart, 'twas a wonder any of them were still alive.

He had been in wretched circumstances before. Slavery and enforced labor amongst the Turks had taught him the value of self-effacement, of patience until an opportune time for action came about. This time at least he had his freedom—and Master Hunt had prevailed upon Wingfield to recognize him as a member of the council just before Captain Newport's return to England in June.

But this—this present ill, he laid firmly at Wingfield's feet. Hoarding the company's resources and only doling out a day's worth of barley gruel at a time. He claimed 'twas for the good of the company, but obviously he and his cronies dipped therein, because they appeared untouched by the sickness and weakness that afflicted the rest.

Smith himself did not go untouched by such weakness. A terrible malaise and discontent such as he had never experienced gripped him at odd moments.

He and two other men gathered fallen branches and dragged them back to the fort, watching the forest all the while. No sign of the savages this time, thanks be to God. Although their worst enemy at this point was not the wild men lurking in the woods but the bloody flux that afflicted them all.

So many had died already. Some of those who had not perished either by attack or disease were recovering—many but slowly—and all hands were needed to work regardless, if able in the least. Others lingered on, driven back to their beds by such extremity of weakness that Smith marveled they still breathed. Bartholomew Gosnold was one of those. Smith was, frankly, worried.

Why were so many of the good men those who were lost?

He and the other men reached the gate without mishap, but he had barely drawn his burden inside before Thomas Savage, one of the surviving boys, accosted him. "You must come," he said, panting. "Captain

Gosnold is not doing well."

His already-rolling stomach took another heave. Then he was in motion, running beside—and then ahead of—the lad to where Gosnold lay beneath a pitiful shelter made of a ship's sail.

Smith knelt beside him, nostrils curling at the stench of sick and the flies buzzing about the man, who remained so insensible to his surroundings that he did not even bestir himself to wave them away.

An ache deepened in his chest. This was so wrong, so unjust. And he was weary of waiting for their president to dole out drips and drops of mercy when it was in the power of his hand to offer some relief.

With a last glance into the waxen, yellowed face of a man he considered a valued comrade if not a friend, he shoved to his feet and strode away.

It was not that others had not tried to appeal to Wingfield, both as president and as a man, but he remained tightfisted about all things that, true, were not easily replaced without another ship from England, but were needful to make food and water more healthful. Sack, aquavit, oil, oatmeal, eggs, and beef—they had brought all with them, but anything that wasn't wheat or barley, Wingfield kept under guard.

'Twasn't far to go, across the fort from the shaded spot against the palisaded wall where Gosnold lay, to the tent, of slightly better construction than Gosnold's, which served for a president's quarters and office. Of course, Wingfield insisted on a level of comfort within, above what the other men enjoyed.

Ignoring the sick feeling swirling through his gut, he marched up to the opening. The guard outside straightened, gripping his pike even while his eyes widened.

"I wish to speak with our president," Smith growled.

The guard swallowed and looked around. Smith knew he'd see nothing but men littering the fort grounds, sitting or lying about or listlessly going about tasks needful for life despite the sickness. He nodded once and ducked under the lifted door flap. "Captain Smith to speak with you, sir."

An audible sigh, then, "Bring him."

Smith was already pressing past the guard. The moment he crossed the threshold, he fixed Wingfield with a glare. "You must release the rest of our resources. The men are dying for want of proper nourishment and medicine."

Captain Edward Maria Wingfield merely favored him with a baleful glare in return. "That is my purview and no one else's."

One step, and Smith slammed his hands flat on the desk in front of Wingfield. The man flinched but then held firm as Smith leaned toward him. "Captain Gosnold lies dying. Your own cousin! Have you no feeling for your kinsman, or does it please you? Serve your purpose, perhaps, being one less adversary to contend with?"

Wingfield's eyelids fluttered.

Smith pressed closer, dropping his voice. "What, indeed, is your purpose here? Are you holding out until more than half of us have died, and then you will sail for England and cry that the venture failed despite all your best efforts?" He shoved away from the desk. "If so, then I offer you congratulations—your plan is a success."

Without waiting for a reply, he left the hut and strode back across the yard to sit vigil at Gosnold's side.

An hour or so later, a man came over, proffering a small jug of vinegar tonic. Thomas Wotten, the chirurgeon, took a spoonful and dribbled it into Gosnold's mouth. After a moment's hesitation, Gosnold swallowed once, coughed, then swallowed again.

It made no difference, however. He breathed his last just before first light the next morning. They buried him with full honors, laying him to rest in an actual coffin and not simply a shroud, with his leading staff laid across the top. Hunt read a heartfelt service, but it was all just bitterness inside Smith's chest.

Wingfield continued to avow that he only had the best interest of the colony in mind, that if he released all the resources, they'd soon gobble them up and then where would they be? Starving, that's what.

Well, were they not already starving?

He ranted on about mutiny and building the kingdom and how he was but a servant to God and the king, seeking not his own interests but only those of others. Smith exchanged the barest glance with Gabriel Archer. He'd have done better to resist the impulse to do so, as it set Wingfield off again.

This time he suppressed the shaking of his head and the wandering of his eye. They must needs do something about their so-called president, and soon.

Chesepioc

Taking lives was never an easy task, whether hunting game or men, even in the heat of battle, and planned warfare required a certain cold-bloodedness that both satisfied and left him feeling a little sick. But warfare was a necessity when it came to the defense of his people. Part of his place as mamanatowic was to keep those under him safe and fed, and they in turn paid him tribute and honor.

Wholesale slaughter, however, shook something deep within him. Even if it was carried out in order to turn aside a calamity so great he had dreamt of it three times. To put an entire region of towns to death, merely on the word of the quiakrosoc, went beyond anything he had known.

And yet, in love for his people—in fear for their lives—he had done it.

"The Chesepioc are no more," he declared, as the rest of his warriors gathered about him.

"Except for women and children," his brother Opechancanough said.

"Those who did not try to fight," another warrior added.

"The women will bear warriors now for the Powhatan," Wahunsenecawh said, "and the children will forget who they were and instead make our numbers stronger."

It was, indeed, the way of the People. He had tried, even while making war on the Chesepioc, to show a measure of mercy and regard for life in sparing those women who had not resisted them, as well as young children and girls.

One thing he did not speak aloud. While carrying out this task, he had been looking for those among the Chesepioc who were different—whose faces were perhaps longer and sharper, the eyes wider, men whose chins betrayed the growth of more hairs than the People bore. A few struck him as not quite pure Tunapewoc, but there were none who appeared purely Tassantassa, either.

It was good. He did not, strangely enough, want to have to face his Woanagusso with the sure knowledge he had slain any of her former people.

A sudden longing to see her gusted through him. He would not go so far as to snatch her up in an embrace—not publicly at least, and relinquish his dignity—but she and the two girls she'd borne him were chiefest in his heart at this moment.

Captives in tow, they made their way back to Werowocomoco. Runners had gone ahead to bid them prepare a feast, carrying a brace of deer and turkeys they'd taken on the way. The fragrance of roasting meat and stewed vegetables carried on the breeze as they approached the town, and as word of their arrival spread, women and children spilled out to greet them as if carried by the aroma themselves.

And there came Mato'aka and Little Flower, ever her shadow, running as fast as their legs would carry them, racing to beat the pack of their half siblings. Mato'aka was then the first to reach him, her small body slamming into his, heedless of weapons or the grime of travel clinging to his arms and legs. They'd washed away all war paint and blood spatters the morning after beginning the return journey.

He lifted her with one arm and held her close, reaching for her sister with the other and greeting all the rest of his children who had turned out.

For a little while, it was a noisy, happy pile, and he could almost forget the reason they'd gone out to war.

Then—there she was, across the way, carrying a basket against her hip, skin gleaming in the sun with either oils or sweat, watching the commotion surrounding him with a quiet smile. After setting down the girls, he made his way toward her, through the press, even as the children continued to clamor for his attention. "Go now," he told them, but gently. "There will be time for talk later."

As he approached Woanagusso, he felt for a moment like a youth untried, but quickly pushed the feeling away. She came into his arms without hesitation and embraced him in return. "I will come to you after we have eaten," he murmured into her ear.

She gave a smile and nod.

They were still feasting, however, when some of his elder warriors and the quiakrosoc approached him. "We must speak of the Tassantassas," they said.

He led them to his yehakan, where the fire had already been stoked and more bowls of food laid out.

They settled in, taking long draughts of *uppowoc*, and he did not wait long before fixing the chief quiakros with a look. "Is it the Span-ish again?"

"No, but these other pale-skinned ones. They seem completely unable to feed themselves. They also have been drinking the river's water rather than find a spring"—this drew derisive laughter from the others—"and are excessively quarrelsome amongst themselves." He shook his head. "It is a wonder they have not slain each other."

Wahunsenecawh chuckled. "Perhaps we should allow them to do just that."

The quiakros peered at him. "You are newly returned from making war on another people. Perhaps they are the next ones you should consider making war upon."

He grunted and took another pull of uppowoc. "I will think upon it."

Jamestowne

Enough was enough already. And today would see an end of it.

Accompanied by Captain Ratcliffe and Captain Martin, Smith marched across the yard to the president's tent, a written warrant in hand. They dismissed the guard and stepped inside.

Wingfield rose, but slowly, that insufferable arrogance carved into his features. "What is the meaning of this?"

Martin held up the warrant. "As stated here, we think you very unworthy to be either president or of the council, and therefore are discharging you of both. Captain Ratcliffe here is president effective immediately."

Wingfield straightened, his face hardening. "Well then, you have eased me of a great deal of care and trouble. You will all recall how many times I have offered you this place, but do also recall that, as His Majesty has instructed for our government, the president ought to be removed only by the greater number of the seven voices of our councilors. And you are but three."

"If we do you wrong," Smith said, "we must answer for it."

He threw up a hand. "Then I am at your pleasure. Dispose of me as you will, without further uproar."

They escorted him to the *Discovery*, the pinnace that Newport had left behind for the colony's use in exploration, for it would not do to have him remain within the town and cause further discord. On the next day, they brought him back for the reading of the articles against him.

While Wingfield stood, dripping with haughtiness as always, they took turns, beginning with Captain Ratcliffe, to name their complaints against him. Ratcliffe's involved the denial of a few items, including a mere spoonful of beer, to relieve him while deathly sick. Smith himself testified to Wingfield's accusations that Smith had lied, and to the defamation of his character, though he was not among the least members of their party. Martin then stepped forward and charged that Wingfield did nothing but tend his own needs and had indeed starved Martin's own son, who had also gone begging for a spoonful of beer to relieve his sickness.

Stiffly, Wingfield turned to Ratcliffe. "Master President, should I answer these complaints, or have you more to charge me with?"

Ratcliffe pulled a small paper book from inside his waistcoat. "These are the full articles against you. Captain Archer, will you do us the favor of reading them?"

"Our council is directed to conduct all business by spoken word and not writ," Wingfield said impatiently. "I am ready here and now to answer."

"It is our intent to proceed in that order," Ratcliffe said steadily, "and read them aloud."

"I wish, rather, that you give me a copy of the articles and time to answer them by writing."

The remaining council exchanged glances and shook their heads. "Nay, but Captain Archer will read here and now."

Wingfield made a dismissive flourish with one hand. "Please yourself, then."

Captain Archer read the articles, which included not only charges of wasting the colony's resources while withholding from those who needed help the most during the outbreak of grave illness, but also aspersions cast on Wingfield's Christian faith, based on his not having a Bible in his possession. Archer had just read that part, not yet even half done with all the charges, when Ratcliffe called out, "Stay, stay! We know not whether he will abide our judgment on all these, or whether he will appeal to the king." He then fixed a severe look upon Wingfield, who had stood with arms folded during the reading. "How say you? Will you appeal to the king or no?"

Wingfield drew himself up again, a look of cunning passing across his face, then schooled to mildness. Smith's skin crawled to see it. But the man only replied, "His Majesty's hands are full of mercy, and so I do appeal to that mercy."

Of course, he would seek the out offered him, especially given the charge of atheism, which must be answered in an English court and not here. Why had they bothered with that one?

Ratcliffe's gleam of eye and hardness of mouth reflected Smith's own feeling. But he only threw up a hand and said, "Commit him again as prisoner to the master of the pinnace. And look to him well. He is now the king's prisoner."

In the days after, a kind of peace—more resignation if not contentment—settled over the town. To Smith's surprise and a gratitude he would not admit to, gifts of food, both meat and corn, arrived every few days from their neighbors the savages. Sometimes he recognized those who came, and other times not.

Strange it was that their manner of dress—or lack thereof—and arranging their hair had become almost familiar.

Shortly after they had sent Wingfield to be kept on the pinnace, great flocks of various fowls settled upon the rivers—ducks, geese, swans, of such variety he had never before seen. They were able to bring down several, sometimes more than one with each shot, and at last, with such plenty, some of the weakest men began to regain their strength. But it was a slow recovery, and illness still came and went even among the chiefest. Himself included.

With Archer, the council took inventory. "Barely eighteen days of provisions left." Ratcliffe turned to the others. "I think it time that I take a few men and go upriver to see what might be obtained from the savages."

Archer lifted a brow. "Do you not mean, rather, the Naturals?"

Laughter followed that, which Smith did not share. Ratcliffe shrugged. "Whatever we call them, it seems we are most dependent upon their good will for our survival. With winter coming, we must needs see what we can do to ensure our provision lasts until such time as supply might come from England." He turned to Smith. "You should go and treat with the—Naturals." The ghost of a smile touched his face.

Smith gritted his teeth.

"It must be you," Ratcliffe said evenly. "None others are well enough for the journey. Specifically, to the mouth of the river, to Kequotan. Trade for corn, and try the river for fishing."

And so the shallop was prepared—the vessel's shallower draft would allow them greater access upriver—and Smith carefully chose his crew. 'Twas a difficult task, when all were in such despair they would rather starve and rot with idleness than be persuaded to do anything for their own relief. At last, however, he had appointed twenty men to accompany him.

"Do you," he told Ratcliffe and Martin most sternly, "see to the building of the houses in my absence. Our tents are rotten, and winter is coming."

They set off downriver and toward the sea and were almost immediately met with stormy weather. Of fish they could catch none, and Smith found himself in a mood as foul as the weather by the time they reached the Indian town overlooking the river. At the welcome that turned out for them, they went ashore, taking along a few goods with which to trade.

Smith's nerves buzzed with both unease and readiness despite the familiarity of the people themselves. Men and women alike came out to greet them. "Wingapo!" they cried, and Smith smiled and nodded, showing his hands as empty and open.

They crowded around him, babbling and reaching to touch his hair and clothing. Sunlight glinted off oiled skin and hair black as ravens' wings. As before, he steeled himself, holding steady to his smile. It was a little easier to pick words out of their talk—or at least he thought he recognized more bits than before. It ought to be easier, with all the study he'd given himself to, to learn their tongue.

There was no beckoning them into the town this time, though, or preparations for a feast. They seemed overeager to trade but held out mere handfuls of corn while gesturing to a hatchet. Smith watched their eyes, noting the calculated gleam and the telltale tightness of their faces. Obtaining needed provisions from these would prove much harder than before.

But he could be crafty as well.

Chapter Three

Werowocomoco

She understood now why he had sought her out.

At least, it was a very strong guess as to why.

The town was ablaze with talk of the strangers who had come to Tsenacomoco. Not the Span-ish—at least, they did not think so—but pale of skin and faces full of hair and bodies that smelled bad under layers of strange and excessive clothing.

She laughed along with the other women about that detail. Would any here recall that when she was first brought to Tsenacomoco, she had also dressed thusly? Perhaps not, since almost the first thing that had been done, after she was presented to the Powhatan weroance, was that she was forced to disrobe and bathe and then given a castoff deerskin skirt in place of her old raiment.

But like that skirt, she was herself a castoff—unwanted, valued only as a last resort, until the moment Wahunsenecawh stepped forward and declared he wished her to become his wife. And oh, what a stir that had caused. She could not suppress a tiny smile at the memory, even now.

More's the wonder he had kept her near him, after, despite all the alliance marriages he had contracted. Despite her bearing him not one but two girls—and she had become caretaker for one of his older daughters as well. Likely it was that none of the other women here at Werowocomoco even remembered her ignoble beginning, although they loved gossip enough that such a thing should have been kept in memory and thrown back in her face when jealousy spurred them to it.

Such had happened often enough in the early days. Wahunsenecawh merely expected her to brush it aside and carry on. And so she did her best to do just that.

About the time it became obvious she was carrying Mato'aka, the women relented. At first, she thought it just the prestige of carrying a child for the mamanatowic—for so he had begun to be called not long after their marriage—but then one of the old women came to her, accompanied by three of the quiakrosoc, with the declaration that the child she carried was marked by the spirit realm—by the manito—to be the next Beloved Woman. She'd not known how to respond to that. It felt a little like being Mary, the mother of Jesus.

Not that there was any chance that her child could be an actual savior or that she was a virgin when the child was conceived. But she was too polite to contradict what the old woman and priests had said.

And then the child was, indeed, a girl. She was given a pair of names—Mato'aka, her common name, and Amonute, her secret name. The quiakrosoc were vague as to the meaning, but Granny Snow had insisted they were good names. And she insisted on overseeing the girl's spiritual education herself.

It did not sit well with her, as mother, but there was nothing she could do about it. She was now part of the People, and this was their way.

Did God even exist as she had been reared to believe? She held memories of attending church and taking communion all those long years before. But here she was now, cut off from that expression of her faith. Was she also cut off from God since she could no longer worship as her elders had always insisted was right and proper?

Even so, a tiny corner of her held on and at least wished to believe that somehow, somewhere, the God of heaven as she had always understood Him still watched over her, still directed her steps, though she be wife to a mamanatowic and her elder daughter be chosen as spokeswoman for the spirits. And so only in her heart did she whisper the prayers that were directed to Him alone.

And now, after years of hearing nothing but the barest rumors of the rest of the company from which she'd been snatched, rumors which left her feeling sick and despondent, the town was atwitter about these newest strangers. These *Tassantassas.*

She wanted to ask Wahunsenecawh about them but was still thinking how to pose the question. The fear had touched her, this last time he'd gone out to make war, that it was the Tassantassas he sought to make a slaughter of. There was no mention of them, however, upon their return—and of the captives he and Opechancanough had taken, they'd brought but few to Werowocomoco. All the captives were of dark enough skin to allay her dread that any survivors from the Cittie of Ralegh might be among them. And yet she wondered. . .

It had been years since she'd allowed herself to think on them overlong. Or to recall names to mind. But the suspicion niggled at her that these newcomers might indeed be more, as the Kurawoten said it, *Inqutish.*

English, her thoughts corrected.

She had been Emme. On a spring day, she was taken, along with Elinor Dare and Libby and a handful of men and boys, and carried away captive. Separated from the others, Emme had been sent to the Powhatan.

She still recalled the terror of those days. In retrospect, she could recognize the respect with which she was treated by the warriors of the People—more respect, she suspected, than Englishmen would have shown.

She could also recall disparaging comments by some of the English, both men and women, toward those they considered savages. Life here was not always easy, true, but when held in comparison to the streets of London, that crowded, filthy, noisy city on the other side of yapám—

How strange that the word which came to her mind for the sea was that used by the People. She no longer belonged among the English.

And yet she could not stop wondering. So when he came to her after returning from making war to the south, she determined to ask.

She saw first to his comfort with food and drink. Once he had finished eating, he did not remain merely sitting on the mats she'd laid for him but stretched out on his side, head resting on his bent arm. Weariness carved furrows in his face as she'd never before seen.

"Are you well, husband?" she asked softly, though the question had already been asked when they'd exchanged their customary greetings.

His lashes rose and fell, and his expression did not change. "Well enough."

She knelt beside him. "How might I ease your burden, my mamanatowic?"

His eyes came open again, glittering softly in the dimness, and at last he leaned up on his elbow, hands folded before him, regarding her. "These Tassantassas. They are of your old people, are they not?"

A chill touched her. "I am not sure, without seeing them."

His brow creased.

"There are many peoples across yapám. It is hard to know for certain of which these are."

He pursed his lips, thinking. "I am told they carry a—thing—" He lifted a hand and waved it like a flag. "It is white, with red across it."

Her heart leaped. St. George's Cross, that was the name of it, as she recalled. It was indeed the banner of England.

"Are you thinking of going back to them?"

She glanced up to find him leaning toward her, gaze intent and mouth thinned.

It was not uncommon among the People, both in the present day and in the old stories, for women to tire of living with their husbands' folk and to return to wherever they came from. And a chief, whether mere weroance or mamanatowic, had the right to send his wives away when they fulfilled their immediate purpose. But for her to choose to leave him?

"You are mamanatowic. You are the one who gives the word for me to go." She hesitated. "Are you wishing me to leave?"

It was a bold question, one he could have met with anger. But he only laughed and leaned back again, though the sharpness in his eyes did not go away.

She must seize the moment. "I have another question for you, my husband."

The corner of his mouth quirked. "You are indeed the mother of our Mischievous One."

She let an answering smile curve her own mouth. "I wish to know. When you went to make war this time, was it on the pale ones? Or any of those who brought me here?"

Humor faded, but it was only curiosity and consideration in his gaze, not anger. At last he merely shook his head.

"Would you tell me true if you knew where they had gone?"

And this time she dared to lay a hand across his.

His fingers stirred beneath, but he did not push her away.

"Do I not love you?" he said, very softly. "Are you not my wife?"

She scooted closer and laid her cheek against his arm. "You do love me. And I am your wife."

"Then why does it matter?"

She blew out a long breath. "I suppose it does not."

His free hand came up to stroke her hair.

The quiakros looked thoughtful and concerned. "It is very troubling. These Tassantassas, at first they are content to trade with the People, but the farther they travel up the river, the more pushy and rude they have become. Their leader, he is a man with hairs the color of the red leaves in fall and acts as though he is mamanatowic. As if the People owe him tribute, and not you."

Wahunsenecawh grunted and paused in his task of affixing a stone point to an arrow. "Can we not delay talking of this until I have uppowoc in hand?"

The quiakros dipped his head in apology. "It is a most urgent matter."

"I do not dispute that." He huffed and gazed off past the man at the activity of the town. "Give me time to think on it."

He barely had time to breathe after making war on the Chesepioc, and his back and limbs still ached from battle. Waugh, but he was not as young as he once was!

And then the way Woanagusso had questioned him about the attacks and her former people. Wahunsenecawh had indeed heard things—some of it doubtless only rumors but much was more accurate than one would think—and thought he knew the fate of at least some of them. Although he could not be sure. Mostly the various other towns thought those newcomers were more cunning and slippery than anyone expected, and it was impossible to say with any sort of confidence where they had gone or were at this time.

He would not be cruel and tell her that all her former kinsmen were dead, but neither would he give her false hope. And he simply, honestly, did not know.

By evening, his thoughts concerning the newer wave of strangers had sorted themselves out enough to bear speaking of. He summoned the quiakrosoc and other councilors to his yehakan. After a leisurely time of smoking uppowoc, he gestured for their attention. "We will let the Tassantassas be for now. Observe their actions and consider them well. But if word comes of them doing more, send to me without delay."

They all nodded. "This is good counsel," the chief quiakros said.

"Think you they could be of those we thought were Span-ish," another asked, "who came and brought slaughter last year and stole away some of our people?"

"If we have opportunity to take this red-haired Tassantassa captive, we should do so, and not only question him, but take him to Tapahanek to see if he was one of those."

"Hm. A worthy consideration as well."

It was enough, at least for now.

"You ought to be well contented, having brought nearly thirty bushels of corn to the fort."

"We will see how long it lasts," Smith said, then clenched his teeth against further speech.

He was not, in fact, well contented. Too aware he was of how desperation forced him to heavy-handedness. And Captain Martin might have so far been an ally, but who knew how quickly that could change?

Dealing with the Indians was like trying to herd small children. Or to manage the lazy and self-important back at the fort. At least patience had paid off with the town of Kequotan situated at the mouth of the river, and God had softened their hearts enough to wish to deal fairly, resulting in Smith's men carrying off sixteen bushels from that town alone.

And then, on their return, they were met upon the river by two kanoes of Indians, inhabitants of Waraskoyack, well upriver of Jamestowne, on the south side. After being entertained by this group, they carried away another dozen or so bushels.

A great hurrah rose from the fort at the sight of what they'd brought. Even the sick and weak crept out to enjoy some of the cakes of bread they'd been given.

But only a few weeks passed before they were once again down to short rations—not above fourteen days' worth. The council met, and motions were made about sending both Wingfield and Ratcliffe, along with Captain Archer, back to England to procure supplies. At least they had built enough houses to shelter them all for the winter. President Ratcliffe and Captain Martin recovered enough from the latest bout of grave sickness to attend, and with much debate, it was decided to send the pinnace and shallop upriver, toward the town of Powhatan, to trade for yet more corn.

Lots were cast this time to determine who should go. One such lot fell to Smith, and while they were outfitting the pinnace, he made a very quick journey to Tapahanek. Only women and children were present at the town, however. They fled at first but were persuaded to return. They would not agree to trade, and with no leave or desire to take by force, Smith left there and turned instead to Paspahae. There, under much threat and hostility, Smith was able to procure nearly a dozen bushels, but the warriors of the town followed them as they continued back to the fort.

They dared not stop even for the night with such pursuit.

Upon their return, the pinnace sat ready. Smith had eight men and himself for the barge, and another five mariners to manage the pinnace, with two landsmen to help with hauling things aboard. They departed on the ninth of November, driven upstream by a stiff wind.

Three forays total they made, meeting and trading most kindly with the inhabitants of the towns along the way, all aided by a warrior of the Chicahamania who offered to guide them. Smith made careful notes on the names of towns and their locations, descriptions of the country around, and, as always, his growing knowledge of their tongue.

He returned the second time to trouble at the fort—the blacksmith, a James Read, quarreling with and even threatening to strike Ratcliffe, the president, with his tools. A jury was drawn up, and Read was convicted and sentenced to hang for mutiny, but while on the ladder with the noose about his neck, he cried out that a dangerous conspiracy was afoot, of which Captain Kendall was the lead. So his life was spared, and a second jury condemned Kendall. This time, the guilty party was marched out and shot for his crime.

The thing gave Smith no satisfaction in the least. They'd had to expel

Kendall from the council for stirring up dissent, so it should not surprise him, but to have to execute the man at such a time?

With the mutterers at the fort much subdued, however, Smith went out for the third foray, still determined to find the headwaters of the Chicahamania River. Of the towns he discovered along the way, their corn was much decreased, yet he took enough to return yet again to the fort.

They were at this point well supplied, but some yet insisted the pinnace should go for England. Smith and Martin both strenuously opposed this and, once the matter quieted, Smith set out—for the fourth time—to finish his explorations.

The country itself was beautiful, even so late in the year. All manner of fowl filled the waterways—swans, geese, ducks, and cranes—and the high banks rose into hills beyond, some forested and some less so, interspersed with level, fertile ground that had clearly been planted during the growing seasons. And all lay inhabited by towns here and there, in full sight of the river.

Often the Indians came to the water's edge and called out to them, waving. Smith hailed them in return, sometimes stopping but often not.

A deep peace and contentment settled into the corners of his spirit. There was nothing he liked so much, aside from a good fight, as ranging alone, or nearly so. And to be the first Englishman to lay eyes on this place? He thanked God often and heartily for the joy of it.

It was a curious thing when her father came to visit her mother and she and Channa and their younger sister, Little Flower, were turned out to seek occupation elsewhere. She had asked Channa once what they were doing inside that was so important they could not have the girls present as well. Channa had merely thrown her a smirk and said, "Talking."

Mato'aka threw up her hands. "About what? I want to talk as well!"

And Channa had merely laughed for a long time and shaken her head.

Mato'aka understood now, and it made being banished from the yehakan even more uncomfortable. But she was still curious, and so she sometimes crept up to the back side of the yehakan and pressed her ear to the wall to listen.

This time, her parents were indeed talking, and not much else. It sounded as if they were almost quarreling, which was even more unsettling—frightening, really—considering her father's position and how quickly he sent wives away who no longer pleased him.

She did not want *Nek* to be sent away.

But the pitch of their voices fell to a murmur, and when she could no longer make out the words, she crept away again.

It sounded for all the world as if Nohsh was asking Nek about the Tassantassas. Why ever would he do that? What information would she give him that the warriors sent out to scout the situation could not?

It was not, however, anything she could ask either of her parents about, since that would betray she had listened where she ought not. It was also not something she could ask Granny Snow—not when Nohsh had told Nek so strenuously inside the yehakan that she must never tell anyone, or he would send her away. So Mato'aka must keep eyes and ears open for clues to more.

Taquitoc was nearly over, the time for gathering and of the leaves changing color. The first cold breaths of *popanow* stole down the neck of her mantle. She and the other women were busy gathering the last of the nuts, mending mats, and gathering wood for the coming winter. On one such trip out for an armload of branches, she noticed a pair of warriors hurrying to Nohsh's yehakan. Their faces were mostly unfamiliar, which meant they must be from a more distant town and were bringing news.

If only she could make an excuse and go listen outside the house! But Nohsh's guards kept watch too well on the entire outside, especially after once catching her and dragging her before Nohsh to be scolded.

Fortunately for her, the whispers swept through the town shortly after. The red-haired Tassantassa and his men were going all up and down the Chicahamania River, pestering the towns for corn. Did they not realize that each town only grew what was needed for each year, and little more? Of course, hospitality was accounted for, but nearly every town ran out of pegatawah and the like before the next year's crop was ready. And with the Tassantassas continually taking from the People, well then, the People faced the possibility of hunger, themselves. Perhaps not with as much severity as these helpless, quarrelsome strangers, but still.

Nohsh had given leave for the warriors to watch the strangers closely, particularly the red-haired one who spoke far too much. Take him, if possible, but keep him alive. Perhaps they could draw from him more knowledge of his people and their intent, since it seemed obvious they planned to stay through the winter. In addition to setting a palisade around their town, they were building real houses.

Nohsh wished an explanation, and speedily.

Early December 1607, the upper Chicahamania River

The river had narrowed and grown markedly shallower, but Smith was unwilling to give up his exploration just yet. "The headwaters cannot be far. It is my guess, by the lay of the land, that the river might issue from a lake or some broad ford."

Two of the men, John Robinson and Thomas Emry, voiced their own desire to press on and continue exploring the country, but half of the men shook their heads.

"We could go back down and secure the barge at Apocant," Smith said, "and there hire a kanoe."

"It would content many of us to wait downstream with the barge," one of the men said. "Then anyone still game for it can accompany you."

Smith took so long considering that some of the men muttered he was losing his nerve for the venture, when in truth, he simply hated giving up the distance gained. But finally, there being nothing for it, they went back downriver some seven or eight miles to the Indian town of Apocant, located at a high point on the river. After procuring a kanoe and two Indians to row for them, he took Robinson and Emry and their provision, leaving seven with the barge, with the express charge for them to remain anchored out in the river and not go ashore until he returned.

Some of the men still argued that Smith and the others should go no further. It was a wild country, they pointed out. The savages here were unknown to them, and well, still savages, despite the seeming friendliness and willingness to trade. But a burning deep within Smith's breast would not allow him to relent.

He wanted—no, needed—to press on and see what lay beyond.

"Do not lay the blame upon us if you are slain!" one of the men said as they parted, climbing back aboard the barge while Smith and the others settled into the kanoe.

A laugh was Smith's only reply.

The Indians paddled them along, one in the rear of the kanoe while the other took the front. Smith could not help but admire their skill as well as the fact that though they carried mantles, they wore only the deerskin drape around their middles and soft deerskin shoes. Their bare skin they coated liberally with some sort of grease, and that provided their only defense against the cold, besides the labor of rowing the kanoe.

The river continued at the same depth and breadth, but in the kanoe, they passed a total of twenty miles—some twelve farther than the barge had been—before calling a halt to go ashore to refresh themselves. Robinson and Emry set to cooking a stew with one of the Indians in attendance, but Smith felt itchy of foot and beckoned the other Indian to accompany him out to survey the land a bit. He hesitated at the fire, fixing each man with a warning look. "Discharge a piece at the first sign of an Indian, and I will come back straightaway. If all is well, I will return soon."

Emry gave him a jaunty grin and salute. "We'll keep our matches lit, Captain! Never you fear."

Smith set out with his guide, a lean, wiry fellow like the rest of his people, looking almost too young to be a warrior yet still taller than Smith by half a head. The youth had a pleasant enough face beneath black hair arranged as the rest of his people—a short crest dividing the right and left, with the right side shaved and the left grown long and knotted in place with the long claws of some creature stuck through.

The land here was low and marshy, unevenly wooded with stretches of tall, coarse grass. He stopped and scanned the area. Not a sound, besides that of birds and other wildlife.

His guide walked a little ahead, choosing the best path. As his own boots sank into the ground and came free with soft sucking sounds, Smith eyed the other man's deerskin footwear with not a little envy. The savage seemed unmoved by the muck and left a lighter track than he did.

Off to the left, a blue heron rose from the edge of the grasses and flew away. Smith traced its flight but remained mindful of where to step.

A shriek split the gathering twilight from where they had come, and a flock of birds rose, scattering. Immediately there followed a flurry of hallooing that he recognized as Indian.

Blast—they were betrayed!

His guide whipped toward him, eyes wide and darting between him and the forest beyond. Teeth clenched, Smith seized him, yanking free one of the garters holding his stockings and using it to bind the Indian's arm to his own. The youth would be his shield, if nothing else. He then drew forth his French pistol and, arm lifted and bent, pointed it at the Indian. "Do not move!"

The Indian gesticulated wildly with his free arm. *"Yoqueme wath!"*

Smith gave their bound arms a jerk. "Have you done this? Tell me, now!"

The youth simply shook his head, wide eyed.

"Take us back, this instant—"

Thwap! Something struck Smith's right thigh, sharply, and he stumbled half a step. An arrow—but in the immediate shock, he felt no pain.

Turning about, he spied two Indians drawing their bows from a short distance away, beneath the trees. With a roar, Smith aimed the pistol at them and fired. One fell and both scrambled away. Notwithstanding his arm being bound, he frantically reloaded. By that time, three or four more figures stood in the shadows. He pulled the Indian in front of him and once again aimed past him and squeezed the trigger.

A small rain of arrows sailed toward them but fell short. Smith reloaded and discharged his pistol twice more before suddenly, looming out of the forest and marsh grasses, came a great band of savages. To his dim astonishment, as they surrounded him and his human shield, they laid their bows on the ground.

One strode out from the others, tall and sinewy, both calm and fearsome. He spoke, and the young Indian Smith had bound himself to hastened to translate. "He say, do not shoot."

Another exchange of words, of which Smith could catch none, until the tall one leaned forward a little and said, "Weroance?"

His Indian shield answered in the affirmative. The tall one gestured toward the river and spoke again. "All slain," his guide whispered. "But you they will spare."

More words from the tall one.

"He offers peace," the young one said.

Smith gritted his teeth. "Tell him, we wish to go back to the kanoe."

His request was delivered, and more urgent gesturing was the response.

"He say, lay down your arms," the guide said.

Smith scanned the crowd—at least a hundred savages, possibly double that. With a growl, he went to take a better grip on his human shield, when his foot slid off the hummock where they stood. He tumbled into the mud, taking the young savage with him.

He had nothing to lose in this moment to cast himself upon their mercies. Struggling to sit up, he threw aside the pistol then unslung his musket and tossed that aside as well before untying the hapless young Indian and holding up both hands to show he was now unarmed.

They pressed in, laying hold of him and drawing him out of the mud. He was led to the tallest one—though they all towered over him—to which one of his guards pointed and said, "Weroance. Pamaunkee. Opechancanough."

One of their kings, then. Smith made a short bow. How could he best use this moment and keep them in awe even though he was forced to disarm?

Holding up one hand to bid them wait, he dug in a pocket and brought forth his compass. "See? This is a compass. Com-pass." He pointed to its face, turning the device slightly so they could observe how the needle floated and swung.

"Waugh!" The exclamation broke out all around as the savages pressed in and craned their necks to see.

Smith went on. "It tells direction—north, south, east, west—and points north." He gestured to each and then lastly to north again, pointing to the needle and once again north, then laid the compass in his palm and offered it to the savage king, who regarded him, eyebrows arched, dark eyes alive with interest. He nodded and lifted his hand higher. "Take it."

Gingerly, the tall savage lifted the device from his palm. Smith cupped both hands to simulate a ball. "Our earth, it is round, thus. North is at one end, here"—fingertips of one hand together to form the ball, he pointed to a theoretical northern pole—"and the moon goes around, while we circle the sun. With this device, and the patterns of the stars"—he pointed at the sky, which grew darker by the moment—"we can navigate the ocean."

'Twas far more than anyone present could absorb in this moment, he knew. But his sole purpose was to catch them off guard, if possible.

The king's gaze flicked toward him, measuring, calculating—oh, Smith could see it clearly. Then with a word, the tall savage set off in the direction of the river. His guards tugged Smith along with them.

There, upon the riverbank where the kanoe was drawn up and the cooking fire yet burned, lay Robinson, slain, with some twenty or thirty arrows bristling across his body. *Gracious God in heaven!* But Smith schooled himself to no outward reaction. Emry was nowhere in sight, nor the other Indian—although 'twas more than possible he had melted away into the countryside before the attack even took place.

One of the savages took up the cooking pot, their king gave the word again, and off they went, deeper into the country.

Smith could not but follow. Above, a quarter moon shone, giving light to the forest gloom. He could see now, as they went, the abundance of fires both near and far. Would they slay him as well at one of those?

He fought to maintain his composure. Wartime he knew, from his time in Hungaria. Captivity as well, when he had been taken by the Turks. But these—these savages, Naturals, whatever name one wished to call them by—they were unlike any men he had known before.

He had cause to be impressed with their orderliness as they marched. The king was well guarded with twenty bowmen, five at each flank and rear and fore, and others armed with wooden swords and cudgels. Two bowmen flanked Smith, and the rest of the warriors followed in file. Two sergeants, or so he presumed they were, kept a running motion around the company, one always toward the front with the other toward the rear, in perfect pace with each other. Their precision quite dazzled him.

They kept marching until at last they came to a town, less than six miles by his estimation from where he was taken—but it was not any sort of town Smith had seen before. The houses appeared to be but mere arbors covered in mats. Women and children came out to meet them, and after greetings were exchanged and much made of Smith, the entire company cast themselves into a circle and began to dance.

In the midst of it, Smith was compelled to sit. How strange were the movements they made, how unearthly and sometimes devilish did their cries and singing sound! Again, he fought to keep himself calm. Was this to be the end? Were they merely warming up for the sacrifice they would make—of him?

Then, just as abruptly as it had begun, the dancing ended and food was brought out, in great bowls and platters. They set before Smith a full quarter of venison and what was almost certain ten pounds of their strange bread. "*Michis*!" they said, gesturing. *Eat!*

He would not refuse.

Shortly after, as everyone went to their lodging, Smith was also led away to one of the makeshift houses. The savage who had accompanied him—one of the captains, it seemed—pointed to a mat spread in one corner, and after Smith lay down, took one for himself between his captive and the doorway.

Chapter Four

Twas passing strange, as the days went by, what kindness they showed him, after his companions had been slain and he expected any moment to meet the same fate. Each morning, three women presented him with great platters of fine bread and more venison than ten men could devour. So much excess, while the men of Jamestowne had languished all summer. But it turned out that his guards were more than happy to eat what he could not.

After initially taking his cloak and all his gear and accoutrements, they returned the cloak, his points and garters, and the compass, along with one tablet and stylus he kept on his person. They observed with much interest as he tied together his jerkin and breeches with the points and properly drew up his stockings and bound the tops with the garters then combed his fingers through his hair and beard in a paltry attempt to see to his appearance. Though eight strong warriors guarded him at all times—even on walks out to the woods to relieve himself—they kept him fed and warmed. In the meantime, he used the tablet to make notes on their language.

Then there were long hours when their king, Opechancanough, sat with him and talked, partly by translation of the young Chicahamania savage, and partly by drawings and gesturings. It wasn't that the Chicahamania excelled so at English yet, but rather that Smith had become more accustomed to communicating with him, and the arrangement seemed the best they had in the moment. The savage king swung between threats to assault the Jamestowne fort and questions about the English manner of their ships and sailing the seas, of the earth and skies and even their God.

Very canny, he was, and possessed of much intelligence. Smith's respect and admiration of him—indeed, of them all—grew by the day.

Then it was revealed to him, when Smith inquired whether there were any other men as he, that away in one of the lands southward, in a place called Ocanahonan, dwelt certain ones clothed like Smith. His heart leapt within him. Did this mean those sent out by Ralegh yet lived?

The savage king went on to explain about the rivers, where the Powhatan dominion began and ended, and about a great turning of salt water some four or five days' journey from the falls of Powhatan, upriver from the fort.

Smith's excitement grew for yet another reason. Surely—surely this must mean another great sea, located to the west? Perhaps on the other side of the mountains they had described?

If he survived this adventure, he'd so many tidings to carry back to the fort!

To the threats against the fort, he responded that they'd ordnance in the fort and mines laid in the fields, and that Captain Newport would surely return and take revenge on them. Partly they laughed, partly they appeared impressed and thoughtful.

On the second day, they had brought him to the side of a man who lay wounded and feverish from a gunshot to the body, apparently during their ambush of Smith. He gathered by their signs that they asked whether he could do anything for the man, but he could not. He tried to make them understand that there might be medicines, as well as the chirurgeon, at the fort, but here?

A letter—he should write a letter to the fort and ask them to take it there. The process of writing it, using a page from his tablet, drew their wonder and curiosity, as he set down not only the great kindness they showed him, but also news of the people of Ocanahonan and of the back sea. That he was safe, but Robinson and Emry were not, and where he had left the barge.

When the letter was complete, Opechancanough astonished him by sending three men to carry the message despite the weather being blustery and cold with rain squalls. It would go to the Paspahae first of all, who would then direct them to the fort. Clad only in the briefest of clothing—the drapes about their loins, soft shoes, and a mantle apiece—they set out.

Please God that it would indeed arrive safely.

The next morning a terrible clatter arose at his door. A single Indian burst inside Smith's lodging, brandishing a wooden sword, and with a shriek flung himself in Smith's direction. Barely in time did Smith's guards intercept the man, and no sooner had they pressed him back and disarmed him, than he drew his bow and threatened to shoot Smith.

The dark eyes were murderous, his features wrought in desperation.

One guard moved in front of Smith, and others once again disarmed the man, this time dragging him back outside. Smith drew a deep breath and resisted the most unmanly impulse to drop to his knees. He'd hardly had time to wake and scrape his thoughts together.

Shortly after, the king himself came, and with the aid of the young Chicahamania, explained that the man he'd wounded with his pistol had died—actually the second to have done so, although the savages had well concealed that they had any hurt from his shots. The man who attacked him was that one's father, seeking vengeance for the slaying. To prevent his fury, they would remove Smith from this place.

His guards bid him gather up his belongings and come, and they set out on the march again, this time northward.

What a curious thing, that they would slaughter his companions but keep him alive—preserving him even from a bereaved father bent upon vengeance. What purpose did they have for him?

A couple of days' march through deep, ancient forests and they came to a town on another river they called Youghtanan. There, about mid-morning, he was taken to a longhouse and seated on one of two mats laid next to a fire. Seven men filed inside, painted in various ugly ways in black and white and red, each holding a rattle made of a gourd. After pouring a circle of ground meal around him and the fire, they began to sing and dance, pausing every so often to lay down two or three grains of corn apiece. One half circle they formed of some six or seven hundred grains—he'd nothing else to occupy himself with but the counting—and then two or three other such circles. Then after each song, they would lay a little stick between every two, three, or five grains. It minded him of nothing so much as an old woman counting her paternoster.

The chiefest of these men, who must surely be some sort of priest, wore a bear's skin and a headdress of bunched weasel skins topped with a crown of feathers. After each song, he would cry out and make strange gestures and mutterings while tossing cakes of deer suet and tobacco on the fire.

What strange incantation did they make over him? At first he felt only the cold brush of terror, during which he marshaled his own heart and spirit in prayer—difficult though it was with such commotion—and finally, simple boredom. And then he would rouse himself back to prayer.

He judged it about six of the evening when they stopped, escorted him outside, and brought him to a feast they'd laid in yet another house.

The next morning, they traveled to another branch of the river, called Mattapani, and then to two other hunting camps—for so he had learned was the sort of "town" he had first been taken to.

In each place, they had a house dedicated to the one great king of the Powhatan. And where did this illustrious figure dwell? Down at the falls, upriver from the fort, was where they had been told.

"I need to speak with your great king," he told Opechancanough. "And then I must return to Paspahae."

He was not sure how much of his request translated, but after a little more than four days' march, they came again to the first town he had been taken to, which was being disassembled with great efficiency. Once all the mats were rolled into bundles, they turned and marched back to the river of Youghtanan.

Nohsh's hunting yehakan was no larger than any others, and as the one time of the year she and her brothers and sisters were invited to stay with him, Mato'aka happened to be near when he invited the lean, young warrior to share the fire and the news he'd brought from Opechancanough. Everyone else he shooed away, however, while beckoning her near.

"Since you wish to be part of all the happenings of our People"—and here Nohsh fixed her with a stern look—"then you may listen in on our talk. This is Koko'um, who has come from Opechancanough with news.

But you must sit quietly, out of sight."

The lean, tall warrior barely acknowledged her with a glance, but that one look was enough to wither her.

At least inside. If she cared about the opinion of one stray warrior.

Nohsh's eyes held that twinkle she had learned to recognize even when his face was carved into hard lines. She whisked away and folded herself into a dark corner, behind a tall basket.

Koko'um, whom she had seen often enough in her uncle's retinue, took his turn with the uppowoc and gave a grave nod. "We have found the Tassantassa with the red hair. We took him alive and have showed him every courtesy. He had a guide who is of the Chicahamania, and the guide told us that this man is a weroance among his people. Opechancanough bid me come ask you when you would be ready to receive him."

Nohsh sucked at his own pipe, his face thoughtful. "We will return to Werowocomoco before the turn of the moon. Bring him a little after the new moon appears in the sky."

Koko'um nodded and took one of the cakes that lay in a basket nearby. "It is good. My thanks, and that of Opechancanough, goes out to you."

Nohsh nodded gravely as well. "So how has this stranger carried himself?"

With a grunt, Koko'um chewed. "He is so far a real man, at least. When we took him, he showed no fear but indeed kept shooting his fire stick at us. Two men were killed, another two wounded, but they are recovering." He swallowed and gestured. "The father of one of those slain tried to take vengeance upon the red-haired man, but Opechancanough took him away to protect him." The roll of his eyes was clear in the firelight. "At Youghtanan the quiakrosoc performed a divination ceremony to see what intent the Tassantassa has toward us."

"And what was their determination?"

"That his intent is not one of evil." Koko'um huffed. "I would not doubt the quiakrosoc, of course. But many of us agree it remains to be seen. We went at last to Kekataugh, who wished the Tassantassa to show how his weapon worked. He took the thing, pretended to load it but broke part of the device, then acted as if he had not intended to do so." Koko'um shook his head. "He watches us with cunning in his strange blue eyes, and then he talks on and on. He seems to think we are but foolish children who cannot understand anything."

Nohsh gave a snort. "One cannot fault him his pride, perhaps."

Koko'um's brows lowered. "Wait until you see and hear for yourself."

"I look forward to that."

Koko'um did not reply, but his glance darted to the shadows where Mato'aka had gone.

"Be on your guard," Nohsh went on. "Continue to show him all courtesy. It may be that we can bring his people in as friends." He took a pull of his pipe. "I would wish that, rather than to go to war against them."

The look the younger warrior gave him was speculating. "Because of their weapons?"

Nohsh lowered his pipe. "We do not know what advantage their friendship might be against others. The Span-ish and the Mandoag."

"The others are taking him to Tapahanek to see if he is the captain of those who came a year ago and slew their weroance and stole away captives."

"Do you think he is the one?"

Koko'um's chin jerked upward. "No. Although I could wish he were, so there would be a good reason to end his life rather than feed him endlessly everywhere he goes."

Nohsh's brow now gathered. "Many who deserve death do not receive it. And many who do not deserve it have their lives ended."

Did he think on the war he had just carried out, on the people to the south?

But Koko'um grunted, lifting his own pipe. "Still, one should be mindful of what is just and fair."

"That is true," Nohsh said mildly. "See that he is brought to me most speedily, then. We may turn for home sooner than expected."

Koko'um took his leave at last, and Mato'aka crawled out from her hiding place.

"Waugh! I had forgotten you were there."

"You did not," Mato'aka said, laughing. "You hardly moved."

Nohsh chuckled along with her.

"So we are going to host the Tassantassa?"

"Yes. What do you think of that?"

"I think—" Her heart beat so fast inside her chest, she could hardly breathe. "I do not know what to think. Is he not an enemy?"

"Mm, Koko'um thinks it is so, but we will see if we can turn him to a friend." He peered at her as he dumped the ashes from his pipe into the fire and ran a finger around the bowl.

"That is a good plan."

"Now you will help your Nek in finishing all the work of the hunt."

"Oh yes, Nohsh."

"And I will make sure that either I or Granny Snow keeps you up on the news, as it comes."

"Thank you, Nohsh!"

He pointed to a mat over to the side, and she curled up on it, tugging a mantle over herself for warmth.

Wahunsenecawh sat for a space and watched the girl settle into sleep. How lively, and how bright she was! Could she indeed bear the burdens placed upon her by the quiakrosoc and the spirits?

He was about to retire to his own mat when a slight, mantle-clad figure slipped inside the door and straightened, her gaze sweeping the interior of the hut.

"Woanagusso," he greeted her.

A smile curved her mouth. "I see Mato'aka has found a warm fire for the night. I only came to make sure she was here and not elsewhere."

He nodded then pushed to his feet. "Will you walk with me a moment?"

They slipped outside, to the cold stillness under the stars. The chill breeze of earlier had fallen, and now he hardly needed his mantle, but still he threw it about his shoulders and gestured for his guards to stay back.

He led her a short distance from the hunting camp. After a moment's listening to make sure none had followed, he turned to her. "I wish to give you warning first. A Tassantassa weroance has been taken captive. They will bring him here so I may see and question him."

Her eyes widened, then her head bowed. "I will keep myself out of sight."

"I think rather you should paint yourself and attend upon me as the other women."

She turned upon him. "I should especially not sit among the other women, where it will be obvious how different I am."

How spirited she was! He laughed softly. "I wished to also tell you that as part of her training as Beloved Woman, I have let Mato'aka hear the news." He hesitated, holding her gaze in the darkness. "You have not told her—?"

"No!" She caught herself, then lowered her voice. "I have told her nothing. To her she is as any of Tunapewoc."

He gave another quiet laugh at her pronunciation of the word—so like the peoples to the south. Bending, he touched his forehead to hers. She leaned into the embrace, and this time the sides of their faces overlapped, cheek to cheek. "Please do not make me appear before him. I do not want to give anyone an excuse to take me away from you."

"Mmm. You have always been a good woman, and my favorite wife," he breathed.

Her arms came around his waist, and he drew her closer.

"In fact, I will now call you Winganuske. Good woman."

She made a tiny sound. Was she weeping? "You honor me, my mamanatowic."

Smith stood still, keeping his face impassive, while the king of this particular town—Tapahanek, he kept repeating to himself to remember—and Opechancanough and all their counselors discussed him as if he were a beef to be quartered and parceled out. One side had pointed to him and asked a question, while the other shook their heads and motioned as if to someone obviously taller.

He did not know whether to be glad they were describing someone else, or no.

For weeks now, they had paraded him as if he were a prize horse, with entire towns turning out to not only stare at him but to touch his hair, skin, and clothing. To examine every bit of his gear. He would often smile and show them his compass, as he had Opechancanough, and prattle on about how it worked, as if they would understand.

That one looked at him now with an expression that bespoke contemplation of some grave matter. What thoughts went through the mind of this savage? Smith chafed against the constraints of language. All that time he had spent studying their tongue—or what he had thought was their tongue—and it availed him but little. He was trying, in spare moments, to truly learn it while among them, as he had during various encounters over the past months. He also continued making notes in the book they'd allowed him to keep, as he had opportunity.

Gracious God, grant me understanding! Or them. In this moment, I care not which.

They beckoned to him, led him to where mats were laid out near the fire, and bid him sit. That, at least, he understood. Food followed—a great feast again, such as he could not possibly finish, but by now he knew it custom to offer what he could not eat to those keeping watch over him. They accepted it with eagerness.

There was venison, roasted then well sodden in a pot with some sort of vegetables. All surprisingly tasty—or perhaps he had merely grown accustomed to the savage manner of eating. They also served a strong, sweet drink he found surprisingly bracing. Bread as good as any he'd had in England. . .and oh, he had missed bread.

A wave of longing for England swept over him. Just as quickly, he pushed it away.

He had endured more than most. His mother dying, then his father. An apprenticeship he'd despised. Then life aboard ship—which was not so bad, when he could avoid the heavy fists of the captain and crew, but he was quick to learn how to sail. Then followed training at arms and combat and hiring out as a mercenary to fight against the Turks because it was, after all, unnatural for Christians to slaughter each other.

Then came being wounded in battle and captivity among the Turks—and oh, the sweetness of *her* face. The lovely Charatza Trabigzanda, who had showed him such kindness. But then she had sent him to her brother. He still did not know to what purpose that was. The brother had proved cruel, and his hopes to return to her were crushed. He'd then taken opportunity to rise up and slay the man and escape on horseback to a Russian garrison.

Returning to his post in Hungaria, he received pay and discharge and made his way back to England. In that same year, Queen Elizabeth died and was succeeded by King James. Sir Walter Ralegh, so long venerated for his efforts to expand the empire, was convicted of treason and imprisoned in the Tower of London. A little later, the long war with Spain ended.

The very next year, he met Bartholomew Gosnold and Gosnold's cousin Edward Maria Wingfield, who persuaded him to join their efforts to establish a colony in Virginia.

Now Gosnold lay dead and Wingfield had foully betrayed the colony by his hoarding of resources. And here was Smith, feasting amongst savages and not knowing whether this hour would be his last.

God, I do commit my soul to You, regardless of what may come. Sustain me. Let me acquit myself like a man, if nothing else.

The desolation receded but a little. How strange was this people, who laughed and smiled and showed him kindness, even after the brutal killing of his companions. What purpose could they possibly have in all of it?

Were they indeed fattening him for slaughter as well? His imagination ran wild with the thought, and he put back the cake of bread he had just brought to his mouth.

He knew better than to let stray suspicions keep him from taking nourishment when it was offered. But this—this—

Breathing deeply, he looked around. The firelight cast faces and writhing bodies into ghoulish shadows, and their whoops and singing—if one could call it such—still seemed nothing less than devilish.

God preserve me!

He could not even pray properly here.

The next day they marched and came to what he was told was the Powhatan king's hunting camp—that is, of the great king over all the other kings—although said personage was not present.

Mamanatowic, they said. Not weroance.

Did he not dwell at the town at the falls? They were a fair distance from there, and Smith did not recognize the country they traveled.

After spending the night in the hunting camp, some of which had obviously been disassembled, they continued on.

They crossed a small river, which his guard told him was called

Payankatank. A little farther they came to the banks of a larger river, called Pamaunkee. Smoke as from many fires arose from the far side, and as they paddled across, a great town emerged, as it were, from the trees.

"Werowocomoco," said his guard, pointing. More words that Smith did not understand, but then, "Yehakan. Wahunsenecawh."

A growing crowd awaited them as they neared the bank. Amidst the barking of dogs on shore, shouts and cries went up from the men accompanying him and those gathered to receive them, rife even to Smith's ears with joy and gladness. The smell of a feast being prepared filled his nostrils and dug a hollow in his gut.

As everywhere else, a sea of tanned faces with glossy black hair and bright black eyes surrounded him, hands reaching out to touch his face, hair, and clothing. He stood, stoic, after briefly trying to smile in return.

Today, it all seemed too much.

Be a man! he admonished himself. What was to happen, would happen, and God surely held him in His hands, regardless.

Mato'aka's heart pounded in her chest. He was here! The stranger was here, and oh—what a curiosity.

Nek had been uncharacteristically short when she'd begged to go catch a glimpse of him. "You will see him later!" she had snapped. "At this time I need your help with the cooking."

Mato'aka danced about, flapping her hands. "But my fingers are sore from cracking so many nuts."

"Stop! Think of how displeased your father will be. I must get the pegatawah ground and you—"

Still unable to contain her excitement, Mato'aka gave a small wail. "Nohsh will be too busy with his other wives. And we worked and worked at the hunting camp—"

Nek shot her a glare, looking both angry and hurt. Mato'aka held herself still at last. "I am sorry, Nek."

But she was already shaking her head. "No. It is nothing more than the truth." Brushing off her hands, she rose to her feet. "Come, we will go together to look. The *apon* can wait a little longer, and we did work very hard at the hunting camp."

Somehow her mother's sudden calm was more of a rebuke than the scolding had been. Even so, she did not hesitate when Nek shooed her on ahead, toward the crowd gathered at the riverbank.

Already some of the group had dispersed, returning to their own cooking and other preparations, but the press was still thick around the man who was but a little taller than Nek.

She glanced over her shoulder, but Nek held back, waving her on with a little smile. Swallowing, she lifted her chin and kept going, though her feet dragged with a sudden reluctance.

Then the press cleared, and she saw him clearly. A short, scrawny body, covered from neck to wrist to foot in a manner of garb she'd never seen before. Bushy, curly hair that was indeed nearly the red of sumac in fall, all that was on the top and sides of his head cropped unevenly to just past his shoulders, while shorter hair, also curled, covered the lower half of his face.

How strange! She had only seen such beards on the eldest of the old. Yet he did not appear so very old himself, and his hair was still bright with no silver intermixed.

He stood, quietly watchful, but did not seem apprehensive. She did not, like the others, push forward to touch him. Looking felt quite enough in this moment.

One of the dogs approached, barking with suspicion, and he held one hand down for the animal to sniff. It did so, then backed away with a muffled growl. The Tassantassa watched it go, then looked up and past the others and caught her glance. His own eyes glinted blue, like the sky, and the skin around them crinkled as if in a smile. It seemed his mouth curved as well, though it was hard to tell through all the hair.

But she smiled also, just in case, and lifted her chin again. And then she turned on her heel and ran back to Nek.

"Koko'um tells me our guest does not know when to be silent."

Lounging upon the sleeping platform while Wahunsenecawh picked through baskets of finery, Opechancanough laughed, long and low. "He speaks much, yes. When he was first taken, he was most desirous to show me a device he carried and to tell me how by means of it pointing to north, his people are able to find their way. I am not wholly certain whether we understood all he tried to speak to us, but he did refer to the earth and seas, and of the sun and moon and stars." His brother snorted. "He thinks our earth is round, like a ball."

Wahunsenecawh angled him a look. "Where would he get such a curious idea?"

Opechancanough smirked and raised one brow. "He will show you the device, no doubt. And you can hear for yourself."

"And the people of Tapahanek say he is not of those who attacked them last year?"

"No, that captain was a big man, as tall as we are."

"Hm." After untangling a string of pearls, Wahunsenecawh looped one about his neck and selected another from the basket.

"He also inquired of the people who had come before, those who landed to the south of us and caused such trouble among the Suquoten and Weopomeioc. I told him of Ocanahonan."

"Do you think he and his people are a threat to us? Or can they be brought in as friends?"

His brother pursed his lips. "I do not know."

One by one, he drew out all the strings of pearls and put them on. The more finery, the better, for such an occasion as this. "I suppose we will see shortly."

As he reached for his great headdress, Winganuske ducked inside, her head and shoulders painted red. "Shall I summon the others, my mamanatowic?"

"Indeed, Winganuske."

She slipped outside again, and Opechancanough shot him a look. "Good Woman? Was she not Swan, before?"

"I may call my wives by whatever name I wish," Wahunsenecawh said, and his brother laughed again.

They filed in, then—two and twenty of his current wives followed by twenty of his chief men, a mix of quiakrosoc and warriors. The women busied themselves making a great stack of mats in the center of his sleeping platform, where he reclined and chose two of them to sit at his head and foot. The others arranged themselves in two rows facing each other down the length of the yehakan floor, on either side of the central fire, women seated behind the men.

Winganuske tucked herself well into shadow at one end nearest his sleeping platform. He nodded with satisfaction that all was ready, and Opechancanough went out to fetch their "guest."

Chapter Five

Smith could not shake the feeling of foreboding. Every step felt as if he were marching to his execution.

'Twas sheer folly, he was sure, to think he could talk his way out of this, but talk he would, if allowed. *Please God. . .* The prayer would not even properly form in his mind, so he resorted to a murmur, beneath his breath. "Our Father which art in heaven, hallowed be thy name. . ."

They neared a domed house, a little apart and longer than the others around it.

"Thy kingdom come. Thy will be done even in earth as it is in heaven. . . ."

The guards immediately in front of him stooped to enter the low doorway. "Go," he was told.

Clenching his jaw, bracing his whole being, he also bent and went in.

Before his eyes could adjust to the dimness, he was nudged and tugged along, just a few steps, before he was bid sit down.

Thine is the kingdom, and the power, and the glory for ever. Amen.

He sank to his knees then sat back on his heels. A fire burned in the center of a spacious floor, its smoke filling the whole interior, but figures became visible—two lines of ten men each lining the walls, with an equal number of women behind them, their faces all painted red and each wearing a great chain of white beads across their shoulders. And there, at the other end, lying upon a bedstead about a foot high—the emperor of the Powhatan himself, glistening with the abundance of great pearls about his neck, and a vast mantle made of *rahaughcum* pelts. His face, beneath a feathered crown, gleamed as if carved from old wood, his dark eyes glittering.

Such pomp! And such a grave and majestic countenance, Smith had never seen. Not in all his travels, not among the Turks, not even in England's own King James.

Smith sank a little further.

"Wingapo," came the Powhatan king's greeting, then more words that Smith thought he understood, but he turned to the young Chicahamania they had continued pressing into service for the task of interpreting.

"What are you called," the young savage murmured.

He cleared his throat to reply. "I am John Smith, of the English." And again, so they could hear it clearly, *"John Smith."*

"Chawnzmit," the king answered, with all dignity. "Wingapo."

He went on, with the help of the interpreter, to assure Smith of his friendship and that he would shortly be released. Then he gestured to those waiting, and in a moment, great platters of food were carried in and set all around them, and Smith was bid eat.

Sitting still and pretending she had no more curiosity about their visitor than anyone around her proved one of the most difficult things she had ever done.

So he was indeed *English*! She had forgotten how vividly red one's hair could be. And after years of being accustomed to how the men of the People kept their faces clean-plucked until old age, she saw this one as nothing short of ugly with his unkempt beard.

His clothing was similar to what she recalled had been worn by the men of her former people, with a close-fit coat over a shirt, but his breeches were of a longer fashion than she remembered, coming to just below the knees, and tall boots with the tops turned down covered his lower legs.

He looked stunned in the face of Wahunsenecawh's finery. When the feast was brought in, his expression shifted to something between gratitude and suspicion, but he ate readily enough, gaze darting between his interpreter and Wahunsenecawh, who was doing all he could to be conciliatory. The young interpreter looked terrified—she was not sure, but someone had said he was of the Chicahamania, who were in recent times considered wayward and stubborn, if not outright enemies.

Wahunsenecawh, of course, lounged as if he'd not a care in the world, but his gaze was intent. As always.

Once he had made the formal welcoming speeches, he asked the Englishman—his way of saying the man's name, *John Smith*, was not far off—why they had come.

John Smith's face changed a little, as if he was thinking. At last he replied, looking first to his interpreter, then at Wahunsenecawh.

After so many years, the words were strange, and at first she was not sure she even understood them properly. She thought he spun a story of being in a fight with the Spanish, of being overpowered and put near to retreat, and coming ashore because of stormy weather. That was part of what the Chicahamania warrior translated. He went on to say that they came to Chesepioc, where the men shot at them, and then to Kequotan, where they were treated kindly. When they asked about fresh water, they were directed up the river, and at Paspahae, they were also welcomed. There they were forced to stay in order to mend their ship, and now they waited for their father Captain Newport to return for them. But he was most desirous to learn of a "back sea," where there was salt water and where his father had a child slain. He supposed that had happened by the Monacan, his enemy.

What a strange account. There seemed something awry with it, but she could not place her finger upon it—and even if she could, she must in this moment keep silent.

Did Wahunsenecawh believe the story? She peeked over at him. He was always the best at keeping his face impassive, but a small tightness about his mouth and eyes told her that he too questioned the validity of the man's tale.

But apparently, he decided to play along. "We will most certainly aid you in taking vengeance on behalf of your father."

He then began explaining to the Englishman what peoples lay beyond the land occupied by the Powhatan, first to the north, then west, and finally south. He told too how they had made war upon the Chesepioc, and the difference in their manner of arranging the hair—that the crown was shaven but at the neck it grew long then was tied up in a knot. Their wooden swords also were different, and longer.

How much the Englishman comprehended, none could say. And her understanding of his tongue crept back but slowly.

That was more distressing to her than she had expected. Why, she could not return to them even if she wished. She would be but a woman of the savages to them.

Wahunsenecawh went on to describe people further south dressed as the Englishman, and those with short coats and sleeves to the elbows, who had passed that way in many ships over the years. He related the distance to places such as Chawanoac and Roanoac, and how far was the great turning of salt water that Opechancanough had told him about.

John Smith thanked him most gravely and launched into his own discourse about the territories of Europe and a great king who he himself was subject to.

So their beloved Queen Elizabeth had died? Sadness touched her heart. If only she dared ask him about that!

The Englishman grew lively in his gesturing, describing battles and the sound of trumpets—here he put his hands to his mouth and gave a loud *doo-doo, doo-doooo*, which had the whole place startling and laughing. Apparently, he had no care for looking foolish before them. And he told of his own weroance, Captain Newport, whose return he awaited.

Still chuckling, Wahunsenecawh extended a hand. "Leave Paspahae and come dwell by me on my river." He waited for the interpreter to translate. "I will give you Capahowasic, and will give you pegatawah, wutapantam, and whatever else is necessary to feed you. You will make me hatchets and copper, and none shall disturb you."

The Englishman inclined his head and said he would think upon it, and again offered thanks.

By this time, the day was waning. Wahunsenecawh assigned guards to accompany John Smith to his lodging. Once their visitor and his guard were sent out, the rest of them were free to get up.

She rose and stretched, glancing about at the others. A little later, she and the other women would go down to the river to wash off their paint, but for now, the food must be carried away and the rest of the town fed.

Three warriors ushered Smith into the house as if in the most royal of rooms, set down his things, and then, after tending his fire and looking at various other things in the dwelling, whisked outside again.

He presumed they'd all be just outside if he saw fit to attempt an escape.

With a great sigh, he stretched out on the bed, which proved surprisingly comfortable. Of course, given how many months he had slept on the plank floors of a ship or on the ground at the fort, with or without shelter over his head, this seemed a small palace indeed.

And what grandeur he had just witnessed! Never had he seen the like. So many chains of large pearls! Such grave majesty. So this was their great king—here, when all this time he and his company had believed the chief Powhatan to be at the town of the same name, up at the falls.

How much else had they misunderstood?

Gracious God, continue to preserve me. I must needs get home! He still expected every hour to meet his death. He'd likely been given up for dead at the fort—it had been some five weeks now since he was taken.

God. . .help me.

"Nek! What did you think?"

Tying one of the baskets up in the rafters, her mother seemed to be holding back a smile. "What do you mean, Daughter?"

Mato'aka gave a stomp. She had been able to see nothing of the proceedings inside the big yehakan, and her father's guards had glared at her when she tried to listen from the outside.

Nek laughed and stepped away from the wall, where she had secured the basket of food just over her head. "There is not much to say. Your father offered friendship, but we still know very little about this Tassantassa or his purpose in this land." She hesitated. "Some have said he acts as if he thinks we are children, or without sense, but he showed little of that today." Tilting her head, she eyed Mato'aka. "And what did you think, when you saw him?"

She scrunched her nose. "He is—ugly. But the color of his hair and eyes is interesting."

Nek laughed. "Take your sister now and go see Granny Snow for a bit."

"But—"

And just like that, Nohsh was at the door. He stepped inside, bare of most of his ornaments and still dripping from his bath in the river, but carrying a pot of bear grease. "Go now," he said, smiling. "And do not linger to listen. I will have to punish you severely if you do."

Amazingly, Mato'aka gave him but one long look and then darted out the door.

Wahunsenecawh sighed, turning toward his wife. "Winganuske."

She smiled and dipped her head then indicated the pot he held. She also had recently bathed. "Do you wish help with the oil?"

He grinned as well. "I do."

She took it from him, and he turned his back. Her hands were warm and sure across his skin. Any of his wives would have been willing to perform the service, and they both knew it.

"Was he speaking truth, do you think?" he asked, quietly enough that if their Mischievous One were listening outside, she'd not have caught the words.

There was the barest hesitation in her stroke. "It is hard to say." She gathered more of the fat into her palms then spread it across his upper back, shoulders, and arms. "What was your thought?"

"He seems too eager to show his own strength. Opechancanough told me that his priests insist their divination showed he intends no harm, but—I wonder."

"Have the priests ever been wrong?"

"Oh, of course. But rarely."

She came around to his front and set to work on his chest and belly. Her expression held an odd tightness.

"He is of your former people, then."

She gave a tiny, hesitant nod. "It has been too long, and I find I barely remember their tongue." She glanced up, even as her hands kept moving, this time to his right arm. "Mato'aka saw him more closely at the riverbank. I only told her what I would have known as one of the Tunapewoc."

"That is good." He hummed a little, enjoying her touch as she worked the muscle even while she oiled the skin. "Is your memory of the tongue enough for you to tell me whether what he said to me is what was translated?"

Her hands fell still at that, and her head bobbled to the side—a gesture of uncertainty. "I am not sure."

"Would you be willing to listen in again and try?"

The glance she gave him this time held a rim of panic. "If—if you wish it so."

He took her hands in his. "Winganuske. My beloved wife." He let the corner of his mouth quirk and his gaze travel over the dullness of her skin. "Do you also need assistance with the oil?"

A tiny nod answered him and, taking up the pot, he circled behind her.

So small-boned she was, compared to the other women, even after two babies. Almost childlike—but with womanly softness aplenty. Her sighs and soft hums allowed him to know that she appreciated his hands as well.

"I do not want to go back," she whispered. "Please never send me back."

He turned her to face him and traced the warmed oil across her face and into her hair, and then downward. "I will not," he murmured.

Her eyes opened to his, dark with stirring. Swiftly he set the pot of oil over by the sleeping platform, then scooped her into his arms and carried her to it.

Deep in the night, while he slept, she blinked awake in the dark and nearly wept.

How could she love him so, when she had to share him with so many others?

And yet, she did. Thoroughly. Passionately.

She thought of what her life might have been if she'd not been taken by the Suquoten. Wed to a man with one of those odd bushy faces—short and stumpy and lacking the lean grace of her mamanatowic.

Her elders had oft spoken of the will of God. Had it been His will for her to be taken? Or was this, in the very least, a grace given her in the midst of a hard situation?

If grace it truly was, how strange that God would use a man so set against any discussion of Him to protect and provide for her. But she was glad He had—at least, glad of this particular man.

Mata'oka rose before the sun, went with the women down to the river to wash and sing their morning songs, and then hustled to help with the cooking.

She was determined to be one of those on hand to help carry food to their strange guest. She wanted another look at him.

Nek was with the others, grinding pegatawah and handing it off as quickly as she could to be stirred into dough for apon. Mato'aka helped with every step of the process then snatched up a platter to receive the cooked cakes as they were done.

There was enough for fifteen men—as was their custom when showing great hospitality. It would not be said that they did not do their best for this visitor as well, no matter where he had come from.

She stood, proudly holding the platter and waiting for the other two to be filled. But when the moment came, one of the women—one of her aunties, or so she called the cohort of Nohsh's wives—took stock of her and the platter and announced, "That should be taken in by a woman grown, not a child."

And before Mato'aka could even protest, the woman whisked the platter out of her hands and hustled away with the others.

Mato'aka scurried after. She would have her glimpse, even if it meant sticking her head in the door with no reason to be there at all.

More food already. Smith would laugh were it not so ungracious of him. After tying his portion of the leftovers in the rafters of his house, they'd come in about midnight, taken the baskets down to offer him more, but refused so much as a bite themselves. This morning, they carried the old away even as the new was being brought in.

He'd not refuse breakfast, however. The cakes were still warm and very good. He smiled and nodded, expressing his thanks repeatedly to the three women who had carried the platters in and even now stood aside, watching him eat.

When they were satisfied he'd well stuffed himself, his guards came in and bid him come. 'Twas the second time this morning—the first had been just before dawn, leading him down to the river, where they insisted he disrobe and wash himself. He'd not show weakness before these savages by refusing to enter the cold water.

'Twas bracing, he'd allow. Perhaps they had something with this habit of bathing every morning.

So for the second time that day, he stepped outside his lodgings and looked around. The town was full of life—women busy at their tasks, accompanied by children of varying ages—all naked, or nearly so, despite the frostiness of the weather. The sun shone brightly, and not much of a wind blew, for which he was grateful.

As usual, he was drawing a crowd. And there, just a few paces away, was a young girl of not more than ten, regarding him steadily with much interest and intelligence in her dark eyes.

She was, he thought, the same one he'd caught gazing upon him yesterday—who'd looked but not approached.

He offered a smile and carefully pronounced the phrase with which he had been instructed and had become much more practiced these past weeks. *"Ka ka torawincs keir?" What are you called?*

She flashed a grin, bringing out dimples in her cheeks and a pert cleft in her chin, but one of his guards preempted her reply, gesturing toward her with a grunt. "Pocahuntas. *Amosens* Wahunsenecawh."

He tried the syllables. "Pocahuntas?" The girl laughed and rolled her eyes, but nodded. *Something*—Wahunsenecawh was the name of their great king. Daughter, perhaps? "*Nechaun*?" he said. *Child?*

She nodded again then chattered something in an exchange with his guard he could not catch a word of before turning back to him and pointing. "Chawnzmit."

He too laughed. Naked she stood before him as the day she was born, save for a chain of white shells about her neck, and as innocent. Her hair had been shaven close around the front and sides of her head, with the back falling only to just below her shoulders. Her skin bore none of the curious patterned markings that many of the other women had.

Did Harriot not mention such a thing—that it was mark of royalty among them? Or was it something they did only with the onset of womanhood?

His guard nudged his shoulder. "Yoqueme wath." *Let us go.* He added what sounded in tone like an explanation or apology to the girl, and they moved on.

The day's conversation was more of the same from the day before. Wahunsenecawh held back his impatience, took his usual care to word questions and explanations, and listened to and watched their visitor. He expressed his desire for their peoples to be the best of friends and received fervent agreement in return. Winganuske sat in shadows, much as Mato'aka had, and later made little comment about the whole thing.

He met with Opechancanough, the quiakrosoc, and all their councilors after. "What shall be done?"

None wished to speak. He grunted in frustration.

"He has expressed his wish to be allied with us," Opechancanough said at last. "Let us welcome him as such with ceremony."

Wahunsenecawh only lifted his brows.

His brother gave a short laugh. "*Huskanaw.* I am sure his people have nothing of the kind. We should give him at least a taste of what it is to be a man of Tsenacomoco."

This thought pleased them all, and they whiled away the rest of the evening planning how it should be done.

As if her dreams were not vivid and troubling enough, Mato'aka was shaken awake and opened her eyes to the face of Granny Snow. She sat up to see Little Flower still sleeping, but Channa and Nek both were awake, with the latter tending the fire.

"Up, Amonute, and prepare your heart to walk in the spirit world this day."

Her heart chose to leap and begin beating very fast in response to that.

As she rubbed her eyes, glancing about again, Granny Snow crouched in front of her. "A ceremony is being prepared this morning for the Tassantassa, like unto huskanaw. I was told by the manito that you are to be part of it."

Sheer terror took her by the throat. "Huskanaw?" she croaked.

"I have informed your father and his warriors that they are not to refuse you entrance. They like it not, but have agreed to not interfere."

Mato'aka swallowed against the dryness of her mouth. "What is it I am to do?"

Granny Snow sat back, softening a little. "It will seem as though they plan to slay Chawnzmit. While they stand over him with clubs, as if ready to slaughter him, you will enter the yehakan and cry out to spare his life. You must make it appear that you are all that stands between him and death. Can you do this?"

Gaze flittering about the room—Nek gave the tiniest smile, but Channa only looked sulky—she nodded. "I can."

"Then we must prepare you while the others are getting ready for their part."

She followed Granny Smith through the town, where preparations were being made for yet another great feast.

So much food! Would they have enough to last through the winter?

But she had never known hunger. Why should she worry?

At the river's edge, she plunged into the water, gasping from the cold and scrubbing her arms and legs. Then Granny Snow bid her climb out and wrapped a soft doeskin mantle around her before leading her away again to her own yehakan. Here she was rubbed down with oil and made to sit by the fire. Granny threw some uppowoc on the flames then chanted a prayer while she waved the smoke toward Mato'aka with a fan of swan's feathers. Then she waited endlessly after Granny went out. She had dozed off before the old woman returned.

"It is time now," she murmured.

From a basket she drew a wondrous mantle, made all of white birds' feathers, and hung it about Mato'aka's shoulders. Then she led her to Nohsh's yehakan. A great shouting arose from within.

Granny Snow bent close. "Remember what I told you. Now go—wait in the doorway until they are gathered as if to slay him."

Four warriors flanked the opening, their eyes bright and faces fierce. As her feet carried her toward them, they neither opposed nor encouraged her progress, and at last she stood in the warm darkness, letting her eyes adjust.

The time had come at last—despite all their avowals of friendship, despite all the food they'd expended upon him, now he would die.

They rushed upon him in his lodgings, so many laying hands upon him and dragging him along, he'd been quite unable to count. Across the town and into the great king's house.

He'd have come willingly if they'd but asked!

As before, their king sat upon a pile of mats on his sleeping platform, two young women on either side of him and twenty others seated down the walls in two rows. Before them sat two rows of men. All painted and ornamented as they had been before.

All here, so early in the morning, to see him slain.

The savages dragged him to just before the fire, where two large, flat stones were placed. Two of the men forced him down, prone across the stones, his cheek pressed to the rough coldness.

There was a shout from the king himself, echoed by the assembly. While the two held him down, two other men stepped forward, cudgels raised, faces made more terrifying by their red paint.

They would beat his brains out. Please God that it be swift—

A high, undulating cry cut across the clamor of the gathering, and all fell silent. The cry came again, with words he could not make out, but drawing closer.

Pocahuntas! came the whisper, echoed across the assembly. He craned his neck, tried to see, but strong hands held him fast.

The king's voice rang out, repeating her name and seeming to ask a question. Hers replied, trembling.

His executors raised a shrill cry of their own, cudgels lifting again. His heart beat so furiously it like to have burst from his chest—

And then it was living flesh that covered his head, thin arms surrounding him, and the girl's frantic words, over and over.

Silence, for a handful of heartbeats. And then a deep laugh, beginning as a chuckle but gathering volume.

The hands that had held him down lifted him to his feet. The savage warriors stepped back as this child, who must surely be favorite of her father the Powhatan, stood beside Smith to face the emperor.

A smile still playing about his lips, he bid them sit. Hesitantly, looking around, Smith did so, and the girl whisked away as food was brought in for a feast, as if nothing untoward had ever happened.

But what had just taken place?

Mato'aka burst out into the cool morning air, gasping. Granny Snow hooked an arm about her shoulders and hustled her away.

"What were you doing? You were not supposed to drop the mantle. Why did you throw yourself upon him like that?"

The old woman's voice was one long scold. Mato'aka could only draw deep breaths into her lungs and try to make her heart stop its terrible racing.

The beautiful feather mantle hung across Granny Snow's other arm.

"But"—she gasped—"I did it! I went in, and I told them to stop, to spare his life, just as you told me."

Granny stopped, her hands coming up to grasp Mato'aka's shoulders, and her face split into a great, wrinkled grin. "Yes! Yes, you did. My little Beloved Woman, you stood firm before them all!"

The old woman's approval wrapped her about like a warm mantle. Suddenly she wanted nothing more but to lie down and sleep again.

There was more feasting, then Smith was returned to his lodging and left to his own devices for the remainder of the day. The next morning, before breakfast, he was taken to the river to wash and then marched out into the woods to a great house he had glimpsed once, a few days before.

He had already cheated death the day before. Why then did such a strange foreboding crawl across him?

They led him into the house, then to a large room in the back where he was made to sit by the fire and left alone. A woven mat divided this room from the rest of the house, and presently he heard footsteps and rustling and then a great howling and lamenting and groaning, all on the other side of the woven wall.

The great king of Powhatan himself, accompanied by scores of men, all of them painted black, came filing into the room and surrounded him.

"*Machic chammay*," he said, pointing between them. Smith knew already the word for friend. More words followed, and one stepped up to translate. "We are now friends, and you will soon go home. But do send me two great guns, and a grindstone. In return I will give you the country of Capahowasic and forever esteem you as my son."

Smith fair goggled at them. After all this, he was now apparently adopted as son?

The very next day he was sent out, accompanied by a dozen guards. One man carried his cloak and haversack, two bore huge baskets of bread, and one led the way, with the others ranged about them to watch. 'Twas but ten or twelve miles, total, across the river from Werowocomoco. Despite this, and the cold and frost and blustery wind besides, his cohorts insisted on sleeping out in the woods rather than pressing on to the fort.

So it was that again, early on the morn, Smith led the approach to the fort, calling out a loud halloo.

The fort was in shambles.

They were elated and encouraged enough, of course, by his return and his report of having been treated kindly by the Powhatan—especially with the promise of more foodstuffs.

But the strongest were plotting once more to steal the pinnace and sail for England. Captain Gabriel Archer, once Smith's ally if not a friend but now fallen from favor, had finagled his way onto the council in Smith's absence, along with Ratcliffe and Martin, and now looked at him with jaundiced eye and, claiming the rule of Levitical law, accused him of the murder of Robinson and Emry. With a handful of supporters, he near persuaded the others to try and hang Smith.

He was having none of it. Emboldened by having survived the trial of these past weeks, he brought the greater number of the men back over to his side—explaining again what had happened on that fateful day on the banks of the Chicahamania River when Opechancanough and his men surprised them—and pointing out that he had indeed brought the Powhatan into alliance with them, where before they lived every day in fear outside the palisaded walls of the fort.

He was saved that very night by the return of Newport with fresh provisions and more men. A worthy and capable personage by the name of Master Matthew Scrivener had come along, who was immediately elected to the council along with Smith and Captain Martin.

In the meantime, his savage guard had returned home, declining to take the heavy artillery Smith had but halfheartedly offered them in response to the demands of their great king. He promised to deliver what Wahunsenecawh had requested as soon as it was reasonably possible. What he did not expect was for a party of them to return four or five days later, laden with provisions.

And skipping along at the head of the party was the pert maiden Pocahuntas herself.

He introduced her and the others to the men at the fort. He did not tell them much of the happenings there at Werowocomoco, however—particularly the little maid's part in it—for who would have believed him?

She walked about the fort, much as she had in the town that was her own home, chatting especially with the boys, trading Powhatan words for English ones. She also, with all her naked innocence, before long had them turning cartwheels with her across the open yard. The men oft stared before looking away with hands covering their mouths, and to those who persisted in gaping, Smith growled a stern warning to mind their eyes and their thoughts, that 'twas only the custom of a savage people and as Christians they were expected to be better—which gave no license for ridicule.

The savages took their leave the next day with many signs of friendship.

Only a day or two later, a great, terrible fire broke out in the fort, destroying all their houses and much of their private belongings and provision.

To make matters worse, a handful of the men perished in the flames, those too sick to move or be moved. More died the first night after the fire from the cold.

Smith threw himself on his face before God, begging relief and comfort.

Chapter Six

Jamestowne, 1608

Winter passed into spring, and somehow, they had survived.

Captain Newport did indeed bring more provision and trade goods, but what had promised to be for the relief of the colony turned into more difficulty. To begin with, the madness for gold had seized many and made them insensible to anything but gathering bucketsful of glittering sand, with the belief that they had found gold dust worthy of refinement. When they would have laden the ship for its return trip with mere dirt, only through much effort did Smith make them throw out the sand and freight the ship with good cedar instead.

Newport insisted in the meantime on visiting the great Powhatan king. Among other things, they exchanged one of the English boys, ironically named Thomas Savage, for a young savage whom the Powhatan king said was very trustworthy, with the intent that each would live amongst the other's people and learn their tongue. A very useful thing, that.

Upon Newport's departure, as a gesture of his regard, Wahunsenecawh presented him with twenty turkeys and the request for twenty swords in exchange. Ignoring Smith's cautions to not be overgenerous with the Indians until they were proved more trustworthy, Newport delivered him the swords without hesitation. Smith himself visited shortly after, but the Powhatan king did not find his wish obeyed when he similarly gifted Smith with turkeys. A flurry of thefts followed as the Powhatan sought to obtain the weapons they believed were owed them. Indeed, the English could hardly go anywhere or do their work about the fort and its surrounding fields without being accosted by Indians who, failing to be given tools and arms upon demand, tried to take them by force.

And however insolent the Indians became about the matter, President Ratcliffe refused to make any order to resist. "The command from England is clear—we are not to offend the Naturals! We should seek to be anything rather than peace breakers."

At last, nearing the middle of April, Newport departed again, taking with him Master Wingfield and Captain Archer, ridding the colony of those two.

Between himself and Master Scrivener, Smith divided the immediate work of rebuilding the town and repairing its fortifications—tasks not yet completed after their fire, so great was the distraction of Newport and his visit to the Powhatan and then the scrabbling about for shiny dirt. Spring had come in full, and Smith organized the efforts to prepare the fields, plant their corn, and rebuild the church and storehouse. While they were thus busied, another ship arrived—the *Phoenix*, thought lost at sea during the storm in January that Captain Newport had managed to navigate, and just now returned from the West Indies.

The captain of this vessel, Nelson, wanted to send Smith and Master Scrivener upriver again to see what commodities they might find and ship back to England, while Captain Martin was all afroth to lade it with more of his supposed gold. Smith resisted, knowing they must take advantage of the season to finish rebuilding the town and fort.

And then, one day, being accosted by Indians demanding his sword and tools, Smith lost patience and fought back. Hunting up and down the island surrounding the town, he captured as many Naturals as he could and punished them with whippings and imprisonment.

As one, they insisted they had been directed only by Wahunsenecawh, the great Powhatan himself.

Werowocomoco, early **Nepinough** *(Green Corn Season), 1608 by English reckoning*

"You recognized Chawnzmit's position as weroance, and he avowed his loyalty to you. Now we realize he is not the one in authority over his people—or at least, not the only one—and rather than give you tribute, he goes all over the place, up and down the rivers, and demands it of the others as if he were mamanatowic. And when he was here last, he refused to lay aside his own weapons, or insist on his men doing so." Opechancanough gave him a hard look from across the fire. "How long will you allow such disrespect?"

Wahunsenecawh waved a hand and took another pull of uppowoc. "And you think it no disrespect to speak to me thus?"

His brother's face softened but little. "I think of our people. These Tassantassas still do nothing but take, despite their promises. What if Namontac and Machumps, whom we sent to be with them to watch and send back word, have now been treated with as much contempt as those who made direct attack?"

"I did not give permission for anyone to attack directly," Wahunsenecawh said, gruffly.

"Hm. Perhaps it would have been better if you had. You are mamanatowic. If you are not strong, then who will be?"

Wahunsenecawh gazed into the fire then lowered his pipe. "We will still extend them love. We have the boy they gave us in exchange for Namontac, as a sign of peace between us and to learn each other's tongue. All others who run away from their town we send back, no matter how they beg to stay among us. It is not right that they hold our men captive. I will send Mato'aka and Ra'hunt, along with a guard and a few more provisions, to inquire and ask for the return of our men. I have ever used Mato'aka as a token of peace when sending provisions, before, so he should know, by her presence, that I mean them only well. Perhaps her being there will soften his heart."

Nek tucked the doeskin mantle about Mato'aka's chin and pressed her lips to Mato'aka's forehead. "Nek! Please, I am not a child."

Her mother smiled. "Let me show you affection. You will always be my child."

Granny Snow was also smiling, but Mato'aka could hardly summon a response.

"Come now, you've been to the Tassantassas town before," Granny Snow said.

"Yes, but never before have I been expected to be the one talking to them. As if I am one of the elders."

Nek laughed softly and embraced her. "If you were able to walk into your father's yehakan in the middle of a ceremonial gathering, you will be able to do this."

"But you were there, then." Mato'aka huffed. "I wish you were coming too."

Another laugh from Nek. "Oh, my little one. I cannot."

"Why not? Other women go, sometimes."

Her mother tipped her head and grinned. "Yes, but I am wife to Wahunsenecawh, and though other men might, your father does not share his wives." She gave another little laugh. "That is, until he wearies of them."

Mato'aka folded her arms. "I hope he never gives you away. I will have to speak with him about that."

Nek laughed again, shaking her head. But were those tears in her mother's eyes?

"I am sorry, Nek. I often speak amiss."

Her mother gave her another embrace. "He will do as he wills, little one. Just know that I love you always."

Thus comforted, Mato'aka set off with the others—a band of strong warriors, every one, including her much-older brother Nantaquas, some bearing baskets between them and others with weapons ready, watching as they went.

Except for Ra'hunt, one of her father's advisors. Despite his misshapen body, he had the sharpest of minds, and no doubt went along to report to her father when all was done. And perhaps to make sure that her part would be carried out as planned.

Their various admonitions still echoed in her thoughts. *Be aware of what takes place around you, but do not stare, and above all do not beg. Maintain your dignity as Beloved Woman. And do not tell them your true name. When you walk among them, you are Pocahuntas and nothing else.*

They had given her the last warning every single time. She did not mind, truly she didn't.

If you tell them your true name, Granny Snow had said, *they will have power over you that you cannot take back.*

When they arrived at the Tassantassas town, there was none of the joy and easy welcome she had received before. Chawnzmit was courteous and seemed glad to see her, but the others were stiff and looked upon them with clear suspicion. And—oh, though Ra'hunt and the others had sternly charged her, it was hard not to stare at the warriors of Tsenacomoco who were tied to the great posts of the strangers' fort so miserably. As if they were slaves, or dogs.

The soft doeskin of her mantle itched suddenly with the day's warmth. But she held herself very straight and still as she had been taught.

Ra'hunt stepped forward to speak to Chawnzmit and the other leaders. He showed as token the shooting glove and bracer that belonged to Opechancanough, who asked that among others, they might release two who had been his own friends.

Flame-colored hair tied back at his nape and beard glistening with sweat, Chawnzmit bowed his head. "It is indeed the glove and bracer belonging to the weroance who showed me kindness even though I was his captive."

His blue eyes were sharp upon each member of their company, but it seemed he avoided looking at Mato'aka until last. When he did, his gaze lingered and softened. "I suppose Wahunsenecawh has sent this, his most precious pearl, to gain my favor in this matter." A wry smile twisted his mouth. "I will see what might be done, then."

In the meantime, food was prepared—not such a feast as Werowocomoco could have furnished, but they were indeed fed and given a house to sleep in. Mato'aka could hardly close her eyes for the strangeness of the sharp-angled roof above her head. On the next day, they were summoned to accompany the Tassantassas to a building they called *church*, where she herself sat on a bench, her father's guard arrayed behind her and against the wall. One Tassantassa stood up and made a great speech before lifting his hands and closing his eyes to intone what she could only gather must be prayers. A chill swept over her. They made their incantations in the open—before the entire gathering of people?

At the end, all the Tassantassas chanted something together. The sound of it brought every hair to stand on end, and tears to her eyes.

If only she could understand enough of their tongue to know what it was they said.

When it was done, they stood, and Chawnzmit ushered them back outside. They were fed again, and then the warriors who had been taken prisoner were released, their bows and arrows and other weapons returned to them.

Chawnzmit looked at Ra'hunt, then at her. "Pocahuntas. Beloved daughter of Powhatan. Go now and return again soon."

The words in her tongue were clumsy, some of them, but it was clear he had taken care to learn them.

How she hoped he did not turn out to be an enemy.

Smith spent the summer sailing the pinnace around the waters of the great bay into which Jamestowne's river emptied, exploring all of the great rivers and not a few of the smaller ones. Many of the people they encountered offered hospitality and treated them as friends, gladly trading food for hatchets and hoes. Others, however, showed either reluctance or outright hostility until Smith and his company displayed sufficient strength to induce them to be biddable. He strove to be no more harsh than was necessary.

He had one near brush with death after being pierced in the wrist by a stingray, but by the mercy of God and ministrations of his physic survived to even make a meal of the creature whose venom nearly proved his end.

And then, on the tenth of September, 1608, a mere three days after his return from the second voyage, by the election of the council and request of the company—after much importuning by the others and long refusal on his part—Smith accepted the letters, patents, and position of president of the colony.

Ratcliffe had been too sick for many months to be effective, except to resist Smith's efforts to protect the colony, and then order the building of a house so grand that Smith referred to it with contempt as a palace. That now stood untouched while Smith saw to repairs on the church and storehouse in preparation for the soon arrival of another supply ship.

The ship arrived with the onset of winter, but again without the joy it might have. Newport seemed almost triumphant when imparting to Smith and the council how he had been commissioned to not return this time without a lump of gold, the certainty of the sea over the mountains, or one of the lost company of Sir Walter Ralegh. All well and good, but Smith had his own questions about where gold might be found—or even if—and whether a salt water ocean truly lay across those mountains, and how far. More recent conversation with the savage peoples made him think what had been described to him was, rather, large freshwater lakes.

Furthermore, Newport had arrived with what sounded to Smith the most ridiculous plan of all: to invite the great Powhatan king to Jamestowne and bestow upon him a host of gifts sent by King James himself—including the plan for a coronation in the English style.

The supply, such as it was, came not without some profit. Newport had hired a handful of men, Polish and Deutsch, to manufacture such things as pitch and tar, glass, and soap-ashes. All that was most necessary and well. But to bring those men and seventy more besides, far less useful than craftsmen and without their own foodstuffs, was not so well considered.

"Oh, but we can get corn from the savages," Newport sallied on, undaunted. "Is their harvest not newly gathered? And did the town not also grow some corn?"

"Some, but poorly, and it is gathered in already and not sufficient to feed hundreds. And if you wish us to neglect the time we have to gather in more by pursuing this—this strange coronation, and spend the supplies we have, well, do not be surprised if we all starve. Again!"

Newport grinned, combing his hook through his grey-shot beard. His twinkling gaze took in the rest of the council. "This land is so full of plenty, it should be no trouble to feed us all. Would you not agree?" He lifted his shortened arm to indicate two men standing nearby. "And what say you to adding these two worthy gentlemen, both seasoned soldiers, to your council, to appease the charge that too few of you have voice in the matters of ruling the colony?"

Captain Waldo and Captain Wynne both gave quick nods to indicate their readiness to serve.

Smith sat back, folding his arms. "I've no particular objection, except that they are heretofore ignorant of our business."

Another wave to dismiss that objection. "They can be caught up on all that in short order. Ratcliffe? Scrivener? What say you?"

Ratcliffe only nodded agreeably. Scrivener lifted one shoulder. "As long as I am able to continue exploring the country unfamiliar to us, I am content."

Smith understood that. Had he not also felt the restlessness to go where no Englishman had ever set foot? To be the first Christian these savages met?

Guilt pricked his conscience at that. If only he had not needed to use some of them so roughly this past summer. 'Twas too difficult at times, balancing spiritual interests with matters of government and keeping order. . .

"President Smith should be the one to go to Powhatan and importune him to come," Ratcliffe said. "He is the one Powhatan knows best."

Smith looked up. They had taken to calling the great chief *the Powhatan* or more simply *Powhatan*. So much easier to say than *Wahunsenecawh*. Half the time the others could not say it properly anyway.

"I doubt not that our president's cruelty toward the Naturals," Newport said, "will rather disincline them to treat with us. His reservations concerning the entire thing will certainly only hinder my journey."

"No, I think I should go," Smith said slowly. "You continue making preparation for going to the Monacan, and I will see what the Powhatan will say."

He chose Captain Waldo and two others to accompany him, plus Namontac and the boy Samuel Collier, who served as his page, and they traveled the twelve miles overland. On the near bank of the river they found Indians willing to bear them across in their kanoe to Werowocomoco.

Little Flower barreled around the corner where Mato'aka knelt, grinding pegatawah. "Chawnzmit is returned!"

Happy to have a reason to leave the grindstone—even for a short time—Mato'aka jumped to her feet and ran after her little sister. Sure enough, Nek called after her, but she waved at her mother and kept going.

At the edge of the town, he stood with five other men—Namontac and four Tassantassas who looked uncomfortable and stared most discourteously, particularly the youngest of them. Mato'aka snorted at the insolence and made her way forward.

Chawnzmit greeted her with a smile. "Pocahuntas! Sá keyd wingan?"

"Wingapo! I am well." She scanned the crowd with him. Some of them she knew, others she did not. "You wish to speak with Nohsh?"

He nodded, and his smile grew tight.

She addressed Namontac—it was easier to seek translation than to speak of details directly. "Nohsh has gone upriver, but we can send for him."

That was readily agreed to, and as Ra'hunt had come to greet their visitors at the same time, he took charge of tending them. Mato'aka excused herself and returned to her work.

She dashed back and threw herself with more fervor into the task of grinding. Nek only rolled her eyes once the reason was known, but she too worked with more urgency.

Channa came next. "With Nohsh not here, we have decided to prepare a welcome for Chawnzmit. All of us young women will do the dance of the wutapantam, and then offer ourselves to him after."

Mato'aka felt her eyes bugging at that. "All of you at once? And what does Tomakin say about that?"

She laughed at the reference to her new husband. "He does not care. As long as I am not chosen. And no, silly—just his pick of one of us."

It was Mato'aka's turn to roll her eyes.

"It is curious," Channa went on. "The other women say that several of the men have expressed interest in them, but not him. Never him." Her eyes held a gleam. "So we will see if tonight changes anything."

'Twas the most hellish thing he had witnessed yet—with the possible exception of the divination ceremony they had performed over him, months ago.

They'd seated him on a mat, beside a fire built in a wide, flat plain, obviously a gathering place of sorts in fair weather. Which today had been fair enough, despite the air holding the tang of coming winter. When a shriek split the air, he'd started up, and his guard reached for their arms. Surely it must be Powhatan come to surprise them, in all his power! But the gathered crowd, Pocahuntas in particular, reassured him that this was nothing to be alarmed at, even though the howling continued.

And then came a troop of young woman—he counted thirty—their naked bodies painted in different colors, wearing nothing but skirts of a few leaves before and behind. The leader wore a beautiful pair of stag's antlers on her head; others bore otterskins on different parts of their bodies; one carried a bow and arrows, another a wooden sword, another a cudgel, and so on. Continuing their fearsome cries and shouts, they ran from the woods and formed a ring about the fire, surrounding him.

They danced. They shouted. They sang. He'd thought himself well acquainted with the savage way of song and dance, but in this they exceeded all he had seen before, in some moments almost stately but mostly with unholy abandon. For all his care in not looking too closely at the women before, this time he could not tear his eyes away.

'Twas almost as if that very thing was their aim.

Nearly an hour it went on, then as they had entered, with shrieks and cries, they went away. Smith let out a long, uneven breath.

He almost did not dare look at the men with him. As he had expected, their expressions ranged from shame and discomfiture to open longing.

Captain Waldo gave a shaky, gusty laugh. "By Jove, that was—singular."

"Do not fail to mind yourself here as a gentleman," Smith snapped.

The older man looked away, a muscle flexing in his jaw.

And then suddenly the young women returned, washed and clad in their customary raiment—brief though that was as well. "Come, come!" they entreated him, surrounding him.

They tugged him to his feet and, half leading, half pushing, drew him away to a house in the town. Well-furnished, it was, but he'd no time to look around before all pressed in upon him.

"Love you not me? Love you not me?" they all began to cry, crowding and hanging upon him.

He could hardly gain his breath. "No—no!"

He tried to extricate himself, but there was not a single inch where a woman's body did not touch—or seek to touch. He put up his arms and closed his eyes.

"Back! All of you! I say nay!"

All the battles and perilous situations he had found himself in—and this was what brought him to wit's end! When he had presence of mind enough to recall their word for *no*, he exclaimed that, repeatedly. *"Mahta!"*

The wave of nymphs fell back, eyeing him with something like disbelief in their faces.

He gasped, feeling as if he'd run ten miles. "I thank you most kindly, but—no!"

One of them looked at another, and broke out in giggles. Soon they all were tittering, and the one who seemed to be their leader said something to the others then beckoned to him. "Come."

And with that, they returned to the fire, where he was seated once more on his mat as the feast was laid out.

His four companions only looked at him with something between envy and alarm. Smith glanced away, his own face burning with the shame of it.

The feast did, as before, hold every dainty it seemed the savages could think to offer. Some pressed more food upon him as he ate, others sang and danced around the fire—none to such alarming effect as before, however. And when nightfall came, they were conveyed to their lodging, yet with none of the discomfortable offerings of before.

Still, it was a while before he could sleep.

All these years, he had kept himself chaste. Not for lack of opportunity, but because the indecency of it rather turned his stomach. And neither could he be persuaded to seek a wife. The time had simply never felt convenient for it.

Would it ever? And what sort of woman would tempt him, if these wanton, naked savages did not?

Memory came to him of Charatza's great, dark eyes, and flawless beauty draped in glittering veils and flowing garments. Sheer folly, he knew now, to think that fair lady of the far east might have been anything to him but a captor—and yet he could not turn away the longing that came with the image of her.

Sleep overtook him at last, and morning came with suddenness. He led the other men down to the river and encouraged them to at least wash their faces.

Captain Waldo removed his helmet and bent to the water, splashing several handfuls, then sat looking around as his beard dripped. "'Tis not what I expected," he said at last. "My old habit of sleeping wherever I must served me well last night, but I vow, I was uncertain for a while."

Smith simply nodded. He'd not admit just how unsettled the women's pageant had made him.

They returned to their lodging to find breakfast being served and had nearly finished the meal when word came that the Powhatan had arrived. A short time later, the summons came to attend the great king.

Namontac accompanied them, and Smith delivered his message of the presents sent to the great Powhatan. "If it please you, I would ask you to come to my father Newport to accept those presents, and also to conclude our revenge against the Monacans."

Today, Wahunsenecawh chose to sit and not recline on his throne, such as it was. He drew a long breath and began to speak, giving space for Namontac to translate. "If your king has sent me presents, I also am a king, and this my land. Eight days I will stay to receive them. Your father is to come to me, not I to him, nor yet to your fort. Neither will I bite at such a bait. As for the Monacans, I can revenge my own injuries. And as for Atquanuchuck, where you say your brother was slain, it is a different direction from those parts where you suppose it to be. But for any salt water beyond the mountains, the reports you have had from my people are false."

Smith nodded slowly. He had wondered whether that would turn out to be the case. What then had he understood from their conversation all those months before?

Wahunsenecawh sat forward then, and with a stick, drew upon the ground. As before, he explained the lay of the land about them, region by region, and this time Smith did his best to listen with fresh ears and look with fresh eyes.

"Those tiresome folk. Are they gone at last?"

Namontac gave him a sorrowful look. "They are, my mamanatowic."

Wahunsenecawh huffed. "How do you bear living amongst them?"

The young warrior tucked his head. "They are not all terrible. Like foolish children at times, but not evil."

"Strange, though. Especially when Chawnzmit did not accept the favors of any of the women last night," Ra'hunt said. Namontac threw him a glance.

"What is this?" Wahunsenecawh said.

Namontac laughed shortly. "Several of the young women danced for him, dressed only in paint and leaves. Chawnzmit looked horrified. His men—" He laughed again. "I think they wished themselves in his place when afterward the women led him to a yehakan and demanded he choose one of them. The women said after that he only refused, so they went on with the feast."

Wahunsenecawh grunted. "How curious." He rubbed his chin. "Presents from their king." He snorted again. "How dare he ask me to come to them for such things? And what do they have that I would value, if they are not willing to bring me swords and guns?"

Namontac looked as if he wished to say something, but kept silent. Wahunsenecawh gave another noisy sigh.

"So, tell me, how fares the Tassantassas town? Is it good, or ill?" When the younger man hesitated, he went on, "Come now. It isn't as if I don't have other spies there. Sit here, and we will have uppowoc, and you shall tell me what you have seen and heard."

Chawnzmit returned a few days later, accompanied by the one he called "father" and a host of other men.

Winganuske wanted to press in closer to look—as everyone else was doing—but in daylight, out in the open, and unpainted, she dared not. Cold enough it was, though, she wrapped herself in a doeskin mantle and hung at the edges.

A great assembly was prepared in the field where the women had offered the extravagant welcome to John Smith. Given the sheer number of onlookers, Wahunsenecawh dispensed with having wives and counselors sit before him, although he arrayed a few of the women and his guard around the mat where he had seated himself. Then the English came, bearing things she had not seen in, oh, so long. A tall, lean white dog on a leash—a *greyhound*, she thought she remembered it being called. A basin and ewer upon a stand, and an English bedstead complete with ticking and curtains. A scarlet cloak and suit, in which, after Namontac had explained thoroughly to him would do him no harm, he rose from his mat and allowed himself to be dressed. Watching, she could only press her hand across her mouth at how he suffered their foolishness while maintaining his own dignity. The shirt, doublet, and breeches appeared too small on his lean, tall frame, but the cloak covered much fault of it all.

The ship's captain, Newport, with his one good arm, motioned to a man, who carried forward a wooden box. They opened it to reveal—was that a crown? And were those real jewels? A murmur went up from the People. She eyed Newport. John Smith claimed to defer to him as "father"—elder and leader—but from the too-bold gestures he made and his overloud voice and the obvious reserve in his manner, this was no man to whom he gave respect.

John Smith, in fact, appeared plainly unhappy at the whole ordeal.

Wahunsenecawh stood, gazing at the Tassantassas and this new toy they had brought. Newport was speaking most urgently, gesturing as if Namontac were not translating furiously beside him. Were they truly attempting to persuade Wahunsenecawh to go down on one knee and offer fealty to the king of England? He was having none of it, though, and stood ever more stiffly the longer they tried to explain. He held out his hand, but Newport shook his head and pointed to the top of his own head and then Wahunsenecawh's.

Her husband, lifting his chin, gazed away into the distance as if he were alone and in deep thought. A chill touched Winganuske. She found herself praying silently for the whole debacle to not end in bloodshed.

Newport grew frantic. After a series of growled commands, two of his men, both of whom appeared to be the tallest and stoutest among his company, stepped with great hesitation to Wahunsenecawh's side and, taking hold of his shoulders, pressed mightily until they'd induced him to stoop just enough for Newport to plunk the crown on Wahunsenecawh's head.

A volley of shots went off from the direction of the river. Wahunsenecawh startled in a flurry—all his guards around him, likewise, but Newport and Namontac and the others hastened to reassure him that it was in celebration of the coronation, not an attack.

Her husband's face lay in hard, stern lines. Winganuske's stomach dropped. He was not pleased by these events at all.

What was it these—these *strangers* sought to do here? Did they not understand that as paramount chieftain, Wahunsenecawh would bow to no one? Death alone would take his seat from him.

He abruptly appeared to collect himself and again smiled and nodded—ever courteous, and offered his old mantle and *mahkusun* to the ship's captain, Newport. And then he addressed the English captain.

"I am informed that your purpose is to discover the Monacans. I cannot lend you any aid toward such a thing. Namontac may go with you if he is so inclined, but that is all. It is too foolish a venture."

Captain Newport looked crestfallen and shocked, but was that a little smile playing about John Smith's lips?

He could not wait for them to leave. Maintaining courtesy in the face of all their supposed honor of him was the most difficult thing he had ever done.

Once the Tassantassas had gone, he pulled the thing off his head and looked at it. The strange yellow metal studded with various stones glittered and shone, in its own harsh way. He supposed they wanted him to be impressed by it.

But the way they had forced him to bow to receive it—anger surged through him once again.

He tossed the mantle aside—that he would wear again, but the clothing underneath? Intolerable. How did the Tassantassas bear having their bodies constrained by such apparel?

As he stripped out of the ridiculous garments, tearing them a little, he tossed a glare at the councilors and quiakrosoc surrounding him. "No more pegatawah. What we gave them today is the last. If they can bring such things across yapám, then they can learn to feed themselves. They are not children, however much they behave so. Neither are they useless simpletons."

A chuckle came from his left. "Are you sure?"

He allowed himself a fierce grin then kicked the strange clothing off to the side. "There. Take those, and all the trinkets they brought—except for the mantle—and store them in the temple." He reached for his deerskin kilt and fastened it in place. "I do not wish to have any of them in my house, before my eyes."

Snatching up the red mantle—something about that did feel luxurious about his shoulders—he fixed a glare upon the men still standing about, their eyes wide. "And if Chawnzmit ever returns, I shall have many hard things to say to him."

Mato'aka overheard Nohsh's tirade and stayed hidden. She did not blame him. The entire thing was so strange, so difficult to watch.

She went to the boy Tommasavach to ask him what was the meaning of all that had happened. He could not explain it and only waved a hand and said the elders of his people often did things they thought wise but appeared stupid to everyone else. They shared a laugh over that.

Both he and Mato'aka—indeed, most of the town—were interested in the white dog the Tassantassas had brought, however. Nohsh himself seemed rather taken with it and very shortly had taught the animal to lie beside him while they took meals so he could feed it from his own bowl. They all thought that a little excessive, but none would tell Nohsh so. And this dog was a creature of far different disposition than those skulking around the town, sometimes used for pack animals. Tommasavach said the *greyhound* might be good for hunting, but Nohsh seemed intent upon coddling it like a child.

Where the Tassantassas were concerned, though, he would hear nothing of it. Indignation bubbled within Mato'aka at how he had been wronged, his goodwill misunderstood and taken advantage of. When she asked Nek and Channa, both agreed it was more Captain Newport's fault this time than Chawnzmit's, but that seemed small comfort when she could see Nohsh still bore the hurt from it.

Chapter Seven

Jamestowne, 1609

The year had begun well enough. The colony was growing. They'd livestock, and provisions, and even a few English women—their first wedding had taken place between one of the workmen and a maid who had come along as a companion to one of the men's wives.

But oh, these troublesome people—both the English and the Naturals. He knew when the delegation from Wahunsenecawh himself had come, early last summer, that it would not remedy the wave of thefts and attacks. He knew also that the savages' love for him—or such as they expressed—was not unmixed with hate. Were they not told, on an expedition up one of the northernmost rivers, of an ambush committed at the direction of Powhatan? And so soon after Powhatan had avowed his love and care for Smith.

The most recent voyage up to Werowocomoco revealed that Wahunsenecawh had commanded an embargo against the English, and none were willing to give up corn unless Smith threatened them. So threaten he did, though he liked it not.

In the midst of it all, he sensed—he was not sure he should even give words to the thought—that it was not merely these people he had to deal with, but their petty gods as well.

He felt his heart tugged back and forth over this matter. He had to admit there was much to admire about them. They were a comely people, their great king very cunning, and his little daughter the most charming of all.

And yet—this darkness hanging over them. Over this entire land, as beautiful as it was. At odd moments it rose up within Smith like gorge needing to be vomited out—except that this was not something of which he could rid himself so easily.

God had been gracious to them, despite fire and sickness and famine. Reverend Hunt had reminded them many times that the love of God never left them, despite how sure Smith was that He was angry with them at certain times. Despite Hunt's own death when they'd barely been in Virginia a year.

But shortly after the ridiculousness of the coronation of Powhatan, Smith had sent Master Scrivener back to Werowocomoco for more corn, only to find the savages more ready to fight than trade. Then Wahunsenecawh had sent word to Smith and offered corn if only he would send men to "build him a house," along with the usual request for swords and guns.

Did they not have enough of those, from their thievery over the year before? But Smith went, assigning two of the Deutsch craftsmen and a few others to the task of building. Of course, after explaining how they'd no swords or tools or such like to spare, he'd also endured a lecture from the chief king, who did not in truth appear so old as to be talking of his own demise, on how he was certain to die at some point. Wahunsenecawh's brothers and sisters would then inherit his place, and he could wish for nothing more but for Chawnzmit and his people to extend the same love to them as Chawnzmit did to Wahunsenecawh. But he knew now that they, the English, had come, not to be part of his people, but to push them out of their place and take the land. So why did Smith lie and call him "father," then nose about into the business of the People, as though he were not under the rule of Wahunsenecawh? Why did he persist in taking by force what he might have had by love? At the very least, it did not dispose him or his people well toward Chawnzmit when they insisted upon coming armed among them. If they were all truly friends, then there was no need for such a show.

Smith had replied that he and his men had kept their vow of love for Wahunsenecawh, but it was Wahunsenecawh's promise they found every day violated. Only because of their love and regard for him did they hold off from revenging themselves. And he might wish them to come before him disarmed, but it was their custom to wear their arms as they did their apparel.

At last, after much talk, they began to trade, but Smith continually refused that which he knew the Powhatan truly desired—more English guns and swords.

With a great sigh, Wahunsenecawh said, "Chawnzmit, I never used any weroance so kindly as yourself, yet from you I receive the least kindness of any. Captain Newport gave me swords, copper, clothes, a bed, tools, or whatever I desired—and he would send away his guns when I asked it of him. None deny to do, or lay at my feet, what I desire, but only you will have whatever you demand. You do whatever you wish, regardless of what respect you claim to have for anyone! Both Captain Newport and I must content you, rather than be contented! But if you are as friendly as you say, then do send away your arms. Then I may believe you. For surely you see the love I bear you, which causes me to forget myself."

Rather did it seem to Smith that Wahunsenecawh bided his time until he could take Smith's life. Smith sent his men to be ready to come ashore, and in the meantime hazarded but a drop of honesty. "You know I have but one God and one king, and I follow none but them. I am here not as your subject, but as a friend. As such I seek to please you as much as possible. By the gifts you give me, you gain more than by trade. If you would visit me as I do you, you would know that our desire for peace is not in vain. Come—bring all your people with you as your guard—I will not dislike that as being overjealous! But to content you, tomorrow I will leave my arms and trust to your promise. I call you father indeed, and as a father you shall see I will love you, but the small care you had of me, though you call me child, caused my men to persuade me to shift for myself."

In the meantime, Wahunsenecawh grew suspicious of Smith's intent and sent all his women and children and their belongings out into the forest to hide, while a contingent of his men surrounded Smith's lodging. Taking pistol, sword, and small shield, he made a run for it and rejoined his own small company. Then a very old man came after them, crying out that he was sent by Wahunsenecawh. They waited while he gave a long speech, mostly filled with dissembling and making excuses, although a gift of a great bracelet and a chain of pearls accompanied it.

When they finally got away—not without a gift of corn as well, to Smith's surprise—they returned to the fort to find that Wahunsenecawh had sent the Deutschmen back to Jamestowne before him, saying they needed more tools and supplies and pretending that Smith had authorized them to be given such things. To compound Smith's frustration, the young man he had left with Wahunsenecawh this time—his own page, Samuel Collier—seemed to be in on the plot.

In the weeks and months after, he wrangled as well with Opechancanough, where again after many speeches, Smith lost patience. In exasperation, he seized the tall Indian king by his scalp lock and leveled his French pistol. "If you will not lade my ship with corn, then I will lade it with your dead carcasses! Are you indeed our friends, or no?"

Much subdued, or perhaps only in shock, the mighty Opechancanough gave the order for corn to be brought, as Smith desired.

That night ended—after so many gifts and baskets of corn that Smith was overwearied with receiving them and retired to bed—with an attack upon his lodgings by some forty or fifty savages armed with good English swords. Once again, Smith led the fight to drive them back.

They returned to the fort to discover a loss most sore: Master Scrivener had taken nine others in a skiff to the Isle of Hogs, so named for where they kept the pigs brought over on supply ships, but a storm blew up and capsized the boat, drowning them all.

The expedition he had sent out to gain word from the Monacan, or whoever would give it, on Sir Walter Ralegh's planters from twenty years ago and more, returned empty-handed. All they could gather were the barest of rumors and of certainty, none, and could only conclude that all must be dead.

In the meantime, such trouble arose from the surrounding Indians that Smith feared for his life. Yet he must carry on as if he had no fear. Must show them strength and bravery. And so he went on.

It had not ended there, however. All too aware that his year as president was coming to a close, he had tried to hand the responsibility off to Captain Martin, who, to no one's real surprise, had arrived again with Ratcliffe and Archer on the third supply. The three had once been his allies, all later exposed as knaves and sent back to England with various returning ships. But Smith, wishing to show his good faith by nominating Martin as his successor, stepped down. Then, after less than three hours—*three hours!*—the other man realized his own insufficiency and relinquished authority back to Smith.

Seven ships of the nine sent out together for this most recent supply had come safely to harbor with them, along with word of a new government to be set up by the Virginia Company. And much of that time the three men, Martin, Ratcliffe, and Archer, had spent fomenting discontent against their own ships' captains, and against Smith himself, before they'd ever set foot on Virginia's shore.

Better they'd been if the ships had never come at all. Because now he'd not only mutiny to contend with, but the addition of yet more people who knew nothing of feeding themselves in this country or of dealing with savages. Although plenty of opinion they had on how the colony's affairs should have been carried out.

He'd leave them to it had he not already invested two long years. Instead, he doubled down on discipline. "He that works not, eats not" had been very effective these past months. He split the company into three groups: one to stay in Jamestowne, one to set up a town downriver, and one to do so upriver, near the falls.

Even now he made his way upriver to the aid of Captain West and his men, who initially had chosen the most horrible place imaginable, near the Indian town of Powhatan. The first location was one surrounded by swamps and frequently flooded when the rains came, although it had been very dry for weeks now. It minded him of the early days in Jamestowne, when they'd no good water and initial attempts at digging a well had failed. Thanks be to God that they did now have a good well.

He drew a deep breath, savoring the clean smell of the river and the earliest tang of autumn. Bright was the blue of the sky, and warm the sun, filtering through leaves just beginning to change color. How he had come to love this country. A sense of satisfaction settled deep in his chest. None had labored on the colony's behalf more than himself. He was hard on the men, true, but ever worked the same tasks alongside them and never sent men where he was not willing to lead. Even many of the faction that Ratcliffe, Martin, and Archer had set against him had seen the truth of the matter and avowed their loyalty to Smith.

And the Indians themselves—he allowed himself to smile a little. They too respected him, after everything. In fact, he was the one they came to when West and his men—and all the others in his absence—went beyond reason in their cruelties to the savages.

This day proved no exception. He'd no sooner landed, greeting the English at the forted town they'd built and named "Nonesuch," before a contingent of savage warriors emerged from the forest and requested to speak with him.

"You sent word to our mamanatowic that if your people built a town here, you would provide protection against the Monacan. But such protectors, they are worse than the Monacan have ever been! If you will not punish them, we will be compelled to take our own vengeance."

'Twas a tiresome business for the next week or so, sorting out who amongst the English were the worst offenders, putting them to the lash, and setting those who were truly worthy in charge. Even then, they had scarcely sailed back downriver before the Indians attacked the new fort. At the same time, the lack of rain caused the river to so dry up that their ship foundered, forcing Smith and his men to return to the fort, this time to beat back the savages and make them stand to parley.

It struck him as strange, as always, that such a thing rather increased their respect for him.

Yes, he could live here for the rest of his life and be content.

They'd freed the ship two days before. Smith had sent them on ahead to Jamestowne, leaving him the shallop in which to return and a crew of four, all solid and trustworthy. At nightfall, reluctant to go ashore, Smith lay in the boat, soothed by the night birds, the rustling of leaves with the evening breeze, and the slight rocking of the vessel. Above him, thousands of stars lay thickly across the sky. At his feet, making their own pallets in the boat as well, were his company.

'Twas a good life. Please God he could continue to guide the colony, put to silence the naysayers, and choose a good man to next take the position of president.

A terrible boom shook the night, and a searing pain dug deep into his side.

Smith opened his eyes to flames—his own clothing afire. Without thought, without hesitation, he dived over the side of the boat, which rocked wildly.

Instant coolness surrounded him, quenching the flames, but the hurt remained, and no river bottom met the soles of his boots. He must be in the deep part.

Thrashing, hardly remembering how to move his arms and legs while in water, he bobbed upward and gasped. Not even a full breath and his head went under again. From the shallop came the shouts and cries of the other men.

His boots—the continual burning of his side—both hindered him from staying above the surface for longer than a moment. But then a hand took hold of him—several grasped and dragged him upward. A scream tore itself from his throat as they pulled him over the side, back into the boat.

He thrashed and writhed, trying to ease the awfulness in his side. Light flickered as someone lifted a lantern. "Great God in Heaven!"

He'd need to punish whoever that was for such an oath—except that it seemed a fitting expression for his own desperate prayer.

"Lie still, Captain," said another, alarm edging his tone, "and let us look."

Clenching his teeth, lungs still heaving, he strove to do so. The pulling back of the edges of his clothing was nothing short of torture, and a groan escaped him.

"'Tis bad, and no mistake. How did this happen?"

"'Twas his powder. Was his pistol match still lit?"

Smith shook his head, roughly. "Quenched it—before we retired."

Hadn't he? He couldn't recall ever making such a mistake before, to leave a lit match where it could accidentally come into contact with his powder, or anyone else's.

Squinting against the light, he saw all the men looking at each other, as if asking the same question.

"Let us make for Jamestowne without delay," came the deep voice of Nathaniel Powell. "We will take turns watching and sleeping."

Near a hundred miles, by way of the twists and turns of the river, did they have to go.

Smith faded in and out of consciousness. There was ever the burning in his side, at one point causing him to dream that Wahunsenecawh stood over him, a firebrand in his hand which he then pressed into Smith's flesh. He came awake from that one with a strangled groan, only to drop off and dream again of falling on the battlefield against the Turks, who then found him and dragged him away to captivity. . .

He opened his eyes to daylight. Always, always the burn. Being awake was too burdensome, but neither could he sleep as soundly as he needed.

They arrived at the fort as the day was waning. Once again shutting his teeth against any cries or groans, he let them help him up and then step out onto shore. 'Twas but a certain amount of steps until he reached his own lodging, but it felt near an hour to make even that short journey. At last he lay in his own bed, gasping against the new wave of agony that getting there had stirred.

The men of the town crowded into his house, bunches of them by turns, asking what he should do. "There is nothing here with which to treat such a grave wound," they said, after pouring a little oil upon it. "Do you wish us to send you to England?"

Deep breaths, in—out—in—out. He could hardly think. "I will give you my word on the morrow," he said. "And think upon who should take my place, lest the town go ungoverned."

Another thought struck him.

"Oh, and lay you my pistol by my hand, with the match lit."

Night came, and more dreams with it. He was once again amongst the Turks, enduring a flogging.

He startled awake. Whisperings came from outside, and the door opened—slowly, carefully, and first one figure slipped through, and then another. They crept to his bedside, and a glint in the gloom showed the presence of a blade in the hand of one.

Gritting against the pain, he palmed his pistol and lifted it across his body, pointing. "Name yourself, knave!"

The two men took such a violent start that they stumbled over one another to get out again. Smith gave a great bellow but did not shoot.

He was sure, however, that it must be Ratcliffe and Archer who had crept in, intending to murder him in his bed.

He said as much to those who came in after, their faces pale. "Aye, we gave guard over your lodging to Ratcliffe, who said he would look after your well-being."

Some looking-after that was.

Dawn broke slowly and with no relief to the burning at his side, which they had reported to him was deep into his flesh, some nine- or ten-inches square. Just over the length of a man's hand one way, and then the other.

He was also quite useless, and when questioned, could not make a decisive reply as to whether he thought he should sail for England. But the matter was soon taken out of his hands. Emboldened no doubt by the fact that he had decided against shooting his assailants in the night, first this man and then that, the whole company of those he had flogged or punished or otherwise used harshly, gathered up to make complaint and accusation of his failures, both as president and before.

He'd not the energy to raise a defense, either in word or deed. Indeed, as the day wore on, he was more and more insensible to it all.

"He'll not survive the voyage back," came the sorrowful voice of Anas Todkill, who had been with him on many a voyage.

"He'll not survive if he stays," said Captain Wynne.

"He'd as lief perish here, than abandon us," another said.

Back and forth they went, and Smith could not summon a response to any.

Dim impressions came to him of being carried on his bed, of the creaking of ship's rigging and call of the crew one to another. Of the floor rising and falling.

He wanted the river. And the forest. He would even welcome the musical voices of the Powhatan people and the deep thrum of their drumbeats.

He awoke instead to the curved walls of a ship. Had he been a profane man, he'd have cursed. Long and loudly.

Dragging himself above decks, he was met with the sun, just coming up to greet them at the rim of the seen world ahead of them—all heaving waves and crying birds.

The wind blew so stiffly, it drew tears from his eyes. He stood at the bow and let it wash the stench from his body and the wetness from his cheeks.

Part Two

John Rolfe

Chapter Eight

Bermuda, 1609

The shipwreck was over. God in His graciousness had allowed them all to reach shore safely, and as the sun rose they slept on the upper edge of the beach, below the trees, within sight of the waves washing endlessly up and down.

John Rolfe sat up, rubbing his eyes with the back of his hand—the only part not covered in sand at the moment. At his side, Sarah lay curled, her rounded belly outlined by layers of wet gown, freckled cheeks rimmed with sand and dark lashes spiky with salt.

Dear, dear Sarah! She had borne the voyage with patience, despite being sick for half of it, and when the storm came that drove them toward these islands, bravely endured the terror of the ship's foundering and the necessity to be rowed ashore.

The ship lay now on her side as well, outlined against the pearly hues of sunrise. Farther down the beach, people had risen and scurried about, no doubt seeing to the needs of the great lord who shared their fate.

Although the lord in question—Sir Thomas Gates, set to be the next governor of Virginia—had labored tirelessly already beside all of them as they strove to keep the *Sea Venture* from going down.

They would need to continue working together, all of them, were they to further survive this adventure.

A little later, it was decided that they would salvage what they could from the wreck and build another ship. Others were in charge of finding food—the seas were full of fish and turtles and crabs, so they need not starve—although water was needful. The island had no rivers or natural springs, but they were able to dig shallow wells and collect rainwater.

He worried over Sarah. She seemed to regain her strength but slowly. The voyage thus far went hard upon her, with much sickness. The shipwreck itself was nothing short of harrowing. Many of them still shuddered at the thought of stepping foot again in a boat of any kind. Yet she would only look at John and say, "If Elinor Dare could face it, so must I."

It only made something inside him feel hollow. She was his wife, near to bearing their child. He ought to be able to protect her and provide for them better than this.

God in heaven. . .

He could not even finish the prayer. What sort of Christian was he?

Perhaps this was only the result of leaving family behind in England—his own mother and brother, and Sarah's mother and father—all of whom were deeply unhappy about his making this journey. If they were unhappy with John, was God also unhappy with him?

Food aplenty they found, both fish and fowl, and fruits in abundance. The shipbuilding came along, and the year wore away even though the season remained warm. What a delightful place this could be!

Sarah's travail came upon her most suddenly, and the babe's appearance followed shortly after—a tiny girl child they christened Bermuda, for the island of her birth. How grateful he was for the presence of other women, to attend them. He'd never have known what to do, despite all his peeking over the stall door in the stables when it came time for mares to foal.

He felt very differently about his own wife and child—and Sarah was no mere broodmare.

Little Bermuda was the sweetest thing. She grew and thrived apace with the finishing of the ships, although Sarah herself did not regain strength quite as quickly as John or the other women would have liked. All frowned and clucked over her, bidding her eat more. But her appetite remained sparse.

With winter's end, the ships were finished and fitted, and after some disagreement over whether or not to actually continue to Virginia, they all packed to go aboard. Not two days out, little Bermuda grew listless and fevered, and within hours expired. They wrapped her tiny body and committed it to the waves, and while Sarah's tears did not cease for a whole day and night, to John's relief, she seemed to gather strength. She did not mention the child again.

At last, on an early morning, a sweet wind blew that gave the fragrance of deep woods, and the coast of Virginia came into view.

Jamestowne, 1610

"We'd have done better to stay on the island," one of the men murmured. "Or better yet, in England."

John and the others surveyed the fort, or what remained of it. Such squalor—the houses ill-kept, the palisade falling in some places, the churchyard burgeoning with new-dug areas testifying to how many they'd lost—and they insisted that was not all. Men and the few women, appearing nearly as skeletons, regarded them with a desperate hunger.

And over all, the stench of death and other filth. John longed to be back out on the open water, where the wind was fresh and pure.

One such victim of near starvation addressed them, hands outspread. "We've nothing for you here. No provision left, nor even seed to plant the fields these past weeks—if the savages would even let us leave the walls of this town. Which they do not, but continually lurk without, and slay any who venture forth to either hunt or gather. Ever since they heard of our loss of Captain Smith, they have not ceased to bedevil us."

It was speedily decided to gather up those who remained—perhaps sixty among the four hundred or so which had populated the town and surroundings the previous autumn—and leave again for England.

When he delivered her the news, Sarah blinked, frowned a little, then nodded without comment. His heart contracted. 'Twas too much to expect, with her still grieving their little one—

He shoved the thought aside and gave his attention to finding room aboard their ship.

They set sail on the next tide. Barely had they traveled halfway down the river to the sea, however, before a grand ship came looming from the mist—a great English vessel with two more following after. 'Twas Lord De La Warre, arrived with fresh supply.

And so, on the ninth of June, 1610, did they return and begin the second settling of Jamestowne.

Mato'aka tucked a strand of hair back up into its knot and, taking a better grip on the handle of her hoe, set back to the digging of holes for the next planting.

How much easier it was, using the tools brought by the Tassantassas. Of course, Chawnzmit had used words like *steal* and *thief* to refer to how they'd gotten them, to which Nohsh had thundered that for how much pegatawah and wutapantam they'd given them, the Tassantassas could spare a few tools. And Nek had only shaken her head.

Regardless, Mato'aka appreciated having them.

Chawnzmit. The Tassantassas said he had died. She could still scarce believe it.

She peered at the angle of the sun. Just a little longer, and they would be done. Nek followed after, dropping in seeds and covering them. Mato'aka focused on getting to the end of the field, where Channa waited with a large gourd full of water, her belly as round above the waistband of her skirt as the gourd.

A flutter went through Mato'aka. Before another turning of seasons, it could be her growing big with child. Granny Snow was already planning her *huskanasqua*, and several of the young men had started looking at her with more intent.

The one who surprised her the most was Koko'um, the captain of Nohsh's brother, Opechancanough. Since she and Nek and Nohsh and everyone had all moved from Werowocomoco, he had come more often and it seemed found many excuses to stop and make conversation with her.

Why in the world would he even be interested, after all his disdain before?

She had posed the question to Nek and Channa, who both laughed.

Channa said there was no accounting for what men wanted, but Mato'aka could tell she was proud that her little sister would soon be considered a woman.

Both were strangely secretive when it came to telling her what huskanasqua would entail, however. Nek merely said she must both grind pegatawah and cook apon, and keep herself strong by running through the fields around their town. And while huskanaw for the boys could last for most of a year, the ceremony admitting a girl to womanhood was not so long.

"After all, you have already crossed over, since your body has begun its monthly change."

Granny Snow pressed her to take more walks in the forest to seek out the spirits, and she was taught the various teas to accomplish both having her heart and mind cleansed to hear them, and to cleanse her body each month before she had a husband who would provide for any babies she might bear.

Not that *that* was yet needful, since she had not yet let any of them take liberties with her. Perhaps she would with Koko'um, after huskanasqua...

Then again, maybe not.

She reached the end of the row, and Channa gave her a cup full of water. "Do you want to hear the latest news about the Tassantassas?"

Mato'aka nodded, slurping.

"Nohsh's plan to starve them out nearly worked. Two of their great winged kanoe came, and they all got into them and went away. But then a day or so later, they came back—with three more kanoe and more people. And now they are rebuilding and trying to have talk with our People."

Mato'aka dipped the cup and drank again. It made her stomach turn to think of the terrible things the Tassantassas had done to some of the other towns after Chawnzmit died.

It still made her stomach turn to think that he was really dead.

He had told her once that if one believed and followed his God, death was not the end, that something called the *sol* flew away to live in something called *hevven*.

Did his sol now live in hevven?

As maddening as he was in dealing with Nohsh and the others, he was not as bad as the others. That had been made very clear after his death. The burning of a whole town in Kequotan, and then the taking of the *weroansqua* of Paspahae and the cruel slaughter of her children—

Later, when the Tassantassas named *Ratcliffe* had come back to Werowocomoco seeking to obtain more pegatawah, the People considered the women more than justified in flaying off his flesh, bit by bit, in retaliation for such gross murders.

Nek had not joined in, and of course neither did Mato'aka—not that she would be allowed, not having gained the status yet of being a grown woman—but she did not blame them.

What a poor excuse he was of manhood. The memory of his dying howls, when he should have been shouting or singing insults at his enemies, still echoed in her thoughts.

She handed the cup back to Channa just as Nek reached them. After Nek drank, she smiled at both of them. "Let us finish the last bit, then go wash in the river."

Nek did like her evening baths, especially in the summer. Mato'aka was not going to refuse to go along, not after planting a good part of the day.

They finished, went to bathe, and returned to the town. On their way back to Nek's yehakan, they passed Nohsh sitting outside his own dwelling, working on a pair of mahkusun. He waved them over with a smile. "Wife! Daughters! I am told by Granny Snow that a very important happening will be soon."

Nek angled her head with an answering grin. "And what may that be, oh my husband?"

"The huskanasqua of our older daughter, of course." His eyes twinkled at Mato'aka. "And a certain young warrior has been hinting about another happening, soon after."

Mato'aka straightened and ran her fingers through her still-wet hair. "He will have to win me first."

Nohsh gave a great laugh. "As it should be, little one. As it should be!"

After more talk, they walked away, and Mato'aka sniffed. "How soon will huskanasqua be?"

Nek shook her head. "Soon."

Mato'aka let out a hard breath and closed her eyes.

Nek's hand settled on her arm. "You are both brave and strong. There will be no difficulty for you to accomplish it."

Mato'aka swallowed past a thickness in her throat and looked up into Nek's warm brown gaze. "But not everyone has the added burden of being Beloved Woman."

Nek nodded, the frown clearing, and gave her arm a slight squeeze before releasing her. "Even so. You will do this."

She was going to die before accomplishing huskanasqua. She just knew it.

It wasn't the extra scrubbing down, or the combing out of the hair, or the painting of her body, or any of that.

Nor even the cooking and cooking, followed by races to the river and back.

It was after, when Granny Snow led her into the forest to a tiny yehakan built just for her and gave her a drink that smelled vile and tasted worse.

Her own skin painted ghostly white, Granny Snow gazed sternly at Mato'aka. "You must drink it, all of it."

So she choked it down. And promptly regretted it.

The whole world swirled around her, first as varying shades of grey, then in vivid colors she had never seen before. A howling took her, and she dreamed she was a wolf—or had she truly changed form?

Then there were shapes about her, tall figures with long hair and flowing clothing. One reminded her of Nohsh at his most stern, his dark eyes cold and glittering as he regarded her. Another was a woman with hair like sunlight and eyes of the sky. She looked at Mato'aka and gave a laugh.

The figures formed a circle and danced about her, slow and stately at first, then faster and faster until their feet flew high off the ground and limbs and hair swirled like mist. Then only lights remained, dancing like the fireflies or sparks from a fire.

And then, with a mighty roll of thunder, they were all scattered by a figure who shone like the brightest winter moon—or the sun itself. He wore a mantle of the whitest doeskin and his hair glittered like snow. His eyes were of fire.

Mato'aka, he said. *Amonute. See, I have called you by name.*

Her heart leaped within her even as she fell to the ground, trembling.

"What are you called?"

But he only gave a gentle laugh and, stooping, reached to touch her shoulder. *You will come to know me. But not yet.*

The town was so much quieter without her. Never mind that Little Flower seemed to try to fill in the space her sister had left.

It had been three days. Winganuske went about her tasks without enthusiasm—weed the garden, grind pegatawah, bake bread, mend baskets—all because she must, but there was no joy.

Chawnzmit had gone away to die, and after the People thought the rest of the English would do the same, more came, and they were terrible. It brought to mind stories she had heard—more than twenty years ago now—of an English captain who had been cruel to the People to the south, the Suquoten.

On the fourth day, she looked up from grinding pegatawah and realized Wahunsenecawh was standing nearby, watching her. "My husband," she murmured, pushing a strand of hair aside.

He came and crouched nearby. "She will return safely," he said at last, pitched only for her to hear.

She could only bob a nod. He continued to eye her, hands resting lightly on his knees.

"Did you ever have anything like huskanasqua?" he asked.

"No. Other than coming across yapám, itself." She glanced about, afraid of being overheard, but there was no one near. "I did not tell her—"

He extended a hand. "I know." His gaze was warm. "She has the blood of the True People. And the best and bravest of yours."

As he rose and walked away, she almost wept. Of all the endearments he had given her over the years, she just might treasure that one the most.

Eight days she spent out at the yehakan, waking and sleeping, drinking only water after that initial tea Granny had pressed upon her. But she did not dream again.

Much she thought about the tall man in white. But every time she considered asking Granny or one of the quiakrosoc about him, she felt a reluctance to do so.

Some visions were not meant for sharing, Granny had already warned her. Was this one of those?

Either way, she could not shake the impression that it was the presence of the Great One in white that had preserved her after drinking that foul concoction.

At last, Granny came for her, conducted her to the creek to wash, and helped anoint her skin with fresh oils before presenting her with a new skirt. Beautiful it was, with careful fringing and sewn about with shell beads.

She had already been growing out her hair, ever since her monthly bleeding had begun, and Granny combed and arranged it for her, tying the length of it back and tucking in a pair of swan's feathers. "That signifies your status as a Beloved Woman," she said softly.

Then she and Mato'aka returned to the town.

As they neared, the smells of cooking foods wafted into the forest. Her stomach gave loud complaint.

Whoops and cries greeted them as they came into view. Mato'aka held in her smile and kept walking, just behind Granny, but the crowd gathered and thickened around them until they reached Nohsh's yehakan. He stood before the doorway, arrayed in his finery—not, perhaps, as much as he'd worn for the coming of Chawnzmit, but still he dazzled.

He kept his expression grave as Granny brought her to stand before him. "The newest Beloved Woman of Tsenacomoco has emerged from the spirit realm! I present her, Amonute!"

A great cheer went up all around, and Nohsh gave her a brilliant smile. "Wingapo, Amonute, Beloved Woman of the True People."

She was given a mat to sit upon next to Nohsh, and the feasting began. Granny had warned her not to overeat, but she need not have worried—Mato'aka could swallow only a few bites of this or that.

As the sun began its descent, the dancing also began. In the midst of the merrymaking, six young warriors, painted and heavily ornamented, pranced out and swirled around the fire.

Mato'aka sat straighter, her heart suddenly pounding. While the entire day was in celebration of her completing huskanasqua, this in particular was for her.

More precisely, to impress her.

There was no faulting their form or grace, nor their deeds of bravery. And each of them sought to outdo the other in their ornaments—one had a brace of bear claws fastened in the knot of his hair, one a whelk shell, one a cluster of rattlesnake tails, and one—was that a dried human hand?

Mato'aka suppressed a shiver.

Their eyes glittered as they whirled past, clearly preening for her benefit. With a little study, she recognized most of them, and relaxed.

One in particular kept drawing her eye. That one also kept boldly meeting her gaze as he skipped and stomped.

She lifted her chin and assumed an imperious expression. She must not appear moved.

With a great cry, they brought the dance to an end and all came to stand before her, roughly fanned out, jostling each other for the best view of her—and that she might have the best view of them.

She fastened her gaze upon each of them. Now she must choose a favorite and join in the dance. There was no commitment attached, but it would clearly mark who she preferred, at least to begin with.

She settled at last upon Koko'um—with the bear claws in his hair and alternating bars of black and white in slashes across his face. He stood, swaying a little but mostly unmoved while the others milled about him.

At her smile and nod, he stepped forward and extended a hand. Taking it, she let him draw her lightly to her feet—and the dance began again.

Chapter Nine

Pota'omec, Cattapeuk (Spring Fish Run Season),
1613 by English reckoning

"Are you not ready? Pocahuntas, why are you still such a child?"

The barb—along with the name—was delivered with a laugh from Miskeh, the chief wife of Yapazus, weroance of Pota'omec, but it still stung. Mato'aka tossed back a laugh in return to cover its lingering burn. "What, because I would rather play with my own baby than gossip with old women? May I never grow too old to appreciate the world around me."

She lifted the baby in question with both hands, pressed her face to the yearling child's bare belly, and blew. Little Fox squealed with laughter.

"I thought you wished to see the winged kanoe of the Tassantassas?"

Mato'aka did, but a strange reluctance curled in her belly. "I do. But Little Fox had to finish his milk. Let me take him to Channa, then we can go see the Tassantassas."

The other woman, only a little older than Mato'aka herself, sniffed and pursed her lips.

For three moons she had lingered here, after coming along as part of a trade delegation on Nohsh's behalf. She was only too happy to oversee the exchange of woven baskets and earthenware vessels for quantities of shell beads—both the more expensive *rahrenoc* and the cheaper sorts. But, although she could not fault Yapazus's hospitality, something in his overeager manner made her wish to be away. And very soon.

She missed Koko'um. And Nohsh, and Nek, and Little Flower.

But first—yes, she did wish to see again this great winged kanoe of the Tassantassas. Perhaps gain word about Chawnzmit—how had he perished?

Channa took Little Fox with a smile as well as a rolling of the eyes, and carried him to where her own son played under the wide trees.

"We will return before day's end!" Mato'aka called after her sister, who merely lifted a hand in response.

If Little Fox needed to nurse before then, Channa would be happy to oblige. It would not be the first time, as sisters, that they had suckled each other's children.

Yapazus and his warriors trooped along as she and Miskeh made the short journey downriver to where the great kanoe lay—and there it was, through the trees, bobbing ever slightly in the water. Its wings were rolled up, but colorful bits fluttered in the breeze like *manaang'gwas*, all over the rigging. Men moved about on the ship and on shore, in apparel so familiar it caused her heart to lose a beat.

"Ai!" Miskeh jumped up and down, then ran forward, heedless of propriety.

And she dared say Mato'aka behaved like a child?

For herself, she kept the same steady pace. She would show dignity even if an elder wife of a neighboring weroance did not.

The Tassantassas straightened and came to attention as their presence became known. Introductions were made. Mato'aka recognized the word *captain* and knew that man was the one in charge of the great kanoe. Argall was his name, nearly as broad as he was tall, with a sharp gaze and equally sharp smile that did nothing to make Mato'aka feel at ease—especially when that gaze lingered on her, taking in every detail of her body. His smile seemed to fade momentarily then return more brilliant than before.

Before the pleasantries were even finished, Miskeh went right to the edge of the river to stare at the great kanoe. "Pocahuntas! Is it not a great wonder?"

She broke from the group to follow her part of the way. "Kuppeh."

Miskeh danced a little. "I want to go aboard and see!" She flitted back to Yapazus. "May I go aboard? Ask them if that is allowed."

Mato'aka longed to roll her eyes, but she forced a smile. This woman was worse than Little Flower.

Yapazus conferred with the Tassantassas and, after much back and forth, turned to Miskeh. "They all agree it is not proper for you to go alone."

Her eyes went wide, and she appealed to Mato'aka. "If Pocahuntas goes with me—will you go?"

Mato'aka did not answer at first. A strange reluctance gripped her. Or was it only that she disliked the woman so strongly?

Suddenly Miskeh was begging—and weeping, of all things. "I wish to go on the great winged kanoe! I have never before been on such a thing. Please do not deny to accompany me, Pocahuntas. Please!"

And on she went, despite Mato'aka's soft refusal.

Yapazus looked at her, most earnestly. "Will you not? For the sake of our friendship—for the love between Wahunsenecawh and I?"

The captain of the kanoe was still watching with that strange intentness. He said something, and it was translated. *If the women would be so kind as to come, we would provide them supper.*

Mato'aka suppressed a deep sigh. She might as well get this over with.

Being a cool day, early in cattapeuk, she and Miskeh both wore doeskin mantles, and she found she was glad of it, for the looks that the Tassantassas gave her. She pulled the garment more snugly about herself and tried to pay attention to the clumsy explanations she and Miskeh were favored with. It was rather interesting, to see the curious way the vessel was put together—the smoothness of the wood, the breadth of the deck, the cords and chains and great, wide wings made of some clever weave.

The Tassantassas beamed with much pride to show off their kanoe. After a while, when they had taken her and Miskeh around every little bit, they showed them into a room where a wide, flat surface on upraised legs held bowls and platters of various foods, and they were persuaded to sit down on the benches on either side.

They ate a little of everything set before them—meats and a strange bread, and something white and soft which they called *cheese*. Mato'aka was not sure she liked it. The piquant drink poured for them, though—that was interesting.

They were feasted until well after dark, and the men most courteously invited them to sleep on board the *ship*, or so they called the vessel. Again, reluctantly, Mato'aka went along when they were ushered into a particular room where pallets and covers lay for their use.

"Is this not exciting?" Miskeh said.

Mato'aka sighed. "My child is going to miss me terribly." In truth, she would miss him and his small warmth just as much.

She slept only in bits, and morning came with the rude realization she did not know where to go to relieve herself. But she did not want to ask.

Miskeh awoke, and with a small smile to Mato'aka, she rose, refastened her hair, and wrapped her mantle about her. Mato'aka had sat ready for some time, but she waited for the older woman to go out ahead of her. Age and position should go first.

When she went to step through the opening, however, a Tassantassa body blocked the way. A grin split his ugly bearded face, and with a laugh, he pushed her back into the room and shut the door. When she tried to open it, it was stuck fast.

"No—let me out!" she cried, with increasing urgency. "Mahta!"

Hearing voices outside, she quieted, pressing against the door, listening. Yapazus and Miskeh were squabbling, and Tassantassas voices added to the commotion.

Then, with much clanking and creaking above, the ship began to move. Biting back a wail, Mato'aka turned and looked about the room. There were no other openings besides the one.

The vessel pitched, making it difficult to stand. She backed against the wall and slid down to huddle, whimpering.

"Winganuske, come!"

The call, edged with alarm, brought her running.

Just outside Wahunsenecawh's yehakan, Channa stood, arms around Little Fox, her own child clinging about her knees. She looked faint with weariness. "I came directly from Pota'omec. The Tassantassas—they have stolen Mato'aka!"

The other women who had gathered to hear and the warriors who currently stood guard for the mamanatowic—Koko'um included—all gave cries of dismay. Winganuske felt her knees wobble.

Wahunsenecawh only shut his eyes, but it seemed he aged at least ten years in that moment.

"Miskeh! That woman, the chief wife of Yapazus," Channa went on, "she has no proper respect of Mato'aka and is jealous of her being *midéwi-qua*. And it is whispered that Yapazus has been too friendly with the Tassantassas. But Miskeh begged to go see the great winged kanoe, and then pestered Mato'aka until she agreed to go aboard with her. They were feasted and given a place to sleep—and then this morning, they would not let her leave." Channa threw up a hand. "Yapazus made a great show of being surprised and horrified, but I saw the Tassantassas captain give him a copper pot."

There was another cry, and Winganuske found herself sinking to the ground—hard.

The cry had come from her own throat.

Her daughter—her elder daughter, the pride and joy of her father, the one who had given her purpose and delight ever since the first kicks inside her—she was in the hands of these terrible, filthy Tassantassas.

Strangers who had once been her own people.

"This," Wahunsenecawh said, slowly, "this is why they are never to be trusted. And yet trust them, I have."

"You brought us here, to Matchcot, to protect us," Channa said. "That was no small thing."

"And yet they have still found a way to steal her from us. I must think upon this and see what may be done."

Winganuske stumbled back to her own yehakan and went through the motions of preparing food for Channa and the little ones. Inside, her thoughts were a welter of half-forgotten prayers.

God in heaven, do You still see and hear?

It was agreed, before the closing of the day, that Koko'um would take a handful of warriors and follow after the Tassantassas ship.

Wahunsenecawh had no peace about the entire thing. And he suddenly felt very, very old.

He thought about how the last few years had gone, since the departure of Chawnzmit. He still was not convinced the man was truly dead. But they had been told repeatedly that he could not have survived the voyage across yapám with how grave his wounds were.

The awfulness of the seasons after, coupled with the Tassantassas' refusal to deliver the tribute he had asked for in exchange for pegatawah, more than justified letting the lot of them starve—or picking them off as they tried to forage and hunt. But then more came the following year, with new weroances even more ruthless than Chawnzmit. Then they had the temerity to buy off the Chicahamania nation, who, while not properly under the Powhatan, had never been enemies.

All that had changed, thanks to the Tassantassas. And right at Wahunsenecawh's back door, despite his move from Werowocomoco.

Opechancanough admitted to admiration of the newest Tassantassas leader, *Tommasdale*, who had actually dared to come all the way to Youghtanan. This one was as bold as Chawnzmit, but taller and broader, and so cut a better figure. Certainly, he was as cunning. Wahunsenecawh had sent him a string of his best pearls, along with the message that the next time a stranger from Paspahae came on official business, they were to wear the pearls as proof that they were sent by Dale, and not merely running away from the Tassantassas.

That had been two years ago, and of men fleeing the hardships of the strangers' situation, especially lack of food, there had been a few, although not as many in the early days. But no one had come wearing the pearls.

And now this. The treachery of Yapazus—that one had ever been slippery. Wahunsenecawh had not felt entirely easy about sending Mato'aka at the head of that trade delegation, but neither could he hinder her carrying out the duties of Beloved Woman for his people. He had warned her to be wary. But this had been unlooked-for.

He sent everyone out of the yehakan, and sitting himself directly by the fire so he could continue feeding it with little effort, he alternately stared into the hearth and crouched, head bent, in prayers he could hardly articulate.

Was there even a god who could hear—who could see—both him and his most-loved daughter, at the same time? Much less one who would care enough to intervene on her behalf?

If only there were. . .

Not long after the ship's departure—Mato'aka could only surmise they were going downriver to the Tassantassas town—the door opened, just wide enough for one of the men to shove an earthenware pot inside. She waited then crept around the edge of the room to investigate.

The pot was empty and smelled bad. She sniffed then pulled her face away. The pot bore the stench of human waste. Was she meant to use it to relieve herself?

While she was debating that question, the door cracked a second time, and a dish of meat and their strange bread was set inside, along with a waterskin. The man pointed at the empty pot and said something unintelligible. When she did not respond, he pointed at his own privates, then at the pot, and repeated the words, laughing, before shutting the door fast once more.

So. At least they did not expect her to release water inside the kanoe, on the floor. This much was good. She would swallow her pride and show them she was not an animal to be kept penned up.

Ignoring the food and drink for the moment, she carried the smelly pot over to a dark corner and made use of it then returned it to beside the door. How much better she felt—although it would be ever so much more so if she could see the open sky and bathe herself as well.

There was no way to tell which direction was the rising sun. She braced herself, feet apart, in the middle of the room, and lifted her arms for morning prayers.

The food seemed to be leftovers from the feast the night before. Not terrible. The drink was a watered version of what they'd been offered during supper. The slight tang did not quite cover the muddiness of the water.

Afterward, chilled, she returned to the pallet where she'd slept. Stacking her mat on top of the one Yapazus's wife had used, she curled up under her mantle and the covers they'd given them.

A while later, the door opened, and the pot was removed. A discussion seemed to be happening outside. She ignored it until the door opened again, wider, and one of the men came inside, with a second at the door. One said something, and the other laughed before crossing the floor to Mato'aka.

She hastened to sit up. There was a look—a gleam in his eyes—that she did not like, as he strode toward her.

She threw off the covers and scrambled away, but he lunged after and caught her by the arm. With a decidedly evil grin, he snarled something she did not understand.

"What are you doing?" she demanded, but he took hold of her with both hands.

As his intent became apparent, she fought back, shrieking. But it made no difference. He was stronger, and overpowered her, then left her huddled against the wall once more, half sobbing and half whimpering.

He went out, laughing and gloating. And throughout the rest of the day, more followed him and did the same.

Another night and a day passed, and the sounds outside the ship changed. Mato'aka lifted her aching head. Were they landing?

The ship jostled and stopped. Two men entered the space where she was kept and, despite her cringing away, hauled her up between them and hustled her out.

How unclean she was! And how every part of her hurt—but especially her overfull breasts and the secret place between her legs. Yet they forced her along, half dragging her, until at last they reached the shore itself. She looked around. The Tassantassa town and fort had changed, but it was indeed the same place.

Oh, how she missed her baby and husband. Nek and Nohsh, and her town and family.

One of the men, presumably a leader, argued with the ship's captain. Mato'aka tried to stand straighter, to lift her chin and gather her dignity about her.

The river's edge lapped just a few steps away. "Please, may I wash?" she asked.

They stopped, looked at her. She pointed to her legs, lifted the edge of her skirt to show the bloodstains streaking her thighs, then pointed to the river. "May I wash?"

The leader's eyes widened, and his already-pale face went more white. He turned upon the captain with fury. The captain threw his hands in the air as if he knew nothing.

More arguing, while her legs trembled so they would hardly hold her. The one man still holding her let go for a moment, and she slithered to the ground.

The leader approached, and her first impulse was to cower and try to get away. He stopped in the act of reaching for her, then pointed to the river and beckoned.

That drew such an outcry, she glanced about. They likely thought she would try to escape. The idea was not far from her mind, truly. But at the moment, she wanted nothing more than to bathe.

The leader beckoned again. She scuttled toward the water and, without removing her mahkusun, eased into the chill, murky edge. Several men crowded close—some of them ship's crew who had violated her.

She flashed them all a look then deliberately lowered herself below the surface and scrubbed hurriedly. Some smirked, still watching, and others half turned away, shamefaced.

She gave the opposite, distant shore one longing glance. Could she make it? The one thing she had always been told about being taken captive was *submit*. Stay alive, whatever that cost.

Captivity was known among her people—but not rape. Yet what recourse did she have, here? Clearly these men knew nothing of decency.

After splashing her belly and breasts to wash off the milk that had leaked, she half waded, half crawled, back to the riverbank. They took hold of her again and led her into the fort, then to one of the small houses, where she was pushed inside and the door closed behind her.

At least there was a fire burning on the hearth. But such a strange hearth—built into one wall instead of in the center of the floor where it could warm the whole house. What a waste of heat!

She would not complain, however. Kneeling in front of the fire, she reached for a small piece of wood and added it then held her hands near the flames.

Such simple comfort. She could almost fall asleep here. . .

The door opened, and—was that a woman? She wore even more garments than the men, with a white thing covering her hair and a long skirt that completely hid her legs. And her breasts and arms were so bound up, how could she move and work, much less feed a baby?

The woman stepped inside, carrying a bundle and a pail. A man followed her, bearing what appeared to be dishes of food and drink. These he set on the raised platform nearby—it was much like that at which they had feasted on the ship—and turned to her.

"Pocahuntas, do you recall me?"

The words from his mouth—her own tongue—were so clear she could not hide her astonishment. "*Tommasavach*—is that indeed you?"

The boy that had been given her father in exchange for Namontac, and who had lived with them for three years, was nearly unrecognizable. The golden-haired youth now sported a short beard, equally bright. He smiled, his blue eyes twinkling. "It is indeed." He hesitated. "Are you well?"

If he had witnessed the happenings at the river's edge, he knew she was not well. "I am not. They have not only taken me prisoner, but they have done me hurt that is not lawful. Me, the daughter of Wahunsenecawh. How do you answer this?"

His smile went rueful, and he looked away, even as his pale skin colored to red. "I am sorry for the behavior of my kinsmen. They ought not to have done this." He peered upward. "This woman, however, has come to bring you food and to help you wear proper apparel."

Mato'aka rose and composed herself before him. "I have proper apparel already, as you see." She frowned at him. "You lived among the True People, and you know this."

He murmured something to the woman and then turned back. "You will be staying with us for a while and must be decently clad, at least while you are here in Jamestowne."

She considered him and the woman behind him for a long moment. At last she gave a slow shake of her head.

Tommasavach's manner became flustered and desperate. "You must. Trust me—it is the best way to keep the men from—from thinking they can take advantage of you again."

She folded her arms over her chest, mimicking the stance Nohsh always took.

He licked his lips and glanced at the other woman. "Please, Pocahuntas. I am trying to protect you."

Such a pleading in his gaze. And she knew that he knew her true name, Mato'aka—was he using the old milk name as a sign that he was on her side and truly did want to protect her?

Do whatever is necessary to survive. . . .

She pulled in a deep breath. "Very well."

He bobbed a nod then addressed the other woman. Something, something—*wingapo.*

The woman also gave a nod and stepped forward. "Wingapo, Po-ca-hun-tas." But there was little actual welcome in her face.

Henrico

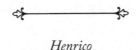

John Rolfe stepped out of the boat—little more than a skiff, it was—and made his way through the press to the merchant's stall set up on the crest of the riverbank. So many people at Henrico today. If he had known it would be this crowded, he'd have stayed at home.

But business must be done, and those who had tasked him with cultivating a particular piece of ground waited for word at regular times.

It helped that there was sharply less threat here, near the Indian town of Powhatan just below the falls of the river, than there had been. Henrico was not yet fully an English town, despite the presence of a church and a tavern, which served a kind of wine grown from grapes that had been transplanted just last year from the wild and grown beautifully enough to be pressed and bottled.

The church, unfortunately, had not been raised soon enough to serve as a burial place, and it was back in Jamestowne he had laid Sarah beneath the ground, late that first summer after they'd arrived.

Three years. It scarce seemed so long, and yet felt an entire lifetime.

As he walked, John tipped his face to the spring sunlight, savoring the warmth and letting it banish the chill of sorrow.

He passed the church and nodded to Reverend Whitaker, who barely looked up from talking with another man. Just a little farther to the tavern, where he took a seat and accepted a mug of watered wine, watching the passersby from under the brim of his hat.

Rafe Hamor came, making long strides, then slid into the chair across from John. Appointed secretary of the colony after the return of the former secretary, William Strachey, to England, the man had become something of a friend.

"You are late," John said.

"So I am," Hamor said cheerfully, also glancing down the street. "Absorbing news from Jamestowne today. I lingered to hear all of it."

John shook his head. "You are worse than a woman, with your love of gossip."

The man flashed a grin. "Say I am worse than a woman of the Naturals, and that would be something."

John rolled his eyes.

The sound of trotting carried across the din of people talking and shouting. Down the middle of the street—or what would be, someday—came a man riding a very neat bay mare.

'Twas a wonder to see horses again after so long.

"Speaking of the Naturals," his friend said.

John's attention came back to Hamor.

"You'll never guess what Captain Argall has done." He squinted at something off in the distance before focusing sharply on John. "He's taken captive the favorite daughter of Powhatan."

"He—what?"

"Aye. Pocahuntas herself." The corner of his mouth lifted, but without humor. "He claims the opportunity simply fell into his hands, that he only intends to keep her long enough to get back what her father and his people have stolen over the past several years."

"What they—" John's teeth clenched on the words.

The first year after they'd arrived from Bermuda had been brutal. More near-starvation, more harassment from the Naturals.

And then he'd lost Sarah as well as the baby.

"The thing is, he bragged about getting that old Yapazus to help dupe her into coming on board his ship, while promising he'd use her kindly. But Powhatan is dragging his feet on paying the ransom. And she is much discontented. Some say she is very sick." He squinted again. "They're talking of bringing her here and letting Reverend Whitaker at her. Teach her how to speak English and instruct her as a Christian."

John winced. The reverend he liked well enough, but expecting him to take charge of a young savage woman—?

"With proper chaperonage, of course."

"Of course," John murmured.

"How comes the tobacco crop this year?"

He nodded, gladly shifting his thoughts. "Well enough. The seedbeds are planted and seem to be growing well. I am waiting for the right time to move the plants to the field."

"And you've workers?"

"I've a few willing. 'Tis enough for this year, at least." He half smiled. "Many think it foolhardy but. . ."

"But last year's crop was promising. And the taste of the leaf, extraordinarily sweet." The other man leaned in. "Where did you obtain the seeds for that Spanish strain?"

John grinned. "That, my friend, is my secret."

He finished his watered wine, and they shook hands and parted. As he walked on, his thoughts strayed back to the dilemma of the Powhatan princess, now held captive, and most unhappily, if Hamor's word was accurate.

Gracious God, be merciful to her. Help her. . .give her a better situation, if possible.

The prayer came reflexively, without thinking. Surprising even himself, though it seemed such did come a bit easier in the past months.

And let this not lead to all-out war between our people and hers.

Chapter Ten

She was not trying to be difficult. She truly was not.

Tommasavach said he was doing his best to help and protect her. It did not seem so, however. And she could hardly bear the feel of their strange, tight clothing against her skin. How was she to know when she took it all off and put on her own skirt again, it would so enrage the woman who kept her that she would come at Mato'aka with a rope, like a whip?

She also was not to be blamed for taking the whip away from the woman and turning it upon her.

The woman fled, howling, and Mato'aka stood, triumphant, until the commotion brought more men, who overpowered her and took the rope away.

One of them knew enough Powhatan to tell her—in the crudest of words, but his meaning was clear—if she would not cover herself, she would learn what that would mean. And again—while the one man held her, the other forced himself upon her, and then the two traded places.

She crawled away to the corner and vomited every bit of the food they'd given her that morning. It was no better coming up than it had been going down.

The woman attending her came back in, made a face at the pile of sick Mato'aka had left, then went out and brought some sort of tools to scrape it all up in. Mato'aka did not move from where she huddled before the fire.

When she returned the third time, she pointed at the pile of clothing

Mato'aka had left over to the side. *"Dress."*

She knew the word well enough now. Lacking the energy to spare for even an insolent look, she tried to get up but found her legs trembling. She pointed at herself. "Wash?"

The woman considered her for a moment, then frowned and shook her head before leaving yet again. This time she brought back a basin and cloth, set it in the middle of the floor, and retreated to the door, where she folded her arms and stood waiting.

Was she sorry Mato'aka had been brutalized again? Or did she think she deserved it?

With what she had seen of these people so far, she could believe the latter.

She stepped to the basin and hesitated. In her own tongue, she said again, "Wash? In the river?" She mimed the flowing of the stream just outside the fort.

The woman pressed her lips together and shook her head, pointing to the basin. With a great sigh, Mato'aka made use of it then reached for the long white garment she knew by now went first.

Afterward, the guards brought her out and made her stand before several men who, judging by their comportment, were the Tassantassas weroances. One, especially, tall man with dark hair whom she learned was called *Tommasdale*, set her most on edge. He looked her up and down as if she'd had no apparel on at all. Suddenly she was glad of the strange clothing to cover her completely. The sharpness of his gaze, bright against his pale cheeks, sent shivers across her skin.

With Tommasavach's help, they questioned her about all sorts of things. How much pegatawah did Nohsh have. How many of their guns and swords, and other such tools. Mato'aka could not answer the latter and would not answer the former—how dare they, and what business was it of theirs? Tommasdale and the other weroances soon grew impatient with her lack of response and sent her back to the house.

"How long do they plan to keep me here?" she demanded of Tommasavach later.

She'd requested him—he had the best command of her tongue, although others did well enough, and he was the only one she trusted at this point.

He looked away, his face turning even redder than it had. Clearly, he knew what had happened to her—again—and it made him uncomfortable even if he could do nothing about it.

"They are waiting for your father to pay to exchange you."

Knowing Nohsh, he might well slay any messengers on sight—or refuse to see them. Although he was never so unreasonable as to do the first, in her memory. "How long does it take a messenger to go and return?"

He spread his hands. "I do not know." His gaze came back to her. "Also, you should know, there is talk of moving you upriver. It would be—better for you. More protected."

She made a scoffing sound. "I do not believe you."

"No, this would—this truly, in my judgment, would be better. You would also be taught our tongue and about our God. That is, if you are willing."

The need to vomit swirled inside her again. "Did anyone ask if I was willing before they forced their manhood upon me?" The words came out harsh and strangled.

Tommasavach went white, then more red than before. "This would be different. And the one they would give to teach you, he is a man of—of honor. He would not do this thing to you."

The backs of her eyelids burned. "I do not believe you," she said again.

He huffed, lifting his cap to swipe a hand across his hair. "Well, they may send you anyway."

She huffed back. "I am not pleased with you. Of all people—you lived with us for three years—"

He took a step toward her. "It is because I lived with your people for three years that I am trying now to help you! But I can only do so much."

Mato'aka stopped, considered his earnest blue eyes and clenched teeth.

Perhaps it was true, and he had no influence on the other men. In fact, she knew that must be true. She herself had only just so much influence on her father, even as the favored daughter of Wahunsenecawh.

But it did not mean she had to be happy about her situation. Or with Tommasavach either.

Not only was Mato'aka taken, but Koko'um had been slain.

The entire town was in mourning. Even Wahunsenecawh refused to eat, nearly refused to speak.

Winganuske kept cooking and doing things because, well, she had Little Flower to think about, and both Channa's child and the child of Mato'aka—but were it not for that, she would either run howling into the forest or curl up on her bed and never move again.

Instead, she found herself doing that for which she had lost the habit a long time ago. She prayed. At first it was simple, inarticulate grief, the silent cries of her heart. But then something broke loose inside her, and the words followed. Not always coherent ones—and almost never aloud—but a constant, sincere plea for Mato'aka's life and well-being.

Channa was clamoring to go to Mato'aka. Both Winganuske and Wahunsenecawh said she must wait. They had so far received only the demand for return of stolen arms, plus more pegatawah—"always pegatawah," Wahunsenecawh said, and she did not blame his bitterness there. Their town always had enough, because of the tributes brought him as mamanatowic, but in other places? Depleting the winter's store of pegatawah meant women and children must go dig in the freezing mud for tuckahoe roots. They made a decent bread, but it was miserable work during the cold season. The very young and infirm could not go.

Besides, the English had been in Tsenacomoco long enough, the People could see that their requests for provision were never ending. Giving aid during the early days was one thing, but they had grown lazy and come to expect it. So it was not simply a matter of paying a ransom for Mato'aka. The Tassantassas were insatiable, and once they'd received what they demanded this time, they would sooner or later demand more.

If circumstances were different, she would have enjoyed sailing upriver on the Tassantassas ship, seeing parts of her father's dominion she had never seen before.

Tommasavach whispered to her that she would actually be closer to Nohsh, by river, where they were going. She was not sure she believed that—or anything he had to say at this point. The relief of having him speak to her at all, in her own tongue, and to be understood was so great, however, even if much of what he said was lies, that she could not bring herself to send him away completely.

All along the riverbanks, the trees were greening, and flowers peeped here and there. Mato'aka felt sick with the longing to run on land. To simply—run. She need not even go anywhere. But they kept such a tight watch on her, even if she had wanted to just stroll about, she was not allowed.

They landed near a small, palisaded town. It was as ugly as Jamestowne, but maybe a little cleaner.

Mato'aka walked, holding her skirts—why did Tassantassas use so much cloth, anyway?—and flanked by Tommasavach and several of the men from Jamestowne. None were those who had forced themselves upon her.

They led her toward a building that reminded her of the one in Jamestowne where the residents went to worship their god. Tommasavach had called it a *church.* He confirmed, as they approached, that this was also a church, and they would be speaking to a man of their God.

So—a quiakros? She was prevented from asking him this, however, by a thin man all in black stepping out of a small house next to the church. Looking eager and yet uncomfortable, he eyed Mato'aka but addressed the others with her.

When introduced, his name was such a mouthful that she merely leaned toward Tommasavach and said, "What am I to call him?"

The young man smiled a little. "Whitaker. He will tell you if he wishes anything but that."

The entire thing set her teeth on edge, but she held herself proudly while all the talking went on around her with increasingly urgent tones.

She could tell that the man, Whitaker, was no happier about the arrangement than she, despite the smile he pasted on and the looks he kept giving her.

'Twas becoming an annoyance, how many times this week he'd needed to take the skiff to Henrico.

John strode through the streets on the way back to the river. The errand had already taken far longer than he'd hoped, and the sun was warmer than he found comfortable. But the sound of strained voices—of the particular pitch that betrayed the effort to not actually raise their voices and draw undue attention—pulled his gaze aside even as he intended to pass the scene.

Reverend Whitaker, surrounded by a cluster of soldiers on what appeared official business, gauging by their stance. And in the midst, the flash of a skirt, and—was that a woman of the Naturals, wearing a gown of English make?

John stopped cold. Then his feet took him toward the gathering before he could even think.

"Reverend! Is there a difficulty here?"

Alexander Whitaker straightened, his gaze seeking him with enough relief to make John's heart sink. "Oh—perhaps. I do have a quandary."

John glanced across the group. Thomas Savage, whom he knew from the first year after they had wintered in Bermuda, famous for his own sojourn amongst the Naturals. A handful of soldiers whose names escaped him the moment he allowed himself to focus on the woman.

Barely above a child, she looked. Yet she held her pert, clefted chin aloft and her shoulders square. Her black eyes snapped, as if she were queen here and her retinue lacking. Glossy dark hair was caught up in a knot, but she wore no cap. Her dark brows were arched, her face round yet angular, her mouth full.

Altogether exotic and not a little fetching.

He started, forcing his attention to Reverend Whitaker once more. "—told them I would gladly help educate her, but they failed to bring a woman to attend her, and my own housekeeper was married this past week. I have no one to help tend a savage in danger of fleeing the moment our backs are turned."

He hazarded another glance at the savage in question. She appeared far too bundled up in that bodice and gown to be able to flee anywhere, but he wouldn't put it past her to try.

Not that he blamed her. "Is this our princess of Powhatan?"

Thomas Savage cleared his throat. "Yes. This is Pocahuntas, lately I believe of Matchcot amongst the Pamaunkee."

She perked at the familiar names, flicked her gaze between Thomas and himself.

He laid a hand upon his chest and gave a little bow. "Wingapo, Pocahuntas. I am—John Rolfe."

Her gaze steadied. "Chawnrolfe," she said, her voice unsteady. She too cleared her throat. "Chawnrolfe."

He offered a smile then turned back to Reverend Whitaker. "'Tis but a temporary solution, I am sure, but we have a modest company out at Bermuda Hundred. I am sure one of the women could be induced to assist with our guest. And you are more than welcome to accompany us to begin your task."

"Well." Whitaker rubbed his sparsely bearded chin. "I think it could serve, since these kind men"—his tone dripped sarcasm— "refuse to take her with them again."

John included them in the invitation. "Come with us and sup before your return. 'Tis but five miles hence."

While they looked at each other, Reverend Whitaker announced, "Let me pack, and I shall return in a trice."

He scurried away.

"Come," John said. "Let us go refresh ourselves at the tavern whilst he makes ready."

Mato'aka sidled toward Tommasavach. "What is happening?"

He shook his head. "Whitaker is not prepared to—to host you with proper hospitality. John Rolfe is offering to do so."

"And this is. . .good?" As they crossed to one of the other houses, she glanced at Chawnrolfe, walking on the other side of her guards and in conversation with them. Her stomach grew sour at the thought of the price he might exact from her for such hosting.

Tommasavach sucked his cheek. Inside the house were many tables and chairs. He drew out a chair and indicated Mato'aka should sit down.

She was still not quite used to their furnitures.

The guards arrayed themselves around her, some sitting and some standing. Someone handed her a cup. She sniffed, then sipped, trying to glance about without noticing all the stares from the other occupants of the room. She was used to people looking at her, as the daughter of mamanatowic. But this—this was a different thing entirely.

Chawnrolfe was the only one who did not gape at her, but after waiting for her to be seated, began talking again with the leader of her guards and ignored her.

"What kind of men are these?" she asked Tommasavach.

He tucked his chin. Well he might look shamefaced on her behalf. "I believe they are good men," he said after a bit.

The guards eyed them. One asked something in an impudent manner, gesturing to her. Tommasavach answered in kind.

She gave him a questioning look. Did she even want to know?

He reddened. "I am sorry that you are having to endure all this, daughter of Wahunsenecawh."

Another sip of her watered drink. "Why did you leave us?"

"They commanded it. That is all I can say."

She suppressed a sound of frustration. There were so many things she had heard but not understood while she was yet a child. Then she was so caught up in the joy of those early days as Koko'um's wife, and the birth of their son consumed yet more of her attention. And now—now she was only beginning to grasp the slightest shadows of the complexity of dealings between her people and the Tassantassas.

The man Whitaker met them just as she was finishing her drink. Her guard hustled her up and back toward the river.

Once there, the ship's crew busied themselves with lifting a smaller boat to the deck. Even after it nestled against the outside of the larger vessel and her guards were beckoning her aboard, she could not bring herself to move.

"All will be well," Tommasavach said. "It is only a little way to John Rolfe's home."

That gave her no comfort. But she was not a daughter of mamanatowic—nor a Beloved Woman—for nothing. She forced her feet, one after another, back up the plank and into the ship.

On the deck, she positioned herself near the front so she could watch where they were going. Whitaker and Chawnrolfe stood nearby, torn, it seemed, between doing the same and observing her.

She wanted to study the two of them as well, but wished not to show interest. Were they not Tassantassas? Their true nature would reveal itself in time, just as the rest of their countrymen.

John had made a point of not watching her while at the tavern, but here, standing opposite her at the bow, just a few paces away, he could not help but cast surreptitious glances her way.

"I wonder what measures they took," murmured Whitaker, at his side, "to compel such a wild creature to wear proper English apparel."

John gave him a narrow look. "Waxing poetic, Reverend?"

Whitaker laughed shortly. "Do you not also wonder?"

The question made him glance toward her again, then at Thomas Savage, who served as her shadow in the moment. "We can ask the lad, once we're ashore. Doubtless he can tell us the most, having lived with her folk before our arrival." He turned to look at the crew and her attendant soldiers, who watched her much as he imagined a wolf would a sheep, then leaned slightly closer to Whitaker. "I wish not to talk of this here."

The other man nodded.

They arrived shortly at the edge of the plantation he helped look after for Sir Thomas Dale—Bermuda Hundred, it had been called. Only recently did the name not waken the ache in his heart.

His own house was humble and not spacious enough to seat all his guests, but he was well used to gathering his workers in a building he'd more or less modeled after one of the Powhatan longhouses. A kitchen lay just outside one end, and rough tables and benches furnished the inside. Today, with the weather so fair, the shutters stood fastened open for the sunlight and breeze to flow through. He ushered his guests inside and gave the word for more drink to be offered and food prepared.

His cook, a burly man more used to the roll of a ship than dry land, assessed the group with a look then nodded shortly and stamped away.

That done, John went in search of the woman tasked as his housekeeper. When he explained the situation, her eyebrows rose nearly to the edge of her cap, and her usually florid face became nearly as white as the same. "Will the savages be attacking here to get her back?"

He could not say the thought had not occurred to him. "I think not. Some of her guard have agreed to stay and keep watch against that very thing." He offered what he hoped was a reassuring smile. "The most important thing is that we show her kindness. Are you willing?"

Returning to his guests, he found a small repast of bread and cheese laid for them all. He tucked himself onto the bench next to Reverend Whitaker and reached for a piece of each. "Lodgings may be tight at first, but you are welcome and no mistake."

The cook worked wonders with a beef stew and pies, then the crew of the pinnace went on their way while the guard settled in with John's workers. He led the other three, Whitaker, Thomas, and Pocahuntas, to his house, where Mistress Leaver was preparing a room for the Indian princess. After a brief introduction and explanation, Thomas translating, the younger woman hesitated, glancing first at John then Reverend Whitaker.

John offered a bow. "Wingapo, Pocahuntas. I bid you good night."

Her gaze lingered on him, then she nodded and followed the older woman from the room.

He poured each of them a cup of small beer then drew out his pipe and set to filling it. "Thomas, what can you tell us about her situation?"

The younger man tasted the brew then cupped the earthen vessel in his hands. "Well, for starters, she isn't just the daughter of their chiefest king. She is one of the—" He dragged a hand through his hair. "Oh, I know not how to say it in our tongue. Midéwiqua in hers. Those who speak with the spirits."

A chill swept John's skin, and the hairs on his arms and neck stood upright.

Reverend Whitaker's eyes rounded. "Gracious! And God have mercy."

"She is, I suppose you could say, a holy woman. Not just her father's darling. And so, bearing that in mind—" Thomas took another deep breath, his cheeks crimson even in the dying light of the setting sun—"you must also know that she's been ravished."

"What? No!" exclaimed Reverend Whitaker. "By whom?"

"Englishmen. Not even one, but several."

John kept silent. He was not surprised. Grieved, yes, but not surprised.

"'Tis what comes of the Naturals being wanton, and our men using them so carnally—"

Thomas waved a hand. "'Tis not like that for them. In fact—oh, I cannot explain it. Only understand that while they see captivity as a matter of course between enemy peoples, they have no tolerance for a man forcing his attentions on a woman. This is a very great disgrace on our part."

"Is there anything we can do?" Whitaker asked.

"Well," Thomas answered slowly, "we can make sure we do not behave as they do. And, watch to make sure it does not happen again."

"Are any of the guilty among the present guard?" John asked.

Thomas gave a single shake of the head. "I think not. But I am not sure."

John sat back. "We will indeed watch. I'll not countenance such misbehavior, at least not here."

"I had hoped you could be counted upon," Thomas said.

For the next hour, he regaled them with tales of his days among the Powhatan and what he knew of Pocahuntas' upbringing and family. Much later, once they'd all bedded down—Whitaker in the second bedchamber and himself and Thomas on the floor—John lay awake, mulling it all.

What a peculiar treasure they had been entrusted with. He could only pray they would prove worthy of it.

Chapter Eleven

She lay awake, listening to the rise and fall of their voices in the other room.

The woman helping her had been surprisingly gentle. The bed provided was comfortable, the room clean but not stripped of all appointments as the house in Jamestowne had been.

The two men appeared about an age with each other, but easily distinguished by Whitaker having hair of a wutapantam brown, with a much thinner beard, and Chawnrolfe's being darker and more curly and thick on both head and face. Both looked at her as if they knew not what to do with her—but neither did she see contempt or condescension in their faces.

Still, it was too soon for such a thing to be promising. If the only reason she had for staying was to protect her own people, then that was still sufficient.

Even so, her arms felt cold and empty without Little Fox to cuddle. How fared her child this night? Did he cry for her? Were Nek and Channa able to soothe him so he might not suffer overmuch from her absence?

And Koko'um. . . She squeezed her eyes shut against her own tears, but still they leaked out, wetting the bedding beneath her head.

When morning came, the woman returned to help her dress. She could hardly bear how soiled and sticky the garments were, but when she asked, "Wash?" the woman only shook her head and motioned for her to get on with the task.

Mato'aka suppressed a sigh and, after combing her hair, tied it up.

The woman handed her a white cap such as she had seen the others wear. Another sigh, this one escaping. She would have to see it as a variation of the ornamentation her own people wore.

John watched as Whitaker set out his things on the table he'd requested—paper, ink, quills, and of course the substantial volume that was his Bible. "You are starting already this morning?"

The other man shot him a quick smile. "Is there any reason to delay?"

"No, I suppose not." The thought of the young woman, up and readying herself in the other room with Mistress Leaver's help, still sent a curl of discomfort through his middle. How strange to think Pocahuntas—*the* Pocahuntas—had slept under his own roof.

"I had an idea, sparked by young Thomas last night. I will begin by telling her a story. After all, the Holy Scriptures are full of them. Even Christ did not despise the use of humble parables."

"Leave us room for breakfast, at least."

Whitaker laughed, even as Thomas entered the house, his arms laden. John helped the young man set the covered baskets on the table. The aroma nearly overcame him.

Such hardship they'd endured, and what bounty, in just a few short years here.

Mistress Leaver appeared with Pocahuntas in tow. Dark circles rimmed the young woman's eyes, but she gazed about, alert, wary perhaps, but also curious. Or so it appeared to John.

Whitaker held up his hands and gave thanks over the food. John peeked at the young woman, who watched the reverend with rapt attention. Did she understand that it was a prayer?

After the *amen,* John indicated the table and beckoned her forward. He had read Captain Smith's account and heard others talk of the hospitality shown by this girl's father and other Naturals. Would she be put off by the English way of things, or would she understand and accommodate the differences?

Thomas was already handing her a plate and explaining in her tongue the various foods—eggs and sausages, small breads, wedges of the leftover pie from last night. Looking resolute, she murmured something and took some of each.

John filled his own plate and tried not to stare. 'Twas not like he'd never seen any of the women of the savages before.

Although, this one was decidedly un-savage, despite eating every food offered with her fingers, as she had the day before. She made neat work of it, he had to admit.

"I thought we would begin the day," Whitaker said, setting aside his half-finished plate, "by the telling of a story." He motioned for Thomas to translate. "Your people tell stories of your gods, and so I will tell you the beginning of the story about ours."

He opened the Bible to the first page of Genesis. "Our holy book begins this way. 'In the beginning God created the heavens and the earth.'"

Thomas translated, but as soon as Whitaker said the word *heavens*, Pocahuntas stilled, staring at Whitaker.

He kept reading. "'And the earth was without form and void, and darkness was upon the deep, and the Spirit of God moved upon the waters.'"

And so he went through the passage, pausing after each verse to let Thomas translate. When he got to the verse that spoke of God calling the firmament heaven, Pocahuntas interrupted. Thomas translated in turn. "So air above us—the sky—is called heaven? If one dies, his soul goes up into the sky?"

"Well." Whitaker rubbed his chin. "That is an interesting question. There are different, ah, places called *heaven*. What she is asking—you are asking"—he nodded at Pocahuntas—"is known as the third heaven, somewhere far beyond our sky, which is only the first heaven."

Thomas struggled through the explanation, and Pocahuntas rattled off something in response. "Pray continue," Thomas said, after a bit of back-and-forth.

He read the rest of the chapter while the young woman listened attentively, eventually eating a little more before setting her plate aside.

Whitaker drew out a paper where he'd begun a sketch. "So here we have the six days of creation. On the first, God made light and separated it from the darkness. On the second, He separated the waters below from the waters above, that is, the seas from the clouds. On the third He made the dry land and every herb that grows thereon."

His paper had been scored into six different sections, each corresponding to a day of creation. In one, rays indicated brightness while shading indicated dark. In the next, a set of double ripples lay below poofy shapes. And after that, an island surrounded on both sides by ripples, and a pair of trees with bushes beneath.

With a smile, he took up his pen and quill and with quick strokes, in the next space, sketched a rudimentary sun, a crescent moon, and several small stars. "Then the great light to rule the day, and the lesser to be over the night."

John leaned forward. Whitaker was a skilled artist! How would he illustrate the others?

"The fish and the birds were on the fifth day."

His quill worked busily, and a school of fish below a small flock of birds appeared.

"And lastly, on the sixth day. . ."

Three animals of indeterminate kind took shape, then the outline of a man, and that of a woman. No detail of course, except that the woman's hair flowed down to cover most of her backside.

He turned the paper and slid it across the table for her perusal. She looked at it closely for a long while then pushed it back with a question and lift of her hand.

"And then what?" Thomas translated.

"I am glad you asked." Whitaker set the quill and corked ink aside then pulled the Bible back to himself. " 'Thus the heavens and the earth were finished, and all the host of them. For in the seventh day God ended his work which he had made, and the seventh day he rested from all his work, which he had made. . .' "

She listened most attentively. How did she perceive it, hearing for the first time? Her eyebrows went up at the description of the creation of man and woman, but she asked nothing until Whitaker had finished the second chapter.

"That is all very interesting," Thomas said, translating. "May I share what my people tell about how the world was made?"

"Shall we go for a walk outdoors?" John asked. "I must needs go look at my crops, but I wish not to miss any of the conversation."

Whitaker readily agreed, and when Thomas communicated it to Pocahuntas, her eyes lit up.

Would she truly be allowed to walk about outside?

Sure enough, when their intent was presented to the guards who had slept about the house last night, a quarrel ensued between them and the three immediately accompanying her. Then Chawnrolfe turned to her and asked, and Tommasavach translated, "Will you give your word not to run? As long as you are treated with honor here?"

She studied them all before replying. If given in good faith, it was most generous. But did they intend to keep their word? Were they even capable of keeping their word? She thought of the long tales told by Chawnzmit and how her elders often laughed later, out of his hearing, and scoffed over what he had said. Of the promises he had made, later broken. And yet her heart had gone out to him—and then he was no longer here and it seemed nothing he had said mattered anyway.

The elders had spoken of a cunning in his face, especially the last few times he had visited Nohsh, that had not been there during his initial captivity. Mato'aka could not remember that, but she knew of what they spoke—she had seen the same in most of the Tassantassas who had taken her.

Except for Tommasavach, who stood even now with a pleading expression on his face. Whitaker appeared intent, his sky-colored gaze steady and almost kindly. But most compelling was Chawnrolfe himself, seeming almost pained. Was that at her situation, or his own, having to host her? Although he had not been compelled to the latter, but had happened by and offered.

It did not help that he was less ill-favored than the others, as Tassantassas went. She had trouble distinguishing the soldiers, they appeared so alike, except for differences of hair color. Chawnzmit, of course, had been immediately distinguished by his red hair, which she had seen in others a few times over the years. Chawnrolfe, though, was as others with hair of brown, so dark it minded her of walnut juice, and eyes of a near shade. And he did not seem so, well, unkempt, as many of the Tassantassas.

But then, there had been Tommasdale. Of note simply because he was stern and menacing and nearly as tall as Nohsh and her uncles and brothers.

She glanced at the soldiers standing by, some looking angry and others more saddened. Beyond them, to the houses and gardens and various animals, all put here by the Tassantassas. She thought about what Nohsh had said about them coming to push back the True People and take their land.

She no longer hurt from the men who had forced themselves upon her, but they had broken her trust. And could that be rebuilt?

Still—to walk about, to feel the wind and the sunlight—

Holding herself very straight and proud, she turned back to the Tassantassas looking at her so earnestly. "I will stay. As long as I am treated with honor."

As Tommasavach translated, Chawnrolfe smiled—she thought with relief—but the leader of the soldiers only threw up a hand and spat something with a tone of disgust. Even so, she was gestured forward.

The town seemed modest in regard to houses where people might live, but the animals were interesting. Some of them she knew, but Tommasavich reminded her what they were called—*chickens, hogs, cows*. And there was a tall, graceful animal he called a *horse*. She thought she had glimpsed a man riding one in Jamestowne.

There were also dogs—treated with much more familiarity and affection than such animals were among her own people—and cats, smaller and more furry than the panthers that warriors sometimes brought back from hunting.

One such cat had a litter of kittens, and Chawnrolfe picked one up and brought it to Mato'aka to hold. Gingerly she took it, cupping it in her hands at Tommasavach's encouragement. "Be 'ware its claws," he said, laughing, and showed her how to cuddle it, very like a baby.

With a tiny *mew*, the thing settled against her and began a rumbling vibration. "What is this sound it makes?" She did not know whether to be amazed or alarmed.

Tommasavach laughed again. "It is *purring*. They make the sound when happy."

The creature seemed to enjoy it when, at his further direction, she stroked its fur. How strange that they would coddle an animal like a child!

But after a bit of that, the thing squirmed, and so she let it go.

Chawnrolfe beckoned them on.

They came to a garden, sheltered near one of the long buildings that housed more animals, where the ground had been scraped completely clean, except for small plants with wide leaves she recognized. "Ai! Uppowoc!"

She crouched beside the plot and reached to touch one of the leaves.

The holy plant of her people! But how had they come by it? And who instructed this man in the growing of it?

But more importantly—"For what purpose is this being grown?"

She shot the question at Tommasavach then glanced meaningfully at the other Tassantassas. After a moment's hesitation, he passed on the question.

Chawnrolfe crouched beside her, brushing his fingers across the leaves—she did not miss it, even in her agitation—with as much care as she. "Toh-ba-koh," he said.

"Uppowoc," she responded, and he gave a little laugh.

"Tobacco."

She lifted her eyes to his, challenging. He seemed to know well what he had here.

He spoke again then glanced at Tommasavach.

"He brought the seeds with him. It is grown in other parts of the world and traded for needed goods."

"And what is done with it, then?"

"Others trade for it, for—for the enjoyment of drinking the smoke."

She glared at Tommasavach. It was well known among the True People that taking the uppowoc was indeed soothing and enjoyable, but to treat it merely as a trade good? Not respected as the treasure it was?

She stood, taking her skirts in her hands. "I would—I would like to walk more now."

And with that, she set off at a sedate but determined pace. Her retinue surrounded her in a moment.

Whitaker asked a question, quietly, and Tommasavach translated. "Would you like to tell us of your creation story now?"

"No." Her thoughts were too much in turmoil. "I do not wish to talk at this time of anything."

John could not fathom why she had suddenly become upset and withdrawn from them. When she set off walking, he thought perhaps she would like to see the river, so he strode ahead and led the way. She followed, cutting her gaze to him but once, then ignoring him. Within sight of moving water, however, she stopped, breathing deeply in, then out.

Were those tears gathering in her eyes? 'Twould be rude to stare.

At last she turned and walked back toward the house and barns. All of them breathed a quiet sigh of relief.

She remained silent and disconsolate through the rest of the day. For the next two days, in fact, despite their attempt to show her every kindness. On the third day, rain kept them indoors, but John left his guest and her little company to go see to the needs of the plantation. After supper and after Pocahuntas had retired for the night, he and Whitaker and Thomas sat around a small fire and quietly discussed what to do with her.

"It seems to be you who offends her," Whitaker said. "She will not say why. I asked Thomas to inquire, but she only turned her face away and refused to speak for the next hour. But when you went out this morning, she enlivened again, and when she'd listened most attentively to the third chapter of Genesis, she had many searching questions about the Fall of Man." He sipped from his cup, looking thoughtful. "I did not expect her to be so quick-witted. She is stimulating, but almost exhausting."

Thomas laughed at that. "You should have seen her when she was younger. A regular dervish, with all the other children of the town trooping along behind her. She would play pranks and get into scrapes, but all loved her." His smile grew nostalgic. "Her father always used me very kindly as well. It grieves me to think I can offer her so little comfort in return."

John leaned forward, hands clasped and elbows on his knees, and gazed into the fire. "What more might be done for her, do you think?"

Thomas scratched behind one ear. "I am sure she misses her family and people. That she is cut off from them is beyond the pale. She was never alone there. None of them are ever really alone, but live in close community." He hesitated. "Too close, sometimes. Even their most private intimacies are often—not private."

"Well, often 'tis nearly that bad in England. Especially in London, crowded as it is."

"True," Thomas said, and blushed more deeply.

"So you are saying perhaps we should send for some of her people to attend her? Would Dale allow that?"

Thomas shrugged, but Reverend Whitaker smoothed down his beard. "'Tis not an unworthy thought. Would they come? And if they came, would they use it as opportunity to attack, or to steal her back? And even if not, would they protest our use of this time to teach her true religion?"

"Let us compose a message on the morrow to send to Sir Dale. If it would indeed comfort her to have someone of her people here. . ."

He trailed off, thinking through all the possibilities.

"If only she would explain what so upset her the other day," Whitaker said.

"It had something to do with the tobacco," Thomas said, slowly.

"Well, that we gathered, but exactly what?" John said.

Thomas shrugged. "Perhaps—perhaps that they consider it sacred. They grow it, not merely for trade, but as a part of everything they do. They throw it in the air before hunting as an offering to their god. Into the river before fishing, and during great storms. They will not speak during any sort of council or other meeting before taking the smoke for a time."

"I have heard of that," John said. "Thomas Harriot wrote about the Indians to the south doing the same." He frequently enough took a pipe full, himself, but how to explain to a Natural that entire peoples across the ocean saw the weed as something purely for enjoyment?

"Well, considering that good King James would also object to its trade. . ." Whitaker laughed.

"To hear tell," Thomas said, "good King James objects to many things, except those vices he himself enjoys."

Both John and Whitaker chuckled. "Precisely," Whitaker said.

Another night, another day. She did not want to get up.

When the woman who attended her rapped on the door and entered, Mato'aka rolled over and curled on her side. At the woman's soft inquiry, she shook her head and put a hand over her face.

There was quiet for a moment, then a soft rustling and the sound of the door closing. The woman's voice on the other side of the door, in conversation with the men.

This time when the door opened, it was Tommasavach. "Pocahuntas? Sá keyd wingan?"

"No," she answered. "I do not wish to get up. There is no reason."

He hesitated. "Will you not come eat? Would you like us to bring you something?"

She did not reply, and he left as well.

It was the coward's way, she knew. But this place seemed to drain all her will and leave her empty.

Would she ever see her son and husband again?

John's missive brought Sir Thomas Dale himself. For the second time in less than a fortnight, he found himself scrambling to provide hospitality. And 'twas easier when it was only Reverend Whitaker and a woman of the Naturals.

"Where is the chit?" Sir Dale thundered, nearly as soon as his feet touched earth from the ship. "I will see her, and no delay."

"She has refused to leave her room the last three days," John said. "Refuses to eat or drink."

"By all that's holy," Sir Dale said, "she will come out and answer to this, or I shall go in to fetch her." He looked at Thomas Savage, standing nearby with rounded eyes. "You serve as her interpreter, do you not? Go tell her."

Young Thomas went, delivered the message, and returned shortly. "She will come." He glanced at John. "Where is Mistress Leaver?"

"Likely over at the kitchen. Go fetch her, please, and quickly."

While they waited, Sir Dale glared holes into John. "What, pray tell, have you been doing with her, and why is she here? Did I not give you, Reverend Whitaker, the command to take her in hand?"

"I have no woman to help attend her," Whitaker said, stammering a little. "God be thanked, Master Rolfe was passing by at the right time and offered his home and the services of his housekeeper."

Dale sniffed. "Yes, and so said your letter after she arrived. But I thought you'd have returned to Henrico by now."

Whitaker spread his hands. "'Tis more convenient to all, here." He gave a short bow. "We are most grateful for your generosity. I believe Pocahuntas will be reasonably content here if only—"

"She is a heathen woman whose only value to us is to gain back what her people have stolen!"

Despite his great respect and dread for the governor, John's hackles rose a little at Dale's words. "Is it of any profit if she languishes in our care and dies? Are we not obligated to use her kindly, as even Captain Argall promised?"

Dale's reply was forestalled by the return of Thomas, with Mistress Leaver in tow. When the woman disappeared inside, he drew a deep breath and seemed to collect himself. "We are the ones who will say what 'use kindly' will mean. So far no reply has been received from Powhatan."

John had no answer for that, though it sat sour upon his belly. Dale folded his arms across his chest and stood waiting in silence.

Presently the door opened, and Pocahuntas appeared, properly appareled and hair tied back, but face pale and her manner altogether lacking any sort of luster. When her eyes fell upon Sir Dale, they widened, but she came forward a few more steps before stopping.

Dale squinted at her, looking her up and down. John did not like how he did so, but neither could he fault Dale for close examination.

"Girl! What ails you?"

Thomas translated, quickly and quietly. Pocahuntas' gaze darted about, and it seemed to John's eye that she folded in on herself as she took in Dale's company.

Were these some of the ones who had ravished her?

She replied at last, her voice but a faint echo of what it had been days ago.

"How can I be well when I am parted from my husband and child?" Thomas translated.

She had a husband and child? No wonder the poor woman was disconsolate!

"You would be welcome to return if only your father would pay the ransom," Dale said. "But apparently you mean so little to him, that he has made no move to do so."

Did a quiver go through her body when Thomas passed on what he had said? She seemed to think on it, and then—

"If your people would not steal our corn, then perhaps he would take your demands more to heart."

Quick as a flash, Dale stepped forward and struck her across the face. She recoiled, then straightened with what looked like fresh resolve.

She had not even cried out!

Her next words were hardly above a heated whisper. Thomas turned white, and then red, and could hardly speak, after. "Is it your habit to let your men force women?"

"What?" Dale looked about, scowling. "Of what do you speak? My men would not do such a thing."

She swallowed before pointing at first one soldier, then another. Dale whirled toward them, furious.

The first of the men smirked. "She offered. You know these savage women often do."

"Or she should have," another muttered.

John glared, but all the men were laughing.

God in heaven! Have mercy, here.

Dale's mouth pressed to a thin line, but either he did not hear all the comments or he chose not to respond. He lifted his chin, regarding Pocahuntas once more. "If you do not mind yourself and cooperate, we will make war on your people. You are old enough to have seen what our guns can do." She did not reply to that, and he went on. "I will allow them to send for one or two of your female relatives, to tend you. But one misbehavior, and you will rue your insolence. In the meantime, you will eat and drink."

She stood, eyes very bright, then followed mutely as they led her away to the dining hall.

It should not surprise her that his men not only lied about what they had done to her, but they made it seem as if she had freely given herself to them.

The look of disgust on the Tassantassas leader's face! While at the same time his eyes gleamed as if he wanted to do the same to her.

The blow was as nothing. It was worth being struck for throwing those words at him. But for these men to think she was only the—the receptacle for their *pocohaac*—that was gross uncleanness. And to think he accused her of insolence! It was nothing compared to their disrespect of women.

Koko'um did not even dare ask her to lie with him while she was nursing Little Fox. Not because he hadn't wanted to, of course. Or because Mato'aka did not want him to. She suppressed a little smile. If Channa and Granny Snow had not strictly warned her—

The ache within surged until she had to bow her head to hide the tears burning her eyes. They were sitting now at the table, but she was Powhatan, of the True People. She must not show weakness here, among Tassantassas who were most assuredly not friends.

Food and drink were placed before her. She sipped carefully. She must also make herself eat.

She must keep herself alive, even if only so she could return to her family.

Survive. Submit. Do whatever is necessary.

It would be easier were these a familiar enemy. She might be taken as wife—but only to one, and they would not dare violate her as some of these had done.

Nor would she be required to sit and take food in the very presence of those who had committed such violation, as if to pretend it had never happened.

She sat back from the table and folded her hands in her lap.

Dale noticed she was not eating and growled a command. Mistress Leaver stepped forward and, while not exactly arguing with him, murmured something that made him relent, scowling.

Was she expected to attend the Tassantassas leader the rest of the day?

When the meal was finished, another discussion ensued, which Tommasavach did not bother to translate, but then he and Mistress Leaver walked her back to the house. The woman asked a question, and by her gesturing, Mato'aka gathered that she was asking whether she would rather sit in the front room or return to her own. Tommasavach confirmed this.

She looked at the two of them. "Th-thank youuu."

The words to express her gratitude were thick upon her tongue, but she knew them well enough by now.

Tommasavach flashed a grin, and the woman also smiled, putting both hands to her mouth. With a little nod, Mato'aka went to her room and to the bed and curled up without either undressing or getting properly under the covers.

She slept, dreaming of the forest and the great river of Werowocomoco. Of Nek and Little Flower and Channa, and of Nohsh, pausing in his labors to play a little game with her.

When she awoke again, the light was gone outside. A rustle at the door and flicker of candlelight brought her upright.

"Good, you are awake," Tommasavach said, and, after setting the candle on the bedside table, whisked out again.

Mistress Leaver entered with a large cup and bowl upon a tray. As she set them on the bed, Mato'aka sat up more carefully. The food and drink awakened her hunger at last.

She reached for the bowl and dipped a bite, holding it beneath her chin, then nearly startled as Chawnrolfe came into the room with Tommasavach at his heels.

He perched gingerly at the opposite edge of the bed, looking as discomfited as she felt. He spoke, and Tommasavach translated. "Governor Dale has gone back to his ship and will leave at first light. He has given me permission to send for a few of your people, but I must know where to go."

She ate another bite, thinking. "Do your people not know where my father has moved his seat?"

He listened to Tommasavach relay the question and nodded. "What is the best way to accomplish this? I could send Thomas, but I think it best to keep him here, for you. Is there anyone else?"

More thinking. The Chicahamania gave no loyalty to the Powhatan, so even though they lived closer than others, any of the Chicahamania might be slain on sight.

"Perhaps ask the Paspahae, if any remain. Tell them—tell them Pocahuntas asks it of them."

Chawnrolfe nodded again. Without his hat, the candlelight gleamed off his dark hair and set a sparkle in his eyes. He looked away, and she glanced at Tommasavach, standing beside him. The kindness in both their faces stirred something deep inside her.

She had not thought to find friends among the Tassantassas. Certainly not with the men. But she dared not refuse it.

Chapter Twelve

"Channa shall go," Wahunsenecawh said. "We will send Tomakin as well, but he must dress as an ordinary warrior and not as a quiakros."

He named a handful of others, and they left the yehakan to go prepare. Wahunsenecawh looked over and saw Winganuske still standing by. "What, my wife?"

She drew breath and gathered courage to ask. "Husband—"

"No. No, my wife, you shall not go." His chin tucked, his dark eyes boring into hers with an expression she knew all too well.

Feeling herself flushing, she glanced away.

"The little ones need you."

She dared flash him a glance in return. "You know I have no milk for them."

"One of the other women can suckle them for a while. They are old enough to not need much."

It was true enough. It was just—oh, her Mato'aka—

He rose from his seat and came toward her. His hand brushed her cheek. "I know you miss her. I do as well. But I will not risk sending you among them."

She must acquiesce. There was no other way.

His arms came around her then, gathering her to his chest. She sank against him, letting the tears fall.

"Do you pray for her?" he asked softly, his breath fanning her neck.

"Yes. How could I not?"

He made a little sound—annoyance, or amusement? "I meant, to your God."

How to answer such a thing? If she remained silent long enough, perhaps he would let it go. But she could tell by the tension in his embrace that he had not.

She huffed. "I—pray."

His arms tightened a little. "Good. She needs all the prayer we can offer."

Rain fell lightly outside, and snugly they sat indoors, with cups of hot drink and small breads the cook had sent, and the great holy book of the Tassantassas lying open upon the table. But the attention of all three men—and probably the woman too—was upon Mato'aka.

She sat very straight on her chair, holding her cup on her knee with left hand curled around it, and gesturing with her right. "And so Nikomis, or Sky Woman, fell, but the great birds of sky water spread out their wings to catch her, and brought her gently down upon the wide back of Turtle. All the other animals came with bits of earth to pat around her so that when she awoke, she had a soft bed.

"Now it was that she had been pregnant when she fell, and before long, she gave birth to a daughter—Winona, or blossom. Winona grew and in time also became pregnant. She gave birth to twin boys, one who came in the usual way and was named Ahoné, but the second decided that did not suit him and tore his way out through her side. He is called O'ki, and his mother Winona died in the process.

"Nikomis took Winona's body, and her head became the moon, with her body becoming the sun and stars."

With that, she lowered her arm and fell silent.

She would not share with them how she now knew that, when she had been sent into Nohsh's yehakan to intervene on behalf of Chawnzmit, she was, in fact, enacting the Grandmother Dance, that of Nikomis, the feast of renewing and re-becoming, to symbolize Chawnzmit himself being reborn into that which he had not been before—a son of the Powhatan.

Instead of recognizing this position as being in subjection to Nohsh, however, he had taken his own way, ignored the will of the mamanatowic he had sworn was his father, and then gone away to die.

She blinked, snapping herself back to the present and three gaping Tassantassas men before her.

A laugh bubbled up from her. "What is it?"

"Is that all?" Tommasavach asked. "I know that is not all."

"That is all I will tell today."

He made a scoffing sound and relayed what she said to the others.

To her surprise, Whitaker smiled. "Thank you."

She gave a single, deep nod. Perhaps she should not be telling them this story. They were not of the True People, those of Tsenacomoco, so how could they understand? And yet she felt compelled to offer something in response to the reading of their holy book. Perhaps it was the need to compare her understanding of gods to theirs, to show that she was not unlearned in the divine and spiritual.

Perhaps it was to remind herself of where she had come from.

Her host had fallen strangely quiet, his expression stiff, as if he did not know how to respond. He had seemed open enough earlier, when Whitaker had read a story about a great flood that overspread the whole earth and killed all but one family and two each of various beasts. She had asked many questions, which Tommasavach patiently translated, explaining that the kanoe, though much bigger than Tassantassa ships, was similarly enclosed, so that those it carried were safe against the storm outside.

She shuddered at the thought of being trapped within such a ship during a storm.

The stories were interesting enough. From the account of the making of man from the soil—and woman from one of man's ribs—to how they had eaten a fruit their God had made to grow in their garden but forbidden to eat, and thus were banished from the garden, she found it all intriguing. The idea of a God over all, who not only sent the sun and rain and good things to eat, but also must be appeased—it was a little like Ahoné and O'ki in one. She would not say so aloud, however. Not yet, before she had thought upon it and heard more.

Chawnrolfe rose, bowed, and excused himself, then snatched his hat from a hook by the door and went outside. She blinked after him before turning back to the other two.

"It is nearly time for the noon meal," Whitaker said. "I think the rain is easing off. Shall we go for a walk?"

She was always glad of a walk. Since the incident of several days ago—the coming of Dale, and the news that her people would be invited to attend her—she found a fresh purpose in living.

And perhaps—perhaps sooner rather than later—she would be able to return to Koko'um and their son.

She would become very tired of the wait. But did not Sky Woman also wait, early in the story she had told the men, despite being weary of it? She was Beloved Woman and could do this.

They had hardly stood from the table, however, before Chawnrolfe came back through the door. A strange look of a different sort was on his face—or perhaps she misread, it was so hard sometimes with his beard. Then he stepped to the side and held the door for someone else.

Someone whose shape appeared very familiar—

"Channa!" she shrieked, as her sister's face became clear enough to be recognized.

The two of them flew together, clinging, laughing—and crying.

Mato'aka could not help it. She had hoped—knew to expect someone—but this was beyond all. She lifted her head, aware suddenly of the room being crowded by others of the True People. "Tomakin! Nantaquas! You have also come!"

They all grinned, but there was something—a hesitation—in the way they responded to her.

"What is it?" She looked at Channa, who was suddenly very grave. Her gaze swept the company again, and—"Where is Koko'um?"

Channa glanced away, her eyes darting about the room. Strangely, all of the Tassantassas had left.

"Mato'aka. I must tell you." But her sister swallowed, gaze darting about again.

She took her sister's shoulders in her hands. "What is it?"

More softly this time.

Channa drew a long, deep, unsteady breath. "When you were taken, Koko'um went after you. Little Fox is safe, but Koko'um—he was slain by the Tassantassas."

The news hit her with the impact of—oh, like when once, as a child, she had gotten in the way of an older boy, who was running, and been knocked to the ground so hard she could not draw breath.

She could not breathe now. Could not speak.

The air at last went into her lungs, searing like the edge of a knife. "Mahta! Say it is not so!"

Channa drew her into her embrace and held her up as a wail tore itself from her throat.

John stood out in the yard with Whitaker while Thomas remained by the door, listening. Mistress Leaver had already been sent to the kitchen for refreshment.

A cry rose, lifting the hair upon his neck and striking coldness into his belly. His gaze went to Thomas, who slowly came farther out into the yard and sat down, heavily, upon a stump.

"Pocahuntas' sister has brought word that her husband was slain."

Something dark and all too familiar swirled within John as the sound of sobbing flowed from the house. "Pocahuntas' husband?"

Thomas nodded, closing his eyes.

"You knew him?" John asked.

"Aye, he was one of Opechancanough's guard, and so I heard, later served Wahunsenecawh. He was—a brave warrior." Thomas gave a sound like a hiccup. "Not that any Powhatan warrior isn't."

John bent his head. The moment seemed too difficult to bear. . .but then, he knew well the anguish behind her cries.

If she had thought herself overcome by despair before, it was doubly worse now.

Koko'um—so brave and strong, so bold in his courtship and, later, in loving her—gone from this world.

At least their son lived, and was safe with Nek and Nohsh.

The Tassantassa woman returned with food for Channa and her attendants. Mato'aka would not eat, even when pressed by Channa. At last her sister simply crawled up onto the bed with her and held her close.

Late into the night, she still could not sleep. And neither, it seemed, could Channa.

"They promised to treat you well," Channa said. "Have they done so?"

Mato'aka held her breath. There was no reason to lie. "I have been treated well enough here. But before, there were men—many of them—who violated me."

Channa jerked upright to look at her. "Mahta! How can this be?"

Tears kept leaking from her eyes. She could not seem to stop them. "They thought to punish me for—for being a woman of the True People. And for my insolence."

Channa lay back down and held her more tightly.

A little later, she asked, "Your monthly woman's time had returned since Little Fox's birth, yes?"

She'd not thought it possible, but Mato'aka's heart sank a little further. "Yes."

"And—has it come since you were taken?"

It had not. And this thing, which she had not allowed herself to think of, until now, broke open inside her.

John was not sure what he had expected—but the grave, courteous, and yet sharply witted comportment of this small band of Naturals was not it.

He had seen plenty of the Native peoples while in Jamestowne, and then again here at Henrico and Bermuda Hundred. There was something uniquely dignified about those who had come to see Pocahuntas—perhaps because they were, as he understood it, royalty, or those married to royalty. The very tall one, her brother, and then the man wed to her sister—both remained watchful and almost ill at ease. Pocahuntas' brother and sister were very affectionate with her, while the brother-in-law was merely cordial. They all sat to meat at breakfast with quiet intensity, thanking him for the fare. After, her sister requested boiling water to make a medicine for Pocahuntas. John felt not entirely comfortable with it, but he could not argue. They were her people and he had agreed to let them tend her.

He went out to see to the plantation, and the brother-in-law, whose name he learned was Uttamatomakin, trailed after. Thomas came along to help translate. John could see that the man was of some consequence, but as he did not volunteer his status, neither would John pry. He showed polite interest at the buildings, livestock, and various tools and devices, but when they rounded the corner to the seedbed where the tobacco plants were nearly ready to be transplanted, the man abruptly took sharper notice.

He asked a question, his words quick, and Thomas answered without consulting John. Uttamatomakin crouched to touch the leaves—much as Pocahuntas had.

Another question. "Why are they here with no room to grow?"

"They will be moved, very soon," John said.

That answer seemed to satisfy him. He asked then if John would show him his field. John saw no reason to refuse, and led on.

The tall Indian surveyed the plot before crouching again and fingering the soil. "You should have moved them already," he said, through Thomas.

"The first year I did not wait long enough, and the plants did not grow well," John explained. "Last year was better."

Uttamatomakin grunted. "Perhaps it is different here, then." He squinted again at the field, then stood and faced John. "Pocahuntas said you and the holy man have been kind to her."

"I have done what I can."

"Thank you for sending to us. We cannot stay, but we are glad to be able to see her."

John gave another short bow. "Before you go, may I ask you about the growing of tobacco—uppowoc?"

The tall warrior's gaze narrowed. He seemed to consider then sighed and nodded. "Ask me what you will."

"And what are you giving me, Channa?"

The two women were alone in the house. Her sister had set the water to heat in the fire and crumbled herbs into a cup. Herbs that appeared suspiciously familiar.

Channa just lifted her head and looked at her.

The tears came again. She had never needed this tea before. She had gone from huskanasqua to being courted by Koko'um—a very short courtship at that—and then marriage, where it was not only accepted but desired that she conceive a baby.

Of course, some women used it so they would not conceive a second baby soon afterward, but Mato'aka had not.

Channa poured the water then came to kneel beside her. She took Mato'aka's face in her hands and pressed her forehead to Mato'aka's. "You know this must be the way of it. Or do you wish to carry the seed of these evil men?"

"Mahta."

"Then do not worry. All will be well. Your body knows what to do, and your strength will return, after."

It was so similar to what she had been told while laboring to birth Little Fox, she cried harder.

Her sister's arms came around her, comforting and steady, until the weeping subsided. Then she pulled away, and full lips pressed together, she stirred the tea and handed the cup to Mato'aka.

Still shuddering a little from the awfulness of the past night and day, she drank it. All of it.

Channa, Tomakin, Nantaquas, and the others stayed a few more days, long enough for Channa to be sure the tea was effective, and then they packed up and were gone. In their absence, Mato'aka felt even more bereft than before.

At least the woman attending her was kind when her bleeding came, and showed her how she and the other women used cloths. Mato'aka would rather have gone out to the woods and sat over a nest lined with mosses, but staying curled up in her bed was no hardship.

For days, she could only think about her family—but especially of Koko'um, his tall strength, his stern and yet bold pursuit of her. The thrill of his touch the first time—and every time thereafter—as he made her fully his.

A touch she would never again feel. A smile, so rare, she would never again see.

Under her breath, she sang a little song, one of longing and sorrow. And she let herself weep when the tears came.

She and Channa and the men had talked of the ransom the Tassantassas demanded. Nantaquas felt it nearly impossible to get back the number of swords they requested—would anyone who now had one be willing to give it up? Even at the command of mamanatowic? And they were weary of having pegatawah taken from them.

She could not blame Nohsh's reluctance to meet their demands. He had tried to negotiate for more time, Tomakin told her, but was rebuffed when he could not provide everything all at once. They did not even have the stores of pegatawah available at this season.

Come evening of the third day, she felt recovered enough to leave her bed—or was it more restlessness at being confined? She crept out of her room to find the house empty, and tiptoed outside. Not even a single guard in sight. Was that trust on their part, or neglect?

No matter. She had not the strength to go far. With a sigh, she leaned against the side of the house and watched the fireflies beginning their evening summer dance.

Would she ever dance again among her own people?

She thought of all the nights she had gone out to watch the fireflies and offer prayers to the manito. It seemed an entire lifetime ago, now.

Even when she tried to pray, the words died on her lips.

Was she completely alone in this place, without even the manito?

"She's grievin', and that's the long and short of it," Mistress Leaver said, most emphatically, as they sat at meat in the dining hall. "You can't blame her, and it wasn't anything her sister did. I am just happy Sir Dale isn't here to try to force her to be out and about before she's ready."

John made a sound of assent. Across from him, Reverend Whitaker merely rubbed his chin and looked thoughtful.

He remembered too well how Sarah remained but a shadow of herself after little Bermuda died. Did she ever truly recover, or had the grief of losing the child taken Sarah's own health?

Would Pocahuntas also decline, or would she rediscover the will to live? She had been doing reasonably well in the days before her family's arrival.

Please, gracious God. . .

He should write Sir Dale a letter to report what had taken place. But how to relate all of it? If the man would not believe she had been violated, how would he respond to the charge that her husband had been killed?

Would their ploy of taking her in order to force Wahunsenecawh's hand be worth the devastation he had witnessed so far?

At the same time, was it his place to question his betters? Or, those he had been taught to regard as such, at least? Dale's manner had not left him entirely comfortable with the whole thing.

"I should take her a tray," Mistress Leaver said. "Even though she's hardly touched anything in three days."

"I'll carry it for you," John said. He gestured at Whitaker and at Thomas sitting farther down the table. "No need to hurry going back."

He was weary enough from two days of final preparation of the tobacco field, then transplanting each of the starts, that all he wished was to stretch out on the floor of the house and fall asleep. Accompanying Mistress Leaver would also allow him to look in on their guest before doing so.

She assembled food and drink, and they made their way through the gathering twilight. Stars peeped from the inky skies above while fireflies winked below, some in the trees and some rising from the vegetation. It was all he could do to mind his feet and not gape at the beauty of the early summer's eve.

As they approached the house, Mistress Leaver stopped. "Pocahuntas?"

A shadow separated itself from the corner of the building, and the young woman's low, smooth voice lilted through the dark.

"We should have brought Thomas," Mistress Leaver muttered.

John shook his head. "Sá keyd wingan?" he called back.

He was only glad she'd stayed at the house. They'd thought her sleeping, without need of a guard at the moment. Although in retrospect, that could have been most unwise.

"Kuppeh," she responded.

"We brought food," he said, nodding at the tray.

She drifted toward them, clad, it seemed, in only a shift with a blanket around her. Her hair fell loosely around her face, but the length of it was covered by the blanket.

"*Minchin*?" he added.

She looked at the tray then smiled at him and turned for the front door.

Inside, at the table, she fell to with what he thought a restrained, elegant eagerness. Or was he simply grown used to the savage way of eating? They really must teach her to use a knife and fork.

Soon, but not this very evening. It was enough for now to sit across the table and watch her. So great was his relief to see her up and taking nourishment, he surely must have been more anxious than he realized over her indisposition.

She watched him in return, openly, almost childlike except for the lingering shadow in her eyes. Was she studying him, trying to divine his intent in regard to her? He could not blame her if so.

"I am sorry we have taken you from your people," he said, quietly. "And I am sorry for the loss of your husband."

Did she understand any of the words?

Thomas and Reverend Whitaker came in just as she was finishing, and greeted her warmly. She smiled, nodded, and shortly returned to bed.

John let out a long breath. Please God that she had understood his intent and was comforted by it, at least a little.

Her bed was warm and soft and comforting this night. Much as the words Chawnrolfe had murmured to her at the table.

What was it he had said? There seemed an understanding in his gaze, a sense of sharing her distress and hurt. Did he too know what it felt like to be separated from family? To lose a loved one? He appeared to have no wife or kinsmen around him.

What had he suffered?

The next morning, he was gone from the house as soon as their morning meal had finished. Mato'aka listened with politeness to a reading from the holy book and then, before they could get very far in discussing it, asked if Tommasavach would take her to Chawnrolfe and translate for her.

Whitaker said she could go, and so the young man accompanied her out to find him.

They found him conferring with one of the keepers of the animals. She tried to wait until he was finished speaking to the other man, but he looked up in the middle of his conversation and stopped. "Pocahuntas?"

She waved a hand and said to Tommasavach, "Tell him to finish speaking."

He relayed the message, and Chawnrolfe hurried through the rest of what he had to say before trotting over.

"May we go walk to see the uppowoc?" she asked.

The younger man translated, and Chawnrolfe nodded, looking uncertain, and led off.

He took them to the field that had been prepared. The plants appeared to be growing well. She let out a soft sigh—how comforting was their familiarity.

She turned to face Chawnrolfe. "I have been thinking upon this. My sister's husband Uttamatomakin said since you have shown me hospitality and have been kind and honorable, I should help you. If you have pegatawah, I would be more help with that, but I can also help with the uppowoc."

Once Tommasavach had finished translating, Chawnrolfe stood blinking for the space of several breaths, then scratched his beard, chin jutted, before speaking. "I would welcome that. Thank you."

She offered a smile and a nod, and he smiled in return.

The next morning, Whitaker returned to the stories near the beginning of his holy book. They had left off before the visit by Channa and the others with a series of stories about a man chosen by the Tassantassa God to leave his country and go to another. In the meantime, both he and his wife grew old and had no children. His wife encouraged him to take another woman to wife to raise up a son, but the second wife grew insolent in her position, and the first wife was jealous. Then God sent messenger spirits to tell him that his first wife would indeed conceive a child of her own—and she did! At the incredible age of ninety. Mato'aka shook her head. How could the translation of that be correct? But it was simply a story, after all.

The child grew, and trouble happened between him and his older brother, leading to the second wife and older son being sent away. The younger son grew, and this time the father decided it was not fitting for him to choose a wife from all the Tassantassas around them, so he sent back to their home country, to extended family, where the emissary met a woman named Rebecca, discovered she was of the proper family, and asked if she would be willing to travel all that great distance to marry a man she had never met.

Also incredibly, she agreed. She made the journey, and when she saw from afar the man she was to marry, she immediately jumped off the beast she was riding and ran to meet him.

Mato'aka chuckled. He must have been very handsome. Or perhaps she simply couldn't bear waiting one second longer to see what sort of man she'd agreed to be wife to.

This portion of the story ended with the man—*Isaac* was his name—taking the woman to the tent left empty after his mother's death and making her his wife. The man loved her and was comforted after losing his mother.

It was a sweet ending, but what of Rebecca? Did she love the man in return? Was he tender, and was she happy as his wife?

She had much to think on from all these tellings.

Chapter Thirteen

Summer blossomed fully, and the tobacco plants grew. John spent more time outdoors, and Reverend Whitaker even moved table and chairs to the lawn, beneath an awning John made, with canvas sides that rolled up or down depending upon the weather. Pocahuntas examined the construction and gave what appeared to be an approving nod.

"She seems much contented of late," Whitaker commented one evening.

John considered his observation. "I think she is merely resigned. Her eyes are still shadowed, and there is something—a spark about her—that is much subdued."

Whitaker hesitated then gave a short nod. "I suppose that could be so."

"Would you be so accepting," John asked, "if you learned your spouse had been slain trying to retrieve you from kidnappers? Or if you were separated against your will from your child?" At the discomfiture in Whitaker's face, he snorted. "Even so."

"I had not thought of it from that standpoint," the reverend said.

"We often don't," John said, soft but fierce. "I must admit, I sometimes question this entire venture. Were it not that I know too well the squalid conditions of London—and other cities back in England—and the pressing need for the Naturals to truly know their Creator, I would think we should not be here at all." He felt the shocked glance Whitaker cast toward him. "We know, of course, that all things work together for good for those who love God, but what of those we have sent into eternal darkness, all for the glory of the English Crown?" He did turn then to meet Whitaker's eyes. "Would you say after beginning the task to teach this particular creature of this land, that she lacks a soul or human dignity and worth?"

"Most assuredly not!" Whitaker said.

"I am glad to hear you say it."

"She is rather the very picture of intelligence and wit. She listens with perfect courtesy, but then challenges me almost daily on my own understanding of the Scriptures." He chewed his cheek for a moment. "Many men could take a lesson from her on diligence in study."

"Indeed."

Reverend Whitaker shot him another glance, looking as if he wished to say more, but when John inquired, he only shook his head and excused himself to retire for the evening.

During the next several days, John came to the realization that in addition to paying attention to the readings and explanations of such, Pocahuntas was also progressing faster than one would have expected with learning English.

Thomas brought her out to the fields for a walk after their morning study was concluded. John listened while pulling weeds among the tobacco. Thomas would give her the English word for something, and she would repeat it. Occasionally he would relay simple sentences, and she would repeat those.

A sudden question, however, made Thomas hesitate, and then laugh. John straightened and looked over. "She asks," Thomas said, gesturing toward her, "how to say, 'Why is he doing women's work?'"

John's ears began to burn. "What?"

Thomas laughed harder, and Pocahuntas repeated the question, looking pointedly at John.

"It is dishonor for men to cultivate the crops," Thomas explained. "That is the women's purview, and they do not welcome help." He grinned. "I recall this all too well from my time with them. I thought I was being kind, but they only ridiculed me and chased me away."

Pocahuntas said something else.

"She also asks if you are quiakros. They are the ones who tend the uppowoc—tobacco."

He tested the strange word. "Quiakros?"

"Their holy men."

The burn spread from his ears to his entire face. "No, tell her I am not a holy man. Although I do try to live in obedience to our God."

Thomas gave him a look, then translated. Pocahuntas's expression grew thoughtful, perhaps curious.

Carrying his hoe, John stepped across to where they stood. "Sá keyd wingan?" he said.

She peered at him a moment longer, then barely lifted one shoulder. "I—am—well," she enunciated carefully.

The shadows still lay deep in her eyes.

He gave her a little bow. "Is there anything we might do to make you more comfortable here?"

Thomas gaped at him. "Are you gone soft on her?" he hissed when John motioned to him to translate.

John's face burned again. Was that what Reverend Whitaker started to ask the other evening? "No," he said, probably more emphatically than needed. "But it does us no credit not to wish to ease her situation at least a little."

That dampened Thomas' amusement somewhat. "True."

He turned to Pocahuntas, who watched the exchange intently, and translated. Suddenly her own expression was more guarded, and she studied John for a moment before replying.

"She says she will think upon it." Another word, then, "Thank you for asking."

Did she dare ask for the one thing she wanted most, aside from her freedom and to hold Little Fox? Chawnrolfe had been kind enough to send for her family, despite the possibility that it would be a war party who came, and honorable enough as well to not turn it into an ambush. Perhaps he would not despise her request, especially since he had invited it.

She considered the matter for several days. Of course, she would need to take Tommasavach with her—which was both a bother and a comfort.

But she wanted to say the actual words for herself. After carefully repeating what Tommasavach told her, she approached Chawnrolfe—but not without her heart fluttering within her like a manaang'gwas.

He stood, expectant and a little apprehensive, while she pronounced the words. "I wish to bathe in the river."

Chawnrolfe's eyes widened. Tommasavach added something, which he said was an explanation of the custom of her people to do so every morning. Chawnrolfe then said he would see whether this was possible.

She knew it was possible. It only remained to see whether they trusted her to not try to escape.

The very next morning, however, at first light, Mistress Leaver fetched her from her room, and with an armload of clean clothing—for they had provided a change of dress for her some time ago—and both Tommasavach and Chawnrolfe accompanying, they walked to the river.

Tommasavach explained that he and Chawnrolfe would be present, but only Mistress Leaver would keep watch. She would alert them if Pocahuntas made any move to escape. They would not be allowed to let her bathe if they did not stand guard in this way.

Fair enough. Mato'aka waited until they had turned their backs, and then, quivering with excitement, she shed her clothing down to the shift—another condition of allowing her to do this—and waded in.

Oh, glorious water! It held the chill that rivers never completely lost even during the hottest days of summer, and after so many moons it felt more of a shock to her body than she recalled, but quickly she went in and sank down to her chin. The garment billowed around her, and she tucked the folds under the surface. How strange that she must keep herself covered, even in the water!

Another moment, and she ducked completely under, scrubbing at her scalp. What sweet relief for the itch and grime of the past moons.

She swam a few strokes upstream then let herself float back. A laugh escaped her as she stood, head tipped to let the water run from her hair and face, then lifted her arms to the sky. "Thank you, Ahoné, for the sun and the rain! Thank you, sun for shining, and river for flowing."

For the first time since she had been taken, she felt clean. Almost—whole.

At last she forced herself to return to the riverbank. Chawnrolfe stood there, eyes wide but alarm already softening to relief once he saw her approach. As she slogged closer, he turned his back.

The Tassantassas were a strange lot. It was not as if she were not already covered.

She let Mistress Leaver wrap her about in what Thomas had explained was a drying cloth, then she padded toward the men. Once again, she pronounced the words as carefully as she could. "Thank you, Chawnrolfe."

He glanced back, seemed relieved again to find her more covered, and smiled a little. "Sá keyd wingan?"

"I—am—well." She offered a smile in return.

So much did it improve her disposition and her attention to their studies, as Whitaker later reported to John, he was glad he'd granted her request. And so it became their morning ritual, accompanying her to the river's edge. She encouraged John and Thomas—Mistress Leaver as well—to join her in the water, with much gesturing. Thomas was the first to do so, shedding shoes but wearing both shirt and trousers. "'Tis very refreshing," he muttered, looking vaguely guilty, likely for being caught enjoying such a savage custom.

John wanted to, but he dared not let off his guard. Or indulge what seemed to be a more intimate activity with a woman so freshly bereaved.

He shook his head. Not that it should matter to him. He had taken it as a divine sign when he'd lost Sarah that he should give singular focus to his labors here.

Pocahuntas laughed, and so did Thomas. John chanced a glance at the water, where both splashed like children. That lad better not have any ideas either. Although he was more of an age with her, and had there not already been a handful of marriages in the new colony? Even amongst the more common laborers? In fact, he was fairly certain something of the sort was brewing between Jem, his cook, and Mistress Leaver, herself widowed shortly after arriving here.

The other thing that discomfited him was the prayer she continued to offer each morning. The sound of her tongue was almost musical, but to what profane deity did she give such tribute? He had exhorted Reverend Whitaker to begin teaching her some proper prayers, but did it truly matter if she did not yet recognize the One True God in her heart?

Or could the words have an effect on her soul and spirit even before she knew and acknowledged the Lord?

"What do you mean, allowing her to play in the water like a heathen?"

Sir Dale's sharp demand brought a prickle of shame to John's skin. "'Twas a small boon to grant her, in reward for diligent study and the help she gives us on the plantation. Would you not agree?"

Dale pressed his mouth into a hard line for a moment. He swung his gaze to Reverend Whitaker, who stood fair shaking in his shoes. "And what is she being taught?"

"We have been reading portions of Scripture every morning and discussing them. She shows great interest and is growing in—"

"Which portions?" Dale was unrelenting.

"Th-the histories, and the Psalms, and some of the teachings of Christ. There has not been sufficient time for her to become a true Christian. She must understand—"

Dale turned back to John. "You say she is helping on the plantation, otherwise?"

He tried but could not suppress a desire to swallow. "Aye, sir. She has much knowledge of growing corn and often joins us in the fields during the afternoon."

"Well, no more of that. I shall myself instruct her during the afternoon." When both of them made sounds of protest, he shot Whitaker a scathing look, then John. "Do not make me a liar for insisting to the naysayers that you both are honorable men, and do not only keep her here for carnal purposes."

Reverend Whitaker drew a sharp breath. John controlled his own response with effort.

"Of course we would not wish to do so," Whitaker choked out, at last.

No more the unhurried mornings of prayers and washing in the river, then taking of food and quiet reading and discussion of the Tassantassas holy book before another meal and walking outdoors or working in the fields. The stern weroance of the Tassantassas had come to dwell for a time, and he was determined Mato'aka would learn as much of their God as possible, as quickly as possible.

It was exhausting. Not only did she miss the pleasure of being outdoors—of sunlight and moving water—but his way of teaching was so forceful.

She could hardly bear listening to the sound of his voice.

He reminded her of the quiakrosoc, harping at Nohsh for this and that. Reminding him not to trust the Tassantassas. Or of Tomakin when he warned her to pay no mind to any talk of their god. That O'ki would find out and come punish her.

The thought made her shiver a little. What if it were so? She had no uppowoc to toss to the wind or into the river. Bad enough that the first time she thought to give a pinch of her food to the fire before eating, her captors had sternly told her to not do that.

How could she appease O'ki if she were not allowed to make even the small offerings? She could barely feel the presence of the manito here. What had they done to the land that even where the Appomatuc dwelt, it no longer remembered the spirits?

In the meantime, the Tassantassas captain kept thundering at her. Tommasavach, horrified, translated, but she could tell he was trying to soften the words.

Repent and be baptized, for the kingdom of God is at hand!

She knew already that the first word meant to turn aside from evil deeds, and the next part was a type of ceremonial washing, but the domain of God part—was it as the quiakrosoc said, that these people were the ones who would sweep aside the Tunapewoc and take over Tsenacomoco? That their god would overcome even the manito?

And if so, what did that mean for her, as Beloved Woman?

Would she even ever return to her people?

While the Tassantassa weroance insisted her father did not want her, that the ransom had not been paid, Tommasavach whispered to her that Nohsh had returned seven of the Tassantassa men he was holding prisoner, along with seven of their guns—ones that would no longer work—and promised to provide corn later, if they would only return his daughter. He claimed that the guns and tools which had been taken from the Tassantassas were either broken or lost. The reply given was that the Tassantassas did not believe they could all possibly have been broken or lost, and neither did they believe Nohsh would hold to his promise if she was returned.

So, neither side was willing to budge.

Mato'aka knew it was not for his own sake that Nohsh refused to return all the Tassantassa implements. Working their fields was easier with those tools, many of which had been traded for, fairly, and since raising crops was the women's work, it was most help to them. Of course, she had not seen that Tassantassas cared overmuch about women.

At least the Tassantassa weroance made his residence in another house, so she had some respite from him. She could see the concern in the faces of Whitaker, Chawnrolfe, and Tommasavach, and as she learned more of their tongue, she knew much of their quiet discussion after she retired for the night was about her and the current situation. Somehow that was comforting, and it gave her strength.

"I plead with you, sir, you must be more gentle with her. Else you shall drive her away from the same Lord to whom you intend her to bend a knee."

Reverend Whitaker's voice was as soft and entreating as John had ever heard it. He marveled at the man's ability to speak the words and yet present them in such a way that might not offend their stalwart marshal.

Please God that he would truly listen.

Already a tall man, Dale brought his head up, gaze fixed on Whitaker. "She needs to have the fear of the Lord put in her and hear the gospel in the strongest of terms."

Did Whitaker wince? " 'A bruised reed he shall not break.' And she has been bruised aplenty."

Dale drew a deep breath, held it, then released it slowly. "Perhaps you are right."

John strove to not show his surprise.

"Furthermore," Whitaker went on, all reasonableness, "if you place any trust in me at all, as a minister of said gospel, I would beg your indulgence.

'Tis not that I object to your conducting readings and examination of the woman—indeed, 'tis a worthy labor on your part, to see her instructed in the Christian faith—but as you have given this task into my hands at the outset, I promise I am not neglecting it, nor will I. And I believe I have found a method of approach she finds—pleasing."

The marshal snorted softly. "It is not within the purview of mankind to find the gospel 'pleasing.' We should only listen and obey."

"Nevertheless. You understand what I am saying? At least in the beginning, she must be drawn carefully, as a wild creature with something good to eat. And then she will be brought to see the wisdom and superiority of Christ to her old gods."

John almost winced at the comparison of Pocahuntas, with all her graceful dignity, to an animal of the forest. And yet untamed she surely was.

To see the alarm in her eyes and then the dullness of her countenance these past several days struck a pang to his heart.

Dale frowned a little then sighed. "Very well, Reverend. I will allow you to return to your method—but you will not object if I attend as I am able."

'Twas not a request. Yet Whitaker dipped his head, as if it had been the good marshal's direction all along.

Dale bent his glare upon John. "Has she at least been keeping her clothing on?"

A faint shock went through him at the mental image of Pocahuntas in—well, less than proper English apparel. He'd not admit to that glimpse or two of her in a wet shift. "She has been the model of chaste womanhood."

Dale snorted again. "I much doubt that, given the report of my men."

"With all due respect, sir," John said. "You are a man zealous for righteousness. How do you know they didn't merely claim it was so, to cover their own misdeeds?"

Dale had started to turn away, but hesitated at that. "I'd not tolerate such behavior."

"Precisely. So why not shift the blame to her, if one were guilty in truth?"

Dale's heavy brows lowered further. "There is no proof."

John lifted a hand and let it drop. "I know only that regardless of what took place before, I have been careful to not let harm befall her here."

"That is commendable enough," Dale grumbled, then left the house.

John exchanged a look with Whitaker, who swiped his forehead with the back of his hand. "I surely thought he'd not listen," Whitaker said.

"God be thanked that he did."

They settled back into a comfortable routine, although John did not dare allow Pocahuntas her morning bathing in the river, at least not while Dale was in residence. And even after, with the entire river's edge so closely watched by various outposts, he suspected someone would discover it and tell Dale, and then they all would be accused of immorality again.

The summer wore away into fall, and everyone at the plantation was called upon to harvest corn. John eyed the tobacco as well. The previous year or two, all had been merely guessed at, and they knew not how to cure it properly. Even so, the crop was well received in England.

Pocahuntas had been quietly offering direction on its care. She explained how the flowering tops were cut off of most of the crop so the leaves would grow more lush. A few weeks later, the lower leaves could be harvested and laid out on the ground nearby to dry, then the process repeated every few weeks thereafter. He had several batches of leaf drying, even now.

After a long day harvesting corn, she joined him at the edge of the field. Strangely she was without Thomas, who customarily followed her everywhere, both for her safety and to help translate and continue instructing her in English, of which she'd grown so quick in her understanding, it continually startled him and Reverend Whitaker.

She tipped her head, chin jutted at the field. "Tobacco grow good."

He glanced at her and nodded. "'Tis nearly time to finish harvesting." He mimed cutting the base of the stalk.

A smile flitted across her face, which after being so pale for a while from her captivity, had darkened again with the sun. Mistress Leaver scolded her for not keeping a hat on, but although she'd start out, she'd nearly always shed it before they'd been outdoors for long.

He supposed he ought to find it repelling but—as the line in Song of

Songs went, she was comely, no matter the shade of her skin.

Even now, he had to force himself to turn away to keep from staring. So fetching she was in her most worn gown, with oversleeves removed and shift sleeves rolled up and bare feet peeking out from beneath her hem. . .her glossy black hair caught up in a loose knot, exposing the column of her throat. . .

When had the day become so unbearably warm?

She gathered up her skirts and wandered along one of the rows, examining the plants more closely. Her sharp eyes had more than once found pests, and she was just as quick to help catch and exterminate them. This time, however, everything must have been satisfactory, for after a row or two, she straightened and shot him a grin. "All good, Chawnrolfe!"

The effect was rather as the concussion of ship's guns to his chest. "John," he managed to say, after what seemed an unseemly long hesitation on his part.

Her eyes narrowed, the smile shifting. Thomas had explained some of the nuances of proper address, he knew, but 'twas the first time he had invited her to use his given name only.

"Ch-awn," she said.

A chuckle escaped him. "J-ohn."

She swallowed, bobbed her head, and tried again. "J-john."

They both laughed. "Kuppeh," he said. "Yes."

And then he forgot how to speak altogether, beneath the sparkle of her dark eyes.

Chapter Fourteen

He would be leaving soon to take tobacco and corn downriver to the storehouse at Jamestowne. He needed to go—needed to put distance between himself and the ever-so-distracting female under his care.

Fortunately, their shallop would not hold more than a bit at a time, so it meant multiple trips. Perhaps by the time he had finished, this fascination would have worn off.

Please God, let it fade. I do not wish to dishonor You.

He went to both Thomas and Reverend Whitaker, asking them separately to watch over Pocahuntas. Thomas looked torn. "I wish I was going with you," he admitted.

John clapped him on the shoulder. "I understand too well. But I need you to take especial care to guard our guest and see that no one takes advantage of my being absent."

Thomas frowned and nodded, but resolve filled his eyes. "I shall."

Deciding exactly how to say farewell to the guest herself, however, proved too difficult, and in the end, he simply avoided doing so. The shallop lay packed and ready, and once he boarded with his personal bag, they debarked.

Fifty miles of early autumn forest stretched on, quiet and beautiful, except for where the other plantations lay. He scanned the shore for any sign of the Naturals and thought of Pocahuntas, she and her people, running free along its edge.

Help me, gracious Lord, fix my eyes and heart on You only!

At Jamestowne itself, he found Dale busy at his marshal duties, reviewing a list of offenders to the laws he had drawn up shortly after his arrival. Dale greeted him warmly, and John gave him the amounts of goods he had shipped downriver and a quick report on how the plantation fared.

"Come, walk with me," Dale said. "Let me show you how Jamestowne grows and prospers."

It did, indeed. John thought back upon their arrival, and the stench and squalor everywhere. Now, the inside of the fort was as tidy as out, and rows of houses were built, with the church and storehouse and all in good repair.

"I have, as you know, had to be very firm with the shiftless and lazy. Smith had it aright when he made the rule, 'he that works not, eats not.' I have only taken it a step beyond."

John nodded. It was true, whatever one thought about his sternness, that the colony had done well under Dale's hand.

The inhabitants certainly were busy today. Men and women alike hastened to their tasks, spurred perhaps by Dale's presence. There were a few Naturals as well, there doubtless to trade—

A more feminine figure caught his eye, sent a jolt through him of—almost recognition. But when he looked closer, 'twas certainly a woman of the Naturals but not Pocahuntas.

Of course she would not be here. 'Twas foolish of him to have even thought it.

"The savages do frequent as well," Dale said, then with distaste added, "including the women. I have it from Powhatan to send them back to him if they stay overlong." He cast John a sidelong glance as they passed through the gates of the fort to where more houses stood in very neat wattle-and-daub English fashion and newly harvested fields stretched beyond that. "If only it were easier to deal with our men engaging in carnal use of their women. They often ignore the ordinance regarding marriage—although no true marriage can be made, I suppose, between a Christian and a savage."

John made a sound of assent. "'Twould rather be preferable if men could practice continence rather than indulgence."

"Indeed."

They passed the houses and stood at the edge of what had been corn, the dried stalks stripped of ears, being gathered even now for fodder for the hogs and cattle.

"Speaking of marriage." Dale glanced again at John. "There are two or three women who would be very suitable, if you were so inclined. Or perhaps there will be more arriving on the next ship."

Something squirmed within him, and the memory flashed of a round, pert face, dusky with the sun, and sparkling black eyes.

"I will not say the thought has not presented itself to me."

Dale smiled a little. "'Tis the one thing about this land, the difficulty that a man should labor to establish God's kingdom here, and not also have the consolation of a wife, as God allows."

Did Dale speak of John's loss, or his own wife far away in England? Either way, he could not but agree. He had no time to reply, however, before Dale turned and clapped him on the shoulder with a broad smile. "Do you see to choosing a woman, in your leisure. 'Twould bring you much comfort up on the Hundred."

John forced himself, after, to look more closely at the women at the fort. None had even half the sparkle of—of a certain guest in residence at Bermuda Hundred. He suppressed a snort. And his Sarah had been peerless. 'Twas not like he held up anyone else as a standard of perfect womanhood.

Yet it was no longer Sarah who haunted his thoughts, day after day.

Mato'aka had never chafed so much as she did now at the shortening of the days and lengthening of nights. It did not help that she, a grown woman, having been both wife and mother and before that, well-guarded daughter of mamanatowic, was penned up like one of the Tassantassa milk cows.

How free was her life before she had been taken, before she knew the depth of how evil the Tassantassas could be. And it was not as if her people did not understand hardship. When huskanaw for the men lasted for several moons, when all were taught to bear blows without crying out, when honor in death meant singing in ridicule of one's enemy even as the flesh was being flayed—or burned—from one's body. Oh no, the

Powhatan—indeed, all the children of Tsenacomoco—knew how to be strong.

But what had been done to her—that was not to be borne. The men who had committed such disrespect to her person would be turned out from among her own people.

Not all men of the Tassantassas were so, thankfully. Tommasavach behaved with honor—and well he might, having spent so much time with the True People. And then there was Whitaker, so mild that she had once asked Tommasavach whether all holy men were so. He looked confused for a moment then seemed to realize what she was asking. "No. Very often they are harsh and fierce, like Sir Dale."

"Do they ever take wives?"

He laughed a little. "Oh, very often. It is just that here, with our king wishing to start a new settlement"—he grimaced, admitting to that which Chawnzmit had denied but Nohsh had long since discerned was the purpose of the Tassantassas—"not many women have been willing to come yet."

He looked a little sad at that.

"Are you wishing a wife, Tommasavach?"

He gave her a smile. "Thomas. Call me simply Thomas."

It was not the first time he'd said so, and since Chawnrolfe—no, *John*—had enjoined her to call him by his short name, she felt more at ease doing so.

"Thomas," she said, and his gaze warmed, much as John's had during the similar exchange.

"Would you ever consider marrying again, after Koko'um?" he countered.

She sighed. "Perhaps. It would depend on the man. He would need to be as worthy as Koko'um."

Thomas's gaze quickly darted away, and his cheek colored. A suspicion rose within her.

"What—are you asking for yourself, then?" A laugh bubbled from her throat, and she hoped it did not sound unkind.

His face went more crimson as he bent his head, as if to hide.

"Oh, Thomas. You are a dear friend of the People—and to me."

"But not worthy," he muttered.

"You are worthy," she murmured. "But I do not see you as more than a brother."

He was quiet for several heartbeats, then at last gave a nod and said what sounded like, "Fair enough," in his own tongue.

The difficult thing about such conversations was the stiffness that always followed for a time, between them. But Thomas never behaved as anything less than respectful. She could wish he were a little older.

None of the other men of this plantation behaved ill toward her, either, although likely not entirely apart from threat of punishment, judging by the looks they sometimes cast her. And so it was that she did not feel safe enough to walk about without being accompanied by either Thomas or Whitaker, or Mistress Leaver, whose short name she learned was Ann.

Or by John Rolfe himself, who had been mostly absent for about the turning of the moon now. And that one—something about him did remind her of Koko'um, especially when he was being most stiffly proper and respectful toward her.

She wished it were possible to converse directly with him, either in his own tongue or in hers. It would be interesting to hear his thoughts on things, without having to speak through Thomas.

Too often she found herself watching him tenderly caring for the uppowoc or seeing to the fields of pegatawah, both with as much care as he tended his people and animals. The earnestness with which he had asked her what comfort he might provide her, and then granting her wish to bathe in the river.

In his absence, she considered slipping down to the water's edge, perhaps under cover of darkness, but he had shown her how vigilantly all borders of their patch of ground were watched and strictly warned her never to bathe alone.

She shuddered to even think of the possible consequences, for his guards she did not trust. Not at all.

More than that, John was the only one she felt truly safe with. She missed him—and with far more strength than was seemly. It was worst in the morning, at first meal, and then again at evenings. Such a quiet presence most of the time and yet, steady and dependable.

He was also the one who kept coming to mind since Thomas' question about marrying again. Plain foolishness, it was. He was Tassantassa and she—well, she was Beloved Woman and daughter to Wahunsenecawh, no matter how they dressed her in these confining clothes or fed her Tassantassa foods.

She was of the True People, and in her heart, she would not change.

John awoke from a dream so vivid, his body still ached, and the shame of it immediately soaked him through.

He was not accountable for what thoughts afflicted him in his sleep, was he?

He'd stayed gone from Bermuda Hundred for the express purpose of breaking off such unholy affections, and barely greeted anyone during the brief times he'd gone back for another load, but it had rather grown worse. Now she inhabited not only his waking thoughts, at least daily and more often hourly, but his sleeping ones as well.

"God have mercy on me a sinner," he muttered, then shifted to a kneeling position on his pallet laid out in a corner of Sir Dale's own accommodations. He set to prayer in earnest, although silently, since the sun had not yet arisen and quiet still lay across the household.

He would continue in prayer until they all awakened, if necessary. Only God could be his help in this. Mankind was too prone to evil. Had not his fellow Englishmen proved that, as they sinned against their esteemed guest, perhaps even more grievously than what they charged her father and people of? The Indians at least had not the upbringing or education that taught them how to behave as Christian men ought. One could not expect a lost people to show the same manners or consciousness of sin that he did, having been reared in the Church.

This must surely be nothing but the machination of the Devil himself, preying upon John's own fallen heart, encouraging him to musings and even dreams that bled of nothing but wickedness. *And so, gracious Lord, deliver me! By Your holy name and the blood of my Savior, Jesus.*

Peace seeped through him just as the sky outside began to lighten. John released a heavy breath and, leaving his bed, he snatched up his cloak and took himself down to the river's edge to wash his face and hands, frosty air notwithstanding.

The memory of splashing and laughter flashed through his mind. Would Pocahuntas be still glad to enter the river, cold as it was...?

Lord, help me! I cannot even rise from prayer and begin the morning without my thoughts turning to her.

It did not help that this was the last trip to Jamestowne he could justify making before spring.

He could send her away—but where, that she would not be vulnerable to more ill use? And returning her to her people was out of the question. Dale had commented just days ago that if he did not hear from Powhatan by the end of winter, he'd drag her up the river to the Pamaunkee and force the savage chieftain to answer the issue.

Surely a father would want his daughter back. Would he not?

But if he did not—or if there were some other impediment to her returning—what then?

He had served temporarily as her protector. What if he made that more permanent?

Wrenching his mind aside from the thought before 'twas half formed, John shook his head. She could be his ward, perhaps, but no more. She was not a Christian. Even now, with nearly half a year's instruction from Reverend Whitaker, she hardly understood their religion, much less comprehended the scope of Scripture. Had Whitaker yet begun to introduce her to Christ Himself and how He had come to redeem mankind?

To be—to be more—was unthinkable. At least, if he valued the blessing of God. Was His displeasure not heavy against the sons of Levi and Israel for marrying foreign women? And how difficult would it be, both for himself and for Pocahuntas, were she to become his wife?

Would she even be willing, so soon after her widowhood? And under such circumstances?

Perhaps he could find another for her to marry. Someone who—

His gut wrenched painfully. Who was not him.

"God above, help me."

Not an oath, but an honest plea.

Ann helped her dress in the cleanest of her gowns, tied the sleeves on over the shift, and after arranging her hair, adjusted everything here and there.

"Why. . .?" She gave up on trying to find the Tassantassa words and simply swept a hand down and up, motioning to her apparel.

Ann smiled. "Master Rolfe is home," she said, slowly and carefully. "A feast is being prepared to welcome him back."

She thought she understood most of that. At the least, that it involved John Rolfe and—

Her heart gave a flutter. John had returned.

Ann walked beside her to the building where they took their meals—*dining hall*, it was called. The men were already gathered there, and two stood off to the side, making music with their strange instruments. An ache gathered inside her. How long it had been since she had sung and danced with her people!

And—there he was, in the middle of a cluster of other men. As she approached, he caught sight of her and went very still. His eyes widened, and for a moment she thought she saw admiration there, and not a little longing. Another flutter rippled through her chest.

For lack of anything else, she offered a small smile. He dipped his head and smiled in return—also just a little, then turned back to the men speaking around him.

He had washed before he came, she could now see. Droplets still clung to his beard and the length of his dark hair, caught at the nape of his neck with a leather thong. She'd forgotten how fascinating she found the curl of his hair. She definitely had not realized how comfortingly familiar he would appear after being away for a whole turn of the moon and more.

Ann drew her to a seat at the end of one of the long tables where she could easily tuck herself and the long skirts in upon the bench. Someone brought her a cup of warm drink, and she thanked them, sipping and looking about at no one in particular.

She could not even see Thomas, who at least could talk to her without hindrance.

The food was brought, and the men all sat, talking and laughing. Mato'aka ate, but hardly tasted it in her fascination of watching them all. Down the table, John laughed as well.

For a moment, it was as if time slipped backwards, and she was at another feast, one where all her people made merry, and one lone, bedraggled Tassantassa sat among them, with hair and beard the color of flame, his eyes dazzled by the spectacle and his ears trying desperately to make sense of the commotion.

And then she was herself, the lone Tunapewoc among all these *Eeng-leesh*, trying also to sort through the experience.

The music stopped only long enough for those making it to eat, and when it started up again, several of the men rose to dance.

She could not help it—her feet tapped along, and her body swayed.

Suddenly Thomas appeared from the crowd. "Pocahuntas, come dance?" The shyness of his smile wrung at her heart.

And why shouldn't she?

She slid off the bench and followed him to the open area just outside the dining hall, where the sun was slipping downward beyond the not-too-distant trees, bathing everything in a golden glow. Thomas danced a hopping, stomping sort of thing, motioning for her to join him. Lifting her skirts, she did her best to mimic him.

Her feet fell into their own rhythm, stamp and kick, both like and unlike what Thomas and the other men were doing. Thomas swung to face her, and they danced opposite each other, an arm's length apart. A laugh bubbled out of her, and Thomas laughed as well.

Some of the other men danced toward them and arranged themselves in a rough circle, taking turns pushing each other out of the way so they were the ones dancing with her. She laughed again.

And then—then it was John there before her, keeping time with her, a strange glow in his eyes and a smile curling his bearded mouth. Her own feet nearly faltered, but she remembered who she was and, lifting her skirts a little higher, gave herself to the rhythm with renewed energy.

The music bounced to a stop, and all of them with it. A cheer rose from the men's throats, and she could only laugh, breathlessly, half bent. Oh, but she was unused to such exertion!

John said something, and the words were lost to the noise around them, but when he beckoned her toward the dining hall, she followed. Behind them, the music started again, but it was slower, almost mournful.

He handed her a cup and gestured for her to taste it. She did so. It was sweet, like grapes, only with a strange tangy bite. What was it? She peered at the liquid, and John spoke again in a tone that sounded like a caution.

"He says not to drink too fast, nor too much," Thomas said, suddenly at her elbow again. "It is called *wine*, made from the grapes that grow wild here. But it is changed. In its present form it will make you not yourself." He laughed a little. "You will either become very foolish, very angry, or very sleepy."

Many things could do that. She sipped again, smiling at John. "Thank you."

His eyes shone, as if he were happy she had spoken the words in his tongue.

She turned back to Thomas, too weary to bring any others to memory. "Tell him, I am glad he returned safely."

Thomas relayed what she had said, and John smiled and bowed.

The moment suddenly felt unbearably stiff. "I should go back and to bed," she blurted.

Darkness had hardly fallen yet, but her head swam, and the strangeness of all of it overwhelmed her again. It had been a while since she had felt it that strongly.

With Mistress Leaver trailing behind, John walked her back to the house. She appeared content with quiet between them, and he was likewise happy to make no conversation.

'Twas probably most unwise, the merrymaking that had drawn them all to dance with her in turn. But it seemed all in good fun, at least in the moment, and he'd discerned no untoward intent in the attention the other men had given her.

And as for himself—oh, blessed peace! Despite his earlier apprehension over seeing her again, his spirit felt light and free. Perhaps God truly had released him from all unholy affection, and he could merely be benefactor to Pocahuntas. It truly appeared to be so.

Inside the house, she smiled and nodded, then went into her chamber and shut the door. A wave of weariness washed over him and, after stoking the fire, he unrolled his pallet nearby and stretched out.

Sleep was slow in coming, however. Consideration of the journey, of the amount of corn taken to Jamestowne and what price the tobacco might fetch this year, swirled together with idle memory of the impromptu celebration the Hundred had held upon his return. Outside, across the yards, the music still played, and when John closed his eyes, he could still feel its pull and see the laughter in everyone's faces.

Not least of all, that of Pocahuntas.

How blithe, how full of charm she was. Captain Smith had written of her and called her the only nonpareil of the Powhatan—and John could well believe it.

Oh, if she would only bend her knee and heart to Christ! And if the rest of her people could be brought to know their Creator and true Lord. He could hardly bear listening to her stories of their profane gods, which others had averred must be Satan himself, but Whitaker had insisted they must show courtesy by being willing to learn of the Powhatan ways and thus better understand them.

He must ask Whitaker on the morrow just where he stood in instructing her. And perhaps, now that the harvest was finished and his trading journey to Jamestowne complete, John could sit in on the reading and discussion again. Perhaps he even could join in and help Whitaker lead her more fully to Christ.

Perhaps he might even be the deciding influence for bringing her to Him.

As quickly as the thought presented itself to him, it fell flat. He must be careful. Only the Spirit of God could move on one's heart and effect true conversion.

But if she could be induced to come to Him. . .oh, the possibilities that might afford.

He closed his eyes, and sleep fell upon him at last.

Chapter Fifteen

She felt sore and achy the next morning in ways she never had experienced before, except possibly after the birth of Little Fox. The thought sent a wave of sorrow flooding through her. But she rose, dressed, and went out to the main room for the morning meal.

Thomas and Whitaker were already there, looking a little weary as well, but both greeted her warmly enough. They were all beginning to eat when John came in and seated himself at the table with a nod.

"We have but a few weeks until our celebration of the birth of the one we call Christ, who is our redeemer from sin," Whitaker said while they ate.

Thomas translated. The term *week* she had learned a while ago—a way that the Tassantassas marked the passing of time, based on their God having taken six days to make the world and then resting on the seventh. But the young man stumbled to explain *redeemer*, until John murmured something and then Thomas said, "He bought us out of the slavery of sin."

Mato'aka sat back. That was an interesting concept. Captivity she understood, and the trading of captives between towns or even peoples. It was indeed the reason she sat here, now. The Tassantassas thought her of value in obtaining certain things from her father.

She was also now familiar with their idea of sin. Their God was perfectly good, like Ahoné, but kept track of rights and wrongs and demanded payment for such, like O'ki. Worse, as they told it, the first man and woman were also made perfectly good but did the one thing God had told them not to, and so the lives of all who came after were now forfeit.

"As we have already read, the Israelites were told to bring animals for sacrifice to cover for their sin. But Christ came to be the perfect sacrifice, once for all."

"I thought you did not believe in sacrificing people," she said.

Whitaker smiled a little. "This is why. There is no more need for sacrifice, whether animal or otherwise, because He has accomplished all that is necessary."

Something about that seized her heart. No more sacrifice? So all that they offered to O'ki—was that needed?

Of course, O'ki was the god of the Powhatan. This *Christ* was the god of the Tassantassas. But she could see the difficulty now between them.

The kingdom of God is at hand.

A chill swept over her. Of a certainty, as she had suspected, this was more than one people sailing across yapám and making towns upon Tsenacomoco. It was one god supplanting another in a land where all had been settled for time out of mind.

She recalled the prophecies from the quiakrosoc to Nohsh, which she had been made privy to after huskanasqua. *The demise of our people will come from the east. Twice we will push them back, but the third time, we shall be overcome.*

"Pocahuntas. Sá keyd wingan?"

John's soft inquiry broke into her thoughts. She lifted her eyes to find one hand pressed flat on the tabletop, the other curled into a fist in her lap.

His gaze was warm and full of concern. But she could not answer him.

"Say on," she said to Whitaker, finally.

He nodded gravely, seeming to recognize how deeply this struck her. He spoke, and Thomas translated.

Long, long generations of a people who were pushed back and forth and suffered and prospered under various rulers, many of them bad. Who as a people were slaves themselves, not just once but twice. Their Redeemer would come, as they were told—a chosen one to free them at last from all their troubles, but they did not understand that at first He had to be a sacrifice. Instead they looked for Him to claim His place right away as king. Mamanatowic, Thomas said. The chief above all smaller chiefs, one whose rule would last forever. But not yet.

She caught a glimpse of what that might mean—a people whose lives would prosper for always, under a good and gracious leader, as Nohsh had been so often. But where Nohsh himself would grow old and die, and another take his place, this mamanatowic would remain forever young and strong.

"When this King of kings first came, many did not recognize Him. Indeed, God had been silent for four hundred years. But let us begin reading what happened."

Whitaker showed first that the Christ was born from the lineage of the great kings, but in that time they were all subjects of another great nation, one that had many gods but mostly viewed their own human king as god. One of the messenger spirits came to a young girl, of age but who had never yet been with a man—another curiosity which had been a point of discussion from the readings before—and told her that she would conceive a child, apart from a man, that God Himself would kindle the life within her.

Mato'aka touched her middle. "How very strange," she murmured.

"And wondrous," Whitaker said, smiling. "The problem was, she was promised to a man in marriage, and when he found out that she was with child—and knew it was not his—he thought to end their betrothal until the same messenger spirit came to him in a dream and explained what had happened. This child, he was told, would be the Chosen One—the Christ, in their tongue. And they would name Him Jesus, which means 'God saves.' And so we call him Jesus Christ."

Whitaker went on to tell how the Christ's adoptive father and very pregnant mother had to travel to a nearby town, which was so crowded they could only find lodging in the building where the animals were kept. Mato'aka curled her lip at the thought. And sure enough the baby was born that night. After wrapping Him in strips of cloth, they laid Him in a feeding box.

But God did not leave them in complete obscurity. That very night, a whole host of messenger spirits appeared in the sky above some shepherds in the fields, tending their flocks—Thomas had to stop and explain about *sheep*, a kind of animal somewhat like the goats that the Tassantassas kept for both food and milk, and indeed the same sort of animal mostly used for sacrifices in the time of their holy book's writing. So the shepherds left their flocks and ran to see the newly born mamanatowic.

Chosen before His birth. Just as she was, for the position of Beloved Woman.

Sometime after, a group of wise men—something between a weroance and a quiakros, Thomas explained—saw a particular star in the sky that led them to the baby mamanatowic as well. But the local weroance, a very evil man, caught wind of it and sought to kill the baby. While His foster father was warned of it in a dream and took the family to safety in a nearby country, the evil weroance slaughtered all the baby boys two years old and younger.

Again that terrible, hollow feeling struck her middle. How awful!

"We will read more tomorrow," Whitaker said.

She lifted her head, a sound of protest bursting from her throat.

The holy man smiled, this time with kindness. "There is still much to talk of. We should not cram it all into one day."

All she wished to do was hear more. But there were the usual tasks of the day to see to, and she would not be lazy and not do her part.

John had brought her water grasses with which to make a basket. The familiar work was comforting and allowed her thoughts to run free—and the morning's reading had certainly given her much to consider.

He could see that she was much moved. And he longed to talk further with her about it but found himself reluctant to push over hard.

As the days went on, however, she drank it all in, grasping spiritual truths more readily than John ever recalled of himself. "She is beyond challenging," Reverend Whitaker admitted one afternoon. "Already she has more understanding than—than some preachers I know." He shook his head, eyes wide. "And yet she holds back from deciding whether ours is the true religion or if it is still her old one she should follow."

John had his own reasons for wishing her to make that decision—and which side he earnestly prayed she would choose—but would not admit to it, even though with each passing day his heart grew more and more entangled.

Her understanding of English grew apace with their studies. Sometimes she would not even wait for Thomas to finish translating before offering a comment or question. They had by necessity become more cautious about stray conversation around her because she perceived just a little too much. John found it both endearing and alarming.

As the winter passed and spring neared, so her restlessness grew, and he could not blame her. Were her thoughts for her people? Did she wonder if her father would pay her ransom and wish her back?

And more, did the looks that sometimes passed between them mean that she felt drawn to him, as he did to her? By necessity he busied himself more with the plantation, overseeing the calving and farrowing, and making sure seeds for this year's crop were still dry and safe from vermin. But his thoughts were evermore fixed upon her, his prayers a fervent and continual offering for her spiritual state and for guidance on how to act regarding his own affections.

Then one day in late winter, a letter came from Dale. He was planning, within the next few weeks, to mount an expedition upriver to demand a reply from Powhatan concerning his daughter—and he would be taking her with him. There would be resolution to this matter, one way or another.

He requested Thomas' presence as an interpreter, since the lad spoke their tongue as if born in that land, and he trusted that John himself would see to their passage to Jamestowne when Dale sent for them.

John's heart beat far too heavily. He stood rereading the letter, out of doors in a patch of late winter sun, when Whitaker emerged from the house and came toward him. "What tidings, Rolfe?"

"Come—walk with me a bit." He wanted no word of this to come to Pocahuntas' ear as of yet.

Once he judged it safe enough to speak and not be overheard, he related the news to the other man.

The scowl that gathered on Whitaker's face was just short of fearsome. "What if Powhatan meets Sir Dale's demands, and she returns to her people? What then of all our effort to instruct her in the faith?" He shot a sidelong glance at John. "And—what of you? Will you speak to her before Dale sends for her?"

John's mouth fell open, and he was still trying to decide how to reply when Whitaker forged on.

"Oh, come, man. We all see how you look at her." He chuckled drily.

"Thomas vows that if you will not declare yourself soon, he shall."

His jaw snapped shut. "No! That is—I will—I plan to—"

He felt rather like gnashing his teeth in the moment.

Whitaker laughed again, then sobered. "You know, many will say nay, but perhaps you have not realized what a boon it could be to both our peoples, were you to take her as wife."

John's entire face burned. "I—the thought has crossed my mind, yes. But can I do such a thing if she does not become a Christian?"

"She is very close to it, in my opinion," Whitaker said softly. "It may be that if you appeal to her privately, she'll be inclined to do so more quickly." He hesitated. "At the least, none of us doubt her attachment to you. The kindness you have shown her will, I believe, bear good fruit."

"Thank you," John said, finally, "for your confidence."

Whitaker patted his shoulder. "You are a good man. And I have no doubt that God is with you in this."

Popanow, the winter, was wearing away, and soon it would be cattapeuk, the time of spring fish runs. Mato'aka felt the coming change in her very bones—even if she did dwell in a Tassantassa house, surrounded by strangers, who somehow felt less and less like strangers the longer she was here.

It had been nearly a full turn of the leaves since she had been taken. Definitely a full turn, when she considered she'd been at Pota'omec for three moons. Such a long time since she had seen Nek and Nohsh.

Her eyes burned. And so long since she had gazed upon her husband and child. She nearly could not recall what Koko'um had looked like, except in tiny flashes of memory.

Channa had said they would try to visit again, if possible, but no one had come. Had they given her up?

And even if they did not—

She could not finish the thought.

Scant solace was found in household tasks. In watching Jem, the cook, prepare meals and assisting as he allowed her. In strolling about, observing the animals with their young, but always within sight of those she trusted.

She felt smothered by the confinement. She wanted to run the forest. To swim the river.

John had not offered again to let her bathe, not in all the moons since he had been scolded by Dale. And speaking of that one—the memory of his voice still drew a shudder from her. She—daughter of mamanatowic! Afraid of nothing and no one.

She took a broom and swept every corner of the house, lastly the porch, and stood gazing wistfully toward the river.

From under the trees—those the Tassantassas had not cut down—came John and Whitaker, walking slowly and deep in conversation. As they neared the house, they looked up and saw her. John first, as he often did, drawing a now-familiar flutter from her middle. But something in his face this time made her catch her breath more than usual.

Whitaker spoke, and John nodded, and the holy man moved off in another direction. John hesitated, folding something in his hands before tucking it into the pocket of his doublet. His head came up, and he came toward her with more purposeful steps.

"Would you walk with me, Pocahuntas?" he asked when near enough to be heard.

She huffed. "I would be glad." The words were still awkward in her mouth, but he smiled, so she must have gotten them mostly right.

He led her back in the direction of the river, under the trees. Just when she wondered when he would speak again—or if—he said, "There is a thing I must tell you. But I do not know how to begin."

She dipped her head in a nod, to let him know she understood if nothing else.

Within sight of the river itself, he stopped, glancing about, then squinted out over the water. "I have had a letter from Dale. He tells me he will be going soon to demand the ransom from your father. And he wishes to take you and Thomas with him."

Her breath caught again. Oh, the strange thoughts and feelings that stirred within her! To see her family again! But then, how would Nohsh receive such boldness? And what if—

"Will he—make war upon my people?"

John turned to face her. "I do not know."

It was likely so, but that was not his decision. Still… "Will you come?"

Something in his expression softened. "If you wish it."

She swallowed, then nodded. He was the only one she trusted to make sure she was not violated again.

"I must also tell you—" He stopped, and to her wonder, his cheeks grew pink as Thomas' often did when they were talking of uncomfortable things. "When we sailed from England, I had a wife. We were shipwrecked and spent the winter on the island for which this plantation is named."

His gaze flicked to hers, then away. In such bright daylight, she could see for the first time that there were green flecks in his eyes.

"Sarah, my wife, gave birth to a daughter while on that island, but the baby died. And then so did Sarah, not long after we reached Jamestowne."

Something in her heart crumbled. Surely she did not understand him aright! To suffer the loss of both wife and child—?

"Because of that, I understand 'tis likely too soon for you to think of another, after the death of your husband, and with such circumstances. But I must ask—"

His words were nearly too fast for her to catch their whole meaning, but when he reached out and took her hands in his, his intent became suddenly clear. And this time his gaze did not waver from hers.

"I must ask whether you would consider staying. Here. With me. Whether or not your father pays the ransom."

She could not breathe—could barely think. His hands were so warm and strong, and she had so missed a man's strength—

"If you agreed," he went on, looking pained, "I would ask you to—to consider becoming a Christian. To believe in our Christ. I should not marry you otherwise. But—but I do want to marry you."

He was trembling as much as she, his breaths also coming hard and quick. And she could only look at him in wonder.

"If—if you were willing, we would ask your father's permission. And I would have to secure permission from Dale." He searched her face. "Would you be willing, dearest Pocahuntas?"

His thumbs moved gently across the backs of her hands. Shredding all her thoughts.

Oh, Nohsh. Oh—Koko'um.

"I must—think upon it," she whispered.

His lashes fell, but not before she caught a flash of disappointment.

"Of course." His hands tightened for a moment. "'Twould be unreasonable for you to not take time to think upon it."

He released her and started to turn away, but she caught his sleeve. He froze, eyes seeking hers again.

How did she tell him that she wanted to say yes? That she trusted him above all others among the Tassantassas? That the honor he had shown her these past moons had made all the difference for her.

She took a breath, let it out sharply. "Mato'aka. Not—Pocahuntas."

His eyes widened, his body shifting toward hers once more.

"I give you my—true—name. Mato'aka."

Whatever else happened between them, she would do that much.

His arms came around her—oh, so warm, so strong!—and he bent enough to rest his forehead against hers. "Mato'aka," he breathed. "Thank you."

He smelled of the fields and of—of uppowoc, smoky and warm and comforting. She shifted, tucked her cheek against his, just for a moment, then stepped away. He let go instantly, his eyes blazing and the green in them very bright.

Lifting her skirts in both hands, she set off toward the house, glanced back at him, and then, with a grin, took off running the rest of the way.

'Twas all he could do to not crush her in his embrace and kiss her senseless, right there.

Did her people even do such things as an expression of love? To kiss?

Regardless, he could not. Especially after she had been so ill used by other men, he must continue to hold himself in check.

He followed after, keeping her in sight as had been his habit for months. His heart still pounded from the sweetness of those last few minutes.

Her real name—she had shared her real name with him. He knew the significance of such a thing. And then to have her in his arms, even so briefly—

Ah, gracious God! How lovely You have made her. And—how I love her. Please help her come to You—and let her become mine as well.

How was he to wait the hours—the days—while she considered and made her choice?

He would not press her. Not when it came to consenting to being his wife—and certainly not when it came to believing in Christ. Nothing could be worse than her agreeing merely because she felt she must.

Mato'aka.

Please, Lord. Oh—please.

She gained the front porch and disappeared inside, but not without a last peek in his direction. He smiled. Drew a deep breath and let it out.

One chair sat on the porch, and he settled into it. His own thoughts were quite frayed.

The door opened, and Mistress Leaver emerged, a drying towel and cup in her hands. She frowned at John for a moment then set her fist on her hip. "So you've spoken to her, have you?"

"Is there anyone on this plantation who does not know how I feel?"

The woman snorted. "Likely not. 'Twould seem we know your heart better than yourself, Master Rolfe."

He laughed weakly then shifted forward to swipe his hands across his face and hair. "I had to. Dale is taking her upriver soon to demand that ransom from her father."

"Ah-h." Mistress Leaver leaned back against the doorjamb. "Our girl has a hard choice to make, does she not?"

After scrubbing at his face again, he stood. "Keep watch over her. I have work to do."

It was Thomas he sought first, however. He found the young man splitting wood for the cooking fire, and beckoned him apart from the others. Thomas set down his axe and came closer, wiping the sweat from his brow with his sleeve.

"Did you know her true name is not Pocahuntas?" John asked, keeping his voice low.

Thomas stopped, blue eyes wary. "Who told you?"

"She did. I mean, we had heard that often the Naturals will not share their true names, because they feel it can give their enemies power over them."

Thomas nodded.

John threw out a hand. "She—she told me 'tis Mato'aka."

Thomas looked around as if to make sure no one overheard, but John had barely spoken above a whisper. Then his gaze came back to John's, but only briefly before he tucked his chin, cheeks going crimson. "My congratulations."

"'Tisn't like that," John snapped. "At least—not yet." He went on to tell Thomas the contents of the letter from Dale.

Thomas gave him a longer look this time. "You'll come as well, will you not?"

"Yes. I'd not leave her at the mercy of the wolves that savaged her last time."

"Neither will I."

Chapter Sixteen

"The time has come at last for Jesus to give Himself as the sacrifice lamb." Mato'aka lifted her head from contemplation of the shimmers in her cup of watered wine.

Whitaker's gaze was mild. "He did come in order to die for us. But most fortunately for us, He did not leave us there."

She blinked. She was still having trouble sorting out her thoughts after John's news and declaration the day before. But it was a new day, a new morning, and time for their customary study.

And continued study she needed, if she was to make any sort of decision.

John was absent this morning. Whether she was disappointed or relieved, she could not say. After lying awake so long the night before, marveling over the fact that John Rolfe of the Tassantassas wanted her—desired her as a man does a woman, yet unlike the others held himself back from the taking—she could hardly hold her eyes open this morning.

How she missed a dip in the river at dawn. But it was the least of things deprived her. . .

Thomas nudged her arm. "Are you listening?"

She sat up straight. Very bad form for her, as Beloved Woman.

A curl of mingled sorrow and nostalgia went through her. If she married a Tassantassa, would she still be midéwiqua?

Whitaker was reading. Jesus and His followers went out at night to a garden to pray. He fell into such agony, knowing what the coming hours would hold, that He sweat drops of blood. His followers, however, fell asleep. Twice He went back and rebuked them. In between, while He sorrowed, the messenger spirits came and comforted Him.

She thought of her huskanasqua. It felt like an entire lifetime ago. She had never dreamed like that again—not so vividly, and never with the presence of the manito.

What would it be like to actually see them as they came and went from the world around them?

Jesus returned to His followers a third time but this time let them sleep until a crowd came to take Him captive. One of His followers in a fury tried to defend Him and with his sword cut off the ear of a servant, but Jesus told him to put his sword away and, reaching out, healed the servant's ear.

Mato'aka's mouth fell open. She should know by now, from all of Whitaker's readings, that Jesus worked strange and wondrous things. But to do this for the servant of one who had come to drag Him away?

"What followed were long hours where Jesus was accused of many things," Whitaker said. "We shall not read them all today."

He did read a passage that told how Peter, one of Jesus' followers, lingered outside where Jesus was being questioned and accused, but denied knowing Jesus when others recognized him. Then a cock crowed, and Jesus turned and looked at him from across the space, and he remembered that Jesus had said this very thing would happen.

He went out and wept bitterly.

Mato'aka also felt like weeping.

Whitaker continued. The Roman weroance ordered Jesus to be whipped. This alone flayed His skin so that He could not even be recognized as a man. Then the soldiers beat Him with their fists, pushed a circlet made of thorns down over His head, and mocked Him as weroance and mamanatowic.

Her heart felt bruised and shredded as well. To think, if the one who had made the world became as one of His own creatures, then suffered them to treat Him thus. Was it not enough for Him to simply die? Must they make His death as agonizing as possible?

Her own people did this to enemies, but not often, and only to those who most sorely deserved it.

This Jesus most certainly did not deserve it.

Whitaker spoke, looking at her with concern.

"We can stop," Thomas said.

She shook her head. "No. Continue."

The Roman weroance gave the people one last chance to spare Jesus' life, but they insisted He should be killed. So the Roman soldiers led Him away to a place where they used great spikes of iron to nail His hands and feet to a large wooden frame—Whitaker drew for her the sign they called the *cross*—and then raised it upright.

And there He hung, while the crowd watched. Two wrongdoers were hung on crosses beside him, and while both joined in with the mockery of the crowd, one came to the realization that Jesus was innocent of what they'd accused Him of.

Remember me when You come into Your kingdom.

And Jesus had answered, *Today you will be with Me in Paradise.*

Her skin prickled as if lightning was about to strike nearby. Just as Chawnzmit said if he died—

"Is that the same place as *heaven*?" she asked.

"Close enough the same that they might as well be," Thomas translated Whitaker's reply.

The difficulty of language made her impatient. She could understand quite a bit of what Whitaker read, but she still needed Thomas to make clear the finer points.

Suddenly, Jesus cried out, "My God, My God, why have You forsaken Me?"

And while those around Him were trying to figure out exactly what He meant, He cried out again, "It is finished," and died.

Immediately the earth itself shook and the sun above became black. All were struck with fear, and even the Roman captain exclaimed that surely this was the Son of God.

Mato'aka realized she had tears streaming down her cheeks. She did not bother to wipe them away.

Whitaker smiled a little. "Bear with it just a little longer, dear one."

"But—it is so unfair! He did nothing to merit all this!"

His smile deepened. "That is the point. He could not be a proper sacrifice were He not innocent."

She sniffled and gestured for him to go on.

Before the end of the day, the followers of Jesus came and took His body and laid it in a borrowed tomb. A great stone was rolled across the entrance. Roman soldiers were set to guard it because they remembered that Jesus had said He would come alive again and they wished to make sure no one stole the body and tried to claim it was so. The morning of the third day, however, another great earthquake took place. Some of the women who loved Jesus had gone to the tomb to see if they could do better at preparing His body, but found the Roman soldiers lying as if dead and other men dressed in blinding white, telling them that Jesus was gone—He was risen. They ran back to where His followers gathered, but none believed them right away.

Peter, who had denied Him, and another named John—no wonder the name was so common amongst the Tassantassas—ran to the tomb. John believed right away, but Peter still questioned.

Mato'aka sat forward on the edge of her chair. "So—did He come alive again, or not?"

Both Thomas and Whitaker laughed. "He did indeed!" Whitaker said and kept reading.

Jesus Himself appeared to one of the women, then to all the followers. Later He appeared to two men walking from one town to another, and they did not recognize Him until He had finished explaining to them how it was necessary for the Chosen One to first die and rise again before He could become the Great Mamanatowic.

"But how did they not recognize Him?" she said.

Whitaker had to think about his answer. "It is said that the power of His resurrection did not only bring His body back to life, but it changed how He looked. Here—let me read you of how He appeared to John, many years later."

He turned the pages of the holy book until he was near the end. "This is from what we call the Revelation, what some believe is an accounting of what will happen at the end of days. So it may be that this is a near description of what Jesus looks like now—or at least somewhat soon after His resurrection."

"John has been exiled for his faith to an island called Patmos. While there, he is praying and has a vision. 'Then I turned back to see the voice that spake with me: and when I was turned, I saw seven golden candlesticks, and in the midst of the seven candlesticks, one like unto the son of man, clothed with a garment down to the feet, and girded about the paps with a golden girdle. His head and hairs were white as white wool, and as snow, and his eyes were a flame of fire, and his feet like unto fine brass burning as in a furnace: and his voice as the sound of many waters. . ."

A gasp tore itself from Mato'aka's throat. *She had seen Him!* The great man from her vision, during huskanasqua! Surely it was Him.

"Keep going," she said when Whitaker stopped and peered at her.

" '. . .and his face shone as the sun shineth in his strength. And when I saw him, I fell at his feet as dead: then he laid his right hand upon me, saying unto me, Fear not: I am that first and that last, and am alive, but I was dead: and behold, I am alive for evermore, Amen: and I have the keys of hell and of death. Write these things which thou has seen, and the things which are, and the things which shall come hereafter.' "

Both Whitaker and Thomas studied her now. She realized she was nearly gulping for breath.

. . .see? I have called you by your name!

It was Him. This Jesus was real—and had come to her at the most important time of her passage from child to woman, having—indeed, having banished all the manito.

"Sá keyd wingan?" Thomas asked softly.

Her throat was so clogged with weeping, she could not find the words to explain, but she nodded.

"I think we are done for the day," Whitaker said. "I will go for our noon meal."

As he passed her chair, his hand rested briefly upon her head, and then smoothed across her shoulder.

Thomas lingered, watching her.

"I wish my people could hear this. Could know Him."

A slow, gentle smile curled his mouth. The blue eyes crinkled. "So say many of us."

John kept himself gone from the house for most of the day, taking his meals with the other men and behaving as if he'd never had any concern with what pertained to their guest.

Mato'aka.

Her name whispered through his thoughts like the softest touch. The look in her eyes when she'd spoken it—the softness of her cheek against his, the answering firmness of her grip.

Once again—how was he to endure until he had an answer from her?

And here he'd thought 'twould be easier once he'd spoken his heart.

Reverend Whitaker came to the kitchen to carry food back for the noon meal and drew him aside for a moment. "'Twas amazing—our guest was much affected by the reading this morning. I feel it needful to let the Spirit of God work as He will and not hurry her yet, but—oh, she may be at the very edge of true belief."

"That is wonderful," John agreed.

Now if she would but give consent to being his wife! But he dare not hurry her on that either.

After lunch he went out to survey the fields. It was too early to plant—they'd a few more weeks before the threat of frost was completely past—but not too early to plan. And even if not, he desperately needed something that would keep him from the house.

She could scarce eat, so full were her thoughts.

If Nohsh paid the full ransom and she were allowed to return to her people, what would she choose? Was she not obligated to go back among them and tell them how she had seen the Tassantassas Christ before ever she had been told of Him?

On the other hand, was it likely that Nohsh would pay the full ransom, in the moment, even with Dale bringing her along? The stores of pegatawah were always nearly depleted by this time of year. And Dale had demanded, what was it, five hundred baskets?

Such a thing, if Dale were not willing to wait until the fall—and perhaps even if he was—was impossible. And to return all the tools and weapons that had been taken over the years, doubly so.

Somehow, though, no matter how things went, she needed to try to get word to her people. Perhaps she could summon Channa and Tomakin again.

That left only John's question to answer.

If she were allowed to return. . .there was the care of her son to see to, but without the benefit of a husband. Not that she would not, as Nohsh's daughter, find a shortage of men willing to step into Koko'um's place at her side.

Yet. . .she found herself unwilling to let John's declaration go unanswered. Was it love on his part, or obligation?

And either way, did she wish to give up the opportunity for an alliance between her people? How many wives had Nohsh taken simply for the sake of binding this or that people under himself, as mamanatowic? Not that marriage to John would mean the Powhatan binding themselves under the Tassantassas, but surely it would bring great peace.

Whitaker and Thomas kept watching her, but she could not even begin to speak her thoughts yet. After eating, she swept the house and the porch as well, but at last put the broom away and begged Thomas to take her to John.

He was at the corn field on the far side of the Hundred when a feminine voice called out his name.

An all-too-familiar feminine voice. His heart leaped.

Walking across the field was Pocahuntas—Mato'aka, rather, with Thomas at her side. His pulse was already pounding an uncomfortable rhythm.

As they neared, Thomas shrugged and gave a half grin. "She insisted I help her find you."

John bit back the smile that threatened to steal across his mouth.

"May we—talk?" she asked, her eyes wide and no hint of humor in her face.

Another uneasy thud echoed through his chest. He nodded. "Of course."

Thomas asked her a question, and she waved him off. As he walked away, John saw that the other men nearby—most of them sentries guarding the palisade rimming two sides of the field—watched him and Mato'aka with too-keen interest.

He pointed to a nearby stand of trees, edging the stream running between fields. "Let us walk that direction."

She gave a grave nod in return and kept pace with him, both hands full of her skirts.

When they were well out of earshot and mostly out of sight, she stopped and swung toward him, her gaze full of feeling.

"When you ask me to stay," she said, slowly, as if choosing her words very carefully, "is love? Or duty?"

Everything in him melted under the expectancy in her eyes. He reached for one of her hands and, stepping closer, placed it palmside against his chest. "My dear Mato'aka. I must say both, but mostly love. I am most unreasonably in love with you."

Uncertainty glimmered back at him, and he smiled. He kept forgetting she did not yet understand English as well as he wished. But she had sent Thomas away, so he must make the best of it.

"Definitely love," he murmured.

With a sigh, her eyes slid closed for a moment, then she nodded again and reached up to touch the side of his face.

He could hardly breathe. "May I—write that letter to Dale?"

The barest nod this time. Her brows drew together. "I must learn better talk."

The ludicrousness struck him of having Thomas always present to translate between them, and he chuckled. "I could learn more of your tongue as well." She peered at him, and he went on, "How does one say 'I love you' amongst your people?"

That she understood, for her expression cleared. "*Nouwmais*," she said, a smile flitting across her mouth.

He repeated it, and the smile went full blown.

"I—love—you," she whispered, and her fingertips combed the edges of his beard.

He was still afraid to presume too much. "Come," he said, taking her hand from his chest and weaving his own fingers through hers, "I've a letter to write. And there are finer points to discuss that I dare not leave Whitaker and Thomas out of."

She understood the necessity of having the other men present, but she missed the private intimacy she'd enjoyed with Koko'um, even in the midst of her people. Here, however, as John later explained through Thomas, such offenses against her had occurred, he wished to protect both of them from evil accusations. And he wished all to understand each other as perfectly as possible.

He explained—as he had tried before but was not sure she'd comprehended fully—that he must make it clear to Dale and others that he regarded any marriage between them as being primarily for the good of the colony and their shared peoples. The current situation did not allow for him to do otherwise. But none of that altered the fact that he loved her with his whole heart.

There was also the situation of whether she was willing, before giving herself as his wife in the sight of God and both their peoples, to declare herself a Christian in a similar manner.

"That would mean you being baptized," Whitaker explained.

She nodded slowly. "I have been thinking upon that. If Dale agrees to our marriage—and my father—then I will also consent to baptism."

Both Whitaker and Thomas grinned at that, but neither appeared as overcome as John, who, as he perched at the edge of a chair, elbows on knees, tucked his head for a long moment, then looked up again with a shy smile and eyes shining with tears.

"This moves you so much?" she asked, and waited for Thomas to translate.

"Yes, indeed. 'Tis an honor that you would choose me—and our God." His gaze remained steady upon her this time, and the smile faded. "Thomas has explained to me that there is a position you hold among your people. That you are—"

"Midéwiqua," Thomas supplied.

"Beloved Woman," she said.

How odd it felt to speak of that here!

"I have no translation for that," Thomas said with a little laugh.

She smirked at him. "Think of something." She turned back to John and Whitaker. "I have seen the spirits, but I have also seen your Christ, presenting Himself as the greatest of the spirits. The Great Mamanatowic, as Thomas has told me He is."

They regarded her with much wonder. "Then if you are baptized, will this position of yours continue?"

She spread her hands. "It is my wish—my hope—to bring word of your Christ to my people, so they may also know. And perhaps it was for that very thing I was born and chosen."

While they thought upon that, she drew a deep breath and went on.

"Another thing I have been considering is that I should take another name. Such things are important among my people. I have the common name you all knew me by—Pocahuntas, by which I was chided for my liveliness as a child, then the real name given me by my father, which you, Thomas, already knew and which I imparted to you, John. There is a third name, that which was my sacred and secret name as Beloved Woman. I will tell you that when I am ready, but not yet."

She waited for them all to nod.

"I have been thinking which name I would like to take after my baptism. Whitaker, many moons ago you read that story of the woman asked to journey a long distance, to be wife to a man she had not yet met. A man who was himself born as a child of a great promise."

The holy man's eyes lit. "Rebecca?"

"Yes. That is it." She said it slowly. "Re-bec-ca. I like the sound of it. And I feel a—a kinship with her, who was taken from her home and did not know what awaited her where she was going." She looked at Whitaker. "Do you know the meaning of the name?"

He swallowed, and his eyes became brighter. "I believe it means, 'to bind.'"

She smiled slowly. She would bind herself both to John and to his God. "It is most fitting, then."

Dale's summons came hardly a week later. Rafe Hamor bore the message in person. "I'm to not waste any time but bring her directly," Hamor said, with no little apology.

"Well, it shall take us a few hours to pack and set the plantation at the ready."

Hamor accompanied John to the house, where, after directing Mistress Leaver to prepare baggage for herself and their guest, he made introduction between Pocahuntas and the secretary of the colony. She gave him a half bow and a grave smile then hastened away to help Mistress Leaver.

John informed Thomas and Whitaker, and all three set to packing.

"You are going as well?" Rafe asked.

"Most assuredly. We'll not send Pocahuntas without a guard to make sure nothing untoward happens to her."

Hamor's eyes went wide. "I heard rumors. . ."

"Even so," John said shortly. "And knowing you are a man zealous for righteousness of God and the good of the colony, I've the need to speak with you privately. Sooner rather than later."

So it was that he acquainted Hamor with how things stood and secured the man's support in the matter.

They sailed downriver at first light, the pinnace providing a very pleasant passage.

At Jamestowne, he expected some difficulty with his insistence on accompanying Mato'aka—and he was not disappointed. To his surprise, Hamor stepped up to argue on his behalf. "The more we have who Pocahuntas feels at ease with, the less you must concern yourself with her well-being, or with having to watch over her."

Dale gave him a long, hard look. "You know that our intent is either to move them to fight for her, if such is their courage and boldness, or to restore the residue of our demands."

"I gathered as much," John said, unmoving.

At last Dale nodded.

A hundred and fifty men he had chosen and gathered, spreading them out across several ships and boats. And so they set off up the river, past the place where he was told Powhatan had once lived—where Mato'aka had made her home, called Werowocomoco.

'Twas not long, as they went, that the Powhatan came out to ask what the Tassantassas meant by this show of force. Dale replied, through Thomas, that they had come to deliver Pocahuntas, who they had brought with them, and to receive their arms, the men who had deserted to them, and corn—or else to fight with them, burn their houses, take away their kanoes, break down their fishing weirs, and do them what other damages they could.

The fiercest of them, so it seemed, answered that if the Tassantassas were come to fight, they were welcome. They were well prepared, and so the Tassantassas should go back downriver or suffer the same fate as Captain Ratcliffe and dishonor themselves in death as he had.

"You translated exactly?" Dale demanded.

"Yes," Thomas said.

"Very well. We shall revenge that treachery."

Chapter Seventeen

Once more confined on board the very ship that had brought her downriver, she could not be at ease with how this was being carried out. But just when she thought she would fly apart from the waiting and watching, John would catch her eye, or at least turn her way when she was held later behind closed doors, and she would be comforted.

He would allow no ill to come to her—not if he could help it. And while Whitaker had stayed behind in Jamestowne, Thomas was also there, although his main task was to help with translation as needed. Ann as well kept ever at her side.

At least she was lodged in a different room this time. She could see out, a little, and hear the exchange between Thomas and those on the shore.

The ship kept pressing upriver, and then as soon as it entered a more narrow channel, where the shore was nearer, a rain of arrows flew from the trees and bushes lining the banks. Ann gasped, but Mato'aka held herself firm.

Was she not still a woman of Tsenacomoco, and even more, of the Powhatan? And daughter to mamanatowic?

The chamber door opened, and the soldiers brought in a man bleeding heavily from the forehead. Their healer, whom they called *chirurgeon*, hastened in after to tend the wound. But as far as she could tell, this man was the only one hurt.

She continued watch as the ship's boats were launched and armed Tassantassas went ashore. The cries and shouts of battle followed, and smoke rose from the nearby town. After a while they returned with much rejoicing and carrying baskets and armloads of various foods and goods.

Her heart lay heavy in her breast as the Tassantassas feasted that night.

Come morning, they pressed on. A cry came again from the shore, demanding an explanation for the previous day's attack and houses burned, and for the Tunapewoc men hurt and killed.

Mato'aka shut her eyes for a moment. To have to return in such a way. . .

"We came to you in a peaceable manner," Thomas called out to them, "and would have been glad to have received our request with love and peace, yet we have the courage and strength to take revenge and punish where wrongs should be offered. And having done so—yet not so severely as we might—we are content and ready to embrace peace with you, if you please."

"We did not shoot! It was not us. It must have been some wandering band who did not know of our purpose, for we would be very glad of your love and wish only to help you in what you came for. What you desire is in the possession of our mamanatowic, and we will immediately send messengers to him, to see what he will do. Only give us the full turning of the sun to see this done."

Dale muttered over that. "They delay without cause. But to show our good will, we shall grant the day."

Even so, the ship sailed on.

The following morning, they brought Mato'aka out upon the deck. Dale pointed to a hill a little ahead of them, where a town could be glimpsed at its crest.

A very familiar town and hill. Her eyes burned, yet she held herself with more strength.

"Matchcot," she said, with as little feeling as she could manage, and Dale gave the command to bring the ship nearer then drop anchor.

So close—so very close! Was Nohsh there still, and Nek? Would she see them this day, at last, and perhaps Little Fox as well?

John was suddenly at her side. "Sá keyd wingan?" he said, very softly.

She gave him the barest nod. What would be the end of this?

What, indeed, did she even wish for that end to be?

When the ship had come as close as it could, they launched the boats.

Mato'aka was herded onto one of them. Ann was made to stay behind, but John and Thomas both stayed close.

A crowd of warriors gathered on the shore and on the brow of the hill, well-armed with bows and arrows, yet standing still, showing neither overt threat nor any fear as the Tassantassa boats drew closer. The gazes of many alighted upon her face and glimmered with recognition, and while some gave her the barest nod, none spoke, except to call out to the Tassantassas and invite them ashore.

A double row they formed as the first boat touched the bank and they were ushered up the hill. At the top, she was flanked by John and Dale himself. "Where is the Powhatan?" Dale called out.

One of the men she recalled as a captain of her father's stepped forward. "Where is your weroance?" he said in response.

Thomas translated busily, as the two faced each other. "We have brought your king's daughter," Dale said, "as he demanded. And where is he, to answer to this matter?"

"We will once more send two or three messengers to our mamanatowic and await his reply," was the answer. "But we are ready to defend ourselves if you are determined to make war. Nevertheless, give us time to know the resolution as desired by our mamanatowic. If by morning his answer does not suit you, then we will fight and let that determine the end of our quarrel."

"'Tis more delay," someone behind her muttered, "to give them time to move their possessions out of our reach."

Indeed, if she understood the words aright, it was not far from the truth. Nohsh would be busy moving his household and the women and children to safety. Why did such a thing offend the Tassantassas?

Of course, here she stood this time, in the midst of the trouble.

"We agree to your request," Dale said. "We assure you that at least until tomorrow, we will not molest, hurt, nor detain any of you. And then, before we fight, we shall give warning by our drums and trumpets."

Thomas gave the translation, and a murmur passed among the assembled warriors. They parted then, and to her astonishment, Nantaquas and Tomakin stepped to the front of the group, looking fierce. "We wish to see our sister," Nantaquas declared.

She was ushered forward. "See," Dale said with not a little pride.

With a cry she let herself be gathered up into their embrace. "I have been well," she hastened to reassure them. "Since you last saw me, nothing has been amiss. I give you my word on it."

A new commotion drew her attention, as John drew apart from her, and with another of his countrymen made apparent preparations to be sent away.

"No! Mahta! Where are you going?" She turned to Nantaquas. "Are you taking him—"

John stepped back for a moment, making a shushing sound. "Peace, esteemed Indian princess. I have been asked to go to your father, if indeed he will consent to meet with us. And see—Thomas is still here. This one is skilled in your people's tongue and will aid me in presenting our case to him."

The smile he gave her was so warm, she had no doubt that it was the matter of their marriage of which he spoke, and not Dale's demands.

She nodded, the fear of it all still fluttering in her chest. John then took a packet from an inside pocket of his doublet and slipped it to Rafe Hamor before shouldering his bag and walking away into the crowd of warriors.

"Sister, we are here," Nantaquas said. He sent a look after John then studied her face a moment more before a wry smile lifted his mouth. "So that is the way of it," he murmured.

Mato'aka swallowed and gave a short nod. "He is a good man and has shown me nothing but honor." She might have no other opportunity to explain.

His smile widened. "It would not be the first time a woman came to love her captor."

"*He* was not my captor," she hissed. "That one, there, was."

Her brother's only response was an infuriating grin.

It was agreed that both Nantaquas and Tomakin would accompany them all back aboard ship, as John and the other man stayed on shore for the night.

John drank in the sight of tall, sinewy warriors and strong faces so familiar and yet, not. These were his beloved Mato'aka's people. Comely of form and expression, every one of them.

Perhaps if her father paid the ransom and she was allowed to return, he'd stay here with her. Perhaps.

'Twas far too tempting a thought.

Gracious Lord, preserve me. Give me wisdom and favor in the sight of these people! And open their eyes to the truth of who You are, if not now, then later. . .but not too much later.

He would, above all, show calm and dignity among them.

There were fewer women than he expected, and no children. Perhaps it was so that most of the town had fled. But he and Sparkes were shown to a house where a fire burned inside, and were seated with all courtesy upon a pair of mats. Two women came and brought both food and drink.

"Wahunsenecawh?" he asked, as they set down platters and cups and withdrew.

Both women smiled—with a stiff formality, he thought—but shook their heads and gestured for them to eat.

He and Sparkes exchanged a glance. "Captain Smith was shown courtesy despite being a prisoner," John said.

"Yes, well, let us hope this does not end for us as it did for Captain Ratcliffe," Sparkes said and, shrugging, reached for a cup.

The drink was sweet and spiced, their food likewise flavorful and sustaining. Other women brought more, after, but they were most pointedly not taken to see the Powhatan chieftain.

At evening meal, Mato'aka sat between her brothers. "Truly, are you well?" Tomakin pressed.

"I truly am. And how is Channa? And Nek, Nohsh, and Little Fox?"

He smiled a little. "They are all well. Little Fox has grown. Your mother and father miss you."

"I miss them as well."

"Even now?" Tomakin's gaze held challenge.

"Even now," she insisted.

He glanced about. "Do you think this will not end in bloodshed?"

She followed his gaze about the table. There, just as Dale was seated at the head, opposite her, Hamor handed him something. The same packet John had shown her, it seemed. Indeed, the Tassantassa captain opened it then sent her a long look before returning to the letter.

"I most fervently hope not," she said.

Deliberately, she shifted in her chair to face Nantaquas so she was not watching Dale.

"What is of such interest with that leaf he holds?" Tomakin whispered from behind her.

Mato'aka held her breath for a moment. "It is a request to—to marry me."

Nantaquas smirked again, but Tomakin leaned forward. "From whom?"

"That Tassantassa they sent up to wait on Nohsh," Nantaquas said.

Tomakin's brows went up. "Your captor?"

"He was my host, not my captor," Mato'aka said tartly.

Tomakin sat back and looked over her head to Nantaquas. "She is besotted."

He only laughed and nodded.

"Pocahuntas!" Dale thundered her name from the other end of the table.

She shifted toward him again, carefully.

"So Rolfe wishes to marry you. Are you agreeable to this?"

Thomas translated, but she gave a nod almost before he was finished.

Dale guffawed. "Well, well! The little bird has caught herself a falcon." And he laughed again.

Cheeks going crimson, Thomas translated that as well. Nantaquas went very still and straight, but Tomakin merely rolled his eyes.

"We will see what comes of our negotiations in the next several hours," Dale went on. "And then we will discuss this further." As the food and drink were carried in, he folded the paper and tapped it against his palm. A smile spread slowly across his face. "Indeed, this may prove the key to resolving the whole matter."

John and Sparkes woke early to the women bringing them even more food. A tall Powhatan warrior ducked inside after them and came to sit on the other side of the fire from them.

"Are we to see the Powhatan king?"

"Mahta. But I am Opechancanough, brother of Wahunsenecawh, and I will see that your request is brought before him."

John studied him, the long and muscular limbs, the strong features and black hair, not without lines or silver—he was strong and hale for his apparent age, just as would be expected of a weroance of the Powhatan.

But more, he could see something of kinship with Mato'aka there. The lively black eyes, the proud intelligence of the face. The dignity of their comportment.

"Please also convey to him that I wish to marry his daughter," John said. 'Twas probably too soon to say so, before he'd expressed permission from Dale, but neither would he let this opportunity slip by.

The Powhatan arched one brow very high when Sparkes translated.

"Pocahuntas?" he asked, as if to confirm.

"Yes. She who is known as Mato'aka among her people."

Sparkes relayed this as well, and John had the satisfaction of seeing complete astonishment—and perhaps a little alarm—on the other man's face.

"I seek of course the good of both our peoples," John said. "But I have come to love her very deeply."

Opechancanough grunted, studying him afresh, then spoke. "I will indeed tell my brother of this as well."

John thanked him, and then they were bid eat before returning to the river's edge.

It was yet early morning, and while Dale made preparations for them to go back ashore, Mato'aka held council with her brothers at the rail of the ship.

"Tomakin, have you ever seen O'ki? With your own eyes?"

He stiffened, flicking a glance at Nantaquas, who shrugged but nevertheless looked interested in the answer. "This is not a thing to be talked of in front of those who are not of midéwiwin."

"I realize that, but where are we to go to talk of it? We may have little time here. And it is of importance."

He looked at her for a long moment before drawing a deep breath and letting it out. "Kuppeh. In a vision, many years ago." He smiled a little. "Many of the quiakrosoc do. You know it is how we conduct our everyday lives, by the guidance of O'ki through dreams and visions."

She nodded. "I ask you because. . .I wish you to know that during my huskanasqua, I had a vision of the spirits—and then of the one we know as the Tassantassas Christ. The one called Jesus. And I have come to believe that He is the true God, the Creator of all we know and love in this world."

Both of them drew up, alarmed and astonished. "How can this be?" Nantaquas asked at last.

"I do not know." She spread her hands. "I do know, however, that I saw Him, and He spoke to me. The holy book of the Tassantassas describes what He looks like, and it was Him."

Both men stared at her as if she had taken leave of her senses.

"What? Do you not believe me? Would I, as Beloved Woman, tell such an untruth?"

"No," Tomakin said slowly. "No, you would not."

"I have thought," she plunged on, "that perhaps this was why I was chosen. To be not only Beloved Woman for our people, but perhaps also to marry John. To be a bridge between our people and his."

Tomakin looked thoughtful, but Nantaquas's lip curled. "To be wife to a Tassantassa, when they do not even know how to respect a woman? You are far too good for any of them."

She put her hand on his arm. "Do not say so, my brother. I—love him."

"Waugh! How can you? A Tassantassa?"

"I told you, he has behaved with honor, and has made others honor me as well."

Again, they looked at her as if they could hardly believe her words.

"We will see what Wahunsenecawh has to say about it all," Tomakin said finally.

"I wish he had consented to come out and see me," she murmured, "or at least let Nek come."

"You know he had to think of protecting the other women and children."

"Kuppeh."

It was the only sensible thing, with the Tassantassas being so bold, for Nohsh to withdraw to another town further inland, taking most of the women, the children, and as much of their belongings as they could carry—just as they'd done before.

Dale had them all ashore and arrayed at the edge of the town before the morning was even half spent. Mato'aka scanned the faces of her people, searching for Nek and Channa despite knowing they were not there.

John and Master Sparkes walked out to greet them, accompanied by several warriors. Relief flooded her limbs just to see him, and he broke out with a smile when he caught sight of her.

He relayed what had taken place to Dale, admirably keeping his attention upon the Tassantassa captain during the conversation until Dale brought up the subject of the letter. Dale gave the order for the others to move back a short space then beckoned Mato'aka and her brothers forward. "On the subject of this proposed marriage, are you, Pocahuntas, willing to become a Christian, for the sake not only of your own eternal soul, but for the well-being of both our peoples?"

Alarm sparked again in the eyes of her brothers, but the joy in John's face—and in Thomas'—gave her strength. "Yes."

Dale looked at her brothers. "Have you objections to this?"

Nantaquas did not reply, but Tomakin lifted his chin and said, "It is her decision. She remains our sister."

"Will you carry tidings of this marriage to your father, and return to us his reply on the matter?"

Both of them nodded gravely this time. "We will do so."

"Very well. We shall depart your river, but for no other cause would we do so without other conditions being met."

Mato'aka embraced both Nantaquas and Tomakin long and well, and after other farewells, they retreated to the ship and set sail again downriver.

For the first time in days she could breathe again, but her eyes burned at having not seen more of her family. With John at her side, they did not insist on her remaining indoors, and she stood at the bow, feasting her gaze on the river's edge she had known and loved.

They would wait three full days and nights after the Tassantassas had gone before moving back to Matchcot. Winganuske could not fault Wahunsenecawh's decision on this. The children, of course, thought it a grand adventure, both Channa's and Mato'aka's boys skipping about the temporary camp and finding all sorts of curiosities to carry back to Channa and Winganuske.

In truth, she welcomed the busyness, since it gave her something to think about besides the threat of the Tassantassas.

Wahunsenecawh was only protecting them, she knew. And yet he seemed unreasonably afraid that she would be discovered, that they still, after so much time, would take her from him.

Opechancanough came to report that the Tassantassas had gone and that the two they had sent to wait upon Wahusenecawh seemed amenable enough. Indeed, the one not only professed love for Mato'aka but knew her true name. Hard on his heels came Tomakin and Nantaquas, confirming that Mato'aka wished to marry this particular Tassantassa.

Wahunsenecawh thought for a long time. "And Dale says it is still his wish for friendship and love between our peoples, for always?"

"He does."

"Bold of him, it is, to have come all the way upriver, with Mato'aka in hand, to make his demand." Wahunsenecawh snorted, but a smile curled his mouth. "I could like him were circumstances changed."

His gaze strayed to where Winganuske sat listening—at his behest, since Mato'aka was her daughter and this concerned her as well.

"There is more, Nohsh." Nantaquas shifted. "Mato'aka tells us that she believes in the Tassantassa God now. That"—he passed a hand over the shaved side of his head—"that indeed, she saw Him in a vision, during huskanasqua. She did not know at the time it was Him, but He did speak to her, and now she knows because of their holy book that it was He."

All the breath left Winganuske's body. She pressed a hand to her middle and tried not to gape like a fish.

Is this true, oh God? That through everything, You have brought her to know and trust You?

Wahunsenecawh slid another glance her way. "What does this mean for her place as Beloved Woman?"

"She told us," Tomakin chimed in, "that perhaps she was chosen for this thing. To marry a Tassantassa and be the one who binds our peoples together." He spread his hands. "I cannot say it is not so."

Wahunsenecawh nodded, very slowly.

"Regardless, it seems to please her, the prospect of marrying him. They both avow love for each other. She insists he has shown her honor, which is more than others have done, and that since the early days of her captivity he has protected her from further harm."

Another nod, and more silence, as he continued thinking. At last he drew a long breath and looked at Opechancanough. "Go to our brother Opechisco and ask if he will journey to be present at her wedding, to represent me and our people. And you"—he addressed Nantaquas and Tomakin—"accompany him to see this done, then bring me word of it after."

"It is good, Mamanatowic," Opechancanough said.

"It is good," Tomakin and Nantaquas echoed.

Part Three

REBECCA

Chapter Eighteen

Immediately upon their return to Jamestowne, preparations were begun for both a baptism and a wedding. Lodging in the house that had been prepared for them before, Mato'aka and Ann labored together to find suitable clothing—or at least what Whitaker and his fellow minister at the church in Jamestowne thought suitable. Ann fussed that they'd not finery to befit the occasion, while Mato'aka wished she had time to make a doeskin dress with all the embellishments she'd had on her huskanasqua garment—the same she'd worn for her marriage to Koko'um.

"And how are weddings accomplished among your people?" John asked.

She smiled. "When I married Koko'um, Nohsh brought me to him, and while we joined hands, a string of shell beads was broken over our heads. Later all the pieces were gathered up and strung again into a chain. That was considered proof of our marriage."

While waiting for official word from Nohsh, they proceeded with the baptism on the first Sunday, which the Tassantassas called the Lord's Day in honor of Jesus rising from the dead.

The first part of the assembly went very much as she was already accustomed, with songs she had begun to recognize and reading of the holy book and what they called a *sermon*, more words of which she found she knew. For the rest of it, she hardly knew what to expect—how to feel—even though Whitaker had reviewed with her the order of service.

"You must know, going forward with this, that most of us have not dreams or visions such as you have borne witness to," he had said.

And she did know. Amongst her people, very few of them—and often only at huskanaw or huskanasqua—did see or dream such things. Her vision had only come to her the once.

When at last it was time and he called her to come forward, a trembling shook her, deep into her middle.

"I present as candidate for baptism the one known as Pocahuntas, also among her people as Mato'aka, henceforth known as Rebecca. We have reviewed with her the order of service and the sacrament of baptism, but to assist with translation, we have asked young Master Savage to stand by as well. May it never be said that she did not fully comprehend all that was taking place, that she has taken the name of Christ under duress or in ignorance."

He led her through the questions and answers, all of which they had thoroughly discussed already. But now—this was the moment when she would declare it in sight of all the Tassantassas.

This was the moment when it became real. . .and irrevocable.

A dozen fears assailed her. What was she doing? Why was she here? And more, why did she so meekly submit herself to this?

And then she recalled unrelenting light, and a Voice that resonated through her being like thunder.

Yes, she would do this. Yes, she believed. Yes, she would renounce the Devil and all his works. Would turn to Jesus Christ and accept Him as her Savior, put her whole trust in His grace and love, and promise to follow and obey Him as her Lord.

At last she was bid kneel, and water was poured over her bent head, three times. She stood again, to receive the sign of the cross on her forehead and covered breast.

" 'Wherefore, henceforth know we no man after the flesh, yea though we had known Christ after the flesh, yet not henceforth we know him no more. Therefore if any man be in Christ, let him be a new creature. Old things are passed away: behold, all things are become new. And all things are of God, which hath reconciled us unto himself by Jesus Christ, and hath given unto us the ministry of reconciliation.'

"Let us now greet Rebecca, formerly known in the flesh as Pocahuntas, now our sister in Christ."

She had been told it was a most solemn occasion, but she could not stop a fierce grin. She had never felt more clean, more alive.

A new creature, indeed!

After, several embraced her—Ann, Whitaker, even Thomas, and then John. A small feast was laid to celebrate the occasion.

Now they must only wait for word from Nohsh before proceeding with the wedding.

On the ninth day after they left Matchcot, a shout went up that a delegation had arrived from Powhatan. With much delight Mato'aka greeted her uncle Opechisco and both Tomakin and Nantaquas again. "Your mother and sisters greatly longed to come as well," Tomakin said, "but we judged the peace between us too new as of yet for the women and children to make the journey."

"I understand," she murmured. "It gives me much joy that you are all here, at least."

Opechisco presented her with a gift from Nohsh—a great string of pearls, each one as big as her thumbnail. A feast was laid for her guests, and the wedding was set to take place the next morning.

Her uncle questioned the absence of a feast and dancing that night, but she explained they'd have both the next day.

Later, she questioned both of them on their thoughts about the marriage, and on Nohsh's thoughts, whether they truly thought it permissible. Tomakin gave her but a grave look, Nantaquas only rolled his eyes, but Opechisco touched her cheek and shoulder and assured her that under the circumstances—she had been taken captive, to begin with, and how many times had the women instructed her on surviving that?—she could proceed. Among their own people, she might be required to mourn another year or more, but here, with the Tassantassas? Their ways were different, perhaps. And did this Chawnrolfe have another wife?

She explained about the death of John's first wife and baby daughter. Opechisco nodded thoughtfully and said he was sure she would be a comfort to him.

And her desire to be a sign of the peace between their peoples was certainly a worthy thing to give herself to.

About dusk, preparation was made for them all to retire. Mato'aka asked for her family to stay in her own house, but as they were settling in, John appeared at the door. "Since we are to be wed tomorrow, may I beg a few minutes of my bride?"

With a smile, he beckoned her outside. "Come for a walk. Just a short one."

He took her hand and led her toward the church. "There is nowhere in this town to steal even a moment alone. And I've no wish to cast out your guests."

Catching the gist of what he said—she thought—she laughed, but not without uncertainty. What was he about?

The sunset glimmered in his eyes as he smiled down at her. "The good reverend is allowing us to step briefly inside the church."

He turned the latch, and the great wooden door gave with only a slight creak. Inside, he pulled it nearly to and then faced her, taking both of her hands in his.

"You—shake," she murmured at the tremor in his touch.

He gave the merest laugh. "Yes." He drew a quick breath, then, "You are certain about tomorrow? That you wish to marry me?"

Ah, so that was it. Koko'um had also trembled, now that she thought about it.

"Yes."

He leaned toward her. "There is a thing—at the end of the marriage ceremony. They will ask me to kiss you." His eyes were great pools of dark, faintly shining, in the shadows. "Have you—that is, do your people—"

With a huff, he turned a little and shook his head. Not knowing the proper words herself, she must only wait.

"It is—I press my lips to yours. I suppose it is better shown than told."

A giggle escaped her throat. "A mother will do so to her child." She reached up to curve her hand about his neck. "Like so."

Panic flared in his face a moment before she pressed her lips first to his cheek, then his forehead.

"This?" she asked.

The unease bled into amusement, then something like longing. "No, more like this."

His hand cradled her face, and he bent, fitting his mouth to hers. It was not merely a press, but a caress—lingering and then gone.

His face hovered, the tip of his nose very close to hers. Were the light better, she could see the green in his eyes.

"That is not so bad," she breathed. "Why do you fear?"

He straightened, slowly, with another half smile. "I did not wish you to be startled tomorrow."

When he began to move away, she reached out and caught his sleeve. He stopped, looking at her.

It was very like the moment when she'd given him her true name. How many more such moments would they have, as they learned to know each other better?

In this one, she hardly even knew what it was she wanted. "Kiss—again?" was all she could manage.

He moved in and accommodated her, until they were both breathless and trembling, and her head felt light and swimmy.

"Tomorrow," he said at last, stepping away. "No more until tomorrow. Now let us go walk outdoors by the river for a short while, then I will see you back to your house."

The day of their wedding dawned at last.

Opechisco would stand in place of Mato'aka's father during the wedding, while her brothers stood as witnesses for their people. After the feast and dancing that evening, they would leave on the tide for Bermuda Hundred, for the planting season was hard upon them.

John readied himself after spending half the morning already in prayer and fasting. Oh, how he wished this to not merely be a match agreed to for duty alone—as much as he'd insisted it was not to satisfy fleshly lust. Although, their shared kisses the night before had sorely tested his resolve in that. Was there room in the middle, however, for honest love between them? Would she even accept him in all ways after having been violated by other Englishmen? 'Twas not something they'd talked of yet. Why had he not thought of doing so the night before? Kissing her had addled his thoughts, for certain, and no matter how pliant she had been in response, 'twas best if he not go into this marriage expecting that which she could not bring herself to give—and he'd certainly not force her.

On the other hand, her expressions toward him in the past several days were tender enough.

How did one cross the gap of language and custom to make a marriage?

In the meantime he was the object of much ribald jesting. 'Twas no different, he supposed, when he and Sarah had wed, but for some reason, this time felt far worse, possibly for all that Mato'aka had suffered.

Mato'aka. . .no, Rebecca. He must remind himself again of the name she'd taken. Scarcely had he grown accustomed to the musical name of the Naturals before she'd chosen a new one for her baptism. Not that it wasn't a right queenly and pleasing name. It simply wasn't how he'd come to know her.

Oh Lord, help me to love her and be a good husband.

He'd prayed that prayer at least a score of times, perhaps two.

When it was time, there was no fanfare, not even any music. He walked to the front of the church where Reverend Bucke stood in his sober black suit, with Sir Thomas Dale, Reverend Whitaker, and Thomas Savage in attendance. Mistress Leaver slipped into a seat at the front, smiling.

And then entered the Powhatan contingent, one brother going before, Mato'aka-Rebecca herself walking alongside her uncle, and the other brother coming behind. All dressed in what he recognized as their own finery—except that Rebecca wore a gown of English make, with the pearls from her father looped about her neck and draping her neat breast, and an abundance of flowers fastened in her hair.

Her gaze sought and held his immediately, and her smile flashed to answer his own.

Up to the front Opechisco led her, Nantaquas and Tomakin moving aside to flank them.

"Who gives this woman to marry this man?" the minister said.

Thomas translated. Opechisco responded, his voice a deep rumble.

"Her father, Wahunsenecawh, mamanatowic of the Powhatan."

'Twas slow, but this way, all in attendance could understand.

John stepped forward, and with grave courtesy, Opechisco placed Rebecca's hand into John's. Her dark eyes flared and sparkled at his touch.

All three Indians withdrew a little but remained standing. Would they truly allow this marriage to take place, or were they merely uncomfortable with sitting?

John left the guarding of the ceremony to others who also stood about and turned his full attention upon Rebecca, her luminous beauty and the softness of her hands in his. The minister gave his sermon then led them through the proper exchanges. All of Rebecca's responses were clear and very correct.

Whitaker had prepared her well for this, in addition to the baptism.

How was it that this lovely creature was soon to be his wife?

Thank You, most gracious God, for bringing us to this time!

It was both like her wedding to Koko'um, and unlike. Her stern and proud Powhatan husband had become strangely tender with her, and with their son, and the look in the eyes of this Tassantassa—the one who had sheltered her, provided for her, protected her, demanding nothing in return—held the same depth of feeling.

A full turn of the leaves it had been since she had seen or embraced one husband. And now, she was taking another.

It was strange, how many words they used in their binding ceremony. There were blessings and prayers that attended a Tunapewoc wedding, of course. But nothing of the promises made between the husband and wife. John seemed not disturbed in the least by saying he would love her and be true to her for an entire lifetime, until death might separate them. How could he promise this, much less keep it?

She did not doubt, however, that he intended to. Had she ever met a man more sincere of heart and purpose?

And then it seemed all was completed.

"Now that John and Rebecca have given themselves to each other by solemn vows, with the joining of hands, I pronounce that they are husband and wife, in the Name of the Father, and of the Son, and of the Holy Spirit. Those whom God hath joined together let none put asunder. Let us pray together. Our Father which art in heaven, hallowed be Thy name. Thy kingdom come. Thy will be done even in earth as it is in heaven. Give us this day our daily bread. And forgive us our debts, as we also forgive our debtors. And lead us not into temptation, but deliver us from evil: for Thine is the kingdom, and the power, and the glory for ever. Amen." She closed her eyes while the words were spoken. She now knew the prayer they closed with at every Sunday service, but it still drew a chill of awe across her skin—and spirit.

Truly this God was the Great Mamanatowic! And how wondrous that she could feel His presence.

When the prayer finished, the minister hesitated with a wry smile, then continued, "Let the bridegroom greet his bride."

Her eyes fluttered open again. This was the moment John had warned her about. He flashed a quick grin, then bent—and she tipped her head to meet his kiss, just—so. Warm and very sweet.

Those attending broke out with clapping and cheering. Her brothers and uncle likewise raised a shout of joy, as was the custom of her own people.

John held on to her hand as they left the church and went to the feast that had been prepared. The same tremor she had felt the night before coursed through him again, and every so often he would look down at her and smile.

After the feast, the music began, and she let John lead her out for that as well. As had happened while at Bermuda Hundred, the day he'd returned from shipping the harvests to Jamestowne, other men asked to dance opposite her, but John always reclaimed his place.

The day passed very pleasantly, with many well wishes from the people of the town, not least of all Dale himself. She was conscious of both John and Thomas hovering, as if to protect her from any untoward attention—and indeed, she was grateful, as it seemed a few of the men tried to be just a little too familiar.

She would be glad when they returned upriver.

As the day wore away, John was drawn off to the side to discuss their time of travel, and Ann approached her. "Pocahuntas—Rebecca—I hardly know what to call you now," the older woman said, laughing.

"Rebecca," she answered with a smile.

"Well. Dear girl, regardless. If we are leaving in the wee hours of the morning, you should try to rest."

Rebecca looked back over her shoulder toward John. She would not, however much she trusted others, go anywhere without him today.

Ann chuckled. "Just as I thought."

"Oh?" Rebecca asked, but Ann only laughed again and shook her head.

Ann waited with her until John was finished speaking, then, with a little smile, she bid them both come. John also hesitated until she said, "'Tis but a few hours until we depart, yes? But until then, there is nothing pressing—and the two of you can snatch a few hours' sleep."

John shot a panicked glance at Rebecca, but she was the one this time to tug on his hand. "Come. Sleep is good."

Her own heart was pounding, however, at the prospect of being truly alone with John. With her husband. Whose kisses had stirred things she had only ever felt with Koko'um.

Ann ushered them to the house Rebecca had shared with her and her Powhatan family. The bed that the two women had shared was fluffed and remade, and her uncle's and brothers' belongings, and Ann's, had been removed. John's haversack lay beside her own.

"Go on," Ann said. "Thomas and I will make sure none disturb you until it's time to leave."

John shut the door and leaned back against it, his eyes round and dark in the dimly lit room. Rebecca reached up to begin removing the flowers from her hair, most of them now wilted, but cast him little glances.

At last he came toward her, and both his hands were trembling as he cupped them around her head. "Will you"—he swallowed—"let me love you and make you fully my wife?"

She hoped he could see her heart in her eyes as she leaned into his touch. "Yes."

Most assuredly yes. But she did not know yet how to say that.

He swooped in, both fervent and gentle, and very much made good on the sweetness of his kisses.

May 1614

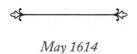

Spring flowed into the beginnings of summer. The crops were planted, and as they grew and flourished, so did the colony, it seemed. All strife ceased between the English and the Powhatan—indeed, all their neighbors. John heard in a brief visit from Rafe Hamor that negotiations had taken place even with the Chicahamania, who made a great show of placing themselves under the English, as subjects and allies.

Rebecca herself appeared contented. John decided shortly after their return to Bermuda Hundred that he would reinstate the morning bathing in the river, since she was now his wife and none could gainsay him. Furthermore, he joined her. Often they went before the sun had properly risen and while the mist cloaked the surface of the water. He was finding it as beneficial to his own refreshment as it was for her.

The only blight upon it all was that Sir Dale had taken it into his head to send to the Powhatan—to Rebecca's father, Wahunsenecawh—and ask for Rebecca's younger sister to wife for himself. The man had a wife in England! How did he think this permissible, much less righteous?

Rebecca stiffened as she heard the news then turned away, muttering something in her own tongue. Hamor lifted a brow at her reaction then spread his hands. "I only carry the message." Hamor was also instructed to take Thomas with him. It could not be helped, he supposed. He and Rebecca had been managing well enough, but the young man's skill with the Naturals' tongue still proved invaluable time and again.

"Well, if Wahunsenecawh has any sense," John said, "he will refuse."

Rebecca whirled and shot him a sudden smile.

"I think 'tis safe to say my wife is in agreement," he added with a wry laugh.

Hamor laughed too, a little nervously. "I shall keep that in mind."

She rattled off a long sentence, and at a loss, Hamor turned to Thomas, who looked suddenly discomfited. "Rebecca asks, why does Dale want her to wife when she is not yet, to Rebecca's knowledge, even of age? Does he truly wish to marry a child? That is very much not proper amongst her people."

Hamor had the good grace to look abashed. "Oh—well—he is willing to wait for her to be of age. Of course."

Rebecca glowered and then shook her head.

John still failed to see how Dale could think it even remotely fitting, either as a husband already or as a Christian. And how did Hamor think it acceptable to be the one presenting the request?

"Winganuske, there is a matter of which we need to speak."

The rumble of Wahunsenecawh's voice in the smoky darkness, close beside her, brought her back to full wakefulness.

"I have had a request from a neighboring weroance. He wishes to marry Little Flower—after huskanasqua, of course. But what is your thought?"

The last of her girls to be grown and make a family of her own? It gave her heart a pang.

She tipped her head so she could see his face. "It is the purpose to which we rear them to womanhood. To marry and be part of the life of the True People."

He nodded, rubbing one thumb against his chin.

"What causes you to hesitate?" she asked.

He had been known often enough to make a decision on his own, without asking the thoughts of the wife in question. Although he'd been kind enough where Mato'aka was concerned, and seeking her opinions on things even for Channa.

"The world is changing," he said at last. "And this past year has been very hard on all of us, with Mato'aka being taken. The Tassantassas press ever harder. Even the Chicahamania have sworn service to them." He flopped one hand, a gesture of frustration. "I am loath to send one of my youngest daughters so far away."

"Who is asking for her?"

"The chief weroance of Mattapani."

"Not so very far. . ."

"Yet too far for my heart." He peered askance at her. "I am not so young as I once was."

She smoothed a hand down his arm, still as muscled as she always recalled. "Yet you have lost none of your strength."

He smiled and arched his brows, preening as he always did under her praise, but with an edge of sadness she had also seen more of late.

"Perhaps let him know it will yet be some moons—"

A rustle and a pattering warned them of another's approach, and outside the yehakan one of the guards said, "Mamanatowic, I beg pardon. There are visitors."

"Come in," Wahunsenecawh answered.

A young warrior ducked inside. "Word has just come of two Tassantassas sent upon business to you from their weroance. They called for a kanoe and are coming across the river even now." He paused. "One of them is Tommasavach."

"Waugh! After so long?" He exchanged a glance with Winganuske, then rose from his bed. "We will talk of this later."

A mantle wrapped about her, she stepped outside to watch him. Rather than head for his yehakan, he set off toward the river's edge in his usual long stride, tossing commands as he went for his wives and guards to all assemble and for food to be prepared.

Was he as eager for news of Mato'aka as she, that he'd break from his customary manner of receiving visitors and go to greet them in person?

Chapter Nineteen

Would they have word of Mato'aka?

He should not go out to greet them himself. Of course, he had many strong warriors at his back—they'd all fallen in behind him as he crossed through the town—but it was beneath his dignity and position to not insist they come to him. But somehow he could not resist going out to watch them arrive.

The splash of paddles told him the kanoe was just reaching the riverbank. Inside were four Tunapewoc and two Tassantassas, illuminated by the torches held by his guards. He did not recognize the one, obviously older, but the younger—

"Tommasavach!" he called out, as they stepped out of the kanoe.

The boy—rather a young man now, sporting the beard many of the Tassantassas wore—looked up, grinned, and waved an arm, then hurried up the hill.

"My child, you are welcome!" he exclaimed, as Tommasavach reached him.

"I thank you, Mamanatowic! How good it is to see you again."

"You have been a stranger to me these four years! I gave you leave to go to Paspahae to see your friends, and you have not returned until now? You are my child, given me by Captain Newport, in exchange for my subject Namontac. And him I purposely sent to King James, to see him and his country and to return me the true report of it all—but neither has he yet returned, even though many ships have arrived here from there. So I know not how you have dealt with him."

Tommasavach seemed to blanch a little at the mention of Namontac. That could not bode well.

Why would these people not give him the truth if they knew it?

He turned then to the other Tassantassa. He was not wearing the chain of pearls given to Sir Thomas Dale as a sign of those sent by him, as instructed. Perhaps it was merely hidden beneath his apparel, under his beard.

Wahunsenecawh stepped close and felt around the man's neck, inside his shirt. The man's mouth fell open, and his eyes widened, but he held still, at least, under the search.

"Where is the chain of pearl?" he asked the man.

The Tassantassa stammered and looked at Tommasavach, who translated. "What chain?"

"The one I sent my brother Sir Thomas Dale for a present, at his first arrival. The chain he said, after our peace was concluded, if he sent any of his men to conduct any business to me, he should wear about his neck, otherwise I had order from him to bind him and send him home as a runaway."

The Tassantassa opened and shut his mouth again but seemed to compose himself. He rattled off an unreasonably long explanation, and once again the boy translated. "I am not unaware of that message from your brother, but he intended that if upon extraordinary and sudden occasion, he should be constrained to send an English man to you without an Indian guide, then in testimony that he sent him he should wear the chain about his neck. But in case any of your own people should conduct any English to you, as did me, two of your own men, one of them a councilor to you, who was acquainted with my business, their testimony should be sufficient and the chain need not be worn."

Well, that was clever enough, even if likely untrue. He must give the man credit for thinking quickly.

Tommasavach looked as if he wanted to roll his eyes but dared not. "This is Rafe Hamor, a man of Jamestowne who sees to the writing of any happening of importance. He was indeed sent by Sir Thomas Dale."

"Come then, and I will hear more," Wahunsenecawh said, and led on to his yehakan. He looked the boy up and down again. "Tommasavach, you are well?"

"I am very well. And are you also well?"

Wahunsenecawh smiled and nodded. They ducked inside, and he took his usual seat on his bed, motioning to two of the younger wives to sit on either side of him. The other women, already present, arrayed themselves as usual in two lines facing each other, with the guards all around.

Tommasavach instructed the newcomer on where to sit while one of the women prepared a pipe of uppowoc. Wahunsenecawh smoked of it first then handed it to the newcomer. At least the man knew what to do with it. He lingered appropriately over it before offering it back.

Wahunsenecawh took it from him. "How does my brother Sir Thomas Dale fare?"

"Very well," was the reply.

"And what of my daughter's welfare? Her marriage, and my unknown son? How do they like, live, and love together?"

He had heard from Opechisco, Tomakin, and Nantaquas that the Tassantassa she married loved her and was one of perhaps very few honorable men among them, but he wished it confirmed from another.

Tommasavach's face grew very lively as he related what the other Tassantassa said. "He says she is so well content that she would not change her life to return and live with you, Mamanatowic."

Wahunsenecawh could not help it—he laughed at that, long and heartily. "And is it so, my son?"

"I cannot say it is as true as he says, but she seems well content with her husband. He is truly a good man and cares well for her. I had opportunity to spend much of the past year with them."

"Tell him I am very glad of it. And now please tell me the cause of your unexpected coming."

The Tassantassa responded, and Tommasavach repeated, "The message is private, to be delivered only to yourself, without the presence of any except the one of your councilors here, Pepaschechar, who has also served as our guide and is acquainted with this business."

Wahunsenecawh gave a sigh then waved a hand. "All of you go, men and women, except for the two next to me."

When they had gone, the Tassantassa said, with Tommasavach interpreting, "Sir Thomas Dale, your brother, the principal weroance of the Englishmen here, sends you greetings of love and peace, on his part inviolable, and has in testimony of this sent you a worthy present by my hand—that is, two large pieces of copper, five strings of white and blue beads, five wooden combs, ten fish hooks, and a pair of knives."

As he spoke, the Tassantassa unpacked a bag at his side and pulled the items out, one by one, handing each to him in turn so Wahunsenecawh and the two women might look at them as long as they liked. Wahunsenecawh set them at his feet in a row and nodded for him to continue.

"Sir Thomas Dale also willed me to promise you, whenever you are pleased to send men to fetch it, he will give you a great grinding stone."

At last! How long ago had he requested just this thing, which would make the work of preparing apon easier for the women.

"And now, great Powhatan, the word of the exquisite perfection of your youngest daughter, being famous throughout all your territories, has come to the hearing of your brother Sir Thomas Dale, who for his purpose has sent me here, to entreat you by that brotherly friendship you yourself make profession of, to permit her to return with me to him—"

"What is this?" Wahunsenecawh said, but the Tassantassa kept speaking.

"—partly because he desires it so and partly because her sister desires to see her. And if her fame is truth, which we are sure it has been, your brother—by your favor—would gladly make her his nearest companion, wife and bedfellow—"

Wahunsenecawh sat forward and opened his mouth again to speak, but once again the man kept going.

Tommasavach's face colored a deep crimson. "He entreats you to hear him out, and then if you please to return him an answer."

He huffed. "Very well." And he made a sharp, derisive gesture for him to continue.

"And the reason for this is, because being now friendly and firmly united together, and made one people—as he supposes and believes—in the band of love, he would make a natural union between us, principally since he himself has taken resolution to dwell in your country so long as he lives, and would therefore not only have the firmest assurance he may, of perpetual friendship from you, but also hereby bind himself to you."

Wahunsenecawh straightened. For all that Opechancanough had expressed admiration, this one was as bad as Chawnzmit ever had been in willfulness and insult. And the one sent as messenger, doubly so!

"I gladly accept your weroance's salute of love and peace," he said, forcing his expression to patience, "which while I live I shall ensure both myself and my subjects maintain and conserve. His pledges I receive with no less thanks, although they are not so generous as those customarily offered me by a greater weroance, Captain Newport, whom I very well love. But the purpose you spoke of, my daughter whom my brother desires, she is promised as wife to a great weroance for two bushels of rahrenoc. It is true she is already gone with him, three days' journey from me."

Hamor spoke, and Tommasavach again looked as if the words pained him. "I know your greatness and power to be such that if you pleased to gratify your brother in this, you might bring home your daughter again, restoring the rahrenoc without any hurt to justice, since she is not a full twelve years old and therefore not marriageable. You would then have, in addition to the bond of peace, triple the price of your daughter, in beads, copper, hatchets, and many other things more useful to you."

Wahunsenecawh eyed the boy he truly did regard as his own son. He hoped Tommasavach might not get sick right here in his yehakan.

The other man—plain enough as Tassantassas went, with hair pulled back at his nape beneath the strange hat the men always wore—sat regarding him expectantly, his face full of pride and cunning, seemingly unaware of the great insult he heaped upon Wahunsenecawh.

What a mistake it had been to regard Sir Thomas Dale as a brother and not a son! Such a one did not merit being regarded as an equal.

"I love my daughter as dear as my own life," he said, "and though I have many children, I delight in none so much as her. If I could not see her often, I could not possibly live—which if she lived with you, I know I could not. I have resolved to never, for any reason whatsoever, put myself into your hands or come amongst you. So I tell you, do not ask me again for this thing. You may return this answer to my brother."

He shook his head and went on. "I desire no firmer assurance of his friendship than the promise he has already made to me—and he already has this pledge from me, one of my daughters to live amongst you, who shall be sufficient as long as she lives. When she dies, he might have another child from me, but she still lives. I hold it not brotherly on the part of your weroance to bereave me of two of my children at once.

"Further give him to understand that even if he had no pledge at all, he should not need to fear any injury from me or any under my subjection. There have been too many of his men and mine killed, and on my part there shall never be more. I who have power to perform it have said it. No, not even should I have just occasion offered, for I am now old and would gladly end my days in peace. So if the Inqutish offer me injury, my country is large enough, I will remove myself farther from you. I hope this much will satisfy my brother.

"Now, because you yourselves are weary, and I am sleepy, we will thus end talking of this business."

The Tassantassa looked unsatisfied, but after Tommasavach spoke to him, he nodded. Wahunsenecawh called one of his men and sent him to find food for their guests. "We did not expect your coming, and as is our custom, we ate the day's provisions, but something shall be prepared for you soon."

He made himself wait until the bread had been brought in, a full basket of boiled rounds about half the size of a man's fist. Tommasavach and Hamor ate some and then dispersed the rest to the guards. Wahunsenecawh then sent for the glass flask of strong drink that Captain Newport had given him some seven years before, which he had kept for such occasions as this. Tipping a small amount into an oyster shell, he gave them each a drink in turn, ordered that lodging should be prepared, and then took his leave.

Winganuske either had lain awake for him or roused easily, expecting him, for she sat up when he entered her yehakan. "Well? What tidings do they bring?"

He stretched himself beside her and drew her body close against his. What sweet comfort she was to him—even now, even after so many years. He released a long breath.

"Tommasavach is well enough. Our daughter—she is by their account very well, and very happy with her new husband. Of all that I am glad. But the other Tassantassa? He is either a pompous dog, or he truly does not realize what he requests." He huffed. "And Sir Thomas Dale is no different. I am very much sorry I ever called him 'brother' instead of 'son,' as I did Chawnzmit."

"Why? What has he done?"

He sighed again. "He wishes our youngest daughter to wife."

Winganuske nearly came upright in his arms. "What is this? Mahta!"

A chuckle escaped him. "That is what I said. I also told him she was already promised to another weroance, three days' journey from here, and that I'd received two baskets of rahrenoc for her."

"Wahunsenecawh."

The chiding tone of her voice drew more laughter from him, then he sighed. "I told him I could not bear to let her go where I could not see her often. So I suppose that settles the matter."

She leaned into him again. "I also could not bear that."

"He had the temerity to claim that Mato'aka is so well content that she wishes never to come live here again."

"And what did you say to that?"

"I laughed. Long and hard. The man is ridiculous." A yawn took him and near split his jaws. "We will provide all hospitality in the morning. But for now, let us sleep."

He surprised her the next morning by continuing to not follow his former insistence on proper ceremony. Rising at daylight, after he had washed in the river, he went himself to greet their guests, again.

Winganuske was up already, cooking. Their guests were sleeping on their mats, but out under a tree instead of in the house that had been given to them. One of the other women giggled and whispered to her that they'd been given a house so infested with fleas, the former occupants had recently moved out. Apparently even Tassantassas were not dirty enough to endure such things, either.

She shook her head and laughed as well. Such a prank would be lost on them—as many such pranks had been over the years—but that would not stop the People from doing them.

The bread was finished cooking—the peas and beans as well, which had been put on to simmer last night as soon as their guests arrived—so those were carried to Wahunsenecawh's house, where he had seated the guests after going out to ask after their welfare. A little later, the fish they'd caught first thing were also finished, and then the oysters and crabs.

By that time it was midmorning, and the hunters returned with both deer and turkeys, which were immediately dressed and set to roast.

In between, their guests emerged again and wandered about the town. The older Englishman, Rafe Hamor, gave a great exclamation and fell into conversation with a young man who appeared in all ways as one of the True People—as Winganuske herself did—after having been taken a few years before. As the two talked, Thomas sidled over to her. "Winganuske, are you well?"

She straightened and greeted him with a smile. "I am very well, Thomas. And you? We have missed you!"

"I am very well." He scratched his beard with one fingertip. "So are you truly sister to Machumps?"

She laughed. "That is what is said, yes."

"He is not very well liked by some of us. I think he is not to be trusted, but he continues to insinuate himself with those he thinks will favor him." Thomas's mouth flattened.

"I am not surprised," she murmured. "But enough of him. Does my daughter indeed fare as well as they say? We heard. . .troubling things, during the last year."

A rueful smile flitted across the young man's face. How grown up he appeared now! "Indeed she does. Early on, yes, there were terrible things. Some of the English behaved most dishonorably. John, the one who became her husband, determined to protect her and keep anything else from happening. It was also he who insisted we send for her family." He peered at Winganuske. "I am surprised you did not also come."

"I had to remain behind and care for the small children." She pointed to one of the little boys running about. "That is Little Fox, her son with Koko'um. Tell her for me, please, that he also does well."

"I will most gladly do so."

She held her breath for a moment. Did she dare say this next thing to him?

"I also heard that—she has chosen to follow the Tassantassa's God."

He nodded slowly, as if measuring her reaction. "She was baptized a Christian just a few days before her marriage."

A huff escaped her. She pressed the heel of her hand to her breastbone. "It is good," she managed to say, at last.

Thomas's brows lifted. "Truly? I did not expect you to respond thus."

"No, that is—I—" How much dared she reveal? "I also believe in the Christ," she said, barely above a whisper. "Tell her so."

"What? How did you come to that?" Even in his astonishment, Thomas also kept his voice quiet. He looked around, as if not wishing to be overheard. "Was it through John Smith?"

She shook her head, hard. "I—I cannot tell you."

Speculation warred with amazement upon his face. "I did not know that any believed, before her."

She too glanced around, but they were alone in the space before her yehakan. She folded her arms and faced him.

The long-held secret was bursting within her. And if even one soul could know, or at least guess. . .

"My belief, it was long held. From my childhood." She leaned toward him slightly. "I may have become one of the True People, but. . .I have not forgotten."

As he gained comprehension, his eyes widened and his mouth fell open.

"You must tell no one. No one! Perhaps not even Mato'aka herself. But you can say to her, well was she chosen to be the binding between worlds and peoples."

Thomas blinked, his eyes suddenly glossy. "You were of the Roanoac Colony."

She gave the barest nod.

He sucked in a deep breath. "I will bear your word to her. Oh, and she is now known as Rebecca. Do you recall from where the name comes?"

Winganuske let herself smile. "Wife to Isaac. Mother of Esau and Jacob."

Thomas bent his head, suddenly overcome.

"Ai, Thomas! Do not weep. God has kept me here and given me a good place." Her smile deepened, though tears stung her own eyes and blurred her vision. "What better than to be favorite wife of mamanatowic?"

He laughed brokenly. "Such—strange turn of events."

"Yes."

The other Englishman came running over at that moment, exclaiming with such energy that she could scarce follow his words. "Thomas,

Thomas! Look, 'tis William Parker, whom we thought lost these past three years!" He indicated a young man who appeared a perfect Powhatan warrior, but who was grinning and nodding. "Come, we must go entreat Powhatan to let him go home with us."

Hamor seemed then to realize that he had interrupted something, for he stopped and looked at Thomas more closely, then Winganuske. "Thomas, is something amiss?"

"No, indeed, it is very well." Thomas swiped a forearm across his face as if he were merely sweating then indicated Winganuske. "This is Rebecca's mother. I was merely relating to her the finer points of her daughter's situation."

"Oh." There were equal parts astonishment and admiration in Hamor's voice as he took her in more fully—his gaze lingering of course upon her bare shoulder and arm, all that lay uncovered by her doeskin tunic, which she wore purposefully with Englishmen about—then he bowed. "'Tis an honor to meet you, lady."

With a wry smile, Thomas translated—not that he needed to, but they must keep up appearances.

"Thank you for bearing us word of her," Winganuske said.

A gleam came into Hamor's eyes. "You would not perhaps consider entreating your husband for your younger daughter, on behalf of Sir Thomas Dale. . .?"

"Mahta. What he has said is true, that we cannot bear to part with her so far away." She put every bit of haughty disdain she had learned from twenty years among the Powhatan into the words.

Thomas fought a grin as he delivered their meaning and then added as if to Hamor alone, "You cannot say you were not warned."

This Tassantassa—Rafe Hamor—was now far more than annoying. He was infuriating.

Hamor had discovered that one of the young warriors come back from hunting, formerly a captive from the area where Wahunsenecawh had been born—and even now Mato'aka and her husband made their home—was indeed Tassantassa as well, despite his adoption of Powhatan ways and dress, from the arranging of his hair to the painting of his skin. *Wil-yam-par-kur* had been his name, and he was all overjoyed to find another Tassantassa in the town. Hamor likewise exclaimed his surprise—and Wahunsenecawh knew why, since every time Dale and the others asked about him, the answer given was that he had fallen sick and died.

Now Hamor was begging Wahunsenecawh to let the young man accompany him home. If he did not, Hamor was obligated to tell Sir Thomas Dale his brother that he had seen William Parker there, and they would then make another journey here for the purpose of fetching him.

His patience broke at last. "You have one of my daughters with you, and I am well content with that. But you Tassantassas can no sooner see or know of any Inqutish being with me, but you must have him away, or else break peace and friendship. If you must have him, he shall go, but I will send no guides along with you. So if any ill befall you along the way, thank yourselves."

Hamor looked as if he had been struck. "I would go alone rather than go without him. I know the way well enough, and other dangers I fear not, since if I do not return safely, you must expect our revenge upon you and your people. In fact, your brother our weroance might have just occasion to distrust your love to me, by your slight respect of me, if you return me home without guides."

Too furious to speak, Wahunsenecawh turned sharply from the man and strode away without bothering to reply. If he stayed, he might indeed open the man's throat.

By suppertime he had cooled enough to summon his unexpected and now most unwanted guests—Thomas notwithstanding—to his house to share his own meal. Tommasavach looked most chagrined but, as before, Hamor appeared oblivious.

They ate, yet he refused to say anything regarding any of Hamor's requests. After they had well eaten, he sent them to their lodgings as before. He stretched out on his bed, alone, after sending away two or three of his younger wives who importuned him.

Much might rest upon how he answered this matter. Knowing the Tassantassas, nearly anything he said or did would doubtless be misunderstood and twisted to mean something completely apart from what he intended.

He prayed for a while, but O'ki gave him no insight.

At last, after it was well dark, he rose and, trailing a pair of guards, went to where the two Inqutish lay again under their tree. He bent and shook Tommasavach. "My son, wake up. I have need to speak with your companion."

Tommasavach sat up, rubbing his eyes, then nudged the older man until he stirred as well. Wahunsenecawh stepped back a pace and folded his arms. "Tell him this. In the morning, Pepaschechar and another of my men will accompany you home. You must convey my request to my brother for these things in particular. Ten pieces of copper, a shaving knife, an iron wedge to cleave apart boards, a grinding stone—one not so big but four or five men may carry it, which is big enough for my use. Also two bone combs such as Captain Newport gave me, for the wooden ones my own men can make. Lastly, a hundred fish hooks, or if he can rather spare it, a fishing seine, and a cat and a dog. If he can provide me these things, I will return his love with a quantity of skins. I am now unfurnished with those but will have them at a later time."

Hamor rubbed his hand across his face again, peering at Wahunsenecawh with frank disbelief.

He did not care—let the man think what he would. "Will you remember every particular?"

"I will remember," Hamor answered.

"Tell me again the list."

Hamor did so, to his faint surprise. Wahunsenecawh grunted a little then said, "Come. I wish you to write it down in a book I will show you."

He led them through the town, mostly dark and quiet, back to his house, where he dug in a basket in one corner until he had found what he desired—a tablet of paper, wrapped in soft doeskin.

Laying it upon the floor near the fire, but not so close that sparks would light upon it, he was satisfied to see the wonder in Hamor's face.

And just as quickly, the expression of the Inqutish turned to more. "I entreat you to let me take this. Such a thing can be of no use to you."

"On the contrary," Wahunsenecawh answered, "it does me much good to show it to strangers who come to me."

With a reluctant nod, Hamor drew a smaller book from his own pocket and wrote the items Wahunsenecawh had specified in both books.

"It is good. Now return to your bed."

After they were gone this time, he fell at last into slumber.

"And after presenting us each with one of these most excellent buckskins, with the two for each of you," Hamor finished, glancing from John to Rebecca, "he himself conducted us to the water side. And so we reached the Bermudas, here, the same night."

Seated beside John, Rebecca sat stroking the tanned deer hide draped across her lap, butter soft and white as snow. She looked up and murmured something to Thomas.

"She wishes to know," Thomas said with a little smile, "if you are mindful of what great honor he has shown you, receiving you himself, and not merely sending for you as he did Captain Smith or others."

Hamor stopped midmotion, lifting a cup to his mouth. His gaze went first to Thomas, then Rebecca, and lastly John.

"'Tis true," John said with a laugh. "He would not even deign to see me when I was there two months ago."

Rebecca said something else, and Thomas chuckled this time. "He did not know you were to become his son."

"There were other extenuating circumstances," John said, and took a sip of his own watered ale.

He'd certainly not fault his father-in-law for seeking to protect women and children. But Hamor must surely be made to realize the unusual nature of the hospitality he'd just enjoyed.

"He is mistrustful and jealous," Hamor complained. "Professing welcome but then becoming angry and difficult when all I did was make most reasonable requests."

All three of them bent raised brows toward him.

"Well, except for the one regarding his daughter. I am not unsympathetic to the plight of an aging parent." Hamor buried his face in his cup a moment then flashed a glance upward. "I do not relish having to take these tidings to Sir Dale, however."

How could a simple deerskin make her miss them so fiercely?

She let the conversation flow over her, the account by this man who most certainly was not aware of how closely he trod the edge of what Nohsh would tolerate from a stranger.

Nohsh must surely have softened indeed, as it was.

Her eyes burned. John made her very happy—truly—but oh, how hard it was to hear the grief and longing of her father, clear even in Hamor's telling of all that had taken place in Matchcot.

Hamor retired to bed, but she could not even think of sleeping.

. . .I am old and only wish to live out my life in peace.

"Rebecca," Thomas said, and she looked up to find him lingering at the table. "Your mother asked me to pass on her greetings, and to say that Little Fox is doing well."

The tears did spill at that. "Thank you," she said, but he did not move away.

"There is—more." He cleared his throat. "She is glad you believe in Christ. In fact—she wished me to tell you she also believes in Him."

"Waugh! What? How can this be?"

"That is. . .too difficult a story to tell. But be assured that she truly believes. And she said you were well chosen to be the one to join two worlds and two peoples."

Warmth flooded her. To have Nek be approving—to confirm not just one decision but two—it was more comforting and strengthening than she could say.

And it gave her hope that the People—all of her people—might someday believe in Him as well.

"Thank you, again."

For a moment, it seemed he would say more, then he nodded and went out to find his bed elsewhere.

In their bedchamber, John was undressing. He turned as she entered and, without a word, held open his arms for her. She dived into his embrace, leaning as close as she could.

How glad she was for this man. For his tenderness toward her, even when he could not fathom her ways.

"I love you, my wife," he murmured against her hair. "Oh, how I love you."

She burrowed her face into the curve of his neck, breathing in his scent of the outdoors and uppowoc. "I love you as well."

He cradled her against him for a moment then straightened, his eyes sparkling. "How would you like to go out to the river for a quick bath?"

Her breath caught. "I would very much like that."

Chapter Twenty

Bermuda Hundred, Spring 1616

"Thomas! Come here this instant."

The tiny boy considered a moment, sucking one finger, dark eyes wide and wispy dark hair standing on end as always. Then he turned abruptly and took off as fast as his chubby legs, peeking out from beneath his short gown, would carry him.

John ran after him, covering the ground between them speedily enough, and swooped him into his arms. The child squealed with laughter, and he chuckled as well. Little Bermuda had not lived long enough to give him chase, and so he savored these moments.

Little Thomas grinned, the deep dimples in his cheeks and chin reminding John so much of the boy's mama, he could not help but melt. And he'd grown so much since John had been gone these past weeks, finishing his survey of the colony's population.

'Twas an honor to be secretary to the colony after Hamor's departure but also tedious in many ways. John longed to have his hands back in the soil, working again with the crops.

He looked over at the mama in question. Rebecca came toward them, slowly, a smile bringing out the matching dimples in her face. Dark hair hung in a long braid over her shoulder, as she often wore it while working around the plantation, and soft mahkusun peeped out from beneath the skirt of her plain linen gown. Simple and lovely—but 'twas the light in her eyes that illuminated his own heart.

"He loves his papa," she said.

John grinned. "His papa loves him. And his mama."

She slipped close, chuckling, and put an arm about his waist. "His mama loves his papa."

Their kiss was cut short by the wiggling of Thomas trying to get down. They both laughed while John shifted his arm to better hold the squirming child.

"So you have heard from Dale?" Rebecca prompted John to continue relating the contents of his latest letter from the man who was now the colony's governor, which had been interrupted by Thomas darting away.

"Yes. We are to at last make preparation for the voyage to England."

Dale had been talking of this journey since shortly after John and Rebecca were wed. The prospect held mixed feelings for both of them. John looked forward to the opportunity to discuss his tobacco with prospective investors, but he'd no great desire to return to the land of his own birth. And Rebecca—who could blame her for dreading such a long journey by ship?

Even now her eyes rounded.

"We will send for your brother and sister and anyone else your father thinks would serve as a proper retinue for you. About a dozen of your people, I would say." He studied her expression. "Would that please you?"

"Oh, very much!" She smiled, but worry still pinched her expression.

He tucked her against his side again. "I'll be with you the entire way. I'll not let anyone touch you."

She nodded, with less certainty this time.

"You will be the toast of all of London." He'd not share his own misgivings. An entire growing season, away!

"But—what if I do not wish to go?" she murmured.

That he truly could not help. "Then I would not blame you."

"Here are the things I wish you to see to."

With Opechancanough in attendance, Wahunsenecawh sat facing Tomakin, his son by marriage.

"Bring me back a report of what their God looks like. And their mamanatowic, and his woman and son, of whom Chawnzmit told us. Count the people, so we may know how strong they truly are."

Tomakin nodded.

"Oh, and one other thing." He took a long pull from his pipe then blew out the smoke. "Take great care to seek out Chawnzmit. They have ever told us he is dead, but you and I both know the Tassantassas do lie much."

"If it can be done, I shall see to it," Tomakin said.

Wahunsenecawh sat back. How weary did his bones feel these days!

"And tell my daughter I send all my love. I wish she would come soon and visit, but I suppose with Sir Thomas Dale summoning them thus, it will be many moons before that is possible."

"I will carry her both your regards and those of her mother."

"It is good."

After, Winganuske came to him. They sat for a time, only embracing and not speaking.

The ship was every bit as terrifying—but exhilarating—as she expected. The presence of Dale himself, now governor of the colony, and Captain Argall, responsible for her capture to begin with, along with at least two of the men she was sure had violated her, all made her cling most closely to John's side.

Being out upon the deck, however, of this huge, wind-driven kanoe and surveying the expanse of yapám? With the birds crying and the never-ceasing motion of the waves?

How great was God, with everything He had made, and how wide the world! And how continually astonished she was to feel His presence so strongly, since making the decision to commit herself to Him.

Little Thomas was fascinated as well, and very quickly adapted to the pitch and roll of the ship's deck. "O-ho," Dale laughed, as she chased after Thomas, headed for the rail. "There is the boy named after me!"

Nantaquas ran quickly past her and snatched up the child before he came to harm. A thin smile stretched Rebecca's lips, and nearby, John's was likewise polite but cool. In truth they'd taken the name from Thomas Savage, beloved brother that he was, but let Dale think it a tribute to himself, and to their former governor, Thomas Gates.

Thomas had stayed in Tsenacomoco—or Virginia, rather. She had to remind herself to use the English name. How strange it seemed, even now, how numerous the Tassantassas—the English—had become in a few turns of the leaves. But there had indeed been peace between John's people and hers since their marriage, and for that, everyone was grateful.

The alliance was once again a bit strained and uneasy, here aboard ship. So many of them, always bumping into each other, but the presence of Tunapewoc—Nantaquas, Channa, Tomakin, four more women and five more men—was comforting.

And John himself too, of course. She could no more imagine her life without him, now—or this tiny boy they had made between them—than she could stop breathing. Her heart still ached for Koko'um and Little Fox, but this—this was where she was meant to be.

They'd good weather on the way out from Virginia, but John watched the skies with anxiousness building apace with the clouds piling up on the horizon. He remembered vividly the ordeal of the terrible storm that left them upon Bermuda to begin with. 'Twas likely too much to hope for a journey without at least one to catch them up on the way to England.

Rebecca came and wound her arm about John's, where he stood at the rail.

"Where is little Thomas?" he asked.

"Channa has him belowdecks. He should be ready soon for sleep."

"Doubtful. You and I both know how he would happily go days without a rest." After exchanging a smile with her, he returned to his survey of the sky. "I fear we may have a rough night and day of it."

She pressed to his side. "I am not afraid."

"Of course you are not." He leaned his cheek upon her head.

After a moment of quiet, she asked, "Do you also fear seeing your family again? And that of your wife who died?"

He had shared with her how he and Sarah had not departed England on the best of terms with their families. "Somewhat, yes."

Her hand smoothed down his arm. "I am praying."

As night fell, his concerns over the storm proved well founded. Thomas was the first to wake and protest the rolling of the ship, and many of their party grew queasy with the wild motion. John gave himself to constant prayer, and judging by Rebecca's whispering, she did the same.

Two days they were storm-tossed, and then on the third, the seas began to calm, the clouds parted, and the sun shone warmly upon them. John had almost never been more thankful.

More than once, Rebecca found herself doubting they would indeed find land across the great expanse of the ocean—but there it was. Clumps of houses nestled among rugged cliffs draped in green, the stone walls a curiosity as the ship nosed her way into the harbor.

"Is this London?" she asked John, quietly, as they gained the dock.

He smiled. "No, love, but Plymouth. 'Tis the main port for seagoing vessels."

Stepping out upon a surface that did not tip and roll was perhaps the strangest thing she had ever experienced. John carried little Thomas so that she might better find her footing. The next strangest was all the sights—and smells—of the wharfside. She stared about her as Dale spoke with a man come to greet them, but when introduced, she turned and bestowed a smile upon the newcomer, whose name they were told was Sir Lewis Stukeley.

"So you are Lady Rebecca, the very nonpareil of the Powhatan, as Captain John Smith wrote!"

He gave the name of her people a strange pronunciation, but she held her smile steady and dipped her head. "I am pleased to meet you and look upon your country at last."

"You are right courteous, and no mistake!" He gazed about at their party. "Captain Smith will no doubt come as soon as he is able to greet you."

Rebecca felt the blood leave her face, and her heart beat unsteadily and painfully within her breast. "What—but he—we were told he was dead!"

"Captain John Smith? Oh no. He had a grave wound, to be sure, but recovered well enough."

She could not seem to close her mouth as she too turned to the others. "Chawnzmit still lives!" she said, in her old tongue.

Only Tomakin appeared unsurprised. His expression hard, he leaned toward her. "Your father suspected as much and told me to find out whether it was so."

They were led then to their lodgings. John explained that they would spend the night here and then the next day be conducted to London by carriage.

Rebecca could hardly feel, hardly hear, so great was her shock that the flame-haired warrior of the Tassantassas yet lived and breathed.

What else had the Inqutish lied about?

London was both more dazzling and terrifying than she had imagined as well.

The carriage ride through the country was interesting. More uncomfortable than being on board ship, in many ways, yet affording a view of fields and towns. Tomakin had seized upon a long stick while in Plymouth and sought to make notches according to the number of people he saw, but with much disgust he soon tossed it away. Rebecca could not help but laugh. Not that she herself was not astounded by just how many inhabitants dwelt in this land, even before they reached London.

Her own astonishment found echo in that of her attendants, nearly all of them exclaiming *waugh!* at some point or another during the journey. And then in London itself—the people, the noise, the great houses made of stone! In the early days, names and places came too quickly for her to remember them all. She was fitted with new clothing, and it was well had she grown accustomed to the English way of dress while still in Tsenacomoco. What was considered proper here proved even more restrictive than what they'd forced upon her in the early days after her captivity—and certainly what she'd worn for everyday dress at home. Those who came to measure and fit her turned up their noses at her old garments. If she'd not suggested her younger attendants take and wear the apparel for worktime, then they'd have taken them away entirely, to dispose of them she knew not how.

Somewhere in the midst of it all, Channa produced a white feather. One single feather from a swan. While they were looking at hats to go with the first three gowns and jackets, Channa pulled it out and handed it to the man in charge of design. He looked at Channa, then at Rebecca.

Feeling the long, meaningful gaze that Channa bent her way, Rebecca asked, "Is it possible for you to use this with one of the hats?"

He bowed. "I can do that."

Later, Channa would only say stiffly, "No matter where you go, you are always Beloved Woman. It is only fitting to have a sign of your position."

Along with incorporating Channa's feather in the brim of the hat, she was given a curious ornament—three small, softly curling white feathers clasped together at the end of a short wand of polished wood. "For brushing away flies," the clothier said. "And it matches the feather in your hat."

Channa looked at it and gave a smile and nod of her approval.

In truth, it was all unexpectedly fun. Rebecca made the acquaintance of Virginia's former governor, Lord De La Warre, and his wife, who seemed delighted to sponsor them in social circles. After Lady De La Warre and the officials of the Virginia Company approved the new apparel, they were taken around to meet various personages. The courtesies and formalities surrounding it all were not unlike those she knew from Nohsh's court in Werowocomoco and Matchcot.

In between, they attended church. How different from the simple services performed by Reverend Whitaker and others in Tsenacomoco. Here the building itself was made in such a way as to inspire awe, and the music! While some of the singing seemed familiar, there was an instrument John called an *organ*, which echoed and rang. Rebecca was disappointed when that stopped and the minister got up to speak.

His sermon was long and, in many ways, difficult to follow and understand. For three years now she had been learning the speech of the English, but this proved she did not know it as well as she had thought. Still, she paid good attention, and her companions did the same.

At odd times, they entertained at the house where they stayed.

Various ministers and other men of learning came to visit them and to ask many questions about her belief in Christ and whatever else they found of interest.

Every day, John reviewed the invitations and requests for audience. There were dinners and balls and parties of every sort. Not every face at every event they attended was welcoming, but Rebecca put on her best look of polite uninterest—as Nohsh often did toward those with whom he was not impressed but was too courteous to say so—and ignored them.

Nothing, however, came from Captain Smith. The days stretched into weeks, and soon the summer was nearly gone.

Then came the day they were ushered to another very tall, grand house, heavily guarded, where the scat of wandering dogs littered the hallways. Rebecca picked up her skirts and stepped carefully. Did the inhabitants pay no mind to such things, indoors? Ann Leaver and the other women had been very fussy about cleanliness even of the dirt floors of the English houses in Tsenacomoco.

They were led into a great hall, lit by many torches and windows set high into the walls. At the far end stood two chairs, now empty, but many groups of people in fine clothing stood about the room.

From somewhere off to the side, a man's voice called out, "Announcing the Lady Rebecca Rolfe of Virginia, formerly known as Pocahuntas, and her husband John Rolfe of Virginia, along with their company of Naturals."

Many in the room turned and stared, but none spoke. They all stood awkwardly for several moments until an attendant came and led them through the room to where an older woman sat beneath a canopy of golden brocade, her gown and hair sprinkled with jewels.

"Her Majesty, Queen Anne," the attendant murmured.

Rebecca curtsied as she was taught, while John bowed, his expression one of astonishment.

Nearby, a cluster of men stood, watching the proceedings. One in particular looked Tomakin and Nantaquas up and down then elbowed another man and laughed.

Something in Rebecca's throat burned. Tomakin's face lay in hard lines, but his eyes glittered as if in fury.

"Pay them no mind," came the queen's voice, firm despite its age.

"They are but spoiled boys."

Rebecca gave another curtsy. "How fare you, Your Majesty?"

A smile creased the woman's heavily powdered face. "Well enough. Thank you for asking, dear girl." She regarded Rebecca with much interest. "How was your journey here?"

"Not without its difficulties, but as you see, we have come safely."

The queen reached out her hand, and Rebecca hesitantly put hers into it.

"You are sweet and darling. Thank you for coming to visit, and for bringing your husband and people. I should like to see you again at some time."

Rebecca dropped into yet a third curtsy. "Thank you, Your Majesty."

They withdrew, and after a short tour of the rest of the palace, they returned to their lodgings to find Thomas wailing inconsolably. After changing out of her expensive clothing, Rebecca settled in to suckle him—and hopefully soothe both of them—while John seated himself nearby with another round of notes that had come for them.

Little Thomas curled into her arms, and they both relaxed. It had been a long string of days with little enough time to cuddle, and she craved some closeness with their boy.

"This is astonishing," John breathed.

She looked over. He'd raked one hand through his hair, then was absently combing his beard.

"What is it?"

"The Reverend Richard Hakluyt would like us to come visit."

"Who?"

He gave a short laugh. "He is a charter member of the Virginia Company. More infirm than he used to be, but he is largely responsible for compiling accounts of many of the great exploratory voyages of our time." John hesitated, eyeing her with an affectionate smile. "Apparently both he and Master Harriot would like very much to meet you, knowing you are a child of one of the peoples Master Harriot heard so much about when he visited some thirty years ago now. Before the Roanoke Colony was sent over."

She was well familiar with that piece of their shared history.

"Master Harriot," he went on, "learned the tongue of your peoples—

at least, of those who lived to the south of Jamestowne. He spent much time among them, learning their customs, and then wrote about all he had seen and heard. I read through his work several times before Sarah and I determined to set out for Jamestowne. He said—he said that we English had much to learn from your people, that your way of life was so healthful and not given to excess, as it is here."

Rebecca smiled and plucked at her skirt then cuddled little Thomas closer.

John gave another dry chuckle. "His name is Thomas as well."

"I should indeed like to meet him."

John nodded. "We shall make plans to go as soon as possible."

He opened the next note, and his mouth fell open, his face going completely pale.

"John?"

He put a hand to his forehead, still staring at the letter. "How would you. . .I mean, would you be willing. . ."

The hand holding the note slowly lowered, and he stared off into nothing.

Rebecca could only wait for him to recover enough to tell her.

"How would you feel venturing to the Tower of London to visit none other than Sir Walter Ralegh?"

Chapter Twenty-One

The two aged men of learning were both sweet and, as the English would say, darling. They made so much of Rebecca and John's visit to them, she felt much abashed. On the other hand, their welcome was so unashamedly warm, it nearly made up for all the difficulty of the journey.

Master Hakluyt rose from his chair, stiffly, his wrinkled face all smiles. A cap covered his grey hair, a simple gown hid any other apparel he wore, and he took Rebecca's hands in both his own. "Oh, what a lovely young woman! Welcome, dear one! I am so happy to be able to see you."

Master Harriot was likewise effusive, although at first he stood back, a cloth held to his nose and mouth. He did not offer to take Rebecca's hand. "It is enough only to see you with my own eyes," he said, lowering the cloth enough to expose a terrible sore and growth on his upper lip and just inside his nose. "My apologies. I have been in treatment by King James's own physician, but I make it my practice not to touch anyone if I can possibly help it."

"I am sorry for your malady," she said.

He smiled ruefully. "Ah well, both Richard and I are old and perhaps not long for this world. But we are both well fitted for the kingdom to come, are we not?" He exchanged a glance with the other man, who had settled once more in his chair.

"That we are, old friend."

"But on to less tedious things. Wingapo! Sá keyd winkan?"

She laughed to hear her tongue, though again spoken so strangely. "I am well," she replied in like manner. "I have brought you this basket.

Will you not eat?"

"Oh, sweet daughter of the New World. What joy it is to hear your tongue!"

As their servant came and laid out tea, John offered packets of the tobacco he had grown. Hakluyt declined, but Harriot accepted with delight. "Oh, happy uppowoc! And how goes the growing of our favorite weed?"

While they ate and drank, he and John each took a pipe, one of a far more delicate make than those used by her people. The visit went long, but both she and John wished to satisfy all the questions both men might have. When at last they begged their leave, it was with much regret on all sides.

"You should come to dinner," John told them. "As you are able, of course. But it would give us much pleasure to visit again."

They said they would consider it, although Hakluyt was more limited in his ability to travel these days.

The next morning, they set out for the Tower. Neither knew precisely what to expect, and they'd brought Nantaquas and Tomakin along, both attired in a blend of Powhatan and English finery.

In many ways, it was like the palace—a heavily guarded stone building—but more austere. John showed the letter he'd received, and they were escorted down halls, all more clean than the palace, and up stairs until they'd come to a particular door. It was unlocked and opened, and after announcing them, the guard stepped back and bid them enter.

Another older gentleman stood from before the fireplace. His clothing was very neat, not as showy as they'd seen at court, and his hair and beard combed and trimmed. Bright blue eyes fastened upon her and widened before a smile overtook his face.

"I bid thee welcome, Lady Rebecca of Virginia! And your husband and—are these your kinsmen?"

He bowed very low, and when their greetings were accomplished, accepted with delight their gifts of food and tobacco. A very pleasant hour they spent with the man whose vision had fueled the founding of Virginia—however mixed were Rebecca's feelings about it all.

'Twas a fair autumn day, still warm, as Captain John Smith strolled with purpose down the street. He'd but a few weeks before the ship sailed for New England, and much business he had to see to—

A tall figure of a man walking beside a young Englishman caught his attention. The arrangement of the hair and the graceful, swaggering stride, despite his being clad half in English garb and half of the savages, was unmistakable for certain.

As he neared, the tall man's head lifted, as he looked this way and that, and his gaze rested upon Smith.

They both stood still for a moment, then Smith hurried toward him. "Uttamatomakin! Is it truly you?" Then, recalling the proper form of address, he said, "Wingapo! Sá keyd wingan?"

A smile stretched the man's lips. "Chawnzmit! It is good to see you."

"And this!" He focused on the man with him. "Could this be young Thomas Savage?"

"'Tis indeed," Savage answered with a grin.

As they asked after each other's welfare, a small crowd grew. "And how does Pocahuntas with the visit?"

Replying now through Savage, Uttamatomakin said, "She is well. Although it was a shock to her to find you were still alive." He smirked. "Wahunsenecawh, though, he suspected. He sent me also to see your king, queen, and prince, and your God, and bring him back word of them all."

What a strange thought, that they should come to England to "see" God. "Our God is not such that you may see Him. He is invisible, made of spirit, but Jesus Christ is indeed the very image of Him in the flesh. But neither does He remain on the earth at this time, only His Spirit, which lives in those who believe in Him." Smith hesitated. "I am sure Pocahuntas could tell you more of this."

Uttamatomakin only gave a grunt.

"And the king, why, I heard that you have seen him already."

"No, we have not seen the king."

"But were you not received at court some weeks ago? I heard tell of it. Queen Anne indeed welcomed and spoke to Pocahuntas—Rebecca—but you were there. They said the king and his courtiers stood off to the side and made fun."

The other man frowned, thinking, then, "Waugh! That one?"

The crowd around them laughed.

Uttamatomakin shook his head. "You gave Wahunsenecawh a white dog, which he then fed as himself. Your king gave me nothing, and I am better than your white dog."

It was, unfortunately, too true. "Our king will never match yours in courtesy or majesty," Smith murmured.

Tomakin eyed him. "I am glad to hear you say so."

"I will come soon to call upon Pocahuntas," Smith said quietly as the crowd began to disperse at last.

"We are being moved out to the country. I do not recall the name of the place."

Thomas supplied the name, and Smith nodded briskly. "I will come as soon as possible."

The estate, called Syon House, nestled against the river in a little town called Brentford. A haven for Queen Anne herself, it became a place of rest for Rebecca, after the whirlwind of summer, attending so many dinners, plays, and balls.

On sunny days her delight was in watching little Thomas lead chase about the lawns, walking with Channa or John, or viewing the river. They'd not been officially allowed to swim, but she and John sometimes slipped out under cover of darkness to take refreshment in its waters.

When it rained, the younger Powhatan women would explore the house with little Thomas, and his giggles and prattling filled its walls with life and joy.

On one such day, as Rebecca sat by the fire, a knock sounded upon the door at the front of the house, and one of the servants answered.

"Are we expecting anyone?" Rebecca asked.

John looked up from perusing a handful of their latest invitations. Before he could reply, a man's booming voice and laugh echoed from the entryway, and a sudden suspicion stole through her. Bolting up out her chair, she gathered her skirts and ran to look.

And there in the spacious foyer, shedding his dripping cloak and hat, was the fire-haired man who had lurked in many of her thoughts. Older, but unmistakable.

She did not quite come skidding around the corner, but nearly so, before halting in the hallway and composing herself.

Was this lovely creature, so properly attired as an English lady, truly his little Pocahuntas?

"Lady Rebecca," the manservant intoned, "Captain John Smith has come to call upon you."

The three associates who had accompanied him crowded behind him, goggling for a look.

She stepped closer, her gaze taking in all but then fastening upon him. Her lips parted.

He gave her a deep bow then another to the man who emerged into the hallway behind her. "Lady Rebecca. Will you not greet me, for sake of our friendship?"

With a sharp intake of breath, her head came up, her shoulders stiffened, and she whirled to put her back to him, covering her face.

What on earth? "Lady Rebecca? Pocahuntas?"

The man shot Smith a look of alarm then stopped to murmur something to her. She answered with nothing but a sharp shake of the head.

He came forward, frowning. "My apologies. Thank you for coming. I am John Rolfe, Rebecca's husband."

"I would have come sooner, if not for a dozen or more other duties that took me elsewhere. Even now I am preparing to sail for New England, so I cannot stay, but I have very much wished to pay your wife the kindness she well deserves."

Rolfe gave his wife another concerned glance then seemed resigned to her mood. "We are honored that you took the time. Shall we remove to the sitting room?"

They followed gladly, and Rolfe showed them to a well-appointed chamber then called for refreshments. Very shortly came a young woman with a child whom Rolfe introduced as his son, and then a pair of tall men—

"Nantaquas!" Smith rose, and the Powhatan warrior greeted him. "And Uttamatomakin."

They made introductions all around then settled again to talk. "As I recall," he said, addressing Rolfe once more, "you've done well for yourself with growing tobacco?"

Rolfe seemed to be more at ease talking of this, and so the conversation went for at least another hour.

Finally he stopped and looked at Rolfe. "I don't wish to leave before she has decided to speak to me."

"I think. . .waiting is good," Rolfe said.

He attempted a laugh. "I confess, I'd regretted to have told others that she can speak English."

Rolfe looked unamused, and he smothered the chuckle.

As if on cue, Rebecca swept into the room. The men all rose from their seats, but it was on Smith she kept her gaze. "I crave pardon for my discourtesy. You promised my father Wahunsenecawh that what was yours should be his, and he promised the same to you. You called him father, being in his land a stranger, and by the same reason so must I do you."

"Ah, no! You must not use such a title of me. You are a king's daughter and I only—"

Her face hardened even more, were it possible. "Were you not unafraid to come into my father's country and to cause fear in him and all his people—that is, all but me? And yet here you fear I should call you father? I tell you then, I will call you father, and you shall call me child, and so I will be for ever and ever your countryman."

Her breast rose and fell with the strength of her passion. Her black eyes shone, and a flush rode the curve of her cheeks, still dusky although winter-pale.

Oh, but she was beautiful!

"They did always tell us you were dead," she went on, her voice catching, "and I knew nothing else till I came to Plymouth. Yet Wahunsenecawh did command Uttamatomakin to seek you and know the truth, because your countrymen will lie much."

The friends who had come with him all stifled laughter. Smith could only spread his hands. There were many of whom that charge was most true.

Pocahuntas—Rebecca—turned upon them. "What? You find amusement in us believing him dead?"

"No, lady," said one, wiping his eyes, "but in your charge that we lie much. 'Tis too true."

She blew out a breath, seemingly disarmed at least a little at his honesty.

"You see me before you, hale and whole," Smith said. "'Twas a grave wound indeed, but I promise you, I did not willingly leave. They sent me aboard ship while I was still insensible from the pain. I believe many of them hoped I truly would die on the voyage, and thus rid themselves of me."

She peered hard at him. "But you never returned. After all your promises to my father. . .and those who came after did terrible things to our people."

'Twas also too true. He had heard some of them.

"I much regret," he said softly, "the slaying of the queen of Paspahae and her children, especially."

Her dark eyes sheened with sudden tears, and her head dipped. "That was but one thing."

Across the room, Rolfe watched, his entire manner stern, no doubt with jealousy on her behalf.

Smith swallowed. For the briefest moment he wondered what could have been had he stayed—might he have been the man to have won this bright, lovely creature?

No one moved. He drew a long breath. "I explained to your father that I could not be his subject—his countryman, under his rule. I owed my loyalty to my own God and another king."

"Then you should not have agreed to be called his son," she said, with not a little fire.

He could not help the smile that came to his lips. "That was at your father's insistence. You will recall I was a captive at the time."

All the wind seemed to go out of her then, and she blinked. "I remembered what you said once about heaven, and I often tried to imagine it, with you there."

An untoward warmth curled through him. Had anyone ever cared for him, thus?

"I am most regretful that you were left not knowing," he murmured. At a loss for what else to say, he indicated his chair. "Will you not sit, Lady Rebecca?"

She blinked again then glided over to take the seat. He pulled an ottoman closer and perched upon it instead, facing her. "Now, I would gladly hear of your voyage and adventures here—but especially how it was you came to be a Christian."

At least she had been able to see him and speak with him.

Rebecca thought much upon their conversation as autumn turned to winter. In the meantime, an artist came to the house and asked whether she might sit for a portrait. First he did only a sketch, but then unpacked paints and canvas, which he was only too glad to show Rebecca and satisfy her curiosity, and prepared for a painting. She dressed in some of her finest apparel, the black brocade with a gold-trimmed red jacket over, finishing with a lace collar, the jaunty cap, and her fan of white feathers.

When he was finished, while she marveled over the painting, he produced a sketched copy for her and John and thanked her for her time.

London, Twelfth Night 1617

"Announcing, the Lady Rebecca Rolfe of Virginia, and her attendant, Uttamatomakin."

Just breathe.

She leaned toward Tomakin. "I am told this is their greatest celebration of the year."

He gave a grave nod, his darting eyes taking in everything.

As they entered, she looked up and found John seated already in the upper gallery. He could come no nearer, being but a commoner (so he said), but she being a king's daughter and Tomakin his son by marriage, they held the distinction of being guests of honor.

They were led to seats at the very head of the table. She was placed right next to the queen, in fact, who greeted her warmly. The king's gaze lingered upon them, and this time he acknowledged Rebecca and Tomakin by inclining his head.

The feast was laid, and the play began. Somehow all Rebecca could see was a much different play, one held under open skies around a blazing fire, where Channa had danced wildly with other women, while Rebecca—yet a child—sought to allay the fears of a certain flame-haired Tassantassa captain.

At last she pushed the memory aside and gave attention to the spectacle before them.

"I've not felt so stirred," she said to Tomakin as the carriage brought them back, "since we were at Werowocomoco."

He snorted softly. "You always were one for the dancing and plays."

"And tonight they had all at once. It makes me miss Nohsh."

She leaned her head upon John's shoulder and closed her eyes.

The entire house lay quiet by the time they returned. John took a candle and led the way to their rooms. On a nearby pallet, little Thomas and one of the younger girls lay slumbering.

She and John helped each other undress, laying aside garments of shimmering brocade and all accoutrements. When at last she stood only in her shift, she loosed her hair and braided it then slipped into bed and curled against John's side.

This was the last of the great invitations. Tomorrow they would begin packing their things and move back to Brentford, where they would await the change of weather so they might sail again for Virginia.

For Tsenacomoco. *Home.*

She closed her eyes against sudden tears.

Would that they did not plague her every time a strong feeling crossed her heart! Would that she could be as stoic as Nohsh and his warriors, as Nantaquas and Tomakin.

Of course, women were not subjected to the long ordeal of huskanaw, either, to harden them. But they were still expected, as Tunapewoc—as Powhatan—to be strong.

She felt anything but, these days. Had months of living as an Englishwoman softened her? She'd best find her strength again, if so, because as soon as the weather turned, they would be readying to leave at last.

"How much longer before we can return home?" she asked one rainy and cold morning at Syon House, feeling pettish for no good reason that she could think of. Thomas had been fussy during the night but now ran about in high spirits. The two younger Powhatan women chased after him, drawing squeals and giggles.

"Late February at the soonest. Or early March." John watched her, his expression grave. "Are you well, dearest?"

"Well enough," she said, looking out a window at the gardens.

He came up behind her, setting his hands on her shoulders. "I also long to be home. As enjoyable as this visit has been. . ."

She leaned back, tipping her head to look at him. "And you have found meeting with Sir Dale and investors to be enjoyable?"

He laughed and slid his arms around her. "All for the sake of Virginia."

A chill touched her. Of course it was. Even her presence here.

"I like not being shown about as a child's toy. Even if it is fun to be tricked out in all my finery."

She referred to the contemptuous comment overheard at a banquet just days ago.

His arms tightened a little. "I wish I could protect you from such hateful things."

At last they were readied for departure.

Rebecca agonized over which of her beautiful clothing to take. Would she ever have occasion to wear it again, at home? And if she left some behind, which would she choose?

At last she let Channa and the other women pack it all into trunks to bring along.

Being on the Thames River, they decided to go by boat, past London, all the way to Gravesend where they would meet the *Treasurer*. The ship would take them from there around to Plymouth, and then—God willing—out upon the ocean and to home at last.

A deep weariness held her as they prepared. Whether it was dread of the journey itself, the prospect of being yet once again on the ship that had carried her against her will away from home and family the first time, or something else entirely, she knew not.

On the river, little Thomas wished only to watch the water, and they were hard pressed at times to keep him in the boat. Even John's patience with the child was stretched by the continual need to keep hold of him.

The weather held, however, and the worst they endured was a fine mist and fog. They reached Gravesend and settled aboard, waiting now only on the tide.

Dinner was a subdued affair. Rebecca looked around the chamber where they had gathered to take their meal and recognized it with a jolt. Perhaps it was some measure of progress that she'd not immediately thought of it the moment they entered. But now, the corners of the rooms seemed to hold living shadows, with memories she'd thought long stuffed away.

Her gut ached. Thomas also was listless and only played with his food. Halfway through the meal, she lifted him and excused herself to her bed.

John's hand came out as she passed him. "Are you well, love?"

His eyes were shadowed as well. She gave a little shake of her head.

"I confess I do not feel so steady, myself." He smiled a little. "God willing we shall be strong enough for the journey itself, yes?"

She could barely respond with a smile of her own. Her gut wrenched again, and she shoved Thomas into John's arms. "Hold him—I need the privy."

Hours of bodily distress and need turned to agony. At last she could hardly leave her bed, and resorted to a chamber pot—which she hated, so unclean did it make her feel, but she could not bring herself to care enough to do otherwise.

The shadows in the corners grew darker, more menacing. She heard whispers and could not discern whether it was those of her companions or something of pure spirit.

Jesus! My Great King, help me!

It was all she could bring herself to pray, but the shadows shivered and withdrew, even if only a little.

"She is no better," Channa said. "Others are sick. Should we go for a physick?"

John leaned hard upon the doorframe of the belowdecks cabin he shared with Rebecca. Cramps wracked his gut as well—in fact, most of them had fallen sick to some degree or another. Tomakin faced him in the gloom, only the occasional tightening at the corners of his eyes betraying that he too felt the malady.

"Have you anything better to suggest?" Tomakin asked.

Both John and Channa, who had labored to tend Rebecca the past few hours despite her own weariness, shook their heads.

"Then"—John sighed—"we must do so. 'Twill likely mean we miss the next tide, but that cannot be helped."

Tomakin entered the room and looked at Rebecca, lying pale and mostly insensible upon the narrow pallet. "She should be taken to the physick."

"I agree." John winced as another spasm gripped his innards.

"I will carry her."

"Let me inform the captain, then I will come as well."

Channa helped John wrap Rebecca's limp form in a blanket then scurried off to tell the others while John made his painful way abovedecks. Captain Argall met his news with a thinned mouth, standing back a little from John as if to avoid catching whatever it was they all had. "We'll miss the tide," he said.

"I know, but she needs aid."

The man waved a hand, and John hurried away in Tomakin's wake, as the tall Indian bore the burden that held the greater part of his heart.

They inquired on the wharf then kept going. Gravesend was mostly a garrison and not much more. After some searching, they were admitted to the rooms of the garrison's own chirurgeon.

She was wrapped and carried, which provided a little distraction from the pain—but also a new distress. Where were they going? Why was everyone around her so concerned?

John murmured to her, and then—was that Nohsh? Only the voice did not seem right.

But she dreamed she was a child again and being carried in the arms of her great and strong father.

"Nohsh, what is it? Where are we going?"

"Shh, child, all will be well."

Darkness, and then light and a bed, and more voices, worried. Bitterness forced upon her tongue.

Then weeping, and anguished prayers.

"Rebecca. . .Mato'aka. Oh my love, my love. . ."

All must die. 'Tis enough that the child lives.

Sobbing. . .

. . .and then it faded. There was a great pressure, then a sense of release, and—

The most brilliant light imaginable burst across her vision. She gasped, and the air rushing into her lungs burned and tingled at once.

And then there was no pain at all. Nothing but delicious warmth, and strength, and comfort surrounding her, along with song such as she might have caught snatches of, once upon a time, but never really heard before. Drum and voice and a host of other instruments, swirling about her and bearing her up—

And then it was He. Robed in brilliance like the sun upon new-fallen snow, a crown flashing with jewels, and eyes of the deepest flame. "My daughter! I have waited so long for this moment. *Wingapo!*"

"My great Mamanatowic!"

She flew into His open arms, and He gathered her in, murmuring over her a name that seemed a blend of all she'd ever worn—yet was new and fresh on its own.

To say he was devastated beggared the extent of his feelings.

They all were. Even the Powhatan warriors—Tomakin and Nantaquas as well—although their grief found expression in one of their strange songs, which John could not understand and none would translate.

Captain Argall looked regretful but said they must go on the next tide. There was nothing for it but to arrange for a quick burial with the church at Gravesend. The rector exceeded all John's expectations, however, when he arranged for Rebecca's body to be interred right there within the chancel.

'Twas the least they could do, he said, for a king's daughter.

The man did poorly at spelling their names, but John was too distracted by the loss—and his own body's discomfiture—to care.

One last look at the face he had loved—now utterly pale and without life, as if it were but a doll or wax statue left behind—and then her body was wrapped, carried to the church, and lowered into the yawning space beneath the slate slabs.

The weeping took him again as her resting place was covered. He was only dimly aware of Tomakin and Nantaquas leading him away.

Aboard ship, little Thomas remained listless and feverish. John took him up and would be persuaded by none to relinquish him, except briefly for needful tending, until they'd reached Plymouth. There they docked, and having several hours yet before another favorable tide, they went ashore to a tavern.

Rafe Hamor greeted them, along with Sir Lewis Stukeley, who had been present upon their landing the summer before. After hearing their news and condoling over the loss of Rebecca, the latter considered the child sleeping in John's arms while they sat at table. "I hesitate to speak this. But perhaps 'twould be better for the infant were he to stay in England for the time being, rather than subject him to the journey while he is yet unwell."

John scrubbed a hand across his face. "Absolutely not."

Argall gave him an unreadable look. "It might not be such an untoward thought. None know better than you the toll a sea voyage can have on passengers who are in ill health to begin with."

He suppressed the desire to snarl in return. As if he needed the reminder of Bermuda.

Tomakin and Nantaquas had gone very quiet, and both wore that stoic look which told him they did not like the turn of conversation.

Channa did not bother to hide her disapproval.

John held little Thomas closer and shut his eyes.

Gracious Lord in Heaven, You know all things. Show me whether this is the wisest course or no.

Only the hard, painful beat of his heart answered, as if half of it had been sheared away and buried at that church in Gravesend. Leaving Thomas would be as cutting out the part that remained.

In the end, it almost seemed the decision was made for him. Stukeley had further suggested that some of the young Indian women stay behind, indeed any of Rebecca's retinue who wished to do so. They could help care for little Thomas, or husbands could be found for them. Three elected to stay.

At quayside, he kissed and held little Thomas until Argall fumed and said they could delay no longer. Then, eyes burning, he whispered his farewell, passed the child to one of the Indian women, and reboarded the *Treasurer*.

A great, gaping maw of pain throbbed in the middle of his chest.

Epilogue

1618 by English reckoning

A brisk spring wind sent the clouds scudding across the sky, and the sunlight spilling around them was not quite enough to warm Winganuske's bare shoulders. Tightening the doeskin mantle about herself, she hurried back to the yehakan of her husband. Though bodily need drove her out for a bit, she did not want to miss the moment. Especially when some of the younger wives were all too eager to be the ones comforting him.

Before she reached the doorway, she could hear him calling out her name. She ducked inside and crossed to where he lay, the great Wahunsenecawh, once so strong and fearsome, now a mere shadow.

"Winganuske!" His voice, now thready, still held a note of its former command.

"I am here, husband," she soothed, slipping aside the mantle to kneel at his side, half covering him with her own body.

His arm came around her, and his gaze, still bright, fastened upon her face. For a moment, the lashes fell, and he released a long sigh.

"I am glad," he said finally.

"And I am glad to be here." She pressed a kiss to the curve of his high cheekbone, not caring who might see such an extravagant token of affection.

His eyes widened briefly. "What is this? You treat me as a child?"

A laugh bubbled out of her. "Not at all, my husband."

"Hm. More of your strange ways of late." But a smile stretched his mouth.

"Nouwmais," she murmured, so only he could hear.

He murmured the word in return, still smiling.

Sitting thus, she nearly fell asleep, when he stirred and announced to the room at large, "All of you, go. Except Winganuske."

His guards and the other wives hastened to do what he said, although not without a sulky glance or two at her.

He waited until they'd all gone, and then his hand curled around hers. "You have been a good woman. My Winganuske."

Her throat thickened so that she could hardly speak. "And you have been a good husband to me."

His eyes closed. "I told my brothers that you are to be free to choose whoever you wish. And—as soon as you wish."

She dropped her head to his chest. The tears flowed freely now. "You—are very generous, Mamanatowic."

He chuckled slightly. "Say—my name."

An uneven breath, then, "Wahunsenecawh."

"It is good—Ay-mah."

She sobbed.

"It has not yet been a full turning of the leaves since our Mato'aka left this world." He hesitated. "You are sure that she truly believed in your God?"

"Kuppeh."

A long sigh escaped him. "Tell me, then. Tell me of your God. If it pleases Him, maybe He will take me to where Mato'aka is."

Oh, how could she even speak? "I will do so, most gladly."

Gathering her thoughts and clearing her throat, she began.

ACKNOWLEDGEMENTS

My deepest thanks on the journey of this story go to. . .

Becky Germany, for trusting me with some fantastic story concepts.

The entire publishing team at Barbour, for being just plain wonderful.

Ellen Tarver, who always gets me and yet pinpoints where the story needs to be clearer and stronger.

Jennifer Uhlarik, for unfailing friendship and prayers—and for reading the very raw first draft.

Lee S. King, also a good and dear friend—for more praying, listening, and reading.

Beth Goddard, for always checking in to see how I'm doing.

Michelle Griep—I could not do without your critiques, or your friendship.

Kimberli Buffaloe—your passion for history has so often helped fuel mine.

My influencer team: Brittany, Kailey, Teri, Jennifer, Susan, Carolyn, Paula, Brenda, Esther, Jeanne, Tina, Andrea, Trisha, Nicole, and Jenelle, for your prayers and enthusiasm, and for being there to answer all-important questions like whether to use a certain character's first or last name in point-of-view scenes.

All those who read and take time for an endorsement or review—you bless me in ways I can't even put into words.

My family, for loving and supporting me even during deadline—especially Meeghan, who happily served as my research buddy; Corrie, for being willing to tackle yet another map (and Paris Eslick for helping finish); and Cameron, who was most present on the home front during the last weeks of deadline.

Troy, of course—it's only ever you!

God, my Savior, first and foremost—Jesus, Lord and King, our Great Mamanatowic Himself.

HISTORICAL NOTE

The Real Story of Pocahontas?

How to write a story about a historical figure who dies young, and still make it redemptive?

The schoolchild version of Pocahontas I learned many years ago was of a young Indian princess who heroically saves the equally heroic Captain John Smith, later marries John Rolfe, then tragically dies before returning home from England. And then, of course, there was Disney.

Only part of what we know of her, or think we know, comes from Smith's writings, which scholars have questioned since the 1800s. He wrote two separate accounts: the first while he was still at Jamestown and sent back as his official report of the colony's early days, likely edited and published without his permission before his return (in 1608); and another, somewhat more embellished, sixteen years later. The earlier account is understandably considered more accurate.

In addition to Smith's writings, bits of Pocahontas' life can be gleaned from William Strachey, who told of Pocahontas turning cartwheels in the open area of the fort, naked, and getting the boys to do the same, as well as making note of her marriage to Koko'um. Rafe (Ralph) Hamor wrote of her captivity and marriage to Rolfe and a little of their life together after. We do know, then, that she lived, what her approximate age was during the initial founding of Jamestown, and that she was a favorite daughter of the Powhatan paramount chieftain. We also know that she was kidnapped in 1613, was baptized as a Christian and took the name Rebecca the following year, and married John Rolfe shortly thereafter. Two years after that, she was taken to England to be shown off by the Virginia Company of London. What I present here in *Rebecca* of the detail and backstory is a fusion of many influences and ideas.

Because the Native viewpoint was very important to me, I started my research with a slim volume titled *The Real Story of Pocahontas* by Linwood Custalow and Angela Daniel, self-described as sacred Mattaponi oral history. (The Mattaponi are one of a handful of surviving Powhatan tribes.)

Though I have great respect for the authors and their work, over the course of continued study, I came to disagree—although not lightly—with some of their conclusions and assertions. To begin with, the idea that Pocahontas' mother was Wahunsenecawh's first wife (and first love) doesn't quite jive with dates, especially not if he was as old as some scholars insist. He could have been in his seventies when he died, although I did present him as a bit younger than that, but still older than Emme. (More on her later.)

Also, I used concepts presented by another Native writer, Paula Gunn Allen, to postulate Pocahontas' possible spiritual position amongst her people and to flesh out their religious views and practices. Where Custalow and Daniel are clear to point out that she would have been a child during John Smith's captivity and later visits, and as such would have had little to no part of any adult business concerning him, Gunn Allen isn't the only one to suggest that any so-called threat to Smith's life, and Pocahontas' intervention, likely had some symbolic meaning rather than any intention of a literal execution. Andrew Lawler of *The Secret Token* was my first exposure to the idea of connecting Smith's "near death" with the rite of huskanaw. Pocahontas' position as future Beloved Woman is pure conjecture, but if she did indeed hold such a place, she might indeed be utilized in such a rite.

As for Smith not writing of it until many years after her death, well, he might have viewed such a thing as too incredible for his audience in his first account, as well as not relevant until Pocahontas herself was known by the wider world.

The existence of her first husband is documented by William Strachey, although written accounts are silent on his fate or on the existence of a child by that marriage. Helen Rountree, highly respected scholar of the Powhatan people, postulates that the marriage was merely dissolved by Wahunsenecawh's agreement to her marriage to John Rolfe, but I thought it likely that Koko'um was killed, as Custalow and Daniel maintain.

I also took seriously their assertion that she was violated by her English captors. They further theorize that little Thomas was not John Rolfe's biological son, and that an obvious culprit would be Sir Thomas Dale (or even Sir Thomas Gates, I think), considering the English custom of naming a first son after his father. If, however, Pocahontas' own family was allowed to visit anytime in the early weeks, I felt she'd probably be encouraged to make use of the abortifacient herbs commonly used among many Native peoples. (For more on that, see my historical notes at the end of *Mary*.)

Either way, it is curious that the details of Thomas' birth are not recorded, given that John Rolfe was secretary of the colony for a while, but then, details regarding the deaths of his first wife and child are similarly missing. I have to wonder whether many of the official records of Jamestown's early years weren't destroyed by fire or other calamity.

John Rolfe is himself something of a mystery, once thought to be one of twin sons born to John and Dorothy Rolfe of Heacham, England. Later legal records show a brother, Henry Rolfe, petitioning for funds from John's estate for support of John's son Thomas. Traditional Native history views John with a measure of suspicion, given the circumstances of Rebecca's death, which they believe is due to poison. After much thought, I decided against that angle. I simply don't see a motive, although I wouldn't have put it past Dale or Argall to strike this last blow at Wahunsenecawh. There is at least one surviving record of someone scoffing over the social favor shown Rebecca and John Rolfe during their visit to England, but as far as anyone trying to prevent her from taking word of "the truth" back to her father of what she'd seen and learned? Anything Rebecca could have communicated could just as well be related to him by members of her retinue—especially Uttamatomakin, one of her father's councilors. Also, John Rolfe mentions in his own account that many of them were sick at the same time. It is interesting that their probable ailment, known at the time as "bloody flux," a virulent and often deadly intestinal malady which also struck the early Jamestown colonists, spread among the Native populations later in 1617, after Rebecca's kinfolk would have returned, and John Rolfe himself attested that several in the party were sick the entire voyage back to Virginia.

Many accounts do portray Pocahontas/Rebecca as being enamored of the English (something seized upon by interpretations written during the Victorian era). Modern interpretations, however, emphasize her captivity and speculate about brainwashing. It's even questioned whether John Rolfe really loved her or whether he married her only out of pity or politics. By his own description, I feel there's no doubt he was nothing short of besotted with her, but did she truly love him in return? We don't know. Could she have? Definitely.

Just as sources don't agree on the actual events of her life, there is conflicting information about which of her two native names, Amonute or Mato'aka, was her regular given name and which was her "secret" name. Paula Gunn Allen and Helen Rountree are at odds with each other on that, so I had to just pick one. Also, because of the vagaries of Eastern Algonquian words and names, I took the liberty of inserting apostrophes to help indicate where there seems to be a break in syllables—such as Mato'aka and Koko'um, variously spelled in primary sources as Matoka, Matoaka, and Kocoum. Speaking of the latter—Strachey only mentions that he was a captain, and while other modern sources say he was actually younger brother to Yapazus/Japazaw, who is also said to be a close ally of Wahunsenecawh, I could find nothing to actually substantiate that.

Wahunsenecawh himself, however, was nothing short of legendary. He is universally referred to in English accounts as "Powhatan"—perhaps *the* Powhatan—but I suspect they did so simply because his given name was so tricky. I also suspect, after looking at all the various spellings and learning that I have about the Algonquian language overall, that the final *-awh* might be some sort of guttural or glottal stop, rendered by some writers as *-ock*. Given that Powhatan is one of those long-dead Native languages, we may never know—although several scholars have made a valiant effort at figuring it out.

For the most part, then, I can only make educated guesses on how the words recorded by Smith and Strachey might have been pronounced. I am indebted to the work of the late Dr. Blair Rudes, who provided Native dialogue to the film *The New World* and offered words for Scott Dawson's Croatoan word list. A lexicon of Virginia Algonquian located at the Custalow family website has also provided valuable insight. (Among other things, I learned that the Algonquian word for woman, *crenepo*, would have been pronounced ke-re-ne-poh.) Overall, however, we only have a smattering of Carolina Algonquian words that survive through Thomas Harriot (he must have compiled his own lexicon, but it was lost), some through John Smith, and some through William Strachey.

Because period spelling was so fluid—and something of a nightmare for modern readers, with a simple "oh" sound most often being rendered "ough"—many inconsistencies exist between historical and modern spellings. I've tried to provide at least one of each in most cases in the glossary.

I've written elsewhere about the limitations of research. An example of this was learning after the completion of *Mary* that Wahunsenecawh would not have inherited the position of paramount chieftain. To begin with, he might not have inherited the position of weroance or chieftain from his father at all, but rather from his mother, given the matrilineal nature of Native society. (Although Rountree contradicts herself on this point. By the same token, Mato'aka/Pocahontas was not necessarily considered a princess and would not have inherited her father's position.) The position of paramount chieftain, however, would have been one he himself built by bringing neighboring towns and peoples under his authority, either by force or diplomacy. He was indeed, as described by Smith, more of an emperor than a mere king.

Also, one alert reader who must surely share my love of obscure historical fact asked me why I had not used the Geneva Bible as my translation of choice for *Elinor*. In part I'd not realized the Geneva Bible would have been used so widely before John White's company set sail—but my difficulty also lay in not having access to an early version of that translation. It is my source in this story, however, for Scripture during the early Jamestown years. Even after the King James Version was made available in 1611, Separatists (of which Alexander Whitaker was one) and Puritans would most likely have stuck with the Geneva Bible.

In addition to many other sources (a nod once again to Scott Dawson for his work on the Lost Colony), I must credit Helen Rountree for her excellent scholarship on the Powhatan people in general and Pocahontas and her people in particular. Her work *Pocahontas, Powhatan, Opechancanough: Three Indian Lives Changed by Jamestown* is the best I've seen on interpreting the entire Jamestown phenomenon through Native eyes, and she's the one who suggests John Smith's name would have been rendered *Chawnzmit* by Powhatan ears, since they likely didn't differentiate between first and last names. I've similarly compressed other English names.

Several volumes proved invaluable as resources on John Smith's writings and biography. My favorite is a compilation by James Horn, which includes not only Smith's accounts but several by his contemporaries (and oh, it was fascinating reading about the nonsense with Wingfield from his perspective!) as well as accounts of the Roanoke voyages. Smith himself was a conundrum—idolized by some, vilified by others, fascinating and maddening by turns in his own writings. Still a young man during the settling of Jamestown—just twenty-seven when they arrived—many argued he had neither the age nor experience to lead well. The case could be made that because he made enough of a difference for the survival of the colony, his untimely departure late in 1609 just might have been what tipped Jamestown into the Starving Time, when famine and Native hostilities decimated the population (a reduction from four hundred-some to about sixty), and archaeological evidence proves they resorted even to cannibalism.

Another interesting fact is that John Smith never married. Given the sentimental tone of his accounts of his earlier captivity by the Turks, one gathers that he had perhaps fallen in love with the mysterious Charatza Trabigzanda, who reportedly treated him with kindness but then sent him to her brother, a man so cruel that Smith was compelled to rise up and slay him. Whether this account was actually true or a fiction he created, no one knows.

We do know, however, something about men like Bartholomew Gosnold, one of the original movers behind the colony. During my visit to Historic Jamestowne in early 2022, my youngest daughter and I visited the Archaearium, which features much of the archaeology of the fort and colony—including forensic reconstructions of human remains, such as Gosnold, who died of illness the first summer, and a boy they deduce was probably Richard Mutton, killed during one of the first attacks on the fort. I knew then that I wanted to at least make mention of these two in my story, and honor their bravery and that of so many others who were willing to cross the ocean for the possibility of a better life.

There is still so much I had to leave out, but here are a few questions in particular.

Could Emme Merrimoth truly have been Pocahontas's mother?

Two words: speculative history.

Do I think it's likely? Not at all. She was a real girl who was probably only twelve or so herself when John White's colonists sailed to the New World and then were dumped so rudely on Roanoke Island (see the first book, *Elinor*). Her fictionalized story thread provided a handy and interesting connection between the Lost Colony and the original Jamestown, but I'm very aware that it is fiction.

Do I think it's possible such a thing *could* have happened, however? Absolutely.

Strachey is the one who lists the names of the wives of Wahunsenecawh still living with him around 1610 or 1611. First on that list is Winganuske, who Machumps claims is his sister. Of course, Emme would not have been his sister, and it is possible the real-life Winganuske had no connection to him at all, either.

Did Pocahontas ever go back to visit her father after marrying John Rolfe?

Speculation on this goes both ways. I think it plausible that she could have—or that the English would have forbidden it because they were worried about Wahunsenecawh keeping her and their "peace" being nullified as a result. There is some indication that John Rolfe visited after her death, for the courtesy of personally carrying that news to her father.

Did Pocahontas ever attend a play written by Shakespeare?

It is very possible, although Shakespeare died the same month she and John and their party set out from Virginia for England. I ran out of time and room, or I would have written a scene where they attend *The Tempest*, the play reputed to have been inspired by Strachey's account of the shipwreck on Bermuda. (Fodder for a bonus scene, perhaps?) We do know that the play performed at the Twelfth Night celebration Pocahontas, John, and Tomakin attended was written by Ben Jonson, another popular playwright of the time.

What really happened to the Lost Colony?

So what, in all this, was the actual fate of the Lost Colony? Strachey says that Powhatan (Wahunsenecawh) was responsible for their slaughter, but it is my feeling this is either sensationalist rumor or outright propaganda on the part of the English. It was clearer that Wahunsenecawh wiped out the Chesapeake, either for refusing to come under his dominion (although he didn't wipe out the Chickahominy for the same) or other more obscure reasons, as I've speculated—but there's no solid evidence that he actually hunted down and wiped out the Roanoke colonists, other than Strachey's assertion. Strachey's main source was Machumps, who it is said killed Namontac while they were on Bermuda. John Smith sent men to inquire of other tribes but could find nothing conclusive. The rumor of captives being kept to "beat copper" for a particular weroance might also have been, as I postulate in *Elinor*, old news in the Native world.

What happened after?

John Rolfe went home to Virginia after Rebecca's death and continued serving as colony secretary and raising tobacco, which became a major cash crop and the main source of the colony's prosperity for many years. He remarried two years later and had one daughter, then died in March 1622. Thomas grew to adulthood in England and finally came to Virginia at the age of twenty, so he and his father never saw each other again.

According to a report by Captain Argall in June 1617, Wahunsenecawh stepped down as paramount chieftain of the Powhatan shortly after John Rolfe's return to Jamestown, presumably upon hearing of Rebecca's death, and did indeed die less than a year later. The next brother in line to inherit his position of mamanatowic was Opitchapam, but age and health prevented him from holding it for long, and Opechancanough was next to take it. After trying to deal the next several years with the rising English population and greater losses of Native-held territory, he at last lost patience and launched the famous attacks of 1622 upon the English settlements. Henrico was nearly wiped out, but Jamestown strangely went untouched. It is unknown whether John Rolfe's death happened during this attack or a little before, but the record seems to point to before.

Uttamatomakin and Mattachanna returned home, but the young women who attended Rebecca (and likely little Thomas by extension) and were given the choice to stay behind in England did reputedly find husbands in the West Indies. Tomakin is said later to have fallen out of favor with his own people. I have to wonder whether Wahunsenecawh blamed him for not bringing Mato'aka home safely, or whether there was some other reason. Maybe Tomakin also eventually softened toward Christianity and thus lost his position and prestige as quiakros, despite insisting he was too old to accept the strangers' Jesus. (As recorded by Samuel Purchas, an Anglican clergyman who was a student of Hakluyt and labored after Hakluyt's death to finish compiling that one's work.) The official report, written by Captain Argall in June 1617 (found in the Virginia Company archives on the Virtual Jamestown website), was that his accusations against the English and Sir Thomas Dale were "disproved," and thus he "was disgraced" with Opechancanough and his "great men" of the Powhatan. Given that Argall was the chief instigator behind the capture of Pocahontas, I tend to take his opinion (i.e., that Tomakin's word was not to be trusted) with a grain of salt. Either way, however, it's intriguing to speculate.

Thomas Savage returned to Virginia, married, and raised a family, living out his life there.

Rafe Hamor also returned to Virginia, married, raised a family, and died there.

Sir Thomas Dale never returned to Virginia, but was assigned to an expedition to the East Indies, where he grew ill and died.

Captain John Smith was continually denied any return to Virginia because of his harsh criticism of the Virginia Company's policies and administration, but he is credited with much of the exploration of New England, laying the foundation for the Plymouth colony's arrival in 1620. He died in England in 1631.

One thing is very sure, however, for those of us who believe in the resurrection of Jesus. As tragic as Rebecca's earthly ending is, if she or any others had genuine faith in Christ, then death isn't at all the end, only the beginning.

As I finished the writing of this story, I felt a deep longing over the Native peoples of America—these brave and beautiful First Nations, fraught with their own checkered history (the varied methods employed by chieftains and nations to subdue others—as all of human history is evidence, really) and trying desperately to deal with the rapid changes of their world. John Rolfe himself wrote that "a good Christian" could not look upon the faces of the Native peoples, who bear the image of God and come from the same mold as other peoples, without being moved by their plight of being so spiritual yet not knowing their true Creator.

And spiritual they are. Indeed, we modern Western peoples, so steeped in science and technology, have done ourselves a great disservice in ceasing to recognize the reality of the unseen realm—or while recognizing it, limiting the actions of God in our own lives. We profess to believe God, and yet we act as though we think His power can't really touch or change us. But I digress.

At its heart, this was always a spiritual conflict. The players may not have recognized it or been able to articulate what they felt, but it wasn't merely English vs. Native. It was, as I explored in the first two books, the struggle of the old gods against the revelation of the one True God. It was the English, indeed all men, being tugged between their own pride, greed, and lust, and the Higher Truth they were being called to.

The making of followers of Christ should happen through love, not coercion. The history of the Church is littered with attempts at the latter, and even those of us who wish to do so much better in our efforts to communicate the pure gospel don't always represent our Savior well.

But the gospel—from a word meaning "good news"—is worth being communicated. A God who is not distant, who not only bent near but became one of us, and who took all our wrongs upon Himself and then also conquered death on our behalf—that is good news indeed.

BIBLIOGRAPHY

Allen, Paula Gunn. *Pocahontas: Medicine Woman, Spy, Entrepreneur, Diplomat.* Harper Collins, 2004.

Axtell, James, ed. *The Indian Peoples of Eastern America: A Documentary History of the Sexes.* Oxford University Press, 1981.

Axtell, James. *The Invasion Within: The Contest of Cultures in Colonial North America.* Oxford University Press, 1988.

Custalow, Dr. Linwood "Little Bear," and Angela L. Daniel "Silver Star." *The True Story of Pocahontas: The Other Side of History.* Fulcrum Publishing, 2007.

Harriot, Thomas. *A Briefe and True Report of the New Found Land of Virginia: The complete 1590 edition with 28 engravings by Theodor de Bry after the drawings of John White and other illustrations.* Dover Publications, Inc., 1972.

Hakluyt, Richard. *The Principal Navigations, Voyages, Traffiques, and Discoveries of the English Nation.* Google Books. Abridged edition, *Voyages and Discoveries*, Penguin Books, 1972.

Horn, James. *A Land As God Made It: Jamestown and the Birth of America.* Basic Books, 2005.

Horn, James, ed. *Capt. John Smith: Writings with Other Narratives of Roanoke, Jamestown, and the First English Settlement of America.* The Library of America, Penguin Putnam Inc., 1984.

Jamestown Rediscovery. *Holy Ground: Archaeology, Religion, and the First Founders of Jamestown.* The Jamestown Rediscovery Foundation, 2016.

Kupperman, Karen Ordahl, ed. *Captain John Smith: A Select Edition of His Writings.* University of North Carolina Press, 1988.

Lawler, Andrew. *The Secret Token.* Anchor Books, 2018.

McDowell, Stephen, and Mark Beliles. *The American Dream: Jamestown and the Planting of the American Christian Republic.* Providence Foundation, 2007.

Moretti-Langholtz, Danielle. *A Study of Virginia Indians and Jamestown: The First Century.* Colonial National Historical Park, National Park Service, December 2005. [available online, http://npshistory.com/publications/jame/moretti-langholtz/index.htm]

Reader's Digest. *America's Fascinating Indian Heritage.* Reader's Digest Association, Inc., 1978.

Rountree, Helen C., Wayne E. Clark, and Kent Mountford. *John Smith's Chesapeake Voyages 1607-1609.* University of Virginia Press, 2007.

Rountree, Helen C. *Pocahontas, Powhatan, Opechancanough: Three Indian Lives Changed by Jamestown.* University of Virginia Press, 2005.

—. *Pocahontas's People: The Powhatan Indians of Virginia through Four Centuries.* University of Oklahoma Press, 1990.

—. *The Powhatan Indians of Virginia: Their Traditional Culture.* University of Oklahoma Press, 1988.

—. *Young Pocahontas in the Indian World.* Helen C. Rountree, printed by J&R Graphic Services, 1995.

Rushforth, Brett. *Bonds of Alliance: Indigenous & Atlantic Slaveries in New France.* University of North Carolina Press, 2012.

Sloan, Kim. *A New World: England's First View of America.* University of North Carolina Press, 2007.

Strachey, William. *A Historie of Travaile into Virginia Britannia.* The Hakluyt Society, 1612, 1849.

Straube, Beverly A. *The Arachaearium: Rediscovering Jamestown 1607-1699, Jamestown, Virginia.* APVA Preservation Virginia, 2007.

Townsend, Camilla. *Pocahontas and the Powhatan Dilemma.* Hill and Wang, 2004.

Quinn, David Beers, ed. *The Roanoke Voyages 1584-1590, Vols. I and II.* Dover Publications, 1991.

Ward, H. Trawick, and R.P. Stephen Davis Jr. *Time Before History: The Archaeology of North Carolina.* University of North Carolina Press, 1999.

A handful of online sites were absolutely crucial to my research as well:

Jamestown Rediscovery: historicjamestowne.org

Coastal Carolina Indian Center: CoastalCarolinaIndians.com

Virtual Jamestown: virtualjamestown.org

The Other Jamestown: virtual-jamestown.com

CAST

Native (historical):

1. Amonute [ah-moh-nuh-tay]: see Mato'aka
2. Channa: see Mattachanna
3. Kekataugh [kay-kah-tah]: brother to Wahunsenecawh and third in line to succession, corule of Pamunkey heartland (Rountree)
4. Koko'um: Pocahontas' first husband, a "captain" (Strachey), believed to be one of the Powhatan elite guard
5. Machumps: Powhatan warrior sent to the English by Wahunsenecawh as an emissary or spy; probably had his own agenda; supposed brother to Winganuske
6. Mato'aka [mah-toh-ah-kah]/ Amonute/Pocahuntas/Rebecca [Pocahontas]: favored daughter of Wahunsenecawh [debate between Rountree and Gunn whether Amonute was the secret name and Mato'aka her given, everyday name, or what]
7. Mattachanna: older half sister of Pocahontas
8. Namontac: exchanged to the English for Thomas Savage, murdered on Bermuda by Machumps
9. Nantaquas (Naukaquawis or Nantaquod, Smith): older half brother of Pocahontas
10. Opechancanough (Opeckankenough, Smith): brother to Wahunsenecawh and second in line but became actual, eventual successor, corule of Pamunkey heartland
11. Opechisco: brother to Wahunsenecawh; attended wedding of John Rolfe to Rebecca; may be same person as Opitchapam
12. Opitchapam: brother to Wahunsenecawh and first in line to succession, in 1607 ruled the Pamunkeys from Menapacute, took the name Otiotan/Itoyatin after 1618 (when Wahunsenecawh died), died 1628 or 1629
13. Pepaschechar: member of Wahunsenecawh's council who served as a guide to Rafe Hamor and Thomas Savage, summer 1614
14. Pocahuntas: see Mato'aka
15. Ra'hunt: councilor of Wahunsenecawh, noted by Smith for his disfigurement
16. Rebecca: see Mato'aka
17. Tomakin: see Uttamatomakin
18. Uttamatomakin (Tomakin): quiakros and councilor to Wahunsenecawh; husband of Mattachanna
19. Wahunsenecawh: paramount chieftain (mamanatowic) of Tsenamocomoco (spelled variously Wahunsenacawh, Wahunsenacock)
20. Winganuske [weeng-gah-nuss-kay]: favorite wife of Wahunsenecawh; kept near even after birth of daughter (Strachey);

fictionalized as Emme Merrimoth from the Lost Colony, during her later life as a captive with the Powhatan [referenced in *Elinor* and *Mary*]

21. Yapazus (Japazaw): weroance of Pota'omec

English (historical):

22. Archer, Captain Gabriel: 1574?–1609/10, one of the original council, died during the Starving Time
23. Argall, Captain Samuel: 1580?–1626, captain of the ship bringing De La Warre to Virginia; credited with first finding and using the shortest route across the Atlantic from England to Virginia (bypassing the Caribbean)
24. Bucke, Rev. Richard: 1573–1623, new chaplain at Jamestown in June 1610
25. Collier, Samuel: one of four boys on the 1607 voyage to the New World; served as page to John Smith
26. Dale, Sir Thomas: 1570–1619; governor, then marshal, then governor again of Virginia; suspected father of Pocahontas' son according to Custalow and Daniels
27. Dare, Elinor: daughter of John White, first governor of Virginia; wife of Ananias Dare; first English woman to give birth in the New World [referenced in *Elinor*]
28. De La Warre, Lord: Sir Thomas West, 1577–1618, governor after the Starving Time; returned to England in March 1611 due to illness
29. Emry, Thomas: one of John Smith's companions on the final leg up the Chicahamania River in November 1607
30. Gates, Sir Thomas: ??–1622, appointed by the Virginia Company of London to be governor; one of those shipwrecked on Bermuda 1609–1610; interim governor in 1610, then again 1611–1614
31. Gosnold, Captain Bartholomew: 1571–1607, captain of the *Godspeed* on the 1607 voyage to the New World; one of the original council; died in the first year from sickness
32. Hakluyt, Richard (the Younger): 1553–23 Nov 1616; minister, writer, translator, and one of the chief supporters of settlement in the New World; named officially recognized clergyman in November 1606 for the new settlement in Virginia but sent Robert Hunt instead
33. Hamor, Rafe (Ralph): 1589–1626; arrived in Jamestown in 1609 with the third supply fleet, returned to England that fall, came back to Virginia the next spring with Lord De La Warre's supply fleet. Served as secretary of the colony 1611–1614 before returning again to England. Back to Jamestown late 1616.

34. Harriot, Thomas: c. 1560–2 July 1621; mathematician, scientist, explorer. Participated in the journey to the New World in 1585 and spent months traveling up and down the coast. His written work about the Native peoples of the New World informed generations to come. *Suffering from cancer of the nose in his later years, Harriot died in 1621 at the home of Thomas Buckner, a mercer who lived on Threadneedle Street near the Royal Exchange. Buckner may have been the "Thomas Bookener" who was with Harriot on Roanoke Island in 1585–1586.* [NPS]
35. Hunt, Robert: c. 1568–July 1608; first preacher at Jamestown
36. Kendall, Captain George: 1570–1608, one of the original council; executed for supposed plot against Ratcliffe
37. Martin, Captain John: 1560–1632, one of the original council
38. Mutton, Richard: one of four boys in the 1607 voyage to the New World, probably the one slain in an early attack (May 1607?; *Historic Jamestowne*)
39. Nelson, Captain Francis: captain of the *Phoenix*, part of the first supply, arrived in Jamestown on April 20, 1608. Returned to England in June, bearing a long letter and map from John Smith, the former later published in London as *A True Relation* and the latter later known as the "Zúñiga map"
40. Newport, Captain Christopher: captain of the *Susan Constant* on the 1607 voyage to the New World; hired only for transport but named to the first council and later participated in negotiations with the Powhatan; lost an arm during the Anglo-Spanish War
41. Parker, William: young man taken captive from Henrico and integrated with the Powhatan until Hamor's visit in 1614
42. Percy, Master George: 1580–1632; brother to the Earl of Northumberland; became governor of Jamestown after Smith's departure until the arrival of Lord De La Warre (Delaware); supposedly devout Christian (*American Dream*) but ordered or at least bore witness to the death of the Paspahegh weroansqua and particularly brutal deaths of her children (*Secret Token*) [did he order them or merely observe when it was someone else's action??]
43. Powell, Nathaniell: gentleman on the 1606 voyage to the New World; writer/recorder of several primary accounts; member of the expedition sent to seek the whereabouts of the Roanoke Colony
44. Ratcliffe, Captain John: 1549–1609, master of the pinnace *Discovery* on the 1607 voyage to the New World; one of the original council; aka John Sicklemore
45. Read, James: blacksmith on the 1607 voyage to the New World; originally sentenced to hang because of an argument with and threats of violence toward Ratcliffe, during that one's presidency
46. Robinson, John: one of John Smith's companions on the final

leg up the Chicahamania River in November 1607

47. Rolfe, Bermuda: infant daughter of John and Sarah Rolfe, born and died on the island for which she was named
48. Rolfe, John: sailed with the *Sea Venture*, shipwrecked on Bermuda, arrived in Virginia on one of the rebuilt ships; second husband to Pocahontas and secretary of the colony; first to successfully grow tobacco as a cash crop
49. Rolfe, Sarah: John Rolfe's first wife, probably died shortly after reaching Jamestown
50. Savage, Thomas: arrived in Jamestown with Captain Newport's first supply voyage in 1607; given over to Wahunsenecawh as a peace exchange for Namontac
51. Scrivener, Matthew: 1580–1609, arrived in Jamestown with the first supply ship, served as the colony's first secretary
52. Smith, Captain John: baptized 6 January 1580–21 June 1631; likely learned some Algonquian from Harriot. Imprisoned aboard ship from the Canary Islands, for thirteen weeks, on suspicion of mutiny. Appointed to the council but not admitted until June 1607. Captured by Opechancanough Nov 1607; released 1 Jan 1608. Elected president 10 Sept 1608
53. Sparkes, Master: Jamestown colonist, accompanied John Rolfe on the visit to Wahunsenecawh spring 1614, any more is unknown
54. Strachey, William: 4 April 1572–buried 21 June 1621; passenger on the *Sea Venture* during its ill-fated voyage to Virginia in 1609, shipwrecked on Bermuda, arrived in Jamestown in 1610. His account of the shipwreck likely influenced Shakespeare to write *The Tempest*; his own accounts of Jamestown, the country of Virginia, and the Native peoples are considered among the most important from this time. His Powhatan lexicon, along with John Smith's, is all we have of that language. He may have learned Algonquian words from Harriot but more likely from Machumps. Served as secretary of the colony until his return to England, probably late 1611.
55. Stukeley, Sir Lewis: Vice Admiral of Devonshire; persuaded John Rolfe to leave son, Thomas, with him after Pocahuntas/Rebecca's death
56. Todkill, Anas: 1580–after 1617; carpenter on the 1606 voyage to the New World; sometime a servant of Captain Martin but a staunch supporter of John Smith; writer/recorder of several primary accounts; member of the expedition to seek the whereabouts of the Roanoke Colony
57. Waldo, Captain Richard: arrived in Jamestown with Captain Newport's second supply
58. West, Francis: 1586–c.1634; brother to Sir Thomas West, Lord De La Warre; arrived in Jamestown with Captain

Newport's second supply [some sources say third]

59. Whitaker, Alexander: 1585–1616; Presbyterian dissenter arrived with Sir Thomas Dale in May 1611; pastored both New Bermuda and Henrico and "taught doctrine sympathetic with Puritan ideas" (*American Dream*); drowned while crossing the James River in 1616

60. Wingfield, Master Edward Maria (mah-RYE-uh): one of the original council, chosen president of the colony, cousin to Bartholomew Gosnold

61. Wotton, Thomas: chirurgeon, listed under gentlemen of the original colonists

62. Wynne, Captain Peter: arrived in Jamestown with Captain Newport's second supply

Fictional, both Native and English:

Ann Leaver: English housekeeper at Bermuda Hundred

Emme/Ussac/Woanagusso/Winganuske [weeng-gah-nuss-kay]: wife to Wahunsenecawh, mother of Mato'aka and Little Flower, originally one of the Roanoke Colony, taken captive by the Secotan and sent to the Powhatan. (Although her story is fictionalized here, Emme Merrimoth was a real member of John White's company.)

Granny Snow: older Powhatan woman and spiritual advisor to Channa and Mato'aka

Jem: English cook at Bermuda Hundred

Little Flower: fictional name of real-life younger sister to Mato'aka

Little Fox: fictional name of probable real-life child of Mato'aka and Koko'um

Miskeh [mees-kay]: fictional name of real-life wife of Yapazus

PEOPLE GROUPS AND PLACE NAMES

(SMITH/MODERN)

Apocant: a town on the upper Chickahominy River

Appomatuc: a town and people near the Falls of the James River, on the south side

Atquanuchuck

Bermuda Hundred: parcel of land claimed by Sir Thomas Dale, formerly the location of the Appomatuc, on the opposite bank from the town of Powhatan

Capahowasic: the town or region offered to John Smith, for the English to dwell in and be under Powhatan dominion, located just east of Weromocomoco

Chawanoac: a "southerly country. . .within two days" of Powhatan territory [Smith]; a region on the mainland of North Carolina, on the Chowan River, above Albemarle Sound; "Chowans" on Smith's map

Chesepioc (Chesapeake): both a region and tribal name; not originally under Powhatan dominion (Rountree)

Chicahamania (Chickahominy): both a river and people group, the former a tributary of the James River and the latter one who resisted giving tribute to the Powhatan but remained independent until allying themselves with the English in 1614

Coree: Algonquian-speaking people and region, on the southeastern coast of what is now North Carolina

Henrico (Henricus): English settlement near the Native town of Powhatan, just below the Falls of the James River

Kequotan (Kecoughtan): town and people group located on the northern peninsula at the mouth of the James River

Kurawoten [kuh-rah-woh-tain] (Croatoan): the people who in 1584–1587 inhabited what is now the lower section of Hatteras Island

Mandoag: another "southerly country" about a day and a half's journey from Powhatan territory; "Mangoags" on Smith's map

Matchcot: a town on the upper Pamaunkee River, the last known capital seat of Wahunsenecawh

Mattapani, Mattapanient (Mattaponi): upper branch of the Pamaunkee River

Monacan: a Siouan-speaking people west of the territory held by the Powhatan, considered enemies and rivals of the Powhatan

Ocanahonan: town or region inland and somewhere on the state line of Virginia and North Carolina

Pamaunkee (Pamunkey): river and people group

Paspahae (Paspahegh): town and people group closest to the Jamestown settlement, just upriver

Payankatank: an upper branch of the Pamunkey River

Pota'omec [po-tah-oh-mek] (Potomac): river and people group at the northern edge of Powhatan domains

Roanoac: Roanoke Island, on the Outer Banks of North Carolina, site of first attempted English settlement in 1587

Suquoten [suh-kwoh-tain] (Secotan): people inhabiting Roanoke Island and inland coastal North Carolina, roughly between the Coree and Weopomeioc

Tapahanek (Tappahannock, Rappahannock): river and people group; Tapahanec on map

Tsenacomoco (Tsenacommacah): Native name for the region called Virginia ("our place"?)

Waraskoyack: place name; on the south side of the James River

Weopomeioc: region and people group on the northern side of Albemarle Sound, a little east of Chowanoac

Werowocomoco: original capital seat of Wahunsenecawh, "where the great king is present"

Youghtanan (Youghtanund?): lower branch of the Pamaunkee River

GLOSSARY

Powhatan etc. words (Carolina Algonquian—CA)

Ahoné [ah-hoe-nay]: the good god

amosens: daughter

apon [ah-pone]: bread made of ground pegatawah (corn)

cattapeuk [kah-tah-pay-uck]: early and mid-spring; during spring fish runs

cohattayough [koh-hah-tah-yoh]: late spring and early summer; planting and weeding season, when crops were tended

huskanaw, huskanasqua: rites of passage for Native youth, about nine months long for Powhatan boys, shorter for the girls

Inqutish: Native pronunciation of "English" [Rudes]

ka ka torawincs keir: what are you called?

kanoe [kah-noh-ay]: Native dugout canoes made of tree trunks

kuppeh: yes (equivalent CA *kupi)*

machic chammay [mah-cheek chah-may]: the best of friends [Smith]

machicómoco [mah-chee-COH-mo-co]: the Great Council [Gunn Allen]

mahkusun: shoes

mahta: no

mamanatowic [mah-mah-NAH-toh-wick]: paramount chief, "great king"

manaang'gwas [mah-nahn-gwahs]: butterfly

manito [mah-nee-toh]: the great spirits

manito'inini [mah-nee-toh-ee-nee-nee]: people of the great spirits [Gunn Allen]; lit. "creative power person"

michis [mee-cheese]: eat

midéwiqua: female practitioner of Native spirituality (midéwinini is the male equivalent) [midewikwe, Wiki]

midéwiwin [mid-ay-wih-win]: the great medicine dance [Gunn Allen]; Native spirituality [Wiki]

minchin [meen-cheen]: food

nechaun [nay-chahn]: child

nepinough [nay-pee-noh]: summer; green corn season; when people fattened on garden produce

nek: mother, my mother

nohsh: father, my father

nouwmais [noh-may]: I love you

O'ki [oh-kee]: the main god to whom the Powhatan make sacrifice

pegatawah: maize (corn; guinea wheat)

pocohaac [poh-koh-hak]: awl; needle; pestle; a man's privates

popanow [poh-pah-noh]: deep winter; coldest and least active time outdoors

powa [poh-ah]: the essence of dreams and visions [Gunn Allen]; possible root of the word *Powhatan*

quiakros [kwee-ah-krohs], pl. quiakrosoc: Native American priests or spiritual leaders

rahaughcum [rah-hah-coom]: raccoon

rahrenoc: white beads made of mussel shells, a type of currency [Smith]

sá keyd wingan: are you well? [sá keyd winkan in CA]

taquitoc: the fall; gathering season [Strachey]

Tassantassas [tah-sahn-tah-sahs]: strangers; foreigners [HCR]

Tunapewoc: the People ("the true, real, and genuine people")

uppowoc: tobacco (also spelled apo'ok)

ussac: crane

waugh [wahh]: expression of amazement (not unlike English "wow")

weroance, weroansqua: commanders; leaders

winganuske: good woman

wingapo: welcome

woanagusso: swan [drawing by John White]

wutapantam: deer

yapám: the ocean

yehakan: house

yoqueme wath [yoh-kway-may wahth]: let us go

HISTORICAL TERMS

aquavit: a liquor flavored with caraway seed

arquebus: a type of matchlock gun commonly used in the sixteenth and early seventeenth centuries

barge: see shallop

chirurgeon: surgeon, doctor

piece: a firearm or other weapon

pinnace: a type of very small sailing ship

sack: a type of dry white wine

shallop: a boat of very shallow draft, either rowed or sailed, sometimes referred to as a barge

shift: a woman's loose garment of linen, worn as an underdress or nightdress

TIMELINE OF THE LOST COLONY AND JAMESTOWN

1584—Amadas and Barlowe make contact with the Croatoan, Granganimeo, and other Algonquian-speaking Native peoples of the New World

1585—Lane's expedition to the New World; Grenville orders the burning of a town of Aquascogoc

1586—after near starvation on a foray inland, Lane leaves Roanoac with Drake's fleet; Grenville returns and leaves fifteen soldiers to hold Lane's fort

1587—John White and his planters arrive on Roanoac Island; White is forced to return to England

1588—White's first and abortive attempt to return to Virginia

1589—White gathers support for another voyage to Virginia

1590—White sets off for Virginia; makes landfall at Roanoac, finds message of "CROATOAN" carved on palisade but is prevented from following up

1592—Ussac (Emme) taken as wife by Wahunsenecawh

1594-5—John White dies?

1606—20 December: First voyage to Virginia departs (Percy)

1607
April: arrived at Chesepioc

22 June: Captain Newport leaves again for England, "leaving provision for 13 or 14 weeks" (Smith)

November: John Smith taken captive by Opechancanough

1608
1 January: Smith released

First and second supply ships arrive

10 Sept: Smith elected president

1609
John Rolfe and his pregnant wife, Sarah, depart from England on the *Sea Venture* as part of a fleet bound for Virginia but are shipwrecked on Bermuda. After spending the winter rebuilding their ship, the company sails the rest of the way to Jamestown.

Third supply (seven of nine ships originally sent out) arrives in Jamestown

1609–1610 (winter)

The Starving Time

1610

John Rolfe arrives in Jamestown, along with Governor Thomas Gates and others

Lord De La Warre arrives shortly after, assumes command of the colony, and enacts a new set of laws

Summer: the colony mounts several offensives against the local Native towns

September: Gates and Newport return to England

1611

March: Lord De La Warre leaves for England to recover his health

May: Sir Thomas Dale arrives with three hundred settlers and assumes command of the colony

August: Gates returns with another three hundred settlers

Henrico is established

1612—John Rolfe sees first success of trial growing tobacco

1613—April: Pocahontas taken captive by Argall

1614

April: Pocahontas is baptized as Rebecca and marries John Rolfe

June?: Rolfe named secretary of the colony after Hamor leaves

1615—Thomas Rolfe born

1616—Journey to England (departed Virginia Apr 21; arrived Plymouth Jun 12)

1617—March 21: Rebecca dies at Gravesend, England

1618—Wahunsenecawh dies

1622—John Rolfe dies; Opechancanough launches the "great assault" against the English settlements in an attempt to stamp out the spread of their towns and preserve his own people

Transplanted to North Dakota after more than two decades in the Deep South, Shannon McNear loves losing herself in local history. The author of four novellas and six full-length novels, her greatest joy is in being a retired military wife, mom of eight, mother-in-law of five, and grammie of seven. She's also a member of American Christian Fiction Writers and Faith-Hope-Love Christian Writers. When not cooking, researching, or leaking story from her fingertips, she enjoys being outdoors, basking in the beauty of the northern prairies.

Daughters of the Lost Colony

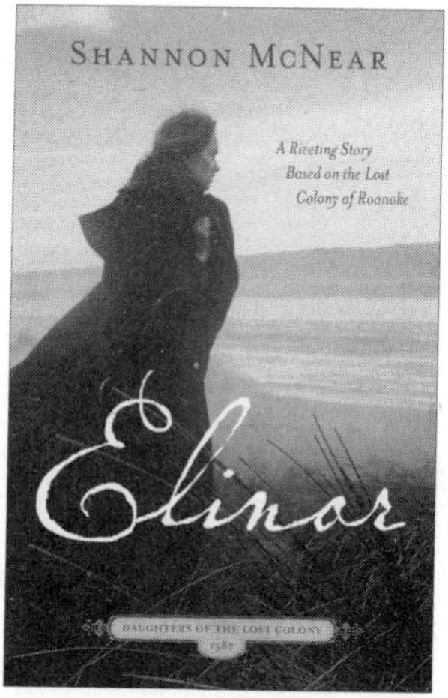

Book 1
Elinor

In 1587, Elinor White Dare sailed from England heavy with her first child but full of hopes. Her father, a renowned artist and experienced traveler, has convinced her and her bricklayer husband, Ananias, to make the journey to the New World. Land, they are promised, more goodly and beautiful than they can ever imagine. But nothing goes as planned from landing at the wrong location, to facing starvation, to the endless wait for help to arrive. And, beyond her comprehension, Elinor finds herself utterly alone. . . . What if one of the Lost Colony of Roanoke survived to leave a lasting legacy?

Paperback / 978-1-64352-954-7

Daughters of the Lost Colony

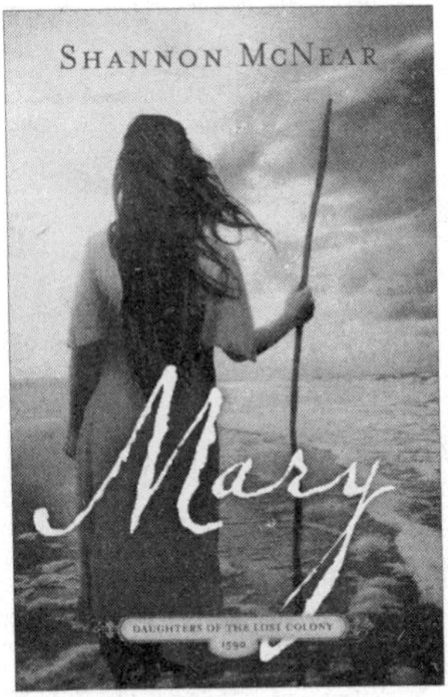

Book 2
Mary

Sparks fly between Mushaniq, free-spirited daughter of Manteo, and Georgie Howe, whose father was brutally murdered by undiscovered native warriors before they'd been on Roanoac Island a full week. As Georgie struggles to make sense of his life and to accept that not all they call "savage" are guilty of his father's death, Mushaniq grapples with her own questions about who Manteo has become. As tentative friendship becomes more, forged in the fire of calamity and attack upon their community, both must decide whether the One True God is indeed who He claims to be and whether He is worthy of their trust.

Paperback / 978-1-63609-386-4